HACKiNG GEORGE

BOB PALMER

DOUBLE
BLUFF
BOOKS

Copyright © 2022 by Bob Palmer
All rights reserved.

No part of this publication may be reproduced, stored or transmitted in any form or by any means, electronic, mechanical, photocopying, recording, scanning, or otherwise without written permission from the publisher, unless for the use of brief quotations in a book review. It is illegal to copy this book, post it to a website, or distribute it by any other means without permission. This novel is entirely a work of fiction. The names, characters and incidents portrayed in it are the work of the author's imagination. Any resemblance to actual persons, living or dead, events or localities is entirely coincidental. Bob Palmer asserts the moral right to be identified as the author of this work.

The author has no responsibility for the persistence or accuracy of URLs for external or third-party Internet Websites referred to in this book and does not guarantee that any content on such Websites is, or will remain, accurate or appropriate.

Designations used by companies to distinguish their products are often claimed as trademarks. All brand names and product names used in this book are trade names, service marks, trademarks and registered trademarks of their respective owners. The publishers and the book are not associated with any product or vendor mentioned in this book. None of the companies referenced within the book have endorsed the book.

―――

Published by Double Bluff Books.

For Berni, who showed me that writing is fun.

Contents

Chapter 1	1
Chapter 2	14
Chapter 3	30
Chapter 4	49
Chapter 5	67
Chapter 6	81
Chapter 7	94
Chapter 8	111
Chapter 9	124
Chapter 10	137
Chapter 11	153
Chapter 12	168
Chapter 13	185
Chapter 14	197
Chapter 15	214
Chapter 16	228
Chapter 17	247
Chapter 18	257
Chapter 19	272
Chapter 20	286
Chapter 21	300
Chapter 22	312
Chapter 23	325
Acknowledgements	335
About The Author	337
Afterword	339

One

Nothing is going to come between George Sanderson and a quiz. Not even gunfire, sirens and a baying mob. His eyeline shifts from the chaotic live TV scenes to the bay window, as if to confirm the events aren't playing out on his street. The world is an uncertain place and it pays to be aware of your situation at all times. But Buckinghamshire folk don't go in for that kind of thing. Unless, perhaps, a proposed bypass, solar farm or Amazon warehouse threatened a chunk of beloved green belt and a rare species of orchid. Besides, he concludes, the torrential rain would have kept them indoors.

He switches channels from the twenty-four-hour news to the cosy world of game shows. And the potential danger to George's wellbeing, already filed in his cerebral cortex under Not My Problem, is averted.

While he waits for a commercial break to end, he opens his laptop and selects the *Demon Of Chess* app. A chess board fills the screen, a game in progress.

'Your move,' says a calm, neutral male voice.

George finds the instruction irritating. He's well aware it's his turn and doesn't need his digital opponent to remind him. He pops a sherbet lemon sweet into his mouth and studies the board.

'If you are struggling, I can enable hints. Would you like me to enable hints?' That voice again.

'Good grief, give me a chance,' says George. 'I'm thinking. And no, I don't need your hints any more, thank you very much. I'm not a child.'

George slides his knight into what he believes is a confident attacking position.

'Now let's see what you––'

'Check.'

'Really? Really?!' George sucks hard on his sweet, assessing the situation. His tactic isn't looking quite so clever now. The TV screen comes to his rescue, exploding with sparkling computer graphics over a brash electronic theme tune. He collapses the laptop with a shrug and settles back into his favourite chair.

But even as the quiz show's slick presenter introduces the contestants, the riot in a minor African republic shows no signs of going away. A rabid horde, accompanied by two ancient British-built armoured vehicles, surges towards the presidential palace – a half-size replica of the White House. Placards, many written in English, read like slogans from a bygone age: *Punish the corrupt! Our land is raped! Death to foreign interference! Mines for the people, not the filthy infiltrators!*

As a news camera pans across the mob, a slight, dark suited Asian man, briefcase in hand, can be seen slipping away against the tide of rage. He glances in the direction of the lens and doesn't look happy. Why would he? Eighteen months negotiating a mega natural-resources deal for his employer, a mining corporation based in one of those huge Chinese cities no one's ever heard of, and just twenty-four hours for it all to fall apart.

A loyal soldier with a death wish confronts the horde. The crack of a single rifle shot rings out. A protester falls to the ground. After a momentary pause in the chanting, the rioters bay for the soldier's blood and stream forward like a shoal of starving piranha. He disappears beneath their stamping feet.

With far better judgement, his ill-equipped colleagues throw off their vintage helmets and join the crowd as it approaches the palace gates. A loud metallic clatter breaks through the din. The rioters stop, turn their attention to the sky. A helicopter that looks fit for the scrap heap rises from behind the domed roof.

Goodbye, Mr President. So long to your share of a billion-dollar cobalt deal.

The Asian man leaves for the airport in the back of a taxi, expression impassive as he barks into his mobile. Before he takes off on a private jet to an uncertain future, he's going to make someone else equally unhappy.

———

Four thousand miles away, uncertainty is filling the thoughts of another Englishman who is not watching a quiz show. In front of him are two computer screens, one showing a live stream of the riot, the other displaying some kind of financial statement. It's the latter that's holding his attention – the former is too painful to watch. Keen eyes are fixed on a particular column of figures that for the past hour have been far too static. Despite refreshing the web browser again and again, the numbers refuse to budge. The man is all too aware that it's something numbers do unless, like obstinate children, someone plays with them. He taps his fingers in random rhythmic patterns on the desk.

In his opinion, he'd fulfilled everything the mining company had hired him for – to discredit the increasingly popular opposition leader prior to an impending election. After hacking the bank accounts of a notorious local gangster he'd transferred the money into the politician's personal account. To complete the scam, he sent an anonymous message to the press leaking the politician's corruption.

It wasn't his fault that a Dutch undercover reporter had recorded a damning conversation between a Chinese fixer and the president's right-hand man. During it, they'd struck an agreement to give the President himself a valuable cut of the cobalt revenues in return for long-term mining rights at a knockdown price. Within hours of the news breaking, the sizeable opposition on the streets is now making its feelings clear.

For the Englishman, the situation is critical. The balance of his fee – $250k – has yet to be paid. The finger tapping continues, joined by knee trembling and intermittent shushing through pursed lips. When his patience runs out, he puts the unruly fingers to good use and sends a message to his contact.

$250k?

There's a three-minute pause before he receives an unequivocal response.

$0. Failure to deliver.

He thumps the desk so hard a pen rolls to the edge, teeters, and falls to the antique Persian rug beneath his feet.

Beyond my control, he types. *Your security was lax.*

Failure to deliver, comes the immediate reply.

Impasse. He can't push back without risking his own life. These people are powerful. Still, he'd earlier scribbled down the reporter's name and the Dutchman would soon join the list of past troublemakers, non-payers and last-minute re-negotiators upon whom he'd wreaked dire retribution. While he viewed vengeance a poor substitute for cash, it went some way towards redressing the balance and strengthened his notorious reputation.

He checks his watch and saunters over to an oak sideboard on top of which sits a half-full decanter and a single whisky tumbler. He pours a generous measure and downs it in one. Berating himself for a tragic waste of a good malt, he pours another. This time the liquid lingers on his tongue while a warm, cosy sensation builds in his stomach. It's been a long day. A long year, even. He yawns, his mouth revealing a gold tooth adorned with a sparkling globule of spittle.

Looking up, Goldtooth scans the Tudor-style ceiling. Intricate lattice work crafted in oak, and gilded. Each panel decorated with a starry sky. It's not the real thing, but he imagines the pleasure this perfect copy has brought to all those who've owned this house. The thought has a calming effect. His home, when he considers it, is the only part of his life that offers him contentment these days.

Even the sensation of winning had lost some of its potency over the past few years. Decades of tension, subterfuge, multiple identities, and the constant threat of discovery by Interpol and those he'd victimised, had left their scars. Any friends were long gone, that's if they were ever real friends. Women arrived, women departed. No children, at least none that he knows of.

He moves outside onto a terrace bathed in the burnt ochre of a sun preparing to dip below the distant trees. Jasmine fills the cool evening air. Long, hard shadows from the vine-covered pergola form a distorted checkerboard on the Yorkstone paving.

He skips from one space to another, avoiding the lines as if re-enacting a child's playground game. The moment is bittersweet, and he wishes he could share its simple joy with someone. Is this what it feels like, he asks himself, to be alone? To be detached from the rest of humanity in his mid-fifties? The next few decades looked bleak. Detecting a moistening in the eyes and a lump in his throat, he banishes the thought from his mind. It's a sign of weakness and that would never do.

Perhaps I should take a sabbatical, he thinks, return to work refreshed? He'd spent more than half of the past three years away from his beloved home. Wouldn't it make sense to kick back and enjoy it for a while without the stress of single-handedly juggling complex projects? Money isn't an issue, so what's stopping him?

The challenge, though, would be to find something to fill his days. What do normal people do? Don't they just jog along from day to day, hypnotised by routine? Work, watch TV, shop, play golf, go to the gym, the pub, the same sunny holiday destination year after year. Sheep. Where's the ambition? A week of this nonsense would drive him crazy, let alone a few months.

What he needs is an activity that involves his heart as much as his mind. To forge a new, meaningful relationship, perhaps. Start a business. Write his memoirs. Maybe donate some time to a worthwhile cause. He pauses at the latter. It would bring him good karma, a part down-payment to readdress the chaos and terror he'd reaped on his victims over the years. Karma offset. Still, no rush to decide right now. The best ideas always float to the top if you give them some air.

'Spare the price of a sandwich, please?' The fag and booze voice is thirty years older than the man it belongs to, and comes with a tinge of hopelessness.

George interrupts his study of the pattern of sprinkled chocolate on his cappuccino and looks up. A damp begging hand invades his personal space. The hand is attached to a damp hooded man. Worse, he has in tow a damp dog of indeterminate breed that's licking George's suede shoes, cleaned only this morning. George wishes there'd been an empty table inside the coffee shop when he arrived. Sitting outside, behind the waterfall that pours over the awning, he's a sitting duck.

He clears his throat and opens his mouth to say something. Then closes it. His gaze moves from the hand to an unfixed point somewhere above and to the left of him. George's fifty-eight-year-old hard drive is processing, and it won't be hurried.

Then he says, 'Hmm. Do you play a musical instrument?'

The man, unprepared for the question, raises his eyebrows.

'Or perhaps you can sing or do a magic trick? Take it from me, it would give some value to your potential benefactors.'

There's undecipherable muttering from behind an unkempt beard.

'I'm only trying to help. It's like those third world charities who don't just chuck food at starving people. They use their donor's hard earned cash to teach them how to become self-sufficient. Makes sense when you think about it.'

The man perks up. 'I could tell you a joke, mate,' he says with new found optimism. 'A sandwich walks into a bar and the bartender says sorry, we––'

George holds up his hand and looks pleased with himself. 'We don't serve food here.'

The man's shoulders slump and his sleeping bag slips into a puddle on the pavement.

'Here,' George says, reaching into a trouser pocket and fishing out assorted coins to the value of twenty-six pence. 'We're both in the same boat, really. No job and all that.'

The begging hand fails to collect the donation as if to say it's not worth the effort.

'To be honest, that's a pretty good return for an old chestnut, you know. As I tried to explain, it's all about value for money.'

'You want me to do half an hour's fuckin' stand up for you, then? Twat.'

He shuffles off to the next table where a slight, well-dressed man has a twenty-pound note in his hand, ready and waiting. Although George can only see the back of this man's head, he can imagine an expression of such revolting smugness it almost causes him to gag.

'Cheers, mate,' says the homeless man. 'You're a gent.' He swivels around to throw a fuck you grin at George.

'Good luck,' says Goldtooth.

'Mug,' says George under his breath, and turns his attention back to the homeless man. He can't be that hard up if he can afford to keep a dog. It's all about living within your means. His logic triggers a painful pang of guilt, and the coffee, despite being constructed to George's exacting specifications, holds no joy for him anymore. He knows he's the last person to lecture others about living within your means. After no income for six months, his savings have taken a terrible battering. He's about to leave when the man with more money than sense turns to face him.

'It's a problem, isn't it,' says Goldtooth.

'I'm sorry?'

'That man who was begging. Hard to believe we still have homeless people here in the twenty-first century.'

George wonders whether to engage. He doesn't want a public argument about begging. On the other hand, he agrees with what the man has said. 'I blame it on the councils for lack of social housing, and successive governments for lack of funds. Mind you, there are jobs to be had, so the homeless aren't totally blameless.' Has he gone too far?

'All fair points. It's good to hear people's views on such complex matters. Do you live nearby?'

There follows the longest conversation George has had with

anyone for a long time. And despite his earlier snap judgement, he revises his opinion of the chatty man. Intelligent, a good listener, interested in others. When George leaves the café, it dawns on him he's missed human company. Any company, for that matter. He wonders if he should buy a dog. The idea is dismissed in an instant because of the running costs. Then he castigates himself for being irrational. Get a grip, George. Get a grip.

He fails to spot Goldtooth following him at a discreet distance. And even if he had, he would have thought nothing of it. They'd got on so well, they'd even exchanged email addresses.

Earlier, sitting outside the café, Goldtooth had been pondering on ways to punish the Dutchman for his damaging exposé. A week after the events in Africa, the story was still running in the media and the journalist's status was increasing daily. Word had it he might be up for some kind of international award. Goldtooth isn't troubled by this. The higher his achievement, the more spectacular his fall would be.

His musings, though, had been interrupted by the behaviour of the thoughtless idiot on the next table. He could barely believe what he witnessed. Asking a homeless person to perform for money as if he was some kind of Victorian fairground freak? What new breed of pettiness and arrogance was that? Unwelcome memories resurfaced: scavenging through supermarket bins, freezing shop doorways, living with invisibility.

And there it was. The distraction his new sabbatical had been screaming out for. If only that insufferable man knew what suffering is – when your life starts to slide away and no amount of pumping the brakes will slow it. What a game this could be. No risk, no pressure, and with all the time he needed to get creative, to push some boundaries, to enjoy the journey. It wouldn't be the karma balancing act he'd envisaged, but that was his head talking again. Maybe he should give his heart a chance. See what it could do. But first things first, and that always meant research.

He followed his prey to the multi-storey car park on the ring road. As George drove off, he noted the car's registration number on his mobile. Then he copied it onto a text and sent it to a high-ranking police officer who owes him a favour.

The information he needed arrived ten minutes later.

George Sanderson
42 Claremont Avenue
HP29 6ST

That would have been enough for Goldtooth, but there was more. Some bonus features.

02731 611347
012291 181560

And a comment from the sender.

The guy's a pain in the arse but no record. Always complaining about speeding cars and noisy kids.

This is almost too easy, thought Goldtooth. He pinged back a quick reply.

Let me know ASAP if anything else turns up.

Once home, he sat at the desk of screens and downloaded an image of a UK ex-Prime Minister in magisterial pose. He sniggered, one hundred percent certain he'd judged George's character correctly. With Beethoven's Ninth thundering in the background on repeat, he carried on working until dawn. When his work was done, he reviewed and tested it across multiple electronic devices. Satisfied, he sent an email to George and headed off to bed, confident that by the time he woke up his target's life would be laid bare before him.

Karma could wait. Game on.

———

There's something insidious lurking in the nether regions of George's laptop. If only he knew it. A string of code as long as your arm has allowed remote access by another computer. The hacking began with an innocuous email that arrived in his inbox at 6 a.m. today. Purportedly from a major consumer website, it contained the kind of invitation a certain type of person can't ignore.

FREE EBOOK: 10 EFFECTIVE WAYS TO COMPLAIN ABOUT ANYTHING. CLICK HERE TO DOWNLOAD!

George clicks the inviting button. Within a nanosecond, the code secretes itself within the laptop's system software. A web page opens: an image of Margaret Thatcher with the caption THANKS JANICE. While George welcomes this unexpected picture of his political heroine, the book itself has failed to download. Assuming some kind of server error occurred, he repeats the exercise to no avail. Perhaps he might have better luck with his mobile? Cursing flaky technology, he finds the offending email and stabs the download button with a firm finger. Maggie's back again, her head cradled in his hand. It feels personal this time, like they have a special connection. The agreeable feeling is short-lived. Where's that damn book? Time wasting and unmet expectations in George's world are things that can't be ignored. And the irony of complaining about an e-book on the subject of complaining, even if it is free, hasn't escaped him. He messages his displeasure to the organisation that never emailed him in the first place.

Meanwhile, another block of code has allowed Goldtooth to access all areas of George's mobile. The double whammy.

———

Goldtooth's nose takes in the intense bitterness of his expresso. It's a ritual he indulges in wherever he is in the world. The first inhale is always the best, like the first cigarette of the day (when he smoked), the first beer sitting on a stool at a Caribbean beach shack (it's been too long), the first hesitant kiss with a woman (even longer).

On the screen before him sits an exact copy of George's computer desktop. It's midday and he assumes George is at work. That leaves him a window of opportunity to take a quick look around. It wouldn't do for George to be at his laptop when a ghostly cursor was flying around his screen. Already Goldtooth can see the man likes order. Only three folders are on the desktop: Household, Personal, Employment. But he knows there's nothing like a calendar to give an instant snapshot of someone's life. And, from what he's deduced already, it's a safe bet George will use one. He takes a deep breath and clicks the calendar icon.

The month of May is almost empty. A disappointment, but also a telling insight. Shopping and a library visit next Saturday morning. Chasing a recruitment agency every Monday. Must be desperate for a new job. He moves forwards into summer. A new series of Mastermind starting in June, and a fortnight later, MasterChef. A dental appointment. A car MOT. Early in September, a single entry reads: *Bournemouth?* He scrolls through to the end of the year. No entries for lunches or dinners or golf with friends. No birthdays. No evidence of a partner. George appears to lead a very solitary life. Moving back in time to the previous December, there's a flurry of activity.

Appointments with a careers advisor, a cancellation of a lawn care subscription, a transfer of car ownership, a review of investments. It seems as if George may be unemployed. Wounded already, smirks Goldtooth. And I haven't even started yet.

Time to exit. He closes the calendar. A forensic examination of the folders and emails can wait until later. He sets an alarm on his mobile for 11 p.m. because George is likely to be one of those early to bed, early to rise people. Time now for another coffee, to flick through the morning's news, and perhaps stick some more virtual pins into a virtual doll of a certain Dutchman.

Two

The traffic stutters to a standstill. An electric window hisses up and stops with a soft thud. Two months have passed since George fell out with the homeless man, and the weather has turned. Cool damp May and June have been replaced by searingly hot July. It's thirty degrees outside, so it has to be hell inside George's ailing car.

He would have liked to keep the window open longer, but he worries about the pollution. To completely seal himself off from the outside world, he presses the air-recycling button. Nothing can get in, nothing can get out. The heat steadily builds. His mind slips back to the previous summer when the Mondeo's air con had functioned perfectly. He wipes his brow with a shirtsleeve and places his clammy hand back on the wheel. Both hands on the wheel whenever possible. No sense in taking chances.

The car in front moves. George transfers his right foot from the brake pedal to the accelerator, applying gentle pressure while simultaneously releasing the clutch with his left foot. He notes with satisfaction the symmetry of both feet moving in opposite directions and yet achieving the same goal – to propel his car smoothly forwards.

Ahead, the road narrows as two lanes become one. As usual, some drivers leave it until the last second to move in from the outside lane. In his wing mirror, he sees a white car barrelling along at speed. George instinctively knows the driver will attempt to push in, so he closes the gap on the Toyota in front. He hasn't left a safe distance behind it, but the situation is under control. He knows his reaction time to an emergency is fast. Given the opportunity, he'd willingly submit himself to rigorous scientific evaluation to prove his lightning reflexes to the world at large.

As the white car draws alongside, he can't help glancing over at the driver. Briefly, they make eye contact. With the single lane section now immediately ahead, and realising there's nowhere for him to go, White Car Man brakes hard and pushes in close behind George. The blare of a horn, at first staccato, then sustained. Headlights flash in George's rear-view mirror. He lets a small smile escape and makes a mental note of the number plate. He has a gift for memorising trivia, having once read a book called *10 Ways to Remember S**t that Matters*. Not that he thinks the driver's dangerous actions are trivial.

Further on, a cyclist partially blocks the lane. Flicking on the right indicator with his middle finger, and with the minimum of movement of the steering wheel, George weaves around the obstruction. A perfect course correction is how he'd describe it. He doubts White Car Man would have achieved the manoeuvre so precisely. He's still there, though, less than a car's length from George's bumper.

George touches the throttle to create some extra space between them. White Car Man closes the gap. George shakes his head, sucks in some hot humid air and exhales it slowly. His eyes swivel up to the mirror again. Ten metres behind, a contorted face stares back.

The traffic starts to flow more smoothly. George selects fourth gear and the revs drop to two thousand two hundred, the point at which he knows the engine runs most efficiently. A digital readout of his current fuel consumption on the dashboard confirms this. He presses a button on the end of the left stalk three times to check the status of the fuel tank. Eighty-seven miles. He'd have to be careful. No unnecessary journeys. There'd been a hike in oil prices and the cost of fuel had risen sharply. His savings would keep him going for a while, but he'd need to find a job soon.

As he approaches his seventh decade, who knew how long that would take? Middle-age and middle-management meant, at best, middling prospects. On the night of his redundancy, sitting alone in his suburban home watching a re-run of The Good Life and mouthing its dialogue for the umpteenth time, he'd acknowledged his own life had reached yet another critical fork in the road.

Now, as he progresses towards the town centre, he wonders if he needs to go back to corporate work at all? Surely there must be other options? I gave my best years to that company and now I'm free. Freedom. Even thinking the word feels radical. Dangerous, even. A squirt of adrenaline into his bloodstream nudges his heart into a higher gear. With White Car Man temporarily forgotten, he allows himself to revel in some possibilities.

Sell up, perhaps, and take an early retirement in...? He runs through a list of countries where a low cost of living would give him a comfortable lifestyle. Spain? Full of Brits like – he glances in the rear-view again – like him, the idiot in the car behind. And he curses the driver for breaking this pleasurable daydream. He refocuses. Maybe Asia? You can eat out for a pound in Thailand, a colleague once told him. Even less, said another, joining the conversation. Great food, friendly people and, he added with a wink, the chance to pick up a new wife.

As George contemplates the pros and cons of such an opportunity, a vivid blaze of red jolts him back into the real world. The Toyota has slowed almost to a halt. The brake lights fill more and more of his vision, and for a moment his brain concocts an illusion in which the Toyota appears to be reversing towards him. As the closing distance between the two cars decreases exponentially, the illusion vanishes. Even as he stamps on the brakes, he predicts a collision looks likely. He's all too aware you can't argue with basic science.

Eight metres … Four metres … Two metres … George stops breathing. He feels weightless. His mind empties. Eyes squeeze shut. Hands brace against the steering wheel. The anti-lock braking has taken over, and the laws of physics will determine the result.

The Mondeo shudders to a halt so close to the Toyota, you could wedge a cheap business card between them.

It's not over. While he simultaneously chastises himself for unusually poor road concentration and pats himself on the back for a textbook emergency stop, there's a massive crunch as the BMW ploughs into the back of him. His car is propelled forward into the space the Toyota has just this moment vacated. The next thing he's aware of is a sharp pain in his neck, followed by the sound of someone hammering on his window.

'You fu'ing dozy cun'! See wha' you fu'ing done!' Although White Car Man's use of consonants is restrained, his upper body shows no such signs of shyness. Arms gesticulate wildly toward his car, the hue of his gurning face shifting from pink to purple.

George still has both hands on the steering wheel, but the fingers that usually exert a mild pressure on the cushioned surface are now squeezing the life out of it. As if the floor of his car has dropped away, and the wheel is all that's preventing him from plunging to certain death into a deep abyss beneath his feet.

'Fu'ing ge' ou', you cun'.' White Car Man attempts to open the door and fails. George always travels with the doors locked. You can't be too careful these days, what with road rage nutters and traffic light beggars and even primary school thugs carrying sharpened crayons or worse.

George still hasn't turned to face his abuser. What would be the point? It might make an unpleasant situation worse. Best to sit it out, settle his racing heart until the man becomes bored and drives off. He has an unexpected urge to whistle a tune, but that was out of the question. Despite valiant attempts, whistling is an art he's never mastered. Perhaps hum a little ditty, then? Yes, that might help. The tune is unrecognisable and there are frequent and unintended key changes. He knows he's some way off perfect pitch, but it's not important. The horns of dozens of stationary cars behind him add some welcome colour to the piece, but a switch in George's head has muted the sound.

The traffic in front has moved on, so there's nothing to stop him from driving off and escaping the madman. But George isn't going anywhere. He'll wait until the BMW has gone and then get out to inspect the damage.

Meanwhile, White Car Man adds extreme frustration to his apoplectic rage. They are not good bedfellows. The chorus of impatient horns heightens his stress. Traffic on the opposite carriageway is bumper to bumper and slow-moving. There's little chance of anyone on George's side of the road overtaking the two stationary vehicles. Behind them, the tailback continues to build.

The man disappears into the blind spot of George's wing

mirror. Perhaps he's going? George slips off his seatbelt. But White Car Man reappears all too soon. This time he's holding a large wrench. The window beside George's head disappears in a shower of glass. Fragments fall onto George's lap. Even as he involuntarily wets himself, he can't help admiring how small and uniform the pieces are. Ingenious. A hairy arm follows the wrench and grabs George's neck. Then a fist the size of a Rottweiler's head lands a blow to the side of his face. The force of it sends George's upper body crashing onto the passenger seat, his head hitting the adjacent door pocket. He lies there motionless. Even the humming has stopped.

The sound of a distant siren. A shout. A lady driver two cars behind gets out and remonstrates with the man. It has zero effect because there's only one person on his radar and he hasn't finished with him yet. She returns to her car, locks the doors, and calls the police. On the pavement, a mother pushing her baby in a stroller scurries past, averting her eyes. The siren continues.

White Car Man tries to pull George's legs through the window. It's not easy because some glass shards are still attached to the edges of the window frame. His hands and arms are already bleeding. He lets go of the legs, the lower parts of which are now dangling from the window, and walks back to the point of collision. Then he returns to the Mondeo, and back again to look at the crumpled front of his own car as if damage assessment is a critical ingredient in topping up his rage. His body, unlike George's, is in perpetual motion, his brain unable to make a firm decision about what to do next. Back and forth, side to side, bouncing from here to there like an out-of-control toy robot with new batteries.

Now he notices the siren for himself. Although it's moved no closer since the collision, he doesn't know that. What he does know, even with his mind hell-bent on revenge, is that if he's caught he'll be facing an assault charge. Fuck that. He runs back to his car. When he turns the ignition, he hears an unusual rattle from under the bonnet before the engine kicks in. This does not deter him. He reverses back a little and forces the BMW into the oncoming traffic so he can pass George's car. More loud horns, and another collision narrowly averted. White Car Man flicks them the finger and takes off in a thick cloud of diesel fumes.

Brave Lady ignores a rare window of opportunity to pass George's car. She can't bring herself to leave the poor unfortunate man without checking on him. Her car creeps forward and stops immediately behind the Mondeo.

George still hasn't moved. He's not dead, comatose, or even seriously injured. He's in Thailand, horizontal on a beach lounger. And despite never having had a cocktail in his life, now seems like the perfect time to have one.

'Hello, are you okay? Can you hear me?' shouts Brave Lady, now accompanied by another man, through the smashed-in window.

George starts humming again.

———

'Let me hazard a guess, you're from Poland.' George prides himself on recognising accents, but these Eastern European ones are tricky.

The Lithuanian nurse in A&E fixes George with a derisory look that seems to infer her origins were of a higher status.

'Actually, the Republic of Lithuania. It is most beautiful and clean.'

'Well, I was close,' he says, salvaging something from his error as she examines his eye. 'Vilnius?'

'You have visited?' she asks, rummaging in a drawer for a lint pad.

'Heavens no. I rarely go further than Dorset. I just know my world capitals.' He pauses, sensing an opportunity. 'Is it cheap to live there? What about property prices? Do they allow foreigners to buy? Is it cold?'

'In Vilnius, best jobs in I.T. Be still, please.' She dabs his pale face with antiseptic. George winces. 'You I.T. man?'

'Accountant. I don't want a job there. At least, I don't think so. It depends, I suppose.'

'You will have stitches and eye will bruise very bad. It is no problem,' she says. 'You will wait now. I fetch a doctor who is stitching. Me, I can stitch. The best. But there is rule here. Must be doctor. Stupid English hospital rule.'

The police have already interviewed George. An officer arrived at the accident scene on a mountain bike. He explained it was the only way to beat the Saturday traffic these days. After George's injuries were judged to be superficial, Brave Lady, who'd stayed to make a statement, offered to drive him to hospital. The officer arranged for the Mondeo to be towed to a local garage. Whilst it was driveable, the rear light clusters were smashed, which, as the officer was keen to point out, made the vehicle unroadworthy and therefore illegal. He took a note of the BMW's registration and phoned it through. The driver had committed a serious offence, he said, and an early arrest was likely, although he couldn't be quoted on that.

At the hospital, Brave Lady, whose name George discovered was Angela and who'd already taken a bit of a shine to him, waited until he'd been seen, and then driven him home. And so it was, with a neck brace and five stitches across his right temple, that George ended his eventful day being looked after by a kindly stranger.

'Shall I make some tea? It's good for the nerves, so they say,' she calls from halfway up the stairs while George is changing his clothes. 'Do you have any camomile? And you must be hungry. I could whip something up. Scrambled eggs, cheese on toast?'

She shakes her head, giggles.

'Silly me. You didn't manage to do your shopping, did you? Do you have any eggs, cheese, baked beans? I can always go home and bring some back. Sorry, I'm rambling, aren't I?'

'No, no, no, not at all. Very kind,' says a freshly showered George emerging from the bedroom. 'I'm sure there's something in the fridge. Let me help you.'

At the bottom of the stairs, Angela takes his arm and firmly leads him into the living room to the nearest armchair. He has two armchairs, and it's not the one he usually sits in, but he's not about to argue with her.

'Don't worry, I'll find everything,' she says. 'Shall I put on the telly for you?'

George checks his watch.

'Perhaps you could pass me the remote.' He points to a side table next to the other armchair. 'Do you like quizzes?'

When Angela finally leaves two hours later, she requests they share phone numbers because 'you never know, do you?'. George didn't know, but went along with it. Adding a new name to his contact list is a rarity. Somehow, it felt like progress.

As he closes the front door, the enormity of the day's events catches up with him. The tremor starts in his fingers. It swiftly travels up his arms into his torso and then down his legs, gaining intensity all the time. He staggers against the wall. His knees buckle and he slides slowly down the wall to a squatting position, his entire body convulsing. A low howl, more animal than human, pierces the silence. Deep in his subconscious, he's seven-years-old again and locked in his bedroom. After an indeterminate period, cramp in his thighs forces him to move. Using the wall as a prop, he stands up and forces himself to take long, deep breaths. Is this a panic attack? He wishes Angela was with him, in case it happens again. He thinks she'd be good in a medical crisis. The observation seems to reboot his brain. He has things he must do. It's been seven hours since the accident and he still hasn't informed his car insurer. Did their terms and conditions put a time limit on reporting an accident? Even though there are extenuating circumstances at play here, his tardiness makes him uneasy.

With his heartrate returning to normal, he pulls himself together and makes the call. First, he must navigate through one of those ubiquitous yet often complex menus. A system to be applauded, he believes, for its efficient way of making sure you were talking to exactly the right department. And, on this occasion, a sympathetic call handler named Lynzee appears to be precisely the right person. Lynzee is so sorry to hear about the accident and asks him to call her back with a crime number once the police had issued it. In the meantime, would Mister Sanderson like her to arrange a complimentary courtesy car? George is undecided. He's comfortable with his Mondeo – it's why he bought it from his previous employer. He knows the position of all the buttons and switches, the power of the engine so he can safely overtake, the overall dimensions so he can glide through most width limits without slowing down, and execute a parallel park in two manoeuvres. George promises to think about it and let Lynzee know A-S-A-P.

Before he goes to bed, he recites some personal information and a few random facts: name, age, address, mobile phone number, National Insurance number, the names of Saturn's moons, the population of Vilnius at the last census, the chances of winning the National Lottery, the date of his redundancy. As there are no hesitations, he concludes he doesn't have a concussion. The A&E doctor had specifically asked him to contact his GP if he developed a severe headache, dizziness, or showed any signs of memory loss. He also advised him to avoid alcohol for forty-eight hours. As George's specified drinking day (nothing excessive) is always on a Friday, and today is Saturday, George had assured him he could easily comply.

He wakes with a splitting headache at dawn, interrupting an unpleasant dream involving Angela screaming at him to sit in the corner facing the wall, as a punishment for losing his school cap. His cotton pyjamas are drenched in sweat. He immediately subjects his memory to another concussion test and passes with 100% accuracy. After downing two Paracetamol – he never takes three like some people because if it was safe to do so the instructions would say take one to three, and not one to two – his confidence suffers a mild wobble due to extreme overthinking. If he has a concussion, then might it be possible he only thinks his answers are correct, when actually they're wrong? He double checks one of his recent test answers. Yes, Google confirms the population of Vilnius is five hundred and forty-four thousand. All is well, confidence is restored, life can go on.

After an early breakfast, he calls his new friend Ray. As it happens, Ray is pretty much his only friend. He has acquaintances with whom he exchanges Christmas cards, ex-colleagues mainly, and a pleasant elderly couple he bumped into on Weymouth seafront. He hasn't heard from the latter in two years and presumes one or more of them have passed away or forgotten who he is because of some form of dementia.

When he and Ray had first met, they discovered a mutual love of chess and neither of them had anyone to play with. As George remarked at the time, a computer is a chess partner without wit or respect. The tech gurus of Silicon Valley with their artificial intelligence and machine-learning might, given the chance, beg to differ. But George is no respecter of a breed of perpetual teenagers living in a netherworld of complex algorithms, ping-pong, sushi, and astronomical salaries. It was Ray who'd suggested they play a few games in a local café, and this offer of friendship flattered George. He suspected Ray didn't have much of a social life either.

He scrolls through his meagre list of contacts and hits the call button. The ringing tone continues for some time. He's just about to click off the call – no point in leaving a voicemail because Ray says it's too complicated for him – when he hears hard breathing and then a voice.

'Yes?'

'Ray, it's George.'

'Of course, of course. Your name's right here on the screen. Silly me. What's up? Do you want another thrashing?'

'I don't want to bother you. Is it a bad time?'

'No more than usual. You know how it is. Martha's in hospital again after another relapse. I'm not sure how much the doctors can do now.'

'So sorry to hear that, Ray. Hopefully, the kids will rally round to take some of the weight off your shoulders.'

'If only that was the case, but they all seem so ... so busy. What is it with the young these days? And when they do visit, they still leave the place in a mess. Were we like that at their age?'

'To be fair, all I cared about was keeping my job. You know, with all that unemployment around. We grew up quicker back then.'

'Tell me about it! I suppose I'm lucky to have a job where the risk of redundancy is low. You know, George, we now get double the planning applications we did ten years ago. The world and his upwardly mobile wife seem hell-bent on home extensions with those bring-the-bloody-garden-inside bi-fold doors, or knocking down some perfectly serviceable nineteen fifties bungalow to create their ridiculous grand design. God, it's tedious. Too late to switch careers now, though.' Ray pauses for breath. 'Sorry, rant over. What can I do for you?'

As George relates the events of the previous day, he feels relieved he's shared them with a friend. This is not something he's been in a position to do for some years, but plagued by the technicolour memories of yesterday's attack, he hoped it would be therapeutic. Ray, naturally, offers his sympathy, and then apologises for still being unable to have him round for dinner until his situation changes. The kind thought is comforting enough for George, and when the call finishes he murmurs, 'Good old Ray'.

———

Four days later, alerted by a local teenager flying a drone, the police find White Car Man sleeping on top of a bus shelter on the outskirts of Merthyr Tydfil. He was arrested and subsequently charged with actual bodily harm, destruction of property, and driving away from the scene of an accident. When the police inform George, he's a little put out that the man is likely to be given bail. Given his multiple misdemeanours, what kind of violent crime do you need to commit before being instantly incarcerated as a danger to the public? Not that George has had too much time to dwell on this important topic. It's been a busy day.

A lady with an impenetrable Glaswegian accent calls from Victim Support. George says no to all her questions, even though he can barely interpret them, because he doesn't want her to call again. A police admin person leaves a voicemail with George's crime number. A contact at a recruitment consultancy returns Monday's call to deliver the news that, no, there still aren't any opportunities in the locality for him at the moment, but to keep the faith. And a nearly new Ford Focus courtesy car sits in the driveway.

It's the latter that George, second cup of tea in hand, is admiring through the window that Thursday morning. He'd taken it for a quick run around the block and found it almost impossible to drive safely because of his neck brace. Nevertheless, the Focus met with his approval, and he thought he'd like to keep it. Then, because he knows he'll soon have to give it back, he convinces himself it will have faults he has yet to discover.

He returns to flicking through the local newspaper on his lap. Earlier, he'd spotted a small piece about his assault. Rather underwhelming, in his opinion. The article contained little detail and concluded with a request from the police for witnesses. A young reporter lacking social skills had called him on Tuesday morning for a statement and asked if he could take a photograph of his battered face. George had refused, believing it sensible not to brandish his injuries to one and all. And who knows how today's click-bait press might spin his words?

It was the front-page leader, though, that had earlier caught his eye. A story he still can't get out of his head. He carefully goes through it again, hoping he'd misread a pertinent detail. It won't change the fate of a baby called Eve, but it might absolve him of being an unwitting accessory to her death. The news item, however, has no sympathy with George's conscience. The fact is, the baby died because of the road rage incident in which he was involved.

He walks over to the kitchen worktop, grabs a reporter's notebook and selects a fine-pointed black pen from an old mug with a missing handle. Bright red, it features the words *George's Ugly Mug!* in a bold condensed font. He only keeps it because it serves a useful purpose, unlike his ex, Cynthia, who bought it for him for lack of any other ideas and then betrayed him.

He makes himself comfortable in the armchair by the bay window and starts to write.

BABY DEATH – REVERSE CHRONOLOGY
Baby Eve dies because…
The ambulance is stuck in gridlock because…
I'm too scared (too sensible?) to move because…
A madman has assaulted me because…
The madman's car hits my car because…
I was late in braking to avoid hitting the car in front because…
My lack of focus on the road ahead because…

George pauses at this point. These are the key events, after all, and it's not looking good for him. But he's seeking absolution for his guilt at any cost. He continues.

I was thinking about where to emigrate because…
My money is running out because…
I was made redundant because…
My high street chain store employer was in financial difficulties because…
Online shopping became popular because…
The internet was invented.

While he'd prefer that the terrible outcome be attributed to Tim Berners-Lee, he reluctantly dismisses the thought. Although he's not directly responsible for the tragedy, his daydreaming had played a major part in the unfolding chain of events. He places the pen and paper down on the side table and sighs. It's difficult to believe, but he made a mistake. A catastrophic one.

Then, using logic and probability, he seeks alternative scenarios for Baby Eve. Would she have lived, even if the ambulance had arrived at the hospital earlier? And if she had, then what would the long-term prognosis have been? She may have been brain-damaged or paralysed from the head down. What kind of life would that be for Eve and those who would need to care for her? Perhaps, he allowed himself to think, he's done the baby and her parents a favour? Negatives into positives. His speciality. After so many rejections throughout his life, it's a testament to his resilience that his sanity remains intact.

'Father Christmas hates scum like you.'

'You want me to send you to school in that dress again?'

'Fuck off, you spaz. No one wants you around.'

'You're as shit as your dad was, but at least he brought home some money.'

'I wasted years on you. Years I'll never get back.'

'We're letting you go, George. It's all about team players these days.'

'You fu'ing dozy cun'.' (Just a reminder.)

With guilt subsiding, he resumes reading the rest of the newspaper. The big story on page three is something he'd previously glossed over. It features a lottery jackpot winner from a less than desirable estate at the edge of town, and it's no surprise that he'd initially lost interest. George is not a gambler and has no truck with those who are. Then he reads this: "'If it hadn't been for the gridlock in Marseden Road, I never would have parked up and gone into the shop,' said an ecstatic Ms Adams, prosecco in hand. 'I only stopped for a cold drink. It gets a bit sweaty in my old banger. But when I got to the till, I saw some chocolate and I couldn't say no. It was like God was telling me to buy things.'"

George's posture straightens. His senses heighten. A million questions whirl around his head.

———

Three

Every action has an equal and opposite reaction. George studies the story of Ms Adams and her stunning piece of good fortune. Could it be? Yes, she bought the ticket the previous Saturday morning, only hours before the entry deadline. And from Wheatley Stores on the corner of Wheatley Street and Marseden Road, the road on which George had been driving. He reads on. "'And for some reason, I had to buy some lottery tickets. Never bought any before, so that's weird. It was like they had my name on them. The rest is history. It's difficult to take it all in at the moment, but I did treat my boyfriend to a Nando's.'"

The paper slips from his hands. Baby Eve and Ms Adams. A death and a fortune. Yin and Yang. Would you Adams and Eve it?

Such is the energy now coursing through him, his leap from the chair might be interpreted as an involuntary reaction upon discovering a stray tarantula crawling over him. But George has an idea. A big one. And those, as a colleague had once coined, are as rare as rocking horse shit. He would have preferred the poo word, but over the years he learnt to be less judgmental of such language in the workplace.

He ricochets from room to room, his head bursting with possibilities. It's like Ray had said when they were playing chess last week – if you can't change the man, change the circumstances around him. It's the kind of thing Ray says.

On Saturday afternoon, he concludes, I was not only an angel of death but a genie in the lamp. I caused someone's wish to be fulfilled, and I didn't even know it. But would the jackpot win have been possible without the death of Baby Eve? The very idea was ridiculous, but who really knows how the universe works? This is stuff beyond a mere accountant's pay grade.

George spends the rest of the day reading up on Chaos Theory. It's mostly gobbledegook but he gets the gist. And the gist tells him he would find it impossible to calculate the required probabilities to make accurate predictions of future events. Even now, he can't guarantee that one queue at a supermarket checkout will move faster than another. There were too many variables. What chance would he have to predict a much more complex event? He notes meteorologists are still next to useless, despite their state-of-the-art satellites and prediction software.

But what if a human intervention could eliminate some of the obstacles and influence the pathway to a successful outcome? George thinks he's on the brink of a monumental discovery: Intervention Theory. Or better, Sanderson Intervention Theory (SIT). He projects the dream further to a time when he delivers a keynote SIT speech to a convention of rapt scientists. Perhaps even a TED Talk?

'Ladies and gentlemen, good afternoon. Those of you who are parents will know that a key milestone in your child's physical development is learning how to stand up unaided. I'm here to teach you the opposite. To sit. S-I-T. Sanderson Intervention Theory. I'm George Sanderson, and I'm going to take you on quite a journey today. Coming?' (Milks wild applause.)

Although it's a Thursday, he celebrates his genius with a gin and tonic. It's not every day you can say you're pushing the boundaries of theoretical physics and taking it into the real world. He sloshes gin into a faux lead-crystal tumbler, purchased in a closing down sale at a local shop which is still, to his annoyance, trading a year later. Throwing caution to the wind, he opens a fresh bottle of tonic. Although there's one open already, he knows some of the carbon dioxide is likely to have escaped over the weeks he's had it. And George wants to see those bubbles dancing like quantum particles on a day out. He's earned it. Perhaps he'll go mad and have two drinks tonight. His eyes sparkle.

All he has to do is work out a modus operandi and find a suitable subject on which to test his theory. For the first time in months, he has something to be excited about, to get his teeth into. He raises the glass and toasts an imaginary audience.

'To Baby Eve. You will often be in my thoughts. And to your family, my condolences. I'm sure it was a terrible shock. God bless.'

He pauses, trying to push out a tear. One almost escapes, but he excuses his failure. After all, he didn't really know her.

'And to Ms Adams, I offer my heartfelt congratulations and wish you all the best with your ludicrously large winnings. Enjoy while you can your predictable purchase of a Range Rover with privacy glass, the double-fronted mock Tudor house with circular gravel drive and underground cinema room and sauna, the succession of unreliable boyfriends and dodgy investments, the Disneyland Florida trip for you and those you think are your friends. I expect it'll all be gone by Christmas.'

His mobile rings as he tips the dregs of the glass down his

throat. George looks puzzled. Almost no one calls him. Even the spam calls are rare these days since he started adopting a complex blocking procedure. Perhaps the car body shop has an update on his repair?

'Yes, hello? One moment, please.' It's a struggle to place the phone at the right angle to his ear because of the neck brace. He consoles himself, knowing he won't need it in a week's time.

'Hello George, it's Angela.'

He's uncertain how he feels about this interruption. Or how he feels about Angela. She'd been good to him, though. Almost achieving the rare status of friend in George's slimmed-down world. And, in her favour, she didn't seem like someone who wanted anything in return. Like money, or a gift of sorts.

'Are you there? George?'

'Ah, yes, Angela. Sorry. And hello to you.'

'I've been thinking. The day after tomorrow is the week anniversary of your ... your incident. And I thought you might like some company. Do you know what I mean?'

George doesn't understand at all because he's already moved on from his bloody assault. He's revelling in organised chaos world and there's no better place for him to be.

'Well, I ... I ... What exactly are you suggesting?'

'Lunch at mine. I love cooking, but I'm not very good at it. No strings attached.' She laughs. George joins in because he senses it's the right thing to do.

―――

The hand is beautiful to perceive, both the writing that flows from the Mont Blanc fountain pen and the delicate fingers that control it. Despite the plain paper, the words adhere to near perfect horizontal lines, individual characters so similar in size and appearance the effect is that of a printed document. Yet this is not some trying-too-hard begging letter or an entry into a calligraphy competition. Goldtooth is simply making notes. And there are pages of them.

It would have been simple for him to create some disorder in George's very ordered life right now – to drain his bank account and cash in his ISAs, for example – but he's looking for a more satisfying punishment. Something worthy of his talents. For a few hours each night for the past six weeks, he's sifted through every single element on George's devices: documents, spreadsheets, bank and savings accounts, emails, texts, web browsers. Yet other than George's current financial crisis, the tedious search revealed little he hadn't already guessed.

But tonight's search through George's internet browsing history has stirred Goldtooth's pulse. Webpage after webpage on chaos theory. What the hell was that all about? And then a second surprise. A new calendar entry: *Lunch Angela 12.30!!* Who's she? Goldtooth checks George's mobile contacts. There's only one Angela and she must be new on the scene. He can see from the call log there have been only a few recent calls between them. To add to the intrigue, Goldtooth finds something odd in the Notes app on George's mobile. It looked like a shopping list headed *Speeders,* under which were three items: *flowers, string, teddy bear or similar furry animal.* It didn't make any sense. George and children wouldn't mix. But who cares? It's given him the idea he's been waiting for.

―――

While the residents of Claremont Avenue still sleep, a furtive figure is tying a large teddy bear and a bunch of flowers onto a lamppost at the end of the street. George strides the few yards back to his house and turns to view his handiwork. That'll slow them down, he thinks.

George has a bee in his bonnet. In fact, he has a swarm. Like people who're unable to respond to a question without beginning their answer with "So". He's noticed the So epidemic has even infected younger TV journalists and politicians. What kind of lesson is that for kids? Then there are those virus-ridden idiots who go into work when they're contagious. It's neither heroic nor clever, and it could be dangerous to older members of staff or those who may have chronic medical conditions. There's more. Contestants with over-inflated egos who go on TV quiz shows lacking the essential skills of storing and recalling miscellaneous facts, thus stealing the place of someone more suitable. But by far his biggest irritant is speeding cars in residential neighbourhoods.

Many years ago, another freak lapse of concentration close to a traffic camera resulted in George receiving a fine and a speed awareness seminar at a local hotel. While most of his fellow transgressors had treated it with some disdain, George enjoyed learning about the effects of a car when it impacts the human body, and the difference just two or three miles per hour can make. He went through those doors an occasional speeder and came out a Highway Code evangelist with a mission.

He's lost count of the number of times he'd motioned to drivers to slow down in his street. He tried taking photos of them on his mobile, but by the time he extracted it from a zipped pocket in his jacket, flipped open the must-have protective case and found the elusive camera icon, the cars had long gone.

Even as he stood at the bay window the previous day talking to Angela, another vehicle shot past. It was the catalyst for his first intervention. A trial run. If road signs didn't slow down these people, then he'd have to appeal to their emotions.

'What a lovely teddy,' the lady at the toy section checkout had remarked. 'For a new grandchild?'

George, clutching an enormous bunch of flowers, just stared at her.

In return, he received an encouraging smile. 'Teddy for the baby? Flowers for mum? How exciting.'

'Oh, I see. Yes, well, not exactly. It's complicated.'

The lady mentally runs through some alternative scenarios. It's the man's baby with a younger woman. The baby is adopted. It's a surrogate baby. There is no baby and the customer is one of those weirdos who collects fluffy toys.

George wouldn't have cared what she thought. He's focused on the simplest of interventions. A single action to create an indirect reaction: the construction of a modest memorial to a child involved in a fictitious road accident. He was sure a fatality on the street would influence the speeders' thick skulls. Of course, it would take a few days to assess the results of his work, but, being jobless, he has all the time in the world. And if his experiment is successful, then perhaps he could look at more complex objectives.

―――

'George! Love the new neckwear.' Ray sits himself down at a corner table in the half-empty café.

'Oh, ha ha,' says George. 'I'm getting used to it now, actually.' He then points to the wound above his eye. 'But this is a bit embarrassing. Looks like I've been in a street brawl. Still, the stitches come out next week.'

'Nasty. I hope they throw the book at that maniac. We need stronger deterrents.'

'Tough on crime, tough on the causes of crime. That worked, didn't it?' George rolls his eyes. 'Anyway, how's life with you?'

Ray appears distracted as he takes out the chess set from his bag.

'Sorry to say it's been a hard week, what with one thing and another.' George assumes Ray's wife had taken another turn for the worse. But he knows better than to press him for details. Ray doesn't like to discuss it.

'Well, if I can do anything ... I just hope there's light at the end of the tunnel,' he says.

'Decent of you, George. We always focus on the light. Darkness is a destructive place to be. Any job interviews in the offing?'

Ray starts to set up the pieces on the board, placing each piece in the centre of each square. George notices one or two could be a little more central, but refrains from reaching out and repositioning them. He wouldn't want to upset his friend.

'As per usual, not a sausage. In the meantime, I've been working on a new project. Chaos, Ray. I'm taming chaos. It's going quite well.'

He delivers the words with ease, confidence, and even, Ray would have detected, no small amount of pride. Today, George thinks, the chess can wait. This is an opportunity to share his new theories with Ray who he believes is the perfect person to spot any holes in them.

'Have you turned into some kind of existentialist? Please tell me you haven't. I liked the old George.'

'Just having some fun. Hoping to make a difference in the world.' He's pleased with the last bit. It came out of nowhere and makes him feel worthy. It also sounds like a tagline for a brand, not that he holds with such frivolous things, but he can see the appeal. George Sanderson, making a difference in the world. Nice.

'Fill me in,' says Ray. 'God knows I need a distraction.'

'Well, it all started when I read the local paper yesterday.'

'You read that rag? I gave up on it. Page after page of adverts padded out by non-news and obituaries of people I don't know. And ridiculous puzzles like that Sudoku nonsense for people who can't do crosswords. Sorry, carry on.'

Ray's outburst takes George aback. Now he wonders how much he should tell Ray who's obviously in one of his darker moods. Maybe just the broad outline of his theory.

'What would you say if I told you that last Saturday I inadvertently caused the death of a baby and created a jackpot winner?'

'I'd say you were quite mad, but you've intrigued me.'

George takes Ray through the discovery that led to his new theory. He leaves the speeders intervention for when they next meet up. He should have some results by then.

'It sounds like you're going to be some kind of incognito super hero,' says Ray. 'You should give yourself an alias. How about The Puppet Master or The Manipulator?'

George laps this up. And as he's on a roll, he unveils some other important news.

'There's something else. Don't laugh, Ray, but I, er, have a date. At least I presume it's a date. I'm not sure, really.'

'Good Lord. Have you been on the internet? Swiping up and down or whatever it is people do these days?'

'Actually, I'm having lunch after this with that woman from the accident. The one who helped me. Angela. She's quite pleasant.'

'You're not going to leave me high and dry, are you, George? Start forgetting your friends and all that?' He laughs. It has a hollow ring to it that George is oblivious to.

———

George pours what's left of the contents of the gravy boat onto his plate. It's somewhat tepid now, and viscous, oozing its way in super slow-motion over the lip to form large gelatinous blobs on a ragged slice of overcooked roast chicken. He suspects Angela doesn't own a meat thermometer, or a decent knife. He refrains from comment because his host has made him feel very welcome. She'd made a considerable wardrobe effort too, wearing what George would describe as going-out clothes.

When he arrived, she'd corralled him through to the living room. She called it a lounge, a word he'd not come across since television test cards and powerful trade unions. A large sofa – he suspected she would call it a settee – overflowing with plump, bright, satin-covered cushions dominated the room.

'What am I like?' she said, as George attempted to find a slot amongst the springy obstructions in which to place his bottom. 'You've been here at least twenty seconds and I haven't offered you a drink.' She paused for him to respond and then shrieked with nervous laughter. 'What's your poison, George?'

George's default poison is, of course, gin and tonic. Wine is for people with more money than sense. He understands the value quotient of beer on a volume versus cost basis, but he doesn't enjoy the taste. In his late teens, he'd once bought a pint of fashionable Australian lager in a pub and sat for some considerable time watching the bubbles disappear. He found it rather fascinating, so the evening wasn't a total write-off.

'Well, I'm driving,' he said. 'Do you have gin? And tonic, perhaps? Just a teeny one, obviously.'

He made a steering motion with his arms. His eyelids closed as he steered off an imaginary road into an imaginary tree. 'Argh.'

Angela raised a beautifully-tended eyebrow at his charade.

When it comes to pouring spirits, she doesn't muck about with pub measures or small glasses. She plonked a hi-ball tumbler, rattling with ice and crowned with a lemon slice, in George's hand.

As she sat down beside him, he shuffled in the opposite direction to retain some personal space. Angela didn't appear to notice. George took a sip of his drink and made a mental note to leave most of it. It was important that he kept full control of his faculties for the next few hours.

During lunch – three courses followed by a cheese of indeterminate origin – the conversation is of the kind typical of new acquaintances, a superficial unpeeling of their lives. George finds small talk frustrating, especially if there aren't any conclusions. Otherwise, what's the point of a conversation? And it doesn't improve when Angela started chatting about her work. He already knew she worked for a local business that manufactures ventilation fans. Now she adds some detail as she clears the table.

'Personal Assistant to the C-E-O,' she says, spinning out the letters like an elocution tutor. 'Chief Execution Officer I call him, the way he gets rid of his staff. The older ones, mostly. I used to work for the ex MD but he retired at Christmas. Nice man. Then his son, jumped-up little squirt, took over and changed his job title.' She leans across the table and places her hand on his forearm as if she's about to divulge a secret. 'Do you mind if I swear?'

'I er ... whatever works for you, Angela.'

'Tosser.'

'Eh?'

'He's a tosser, George, no other word for it, and he makes my life a misery. Who knows how long it'll be before I'm replaced by some dolly bird?'

George's ears perk up.

'I used to feel a bit sorry for him,' Angela continues, 'what with Reg on his back the whole time, and the whole nervous breakdown thing, but now...'

Suddenly, she has George's full attention. He waves his knife at her to continue.

'Pushy wife too. Got him to borrow company money to buy a place in Barbados. I heard them arguing about it on the phone.'

'Does his dad know about it?'

'Doubt it. I saw the paperwork later. Reg always put the company first. He wouldn't borrow company money without paying any interest.'

George nearly chokes on the lemon slice he's currently extracting the juice from.

It's only when Angela's mobile buzzes that there's a break in the conversation. She checks the call, declines it. 'Jackie, my sister,' she says. 'Chalk and cheese, we are. But she's the only proper family I've got. Lives in South Shields.'

Home to the world's first electrically powered lighthouse, recalls George. He'd like to mention it to Angela, but the phone call has created a natural break and he now has more important things on his mind.

'Goodness,' he says. 'I've probably overstayed my welcome. I really should be off and leave you in peace.'

'Don't be so soft. You can stay as long as you like. I'm not going anywhere.'

'I must, Angela. There's a couple of things I need to attend to. Perhaps ...,' he coughs into his hand, 'perhaps I could reciprocate sometime soon? A lunch maybe? Dinner? I'm quite flexible these days.'

Angela would like this very much, and George sees how his clever invitation has given him the chance to extricate himself from her clutches without appearing to be rude. It's not that he hasn't enjoyed her company. He can see an opportunity here for some kind of ongoing relationship. But right now, his head his buzzing with his next intervention.

One good turn deserves another. Puppet Master to the rescue. Project Angela is born.

PROJECT ANGELA
Mission:
– To protect Angela's financial independence by ensuring she holds on to her job

George sits at the dining room table, typing up some handwritten notes from Saturday evening. The room is more of an office these days, ever since Cynthia left him for Geoff, the divorced salesman who talked him into replacement windows. It turned out to be a very expensive transaction, what with the cost of solicitors and split assets added to the windows and their installation. Her departure did have a silver lining. The savings he's made from her reckless spending subsidised his losses. For fun, he'd worked it out on a spreadsheet in a Bournemouth guest house last year and was pleasantly surprised.

Cynthia is a distant memory. While he bears her no ill will, he hasn't forgiven Geoff, who'd accomplished as good a sales pitch on his wife as he had on him. Moving on was important, though. Why poison the present with a past you can't change? He'd read that on a tiny slip of paper inside a Zen-themed Christmas cracker and banged on about it to anyone who would listen ever since.

He helps himself to another biscuit from the 99.99% airtight – or your money back – container. Plans can be complex and it's hard to predict how long it will take him. So far, he has the basic background, mostly hearsay from Angela, plus some information from a search on the Companies House website. He continues typing.

Potential Sub-mission:
– To evict her boss (and install a good one?)
The Target:
– Michael Finguish, CEO Finguish Fans
Background:
– Reginald Finguish retires as Managing Director of Finguish Fans. He's still the majority shareholder.
– The company's last set of accounts showed a net profit of £317,583 on gross revenues of c£4.5M.
– In January, Reginald's son, Michael, takes the helm, giving himself a 50% pay rise and taking a £300k interest-free company loan, repayable in 10 years, to buy a holiday home in Barbados.
– The company's current bank balance according to Angela is £80,000, down from £430,000 (NOTE: Commercial suicide! Well below a sensible figure for operating cash. It would only take one bad debt…! Surely his father wouldn't have countenanced such a thing?).
– Current staffing policy: MF has made 7 older staff redundant, citing change of job description and hires cheap young labour to carry out similar tasks but often to lower standards. No ex-employees ever questioned the validity of their redundancies, though the justifications may be flawed and possibly illegal.
– Conclusion: MF is a real danger to Angela, other loyal employees, and the success of the company. Also, a potential danger to himself? (How will he survive under the pressure he's putting on the company and himself? Previous mental health issues!!)
– Intervention strategy:

George hits a wall at this point. This is the difficult bit and it needs the kind of clear head that only mornings can offer.

Angela's Sunday morning conversation with Jackie has already nudged the twenty-minute mark, monopolised by her sister who's having trouble with her thirty-year-old live-in son and his partner.

'It's like she thinks it's her house now. There's stuff I've never heard of all over the bathroom. Never offers to cook or clean up. Lazy cow. And he just lets her. Too busy lying on his bed on the phone half the day. Doing what, who knows? Just says it's business. You did right to stay single, Angela. Less complicated.'

'Well, I've––' says Angela, but Jackie hasn't finished.

'Doesn't matter what I say, they don't listen. He could get a proper job. He's got a brain, he has, but he won't use it.'

Angela is nothing if not determined. 'I had a friend round to lunch earlier. He's very nice. Respectable.'

'A man?' There's a long pause while Jackie switches focus from herself to her sister. It's a difficult manoeuvre. 'Are you sure?'

'Of course I'm sure. The one who was assaulted. I did tell you about it. He's called George.'

'It all sounds very unsavoury. Are you sleeping with him? You would tell me, wouldn't you?'

'What a question! Really, Jackie. And no, I'm not. I've only known him a week.'

Jackie is happy about this. She hasn't had sex for four months since Peter, her husband, started watching porn and demanding too much from her.

'He's not married, is he?' she says.

'Divorced.'

'The worst. Bet he watches porn on his computer. You never know what disgusting things he might ask you to do.'

At the top of a new document on George's laptop is a single word in a bold font.

RULES.

If this intervention is to go ahead, then he'd need to set some parameters or it wouldn't be a genuine test. Rules are what bind civilised society together and he's adept at following them. There's enough anarchy on the streets as it is, and he believes he'd be the perfect person to write some. They'd be simple, sensible, and with no chance of misinterpretation. After thirty minutes, he hasn't got past rule one so it's not going too well.

1. Indirect action(s) only.

George is well aware that his accident only indirectly caused the key events to take place. It's not as if his car had been in a collision with the ambulance, or that he'd been in the corner shop and recommended to Ms Adams that she try her hand at the lottery. This simple rule means that, in order to keep Angela in employment at Finguish Fans, he can't simply roll up to Finguish Junior's office and poison him. Or fiddle with the brakes on his flashy Jaguar SUV, hoping he'd smash into a brick wall.

Searching for further rules is put on hold due to an emergency. He's been so focused on his work, he hasn't realised his bladder is full. The need to urinate is now so urgent he makes it to the toilet with only seconds to spare. It's a good job he had the foresight to open his zip on the way or there could have been a nasty accident. It takes a minute to empty himself, his prostate not being what it was, which gives him ample opportunity to contemplate his penis. He's only glimpsed a few others for comparison since those best-forgotten afternoons in the school changing rooms, and he's quite happy with what he has. It's a nice enough shape and size, and when erect had even satisfied Cynthia – at least in the early years. As he walks back to the dining room, he considers the double-glazing salesman's manhood. Did he have one of those huge monstrosities that some women enjoy? He wishes he'd asked Cynthia at the time. It's good to have all the facts.

The short break must have refreshed his mind. Back at his laptop, two rules come along at once.

2. The action(s) must be, to the best of my knowledge, lawful
3. The action(s) must not directly or indirectly cause serious physical or mental injury or death

Satisfied, he returns to planning what kind of intervention he'll use for Project Angela. Getting Finguish Junior to leave the company would be tricky and there might be a sting in the tail. Who knew what his replacement would be like? They might be even worse. And that would require a second intervention in order to ensure the quality of a new boss. But what if – and George thinks he's onto something here – what if he could somehow coax Finguish Senior out of retirement?

This felt more achievable. Angela liked her old boss and he'd treated her well. George also predicts that Finguish Senior, like many retired entrepreneurs, might struggle with his newfound freedom. Letting go of the baby he'd nurtured for decades would be hard. If he realised how his son is now running the business, that might provoke him to return. But how to do that indirectly? George comes to the conclusion that he needs to understand more about the man in order to create the right strategy. And the internet is always a good place to start.

———

Goldtooth taps the name Peter van de Hoek into Google, hits the Return key. There, a dozen new entries, all from newspapers and online bloggers. Oh, the joy.

He hadn't rushed to get his own back on the Dutch reporter. It called for a more considered approach because it was important he didn't implicate his Chinese clients, whatever he thought of them. No point in making unnecessary enemies, especially now he was enjoying the stress-free life of his semi-sabbatical. After three weeks and a not inconsiderable sum of cash, he'd sourced and hacked the man's personal mobile phone. Luck was with him. Scrolling through the messages, he uncovered some eye-opening details of the reporter's secret relationship with a Belgian pig farmer and reality TV star of the notorious show Blind Wedding. A man famous only for taking a chance on the disturbed ramblings of a trainee chiropodist he'd never seen and marrying her four hours later.

Two days ago, Goldtooth had copied the relevant text and revealing pictures from the phone and sent them to every news outlet in Belgium and the Netherlands. He knew results would not be instant. Facts had to be checked, but not, he predicted, at the expense of getting the story out as fast as possible.

He clicks on the first search result, from Belgium's Het Laatste Nieuws, and has Google translate it. It's a brief article, but size isn't everything.

TV'S PIG MAN CHEATS ON TOE GROOMER WIFE WITH TOP REPORTER

Goldtooth licks his lips, reads on. All the salient details are there, including the reporter's name and an image of both men naked. To preserve their modesty, the newspaper had added white panels over the offending appendages with the text: *Nothing to see here*.

He moves on to a report from the leading Dutch paper, De Telegraaf, the one he imagines Mrs van der Hoek might read.

OINK! OINK! HERO COUP JOURNO PREFERS PIG LIFE TO OWN SOW

Good enough, he concludes, and wishes he could be a fly on the wall at the van der Hoek residence. And if the fallout from that didn't result in an expensive divorce settlement, then he'd dole out another, more severe, punishment for wasting his time. Like hiring one of his cut price yet reliable Albanian contacts to pop round to the Dutchman's house and say hello in his own special way.

Now he can put one hundred percent of his energy into making someone else's life a misery. While George's misdemeanour wasn't in the same league as the Dutch reporter's, it had felt much more personal. And like a Gurkha who must draw blood once he unsheathes his kukri, Goldtooth's game must continue until George has been punished. It wouldn't do to have any sympathy for him. Not with what he's planning.

―――

Four

8.00 a.m. on a drizzly Monday morning. George, anorak on, hood up, lurks on the pavement close to the teddy bear memorial. He may be a local resident, but his actions, or lack of them, are likely to prompt some suspicion. George is unaware of this. He's engaged in recording the behaviour of car drivers. In the fifteen minutes he's been standing there, pen and notepad in hands, only three cars have passed. Frustratingly, they've all been driven at a sensible speed even before they had the opportunity to see the memorial. He'd have to wait until the road got busy to see what the idiots might do.

After a few minutes, a young mother with two young kids in tow stops beside the memorial.

'See that,' she says, gripping the shoulder of the older child and pointing to the bear.

George's ears prick up.

'That's what happens when you don't look before you cross the road.'

The kid looks quizzically at his mother, as does George.

What kind of blurred message is that, he thinks? Teddy bears and flowers miraculously appear on lampposts when a child fails to observe a basic safety rule? Where's the jeopardy?

Nevertheless, he's pleased the mum had bought into the idea that there'd been a real fatal accident, but annoyed that she assumed it was the fault of a child. It's the cars going too fast, you stupid person, the cars! His right hand delves into a jacket pocket and pulls out a bag of sherbet lemons. One, perhaps two, will calm him down.

Locating vintage sweets on the high street these days is almost impossible. His local supplier had sold up and retired without giving him any notice. So much for brand communications, grumbled George when he turned up one day with a single sweet left in the bag, only to find a betting shop. Hardly a cliff-edge situation for many, but these matters are important to him. Online shopping, despite its popularity leading to his current unemployment, came to his rescue but sweets in packets never seemed to taste the same as those from jars.

While he's waiting for the traffic to build, he tests his geographical knowledge by reciting the names of world capital cities, from north to south. It could be useful one day. As he reaches Honduras – Tegucigalpa, of course – a vehicle approaches. The notebook is back in action.

When George returns home an hour later, he can't in all honesty say the experiment has been an unqualified success, but there are glimmers of hope. Of the fifty vehicles that passed him, ten were speeding in his opinion, and of those three reduced their speed after the memorial. One even touched the brakes. All in all, a decent result. Only a speed camera or road humps would have been more effective. And as some of the regular speeders probably haven't noticed the memorial yet, there's every chance the success rate will increase.

Buoyed by his minor triumph, he fries up some eggs and

bacon for breakfast. Then, wishing to mitigate his guilt and achieve some kind of nutritional balance, drops two slices of wholemeal bread into the toaster. While he waits, he types Finguish Senior's name into Google. As he scans the results, he riffs on a mid-seventies novelty chart-topper most people around at the time are desperate to forget.

By mid-morning, he's completed his brief biography of Angela's boss: a few business awards, local sponsorships, a little charity work, and some nimby campaigning. Hardly Wikipedia stuff. It's not much to go on. As he reaches for his mobile to call Angela, it starts to ring. He spots the caller's name but waits until the sixth ring to pick up. It's a habit he developed at work. If you answer promptly it might appear you have so little to do, you're actually waiting for the phone to ring.

'Angela.'

'Hello George. Just calling to see if you're okay. Is this a good time?'

For what, thinks George. A silly expression, but he's prepared to overlook it.

'Yes, absolutely. In fact, you've been on my mind this morning.' He wonders if he's giving her the wrong idea. His fears are instantly founded.

'Ooh, I am honoured. Was it about coming to lunch?'

'Well er, yes, and I was thinking about your boss, actually.'

'You want to invite him too then?' Peals of laughter from Angela.

'Ha ha. No, I've just got a little idea up my sleeve that might help you. Early stages and all that. Listen, as we're talking perhaps I could pick your brains for some info about his father?'

'What do you want to know about him for?'

'Humour me. Does he have any hobbies? Married? Divorced? Any other kids? Grandchildren? You know, personal stuff like what he gets up to now he's not working. Do you keep in touch?' George wishes he'd talked to Angela before spending hours of online research with so little to show for it.

'Funnily enough, I saw him a couple of weeks ago at the doctors' surgery, but it's not like we're friends or anything.'

'Did he say what was wrong with him? Anything ... serious?'

'Something to do with his knee, I think. They'd told him he'd have to stop playing golf for at least three months. Lots of physio. That won't be easy for him, you know. Spent all his spare hours on that course, he did.'

'So he's going to be bored.'

'Bored? He'll be driving that poor Anne up the wall.'

'His wife?'

'Second wife. The first ran off with a local councillor. Anyway, Reginald's not a man who can sit still. Has to be doing something. I don't know how she copes now he's retired, I really don't. Patience of a saint.'

George's pulse quickens. 'The son. Is he hers?'

'No, Reg only married Anne about fifteen years ago. I know Michael wasn't keen. Still gives her a hard time, I think. Not his mum, see? George, what are you up to?'

Humming from George.

'Oh, one other thing,' says Angela. 'Not sure if it's useful, but he and Anne really love Barbados. They've been going there for years. I'm sure that's why Michael bought ...'

Bingo! George has found a way in. And Anne could be the catalyst. He needs to put some flesh on the idea, but he can see possibilities.

'Angela,' George lowers his voice for maximum impact, 'if I could arrange for Reginald to return to work, is that something you'd like?'

'How on earth could you do that? Are you going to lean on

him? I think that's the word gangsters use, isn't it?' She giggles, trying to imagine George as a bad boy.

'Good Lord, no. Do I look like a criminal?' He lets it sink in. 'But what if I could, er, make such arrangements?'

'Then I'd say do it. Reg could be a pain in the bum sometimes, but he was fair, and he cared. A lot of people would thank you. Especially me.' Those last two words hang in the air like an invitation to the kind of party George isn't used to being invited to. 'Now about lunch, or was it dinner?'

―――

The mid-afternoon school run has started. George moves from his previous static observation spot in the street after a few suspicious mums gave him a very wide berth on the pavement. The red welts and bruising on his face probably don't help. Now he's pacing up and down pretending to make a business call, in the hope it makes him appear less dubious.

'... Well, I really think we need to include Gareth on this ...'

'... Check the September ROI spreadsheet – it's all there ...'

'... But the numbers don't lie! I copied in Jim and he agrees with me ...'

'... Circle back once you have the net figures ...'

He may be talking nonsense, yet he finds it strangely empowering. It's been a while since he used office speak and he misses it. An attentive bystander would notice how his posture has changed – chest out, shoulders back, chin up, although the imposing neck brace helped with the chin part.

His current self-assurance is a far cry from the sixteen-year-old who'd left school with a brace of O Levels and even fewer friends, and if it hadn't been for a solitary teacher who took pity on him, he may have disappeared without a trace into one of those invisible jobs reserved for underperformers.

Mrs English, counter-intuitively, taught maths and saw promise in his natural talent for logic and numbers. She encouraged him to retake the critical subjects and organised a visit to a local accountancy practice. It was the motivation George needed, although she would never have guessed that one day he'd be using his talents in quite such an unusual way.

As the traffic builds, he has to pocket the phone in order to make notes. His fingers are simply too large to use the mobile's keypad efficiently. Besides, a pen and pad would make him look more official. He doesn't want to be perceived as being the weirdo some mums were already silently accusing him of. Over a forty-minute period George compiles his second set of data, and the results reflect those of the morning session.

With the evening rush hour still some time away, he returns home to refocus on getting Reg Finguish his old job back, whether he wants it or not. The idea that's bouncing around inside his head needs a sense check. Angela's future, and possibly his, depends upon joined up thinking.

―――

The blond-haired boy might be ten years old. With an air of innocence, he's looking directly down the barrel of the lens. A man, old enough to be his grandfather, stands directly behind him, their bodies touching. Both are naked. Accompanying this image are twenty-seven others of the couple, all in a folder labelled 'Bournemouth'. The folder is hiding in another folder marked 'MISC' somewhere in the depths of George's laptop. George is totally unaware of it. And it's unlikely he would, because he rarely files anything in that folder. MISC is for lazy people.

That's just the way Goldtooth wants it. Phase one of *Project*

George – The Revenge is complete. Now for phase two. The tricky bit.

———

Is it an indirect action? Check. Lawful? Check. Not physically hurting anyone? Check. George is shortly to enter the Caribbean property sector and his idea has passed the intervention rules with flying colours. Bold and sophisticated, it came to him as quickly and fully formed as an Elton John melody. His new business, Buy Barbados, may only be words on a page at the moment but over the next few days he aims to turn it into the kind of bait Anne Finguish can't resist.

The first item on his to-do list is to place an advert in a publication he believes Anne is likely to read. It's a weekly local arts and culture magazine delivered free to local residents in high-end postcodes. The website gives George some basic info but he needs to check some critical details with the advertising executive.

'Artima magazine advertising. Fiona Smallbone speaking.'

'Good afternoon, my name's Anderson.' Pause. 'James Anderson.'

George suppresses a laugh at his 007-like introduction. The pseudonym is important, though. The last thing he wants is for any of this to be traced back to him. It could ruin everything.

'I have a new property business I'd like to advertise as soon as possible,' he continues. 'Is it too late to get a quarter page into next week's issue? FYI I'd like you to produce the advert for me.'

'Not a problem, Mister Anderson, and thanks for thinking of us. If we're designing the ad we'd need the copy by 11 a.m. tomorrow latest. Would that be okay?'

George wonders if he isn't being a little optimistic. After all, he knows nothing about the property market in Barbados or even how to write an ad. Still, how difficult can it be?

'Absolutely. And could you confirm you deliver your magazine to the AL2 1AD postcode please?'

'Let me just check for you, Mister Anderson.'

George looks at his watch, fidgets. Ten minutes before he needs to hit the streets again and gather some data.

'Yes, that's one of our areas,' says the lady. 'May I ask what you're selling? It's just that we do reject certain types of advertiser. We don't want to upset our readers as I'm sure you'll understand.'

'Quite right too. I'm one of them. I don't think they'll have a problem with my upmarket real estate in Barbados.'

'Oh, how wonderful. Bang on for the Artima demographic. Click-throughs from our clients' ads to their websites are higher than average, you know. Would you like to reserve your space now? It's £90. I can offer a good discount for multiple insertions if that helps.'

'Just the one for now,' says George. 'Suck it and see. First rule of marketing.' George is guessing here, but confidence is everything.

There follows an awkward moment when the lady asks for payment over the phone. George hasn't considered this particular obstacle to his anonymity. He offers to pay in cash and drop it in with the advert copy. It feels a bit low rent, but he knows the lady will be only too pleased to have a new up market advertiser.

―――

The curse of the cashpoints when you really need them. On his third attempt, George finally finds one that works and that doesn't charge him a premium for using it. He withdraws £90 and puts it into a large brown envelope along with the advert copy and instructions on what kind of picture he'd like Artima's design team to use. He thinks Anne Finguish will find it very appealing. At least, until she reads the small print. Fifteen minutes later, he posts the envelope through the magazine's letterbox. Plenty of time for a shower, breakfast, and be out again before the school run.

Writing the copy last night had been easier than he thought. He looked through a few Barbados property sites, pinched a few choice phrases, and added some crucial words of his own. Who needs expensive advertising agencies when you could do it yourself for free?

For the next few days, and in between his speeders sessions on the street, George immerses himself in the Caribbean property market. He's been in a quandary over the website. Every business had one these days and he knew that if Reg read the ad, the first thing he'd do is to check out the company. But after the cost of the advert, George isn't about to blow more of his dwindling cash reserves on hiring a website designer. When he finds an online resource that could help him design the site for next to nothing, he does it all himself. It's a tight schedule. The site must be ready by the time Artima is delivered on Friday. He works long into the nights, watching how-to videos, writing the text, and copying property images and information from other websites. On Thursday evening, he clicks the Publish button and the Buy Barbados website goes live to the world.

George still finds it difficult to relax. There are many variables that could upset his plans, most critical of which is whether Anne Finguish would actually read the magazine and spot his ad. His thumbnail character assessment of her said she would. Barbados is a buzzword in the Finguish household. Fingers are crossed. Tomorrow is the magazine's distribution day. It's also his dinner date with Angela. He surprises himself by acknowledging he was very much looking forward to it. He couldn't quite pinpoint why, and that puzzles him.

———

George has planned the menu carefully, confirming beforehand things Angela doesn't eat. It's a short list: offal. George is happy with this. He's not a fan either, and can't understand the fascination the French have for it. Another good reason to give that anarchist-ridden country of amateur philosophers a wide berth.

Keep it simple, George, he'd said to himself. Italian, perhaps. That's always straightforward, and who doesn't enjoy pasta? Cheap too, if you selected the right recipe. While it's been years since anyone had come to dinner, it's not as if he suffers from a lack of confidence in the kitchen. Cynthia had little interest or skill in cooking and George had taken over the chef's mantle early in their married life. It was that, or baked beans and tiny sausages from a single can, one of her specialities.

Earlier, he'd entered the final day of car stats onto the spreadsheet and analysed them. He can say with certainty that his ingenious memorial had slowed thirty percent of the traffic in the street. And on a total budget of just £30. Surely that would gain the attention of the local council and constabulary. Perhaps even his MP. If a proper scientific test subsequently proved his theory, then this could be an initiative to roll out nationwide. Perhaps even worldwide. Imagine the lives saved. Thankfully, he stops pontificating on the what ifs before he awards himself a Knighthood or a Nobel Prize for Road Safety Psychology.

———

While George prepared for his evening with Angela, Anne Finguish had been enjoying her favourite time of the day. The golden hours between stacking the dishwasher after lunch and starting to prepare dinner. The heatwave now over, she lounged on a sofa in the conservatory with her current book, a historical romance. There were only twelve pages left to read, and she'd enjoyed it so much she didn't want the story to end.

To delay her gratification, she picked up Artima, delivered only an hour ago. The smell of fresh printing ink drifted from the pages as she flicked through it. Advertising filled half the pages, but Anne likes this kind of advertising – the latest kitchens and bathrooms, cruises and escorted tours, upmarket property and garden designers. She and Reg aren't super-league wealthy, but they have enough money to make life more than comfortable.

Opposite an article about a young, local opera singer made good were four quarter-page adverts. Investment consultant, tree surgeon, driveway installation, and a company selling houses in Barbados. And within the latter, with its stunning view of a tropical beach scene, a very familiar name pops out.

Anne strides into the living room where Reg is snoozing. She shakes him gently at first, then firmly.

'Reg. Reg!'

He blinks, sees his wife staring down at him.

She thrusts the magazine into his hands. It's open at the offending page.

'I think you should see this,' she says, tapping her finger on the ad.

Reg scans it quickly, barely taking it in.

WINTER IN THE UK OR WINTER IN BARBADOS?
OWN A PIECE OF SUNNY REAL ESTATE TO ENJOY
WHENEVER YOU WANT.

*Beachside properties from just £299,000. Discount inspection flights, free legal work.
Visit www.BuyBarbados.uk and never look back.*

'What's your point?' he says.

'Look closer ... the small text at the bottom.'

Reg is already not in the best of moods, due to missing his usual Saturday foursome at the golf club. But this – this! – is something else.

The best investment I've ever made.' M. Finguish, Bucks'

'Did you know about this?' Reg says, turning to Anne who's still hovering nervously behind him.

'Maybe it's a different Finguish?'

'How many effing Finguishs have you heard of? It's him. How can he afford this, then? I know what his salary is, at least I think I do, and he's always stressing over his mortgage.'

'It does seem a little odd.'

Reg pulls out his phone, and brings up a web browser, and taps in the company name. Less than a second later, a sizable villa set amongst lush foliage appears on the screen. Reg scrolls down the page, past the intro, past some property listings, past 10 Reasons Why You Should Choose Buy Barbados, to a testimonials section: four boxes, each with a quote from a customer. It's no surprise that one of them is Michael. (Compared to the puny size of the quarter-page ad, the website's extra space has allowed George free rein to add some meat to the bones.)

'I've always loved Barbados, ever since holidaying there as a kid. Since my parents passed away, I was lucky enough to have the money to buy a house in the Royal Sun resort. The purchase is a fitting memorial to mum and dad. It's the best investment I ever

made and Buy Barbados made it easy for me.' MICHAEL FINGUISH – Bucks

Silence descends like a thick fog in the Finguish home. At the base of the phone screen, Reg's thumb has developed a tic. He can feel his blood pressure, already held in check by two medications, skyrocketing. There's a faint ringing in his left ear. He tries to speak, but his jaws are immobile. With some effort, he manages a lateral movement of his phone arm towards Anne. As she prises the phone from his grip, it's as if a straitjacket has been removed.

Reg jumps out of the chair.

'What the fucking fuck?'

'Calm down, Reg. You're supposed to be resting that leg.'

'Read it. Go on, read it! Then see how you feel. Jesus!' Reg reluctantly eases himself back down into the chair.

With Reg's heavy panting adding a suitably atmospheric soundtrack to the moment, Anne reads the Michael's quote. 'Oh, my God. This has to be a joke.' Her voice is barely above a whisper.

'Joke? It's on the website for all to see. Of course it isn't a joke. We're dead, Anne. You and me. Dead and buried.'

'But where's the money come from? We only gave him enough for a deposit on the house.'

'Exactly. Unless he's some kind of drug baron on the side, there's only one place it could have come from.'

Ann looks blank. She's never really been interested in the business. Looking after Reg has always been her priority.

'From the company. From the fucking company! That's where he got it from. Must have.'

'I still don't believe it. He would have told us, surely.'

'You reckon?!' Reg isn't going to calm down anytime soon. 'Last week I heard there'd been a few changes that pissed off some damn good people. Who knows what's bloody going on down there? I need some air.' With that, Reg limps into the garden.

'Your stick, Reg! You need your stick!' Anne is close to tears.

———

'Come in, come in, come in,' says George, opening the door to Angela. There'd been a moment when neither of them knew whether to shake hands, give each other a peck on the cheek – one or two? – or do nothing. They settle for the latter, laughing the moment away.

'You look very nice,' says Angela, who George notes has again made a considerable effort herself. She pats his Marks & Spencer plaid shirt. 'Suits you.' Then, looking up, 'What happened to the brace?'

'Oh, that. I think my neck's better now. I only wear it during the day. Gets itchy.'

'The bruises have nearly disappeared too. I expect you'll soon have all the ladies flocking around you again, won't you?'

As they move into the living room, George is both flattered and just on the right side of terrified. His attractiveness is not something he considers very often, there being little opportunity or desire to test it. He barely notices the ever-deepening crows' feet edging his eyes, or the greying hair, though he carries a mild element of pride that he still has plenty of it.

'I'll have to fight them off, won't I?' says Angela, removing her coat.

'Well, I doubt that––'

'Aren't you going to offer me a drink, George? Tell you what,' she says, pulling a bottle of white wine from a supermarket carrier bag, 'I'll start with this. I left the car at home and took a taxi so I won't need to ration myself.' She beams, and George notices she has good teeth. Teeth are what first attracted him to Cynthia, but look how that turned out.

'Yes, of course. Very pragmatic. Do sit down, please.'

'Such a gentleman. You're one of a dying breed,' she says.

Having broken the ice with Angela seven days earlier, he's feeling a tad more relaxed this evening. Leaving her in the living room peering at the contents of his bookshelf, he checks on the lasagne. He's so focused on what he's doing he fails to notice her at the kitchen door, empty glass in hand.

'I'm lonely,' she says. 'Tell me you need a hand.'

George is unsure how to respond. Cynthia had never once offered to help him, instead concentrating on the more important aspects of her life, like watching reality TV or shopping online or probably planning clandestine trysts with her smooth-talking lover.

'Three minutes,' he blurts out, his eye on the timer. 'Three minutes, and then it's all done. Plus one more minute to serve up, so actually four minutes. Nearly there, Angela.'

'Looks like I'm surplus to requirements, then. What's a girl to do?' She gazes around the room. 'You do keep a tidy kitchen, don't you?'

'The secret is to clear up as you go. You can't work in chaos.'

'I heard that being untidy is good for your brain.'

'Not in this house, it isn't.'

This might come across as a little rude, but George is unaware. He's already downed two large G and Ts, one before Angela arrived and another in the past few minutes because of a sudden, intense thirst. The drinking doesn't stop there. Angela's budget Sauvignon Blanc is quickly dispatched during the meal. Even George enjoys a glass, despite his deep-seated misgivings of squashed grape. Now he's up for more alcohol, and tongues will loosen further.

'G and T?' he asks.

'Will it make me cry? The last time I had one was, let me see now, about thirty-five years ago. I'd just split with a boyfriend. My best friend took me to a pub, and I had too many of them. Cried my heart out, George. It was very embarrassing.'

'Dear me. Yes, I'm sure it was. You haven't just split up with another, have you?'

'Chance would be a fine thing.' She pushes her wine glass towards him. 'Go on then, you've persuaded me.'

The amount of alcohol she's consumed is affecting her decision-making processes. What's more, she knows it and doesn't care. They've covered a lot of ground in their conversations, as new friends do, and she's been quite open about certain aspects of her private life that perhaps she would normally have revealed later in a relationship.

George, on the other hand, has been less forthcoming, particularly about his mysterious plans for her ex-boss. Despite a thorough grilling by Angela, all he would admit to is that 'Today Is the Day'. Then he'd added the word 'hopefully'. Some people might have found this annoying, but to Angela it only made George more interesting.

As the evening wears on, George is just sober enough to realise his speech is slurred and he worries Angela will notice. Had he known she's thinking along the same lines, he'd probably have poured himself another G and T. He hasn't been this drunk in decades, and decides he's quite partial to it.

He judges the evening to be a success so far. And Angela helping him clear up feels like the icing on the cake. It feels like a proper, adult partnership. As he closes the dishwasher door, he almost stumbles over her and feels a hand gripping his arm to steady him. And the hand stays attached for a second longer than is entirely necessary. He mumbles an apology, but even George can feel a new dynamic in the relationship. A meal for two has turned into a date. Angela, of course, is ahead of him already.

When the mantelpiece clock strikes midnight, the conversation pauses as if both of them are fearful something might happen. Now her phone beeps.

'Taxi should be here in a minute.' she says, trying to push an arm into a wayward sleeve of her jacket. 'We had a laugh, didn't we?'

'It's been the best evening since ...' George can't remember an evening better than this since an accountancy conference dinner some years ago, but thankfully bites his lip before the words come out. 'We must do it again soon. Please. Angela. Yes.'

When the taxi arrives, the goodbyes are even more awkward that the hellos. Two people tentatively gripping each other's shoulders and leaning in to kiss each other's cheeks, but instead clashing noses. More embarrassed laughter as Angela weaves her way down the drive into the hands of a man whose local road knowledge comes from a free app on a recycled smartphone attached to the dashboard of his third hand Toyota Prius.

George closes the door only after the taxi drives off and staggers into the downstairs toilet. He unzips his fly, pulls out his penis and masturbates as furiously as a teenager.

———

While George sleeps, Goldtooth has checked into his laptop to see what he's been up to. Of particular interest tonight were the Speeders Intervention summary and Project Angela, the latter gaining a respectful nod from the virtual peeping tom. He'd been wondering if his target would ever do anything remotely interesting.

Now his slender fingers touch-type the Buy Barbados website address. It takes only a split second, yet the process is beautiful to behold, like a blind concert pianist totally at home with their tool of trade. Dancing eyes scan the website homepage, the forefinger of the right hand clicking through the menu, constantly scrolling down the pages. Everything in motion. Finally, the fingers come to rest at the testimonial section.

'... Buy Barbados made it easy for me.' MICHAEL FINGUISH – Bucks

Georgie, Georgie, who's a clever boy then. Add a ruthless streak and he'd have all the attributes to be a useful business partner. He chuckles at the ridiculous thought. Best to sit back for now, observe, see how it plays out. Then act.

———

Five

While the kettle is boiling, George opens up his laptop. Normally he wouldn't touch it until after breakfast, but today is different. Someone might have messaged him via his new Buy Barbados email address. With some trepidation, he clicks the inbox button. Bam! One email. Sent last night. He opens it. At the top: *r.finguish@safer-mail.online.* He leans back in the chair. He can barely bring himself to read it. This could go either way. Deep breath, George.

Hello, I've been recommended to you by a relative, Michael Finguish. He speaks very highly of your company and knew my wife and I were interested in purchasing a similar property in the Caribbean. I gather Michael bought the property for cash so what kind of discount could I expect if I were to proceed in the same way? I look forward to hearing from you at your earliest convenience.
Best regards
Reginald Finguish.

If George could have hummed *We are the Champions,* he would have done. Instead, he waves his arms in the air like an eight-year-old who's just scored a goal against his dad, something he'd never had the opportunity to do. He wishes Angela could have been there to witness this triumphant moment. He knows there are still hurdles to overcome, but the intervention is on the right track and that's what matters. It's clear Reg is fishing and George is happy to oblige with a well-worded reply.

Dear Mr Finguish

Thank you for your enquiry.

Barbados is indeed a wonderful choice for a second home – as I also explained to Michael, not that he needed any convincing! I was very moved to hear about the tragedy surrounding his parents. I'm sure the whole family misses them terribly. At least some good has come of it. I gather the Barbados government has since allocated some budget for anti-shark measures. Very generous, I thought, as sharks are extremely rare in that area. Indeed, one is far more likely to be lacerated by a boat propeller.

The Royal Sun Resort and environs has just about everything one needs, whether you're staying for a week or a lifetime. Properties inland start at around £250k, more for beachside locations. For a small villa such as the one Michael recently purchased, you're looking at asking prices of around £350-400k or more. Cash buyers are always much sought after, so I know you would be in an exceptional bargaining position. Depending upon the individual seller, a 10-20% discount would not be abnormal. I seem to remember Michael achieved something in that range.

Please let me know if there are any specific properties you're interested in and don't forget our low-cost inspection trips. I know you wouldn't be disappointed.
All the best

James Anderson
Managing Director, Buy Barbados

George gives it a final read-through and hits Send. He doubts he'll receive a reply. The email contains all the information Reg needs to confirm his fears. For now, his work is done. According to his intervention checklist, Reg's next step should be to make discreet enquiries into the Finguish Fans accounts. He won't want to confront Michael at this stage because there's no evidence yet of the source of the holiday home cash. What Reg needs is someone trustworthy, and with access to the financial records. And that means Angela. It'll be just like the old days.

He checks his watch. Ninety minutes before he meets up for a chess session with Ray in town. In his current state of euphoria, he feels optimistic enough to predict a significant, and his first, victory over him. If he knew what Angela was planning for her shopping expedition, however, he may have been somewhat distracted.

———

The black bishop in Ray's right hand flicks over George's white king just a little too hard. It rolls off the board, hovers at the edge of the table for a moment as if contemplating its next move, and falls into George's lap.

'And that's checkmate. Sorry, my friend. You started well,

but made a bit of a hash of it in the middle. That intervention stuff must be taking its toll on you.'

George rocks back in his chair, clutching his chess piece, and exhales loudly. He's unsure whether to take Ray's assessment of his play as some kind of back-handed compliment.

'I have been rather focused on it, to be honest, so maybe you're right. It's a different kind of thinking, you see. More involved, more players, more of a chance for chaos to rear its head.'

George appears to be attempting to elevate his own level of mental agility above that of Ray's merciless chess play. There's an atmosphere of real competition here, but will Ray notice? Of course he does.

'Yes, I'd imagine it would tax all but the most brilliant of minds. So, what's the latest? Any successes?'

Ray's mild jibe completely escapes George. He's wondering whether to tell him about the mixed results of the Speeders Intervention, but Project Angela is much more sophisticated.

'There is something. I've moved into real estate. Barbados.'

'Didn't I spot an ad in Artima magazine yesterday? Very enticing picture. Don't tell me that was yours?'

'The very same. Shark bait.' George smiles, impressed with his metaphor. 'And I've had a nibble already. Another game?'

'What, and leave your story hanging there? Spill the beans, George. I want to know every detail. It's not every day I meet a mastermind.'

'Well, if you insist.' He takes a sip of tea, swills in around his mouth. 'Funnily enough, it started with Angela.'

―――

Normally on a Saturday afternoon, Angela would clean the house after a supermarket visit. But today she's clothes shopping, planning for when she next sees George. Nothing too revealing, yet accentuating the curves of her body. Conservative, but with a twist, an edge. It's a little presumptuous because neither party has yet to extend an invitation, but she's hopeful. Store after store, rail after rail, she rummages through dresses, skirts, tops, and trouser suits, before settling on a dark red dress. It comes with a sizeable slash on the right-hand side up to midthigh, and a neckline that displays a tantalising amount of cleavage. The shop assistant tells her she looks ten years younger in it, and asks who the lucky man is she's trying to impress. Angela blushes, but mainly because she knows what she's about to buy next.

The last time she'd lingered this long in a lingerie section was never. Some years have passed since she'd someone in her life. After her first serious relationship with a man she truly loved ended – he'd run away with a married man, rather uncommon in those days – Angela has been sceptical about relationships. She'd seen other men since, but all of them had let her down, one way or another. In her eyes, George created the impression of being different. He hadn't made an obvious play for her, yet he appeared appreciative of her company. A thoughtful man, and certainly a bit of a control freak, but that didn't overly bother her. Most of all, he seemed genuinely interested in her as a person. Naturally, she hoped he thought about her body as well, which is why she'd ended up here, studying the more exotic lingerie on display.

Her day-to-day underwear looked so uninviting by comparison. But it was a question of balance. While she wanted George to find her attractive even after she'd slipped out of the new dress – and she'd sensed last night that the moment would happen sooner rather than later – she also didn't want to frighten him off. A deeply conservative man like George might not respond well to the kind of underwear a porn star might wear. Or would he? She knew which side of the fence her sister would sit on.

Angela has looked after herself, unlike some women of her age who, in her opinion, let themselves go. Fuller of build now than in her twenties, she still retained an hourglass figure. As she'd prepared for bed the previous night, the body she'd seen in the full-length mirror gave her renewed confidence. Fully naked, feet together and arms hanging loosely by her side, she tried to imagine what silk might feel like against her skin. And whether to follow current fashion and drastically trim her pubic hair. Mostly, she thought about being cuddled.

———

Angela's mobile rings as she bustles through her front door, clutching a brace of shopping bags.

'Hello,' she says, letting them slide to the floor.

'Angela? It's Reg. Reg Finguish.' It takes Reg less than a minute of small talk to get to the point. 'Listen, as you know, I'm still the major shareholder in the business and I'm a bit concerned about something that's recently come to my attention. Now this is strictly between you and me, okay? Can I trust this will go no further?'

Angela loves a secret as much as the next person, but not as much as Jackie. 'Of course. Just like the old days.'

'Ah yes.' Reg is instantly transported to the cosy office he shared with her. 'The old days.' For years, he'd harboured a secret crush on his personal assistant, yet his honour and loyalty had always prevented him from acting upon it.

'Are you still there, Reg?'

'Yes, yes, I am. Sorry. Angela, you know that holiday home that Michael has just bought?' Reg thinks he's very clever posing the question as a statement because it implies knowledge of it.

'Yes, but I don't know much about it. Can't you ask him?'

She hears a bang at the other end of the line. It's Reg kicking the coffee table with his good leg.

'Reg?'

'I'm here. Okay, big favour please. I want you to print out the September accounts balance sheet and bank statements for the past six months. You know where to locate them on the system. Don't email it, print it, and call me when it's done. Is that alright?'

Angela agrees, but she's uneasy about the task. A secret is one thing, but subterfuge pushes her moral boundaries. However, it's now obvious to her that Reg must have at least an inkling about Michael's loan for the holiday home. And anything to get shot of that arrogant arse would not only be good for her, but for the entire company. Who knows, she thinks, Reg might even return. She texts George.

Dear George, Michael Finguish might be in trouble. Good riddance! Fancy going for a walk tomorrow afternoon? A

―――

The path over the common winds through a stand of ancient oak before heading to the crest of an escarpment. Here, beside the path and bathed in dappled sunlight, is a wooden bench donated by the family of a local man who'd spent many happy hours staring across the patchwork of fields below him. After a rather muddy forty-minute walk, George and Angela have just reached it.

Her news had excited George, and he actively encouraged her to do as Reg has asked, despite her continued apprehension over becoming a spy. What he hasn't mentioned yet is his involvement in the affair, and Angela has apparently forgotten about George's promise to arrange for Reg's return to work. He'd like to tell her, but it's too early in the game to show his hand.

So far, he's had two other emails expressing interest in the Barbados properties, and George finds some satisfaction in this, knowing that his marketing actually works. The messages are sitting in his inbox awaiting a response. They'll never be answered because George plans to delete the website as soon as he knows Reg has the company accounts in his hands. And it wouldn't matter if Reg tries to show Michael the website and discovers it's disappeared off the face of the ether. The damage will have been done once he sees the evidence on the balance sheet.

'I love this view. It makes me feel small.' says Angela. 'In a good way,' she adds. 'It's been a while since I've walked up here. Used to come a lot.'

'Me too. We probably passed each other at some point.' George realises the car accident and assault had precipitated another outcome he hadn't considered before – meeting Angela. 'Strange how things work out, isn't it? And who'd have believed you now have the opportunity to take down your idiot boss. You wouldn't have predicted that a few weeks ago, would you?'

'If there's one thing I've learned, it's that you can't predict anything.' She stands up and stretches her legs, not noticing the smug look on George's face. 'My place for tea?'

'Why not. I'll tell you about my speeding cars intervention on the way.'

And he does. The whys, the hows, the stats, all in micro-detail. Even easy-going Angela switches off. When they arrive back at the car park, she's had enough.

'It's all very clever, George, but what happened in the end?'

George fumbles in his pocket for the car keys. The repair shop returned his old Mondeo yesterday. New boot lid, bumper, lights, exhaust. It was touch and go whether the insurance company would write it off but George is happy to see his old friend again, whatever its foibles. He holds the door open for Angela.

'I'm wittering on, aren't I? Apologues.' He hates saying sorry, which is why he subconsciously invented a new word which generally satisfies the apologee, yet allows him to escape the responsibility of actually admitting he's made a mistake. So far, not a single person who's been on the receiving end has pointed out that apologue is an obscure word meaning 'fables', which in George's usage would make absolutely no sense at all.

'It's fine, George, really. It was just getting a bit ... complicated. You must think I'm really thick.'

'Perish the thought. Mea culpa,' he says, still refusing to apologise properly. He rattles out these words like they mean nothing to him, and he doesn't even realise he's doing it.

———

In the time between buying her new dress and lingerie yesterday, Angela had passed a small concession selling chocolate brownies. She bought four, earmarking them for weekday afternoon snacks. But that was before George came around. Now, back at her house, he has a sizeable chunk in his mouth. Angela has asked him a question about how the police were progressing with his case, and he's totally incapable of answering without soft brown shrapnel flying from his mouth onto her carpet. He sips some tea to help wash it down, simultaneously holding up his forefinger in the direction of his host. The seconds tick by.

'I've not heard anything lately,' he finally answers, 'but they told me it would be a few months before it came to court.'

'And the maniac's still out there. That would scare me.'

It bothers George too, but won't let on. Instead, he says, 'Well, he'd be stupid to try anything, wouldn't he? It would make a bad situation even worse for him.' What he really thinks is maniacs don't act like normal, logical citizens. In the heat of the moment, they seem to be unaware of the potential repercussions of their actions.

'Another brownie?' says Angela. 'I won't eat it. Trying to keep this body in check.' It's a statement that comes with a hidden invitation for George to first look at her body, and then to say something nice about it.

His eyes dip from her face to her breasts, then return. 'I think, er ... You've got nothing to worry about on that score. I'm the one who should be abstaining. Yes, indeedy.'

George is enjoying himself in his own quiet way. He'd planned to have a quick cuppa and be on his way. After all, there were letters to local authorities to compose, the weekly ironing, and his household accounts spreadsheet required updating. But Angela appears to have weaved a procrastination spell over him. He's well aware that his tasks are being overlooked, yet he doesn't want to leave the warmth and, dare he even think it, the excitement of Angela's company. It feels, well, a little weird.

'You're not so bad yourself, George,' says Angela. 'All you need is a little looking after.'

'Ha ha, are you offering? Cynthia said that once, I seem to remember.' His face reddens at the mention of his ex. The woman who'd helped build his confidence, then shattered it over a splendid Pad Thai in a well-reviewed local restaurant – the one thing for which George would never forgive her. How could you revisit a place after something like that had happened? To compound the problem, the only other Thai in town flattered to deceive. All the frills but hiding an inadequate chef and rodent droppings.

'Cynthia's loss is the rest of the world's gain,' says Angela, smiling. She's unsure whether she's overcooking things, but ploughs ahead anyway. 'Do you ever see her, George? Must be difficult.'

'Thankfully, no. I gather she moved to Burnley where Geoff got a job selling solar panels. I don't think they get much sunshine up there, but if anyone could convince the punters, it's Geoff.' It's a testament to George's continued admiration of Geoff's skills that he's still prepared to big him up. Angela thinks that if she were in George's position, Geoff's name would have a permanent prefix: Fucking. And, like George, it's not a word she uses lightly.

'You're amazing, you know.' she says. 'How something like that could happen and you rise above it all. I wouldn't be so understanding.'

George wishes he'd not used the Cynthia word now. It's broken the spell in the room and he knows his pleasant afternoon is all but over. He'll recover, of course, but now he needs the distractions that only his home can offer him. Angela can feel the change in atmosphere too and sensibly lets events take their natural course.

As he walks to his car, she calls out, 'Call me. *You* call *me*. It's a two-way street.'

He gives her the thumbs up and says, 'And don't forget about Reg! It's important.'

The TV image flickers again, then loses colour intensity. George tuts and puts down the iron. He turns the TV off and back on.

It's not the first time he's had to do this during his shirt ironing session. It's difficult enough switching his focus between flattening creases and keeping up with the documentary, without worrying about the TV picture disappearing altogether. He's learning about a Scottish ex-entrepreneur who'd left the civilised world to live a self-sufficient life in Thailand's back-of-beyond. George thought the man looked quite unwell. As the man eulogised on the benefits of his new life, George became more and more sceptical, convinced it was simply bravado for the cameras. Understandable, though. Why would you own up to making a terrible mistake? He mentally removed Thailand from his list of boltholes. A shame because he enjoyed the food. Besides, now there was Angela. And, by the tone of her last request, he'd better get his act together if the relationship was to continue.

He'd never been the most proactive with the opposite sex. And when he had, things usually went wrong. One Valentine's Day, in his third year at secondary school, he'd bravely secreted a card into the bag of a popular girl called Cheryl. When she found it, a cluster of classmates – including some boys who were competing for her affections – crowded around her. At this point, George retreated to his usual position at the back of the room, blushing even before Cheryl opened the card. A knockback was always likely, but what happened next was much, much worse.

'It's from Georgie! You got a card from Georgie!' squealed one of Cheryl's girlfriends. 'Georgie loves Cheryl. Cheryl loves Georgie.' The rest of the George's class took up the chant that Cheryl's posse had begun. 'Cheryl loves Georgie, Georgie loves Cheryl.'

Cheryl turned a violent shade of cerise. 'No, I don't.' Pause. The chanting resumed. Her response plainly didn't satisfy the mob. 'I hate him,' she said. 'I hate him,' she repeated with more conviction. What else could she do? It was all about self-preservation, and George had to be sacrificed.

But that was only the start. 'Rip it up, then!' someone said.

'Rip it up! Rip it up! Rip it up! Rip it up!' Thirty children can make a lot of noise. George looked over to Cheryl and gave her a hint of a wry smile. A gesture that seemed to give Cheryl permission to extract herself from the most embarrassing moment of her life to date.

She ripped up George's card and let the pieces drop to the floor.

After the cheers subsided and the class distracted by something else, Cheryl glanced back in George's direction. The smile still hung on his face, unchanged. No one would have known what was going on in his head.

He never made the first move ever again. The few girlfriends he'd had were only a result of persistence by the girl. Cynthia, who'd wasn't the brightest of souls, saw George, then in his twenties, as a fast-track meal ticket out of her local estate. Wasting no time, she'd seduced him in the bathroom of her parent's house within minutes of picking her up for what he'd thought was going to be a tentative date at a local restaurant. Wham, bam, thank you Cynthia.

George resolved to call Angela the following day to make some plans. He guessed it didn't matter so much what the plans were, as long as some were made. Leisure arrangements were plainly important to Angela. In the meantime, he texts her: *Tea and cake yummy. Call you tomorrow night. Good luck being a spy! x*

He stalls for a moment, wondering whether to delete that sign-off kiss. George's head says the kiss takes things to another level. Was that bad? Good? Too presumptuous? Was one kiss enough? Did men add kisses? This is awkward territory. In the end, he bravely sticks with it and hits Send. If he'd looked in a mirror, he would have seen the thirteen-year-old George in the classroom on Valentine's Day.

———

Angela drives into the office car park half an hour earlier than usual. That would give her plenty of time to find the relevant documents in the system, and print them. In the old days, Reg, a seventy-hour week man, would have beaten her to it, but Michael rarely made it in before nine. But today is different. Michael's Jaguar is already in his assigned space. Angela curses, and now has to think of an excuse for why she's so early. Turns out it's Michael who does the explaining.

'You just caught me. I'm not feeling too good today, so I thought I'd grab some work and take it home. I haven't checked my diary, so please could you rearrange anything. And no calls unless it's urgent, okay?'

Perfect. She has all the time in the world to carry out her mission undisturbed. Even before he's reversed the Jag out of its space, Angela has located the files and pressed the Print button.

———

Six

Over a boiled egg and soldiers breakfast, George reads through a draft of his speeders intervention letter to the relevant authorities. He'd written a page of notes the previous night and had slept on it. Literally slept on it. He'd been led to believe by some pre-internet age guru that placing important work under your pillow triggered the unconscious mind to cogitate on the subject whilst sleeping. In bed this morning, sipping hot tea, and with a radio talk show in the background, he'd scanned through the creased notes again and congratulated himself on a well-constructed argument. Sensibly, he's been careful to focus his pitch more on the principle of his intervention, rather than the unscientific stats he compiled.

Later that morning, he propels three envelopes through the slot in the mailbox at the end of the road, ready for the noon collection. One to the Chief Constable of the county police, one to his Member of Parliament, the other to the head of the County Council's Highways Department. George believes the recipients will take a personally signed letter more seriously than an email.

As he walks home, he detects a vibration in his jacket pocket. It's a text from Angela: *I've done it! Meeting Reg at lunchtime to give it to him. Chat later xxx.* George is thrilled for two reasons. Michael's role in the company could be history in a matter of hours, but more importantly Angela has taken George's text kiss and trebled it. It's been a good start to the week, he decides, though the onerous nature of his next task tempers his mood.

Every Monday, George updates his household accounts and checks his bank statements and other small investments. For a man well-acquainted with numbers and who keeps such a tight rein on himself and his life, he can be surprisingly blinkered with the all-important overview of his own finances. His redundancy payment is long gone, and he'd resorted to periodic sales of some investments to keep him afloat. When he was first laid off, he predicted there would be enough cash to tide him over until he started another job. But with the pressure off, he'd relaxed a little too much. In his defence, he'd applied for every suitable position available but received only one interview. As a result, his confidence took a battering. And to compound his financial position, he doesn't believe in claiming unemployment benefit. He still has his pride. Anyway, the benefits office would only push him into becoming a supermarket delivery driver or suggest he retrain as a barista in some hipster coffee shop.

Reluctantly, he clicks on the total cell in the negative column on his spreadsheet. Then does the same in the positive one. There's no putting his head in the sand today. The figures staring him full in the face aren't pretty. A quick mental calculation reveals he has less than two months' money left. After that, he'd need to cash in some of his pension or sell critical assets. Perhaps starting with the car, then the house. Ah, the house. He let the thought dwell there for a moment. It was his house, the one he'd managed to keep even after Cynthia left him and demanded her share of its value. He'd tightened his belt, forgoing luxuries like holidays, and only in recent years had paid off both Cynthia and the mortgage. He'd worked hard for that house.

Now his thoughts drift to the local lottery winner. So many millions, and all courtesy of him. Swift action is called for. He jots down an Options for Income list.

―――――

Reg has bagged a window table in the Marsh & Parsons coffee shop. He mulls over why so many independent establishments like this now have names like solicitors or estate agents. They make coffee, not contracts. But when he looks around at his fellow customers, many of whom are glued to their laptops, he supposes it is a kind of office after all. He sits back and tries to relax. He's been unsettled throughout the weekend, finding it difficult to take his mind off being shredded by a shark. Worse, he'd had to endure the weekly call from Michael on Sunday night without bringing up the Barbados fiasco, much as he wanted to. He feigned a coughing fit and curtailed the call before the throbbing vein in his left temple exploded.

The door opens and Angela walks in. He stands up, pulls out a chair.

'Angela, good of you to come. Do you have time for something?'

'Why not. Michael's working from home today – he's not well – and I don't think anyone else will miss me for a while.'

'Not well? He sounded fine last night when I spoke to him. What'll you have?'

Whilst he's at the counter, Angela retrieves the folded financial statements from her bag and slides them under the saucer of Reg's cappuccino as if she's leaving a tip. No one in the room notices, such is the nonchalance with which she does it. While still uncomfortable with her actions, she has to admit the task he'd set her has added an element of excitement to her day.

Reg returns with her skinny decaf cappuccino, hold the chocolate. He thinks he's ordered it correctly, but isn't entirely sure.

'Thanks for doing this,' he says, frowning as he scans through the accounts summary. 'Just as I feared. I thought I could trust him to take good care of the company. Not your problem, though. By the way, I hear Linda was made redundant recently. What's the story on that? I know it's hard getting good marketing people.'

'Let's just say she's attractive. I really shouldn't say any more.'

'Of course, of course. Very unfair of me. You've done enough already.'

Angela plucks up the courage to get her fears off her chest. 'I'm worried, Reg. I'm worried that I'll turn up one day soon and it'll be my turn to go. I like my job and I'm good at it. And I still have ten years until retirement. Who'd give me a fresh start at my age? You know how it is out there.'

Reg lays his hand on her forearm. 'Listen, I'll do everything I can to make sure that doesn't happen. You trust me, don't you?'

'Of course I trust you, but I don't trust – and I'm sorry to say this – I don't trust Michael.'

———

With a hummed approximation of the theme tune from a TV thriller series his parents religiously watched when he was a boy, George celebrates the completion of his Options for Income list. For better or worse, he's happy to have the facts out in the open. Change and challenges lie ahead, but there's a certain excitement that comes with them.

The recruitment companies have been useless, and the prognosis is poor. The option of relocating somewhere with cheaper housing had obvious benefits, but he'd be leaving Ray and Angela behind. Downsizing locally, though, would solve that problem. Devising a new intervention that would make him a lottery jackpot winner was reluctantly discounted. Too many variables. The final option on his list, going freelance, looks to be the most sensible and, in the current circumstances, the most doable. With thirty-five years' experience of company finance, he has a lot to offer, and with all these so-called start-ups popping up all over the place, surely there'd be no lack of potential customers. He could advertise – grudgingly – in the local newspaper or that Artima magazine perhaps, although he'd have to watch the cost.

Most people would kick off a business by asking their circle of friends and family to put the word out, but George isn't most people. He has Angela and Ray. At a stretch, a few others he saw irregularly. Hardly what you'd call a network.

He looks at his watch: too early to call Angela. She won't be home for another hour. He prints out the list, grabs a pen, and settles down in a chair on the sunny patio. He casts his eyes over the neatly manicured lawn. Despite the unusually hot summer, it's still a vibrant green. George invests considerable time on his garden and he wishes his neighbours took as much pride in theirs – especially Robert and Mary next door. They seemed to be averse to the outdoors, hence the weed-ridden borders and overgrown shrubs. He puts it down to their advanced years and an unhealthy obsession with obscure academia and psychedelic knitwear patterns. Possibly even psychedelic drugs when they were younger.

He continues making notes until an oven alarm and the aroma of a Chicken Provencal casserole wafting through the open patio doors alert him to the time. He pulls the phone from his pocket and calls Angela. It rings six times and switches to voicemail.

'This is Angela. Please leave a message unless you're a stalker.'

'George calling secret agent, over.' George thinks she'll be amused by this. 'How did it go? Call me. Thanks.'

His call to action sounds very relaxed, but actually he's annoyed at Angela for not picking up. What's the point of having a mobile phone if you don't answer it? As he clicks off the call, he lets out a little yelp of frustration and marches indoors to stab the chicken thigh with a thermometer. There's no need for him to do this at all. The casserole has had the requisite time, but George doesn't trust the supermarket chicken you buy these days. One in three are found to contain Salmonella or E. coli, so he isn't taking any chances. The thermometer reads seventy-five degrees Celsius. Perfect. He ladles half the contents onto a plate, along with some green beans, and the rest into a plastic container, earmarked for consumption on Wednesday.

The moment he sits down to eat, his mobile rings. This is most inconvenient. George hates to be disturbed while he's eating, and for twenty minutes afterwards when relaxation is vitally important for digestion.

'Yeeesss?' he says, rather impolitely.

'Oooh, who's in a strop then?' says Angela. 'If it's not a good time, George ...?'

George silently curses himself for not bothering to check the caller ID before he picked up. 'Angela, forgive me. I was just distracted. How are you?' He looks longingly at his dinner plate, which he knows will now have to go into the microwave to heat up again.

'I had a nice coffee with Reg at lunchtime. He's not happy, George, not happy at all.'

'So he's seen the numbers then?'

'Put it this way, I wouldn't want to be in Michael's shoes. And he said my job is safe. My guess is it'll all go off tonight. Reg isn't the kind of man to postpone something like this.'

'That's brilliant news.' George is up from the table and walking around the room like an animated spin doctor. 'Must mean he's thinking about coming back to work then. We must celebrate. What about a Chinese? Even better, let me order a takeaway and you can come here. Tomorrow? What do you think?' George has barely taken a breath. This is reckless talk, and a younger version of himself would have taken him to task. But now he's thrown Angela a very tasty bone, and it's pounced upon immediately.

She sees George's enthusiasm and raises him. 'Or even tonight. I know it's a school night and I've only just got home, but I could be with you in an hour.'

George looks down at his untouched plate. It's not what he planned, but he doesn't want to disappoint her. 'Anything in particular you want me to order, or shall I surprise you?' He's rarely surprised anyone with anything, so the words actually surprise George himself. Something's happening to me, he thinks, and it's not altogether unpleasant.

The moment the call finishes, he logs on to the admin area of the Buy Barbados website and presses a small red button on the top right-hand corner of the page. A window pops up:

ARE YOU SURE YOU WANT TO UNPUBLISH YOUR WEBSITE?
NO ONE IN THE WORLD WILL BE ABLE TO SEE IT.

George clicks Yes. It's as if BuyBarbados.uk never existed.

———

While George is checking through his proposed Chinese takeaway order for the third time – Crispy Duck is now back on the list, having been deleted initially for being too obvious a choice – a Buy Barbados bookmark on a web browser is clicked. It reveals an on-screen message: Page not found.

Goldtooth knows it can only mean one thing: the website has done its job and is no longer required. He's not at all surprised. George's homespun project to save his little lady friend had been ingenious and well executed.

Perhaps he could use Buy Barbados for his own ends? To turn George's victory into his downfall? He's been struggling for days to find a neat way to spread the word about the squalid images he placed on George's laptop. Now he has the perfect vehicle.

He makes a note on his pad: Business cards.

———

Reg slams the front door behind him.

'That you, Reg?' a voice calls out.

'Who the hell else would it be?' He limps through to the kitchen where Anne is rearranging some flowers in a vase.

'It's just a figure of speech. I see your mood hasn't improved then? How was Angela?'

Reg slaps the now crumpled company balance sheet on the worktop. 'She's fine. See that big hole there,' he says, tapping his forefinger at two vastly differing numbers, 'that's the house in Barbados.'

Anne makes a show of studying the sheet but she has no

idea what she's looking at. 'So what happens now? You're not going to let him get away with it, are you?'

'Damn right, I'm not. You know what this means, don't you?'

Anne thinks she knows the answer, but can't say it in case she reveals her obvious enthusiasm. Reg won't give her the opportunity, anyway.

'I'm going to have to go back to work, at least for a while. Sorry, but there it is. Someone's got to sort this mess out.'

'Oh, you poor love,' says Anne, holding back a huge smile as she waltzes towards the kettle. 'Cup of tea? Biscuit?'

———

A scooter with a large black box on the back is buzzing its way towards George's house. Judging by the skill with which it's being manoeuvred, the rider has learned much from action movies and video gaming. Amber traffic lights appear to be a signal to speed up, red ones an excuse to intimidate other drivers by staring at them from behind a black-visored helmet. And the broken white line existing only to show where the middle of the road actually is, should anyone be interested.

George glowers at his watch. Mr Huang's wife or sister or daughter or cousin – he never could discern between their voices – had assured him they would deliver the meal within thirty minutes. Yet here we are, less than two minutes from the deadline, and no sign of it. He's totally unaware that the tighter the deadline, the better the scooter rider performs. Even seemingly impossible delivery windows don't faze him. One-way streets, pavements, speed limits, are all fair game. Traffic-calmed roads, a particular favourite, are an opportunity to 'get some air' under his wheels. Rain, hail or snow are no barriers to performance. They merely serve to make the journey more engaging.

The rider only wishes he could add an element of combat to his journeys, preferably with guns and zombies. He doesn't need to check his watch like George. He can predict his ETA to the second.

George hears a triple beep from his driveway. Checks his watch again. Nods approvingly, then opens the front door. He looks down at the huge racing helmet that sits atop a diminutive figure.

'Chinese,' says a muffled voice.

'You old enough to drive?' says George, stooping to take the large bag.

'Course.'

'Well, thank you.'

The rider flicks open his visor. A boy's blue eyes, unsullied by life, stare out.

'Er, thank you very much,' says George.

The rider doesn't move. 'Delivery man's tip,' he says. 'They pay shit,' he adds, justifying his request.

'Well, they don't mention that on the menu. I've read the small print, what little there is. There's just a delivery charge which I've already paid.'

'Everyone pays the tip, mate. They just do.'

George realises he could be standing there for some time if they carried on arguing. It might even end up with a brick sailing through his window one day. He instinctively fishes around in his pocket for some change, but it's a pointless exercise. He'd decided at the beginning of the year to give up carrying around cash. Even buskers owned card machines these days, not that he'd ever given money to that pack of guitar-wielding wannabees.

'One minute,' he says, and rushes into the kitchen to raid his emergency coin tin. He picks up a handful of coins, removes the most valuable, and returns to scooter boy.

'There you go. And don't go spending it on cigarettes, alcohol or drugs.'

The boy grunts a thank you and straddles his scooter.

'Open a stocks and shares ISA!' George shouts as the boy takes off. 'You'll thank me when you're older.'

Angela is warming two plates under the grill in the kitchen when he returns. 'That smells good,' she says.

'Shenzen Spice,' says George, 'the best in town according to the reviews. And now the most hygienic. They were prosecuted six months ago, so they had to clean up their act. I bet you could eat off the floor there now.' He holds up the bag. 'Shall I take it through?' Normally, this is not a question George would ask in his own house, but he feels it's only polite.

Angela, hands now clad in George's Souvenir-from-Corfe-Castle oven gloves, pulls out the plates. George looks on, trying to get to grips with the image of someone else wearing them. It feels intimate in a way that he's not felt for a long time. 'Yes, do,' she says. 'We're ready here.'

They sit on adjacent sides at one end of the dining table. George had heard it's more romantic than sitting opposite one another and laid the table accordingly. His alcohol regime has faltered again. He'd been quite prepared to drink water. Then Angela arrived with a bottle of wine and it would appear rude if he didn't join her. He was even developing a taste for Sauvignon Blanc, much to his surprise.

He holds up a glass. 'To you, Angela, for bravery in the field.'

Angela reciprocates. 'To you, George, for the encouragement. I'm not sure I could have done it without you.'

'Well, far be it for me to say but ... I'll let you into a little secret. Have you heard of BuyBarbados.uk?'

Wary of his previous inefficiency in the laborious telling of the speeding cars intervention, George now relates an impressively short synopsis of Project Angela. When he finishes, he raises his glass once again. 'So, to Reg, saviour of Finguish Fans.'

Angela can barely speak. This good-hearted man, someone she'd met only a month ago in terrible circumstances, had gone out of his way to help her. And he'd asked for nothing in return. 'Oh, my God,' she breathes, 'do you ... do you do this kind of thing often?' Even as the words came out, they sounded slightly ridiculous, but she secretly wanted to confirm that, in George's eyes, she's been singled out for special treatment.

'You're only my second experiment, Angela. We still don't know if it's going to work out the way we want. Let's pray that it does for your sake.' He lays his hand gently upon hers.

'You must have an amazing brain. I saw your chess board. I bet you're good at that.'

'Well...'

George is about to say something he may regret. Worse, it's a lie. An unnecessary one, but he's on a roll with Angela and wants to keep up the momentum.

'You remember I mentioned my friend, Ray, the poor soul with the ill wife, the one who doesn't get out much? He's a skilful player, very experienced, but I can see through his strategies plain as day. I let him win most of the time because I know it's important to him. You don't want to kick a man when he's down.'

———

The lovingly constructed code that allowed Goldtooth remote access to George's laptop contains something even more intrusive. The ability to switch on George's laptop camera.

While George and Angela had been enjoying their meal, little did they know the entire event was being watched on a live stream. When George was laying the table, he'd moved the laptop from where he'd been working and placed it on top of a sideboard, the screen still open. The wide-angle camera lens captured the critical part of the room. It had been a lucky break for Goldtooth who'd spotted the number of the Chinese restaurant on the recent calls list on George's mobile. One quick call and he'd put two and two together.

He'd poured himself a drink and settled in the chair, eager to watch the evening unfold. But he was totally unprepared for what he witnessed. The way the conversation flowed. A laugh here, a light touch there. So comfortable with each other. So – and it pained him to think it – happy. And he might have coped better if George had dialled down the grandstanding about his precious and oh-so-clever Project Angela. And there was something else he said. An out and out lie. And the longer Goldtooth watched, the emptier he felt, as if George was sucking the life from him. And the more he thought about it, the more pain he wanted to inflict on George. And Angela, the interloper. She must suffer too.

It was time to unleash the might of *Project George – The Revenge*.

Seven

Goldtooth's games had started when he was still in short trousers. Even before his parents waved goodbye to him at the boarding school entrance, he'd devised ways to make them pay for their decision to rid themselves of their only child for much of the year. The school, in an old Snowdonian country house, had been trendy in the mid 1970s. It expounded the values of individualism above academic achievement. A perfect fit for hippie parents who initially followed the movement's values of peace, love and freedom, but subsequently embraced the very system they claimed to despise.

Their tiny mail order business selling colourful Indian-made clothes had taken off. Within five years, the company became a high-street fixture and earned revenues in the tens of millions. Amid his parents' long working hours and global travelling, the unplanned and probably unwanted Goldtooth became an inconvenience. It was something even a young boy could detect.

He'd started with the traditional game of playing one parent off against the other, and over the following years he perfected it. Whatever he asked for, he received. To strengthen his control, he moved onto his fellow pupils, blackmailing those who transgressed the few rules the school actually upheld. He rose quickly in the hierarchy, both admired and feared, even by the older pupils. Although his reputation hadn't escaped the notice of the teaching staff, it was tolerated. Such behaviour was surely a childish phase he would grow out of.

When the adult Goldtooth finally emerged into the real world, he was fully conversant in extortion and manipulation. While his peers set off for university or job interviews, Goldtooth was already looking at devious ways to make some serious cash from his talents.

Friends and associates were merely tools to be used in his plans. What other use would they have?

An hour after Reg left a voicemail on Michael's phone, the call is returned. His heart cranks into overdrive. He'd like to settle this right now to minimise the stress, but he believes it would be better to do this face to face. Gripping his mobile like he's never going to let it go, he punches the big green button.

'Dad, you called.'

'Michael, thanks for getting back to me. Are you in the office tomorrow morning? I'd like to discuss something with you.' Reg hopes Michael doesn't notice the slight tremor in his voice.

'Should be. Wasn't feeling too good this morning so I worked from home. What's up?'

'Nothing that can't wait. How's Sophie and the kids?'

'Yeah, they're good thanks. Rupert got a gold star for his times tables today. I think he's going to be as good at numbers as you. Anne okay?'

Reg thinks Michael's not so shoddy with numbers either, but lets it pass. 'Yes, she's fine thanks. Sends her love.' Anne, who's preparing the dinner, scowls over her shoulder. 'I'll pop in about ten if that's convenient.'

———

A large Mercedes drives smoothly into a visitor's parking space at Finguish Fans. As Reg exits his car, he grabs the Artima magazine from the passenger seat.

'Can I help you?' says a glossy girl with a dash of indifference as he walks into the reception lobby.

'Good morning,' says Reg. 'Where's Sue then? Holiday?'

'Don't know any Sue. I'm new, me. Who've you come to see?'

'Michael Finguish. He's expecting me.'

'What's your name?'

'Finguish, Reg Finguish.'

There's a pause as the girl registers the similarity of the names. 'You his dad, then? He doesn't look like you.' She giggles.

Reg sighs. 'Just let him know I'm here, please.'

The girl taps three digits on the keypad. 'Michael, your dad's here. Shall I send him through?' She looks up at Reg and smiles sweetly. 'He says you know the way.'

Reg limps down a short corridor and stops outside a door which is signed Michael Finguish, Chief Executive Officer. It's a business of less than fifty people, he thinks, not a giant multinational corporation. He shakes his head in disbelief and walks in. Michael stands as he enters.

'Hi Dad, good to see you.' He gestures towards a chair. 'Everything alright?'

'Michael, I want you to take a look at something.' Reg

opens up *Artima* at the appropriate page and tosses it onto the desk. He won't sit down yet. He's too fired up. Michael picks up the magazine.

'What am I looking at?'

'The ad, bottom right-hand corner. Ring any bells?'

'I don't ... That's my name on here!' Michael is trying to get his brain around how his name has appeared in an ad from a company he's never heard of. 'This is ... this is ... ridiculous.'

'So you don't own a property in Barbados, then?'

'Well, I ... I've been meaning to tell you about it. Just didn't get around to it. The deal's only just been done. Quite an opportunity, actually.'

'I'm sure it was, given that it was paid from an inheritance.'

Michael looks confused. 'Inheritance?'

'Yes, the one from your deceased parents. Remember them?'

'I've no idea what you're talking about. What deceased parents?'

'The dead ones, obviously. I seem to recall your words on their website: the purchase is a fitting memorial to my mum and dad. Are you saying you don't remember that?'

Finguish Junior is lost for words.

'Shark attack? Ring any bells?'

As Michael continues to look confused, Finguish Senior moves in for the kill.

'I'd like to look at the last quarter's accounts, please.'

The colour drains from Michael's face. 'The accounts? Why do you want to look at those?' The situation clearly calls for some bravado. 'And who's running this business now, anyway?' He throws the magazine back in the direction of Reg. 'You promised me you wouldn't interfere.'

'As the majority shareholder, I have every right to look at the books.' Reg moves around the desk so he's standing beside

Michael. He places his hand on the mouse. 'Do you want to bring them up, or shall I?'

Michael acquiesces, and petulantly flops back in his chair. Reg finds the relevant spreadsheet, points to the evidence.

'What. The fuck. Are you playing at?'

Silence.

Reg isn't finished. 'Here's what I think has happened. Feel free to correct me if I'm mistaken. Getting yourselves strapped into a huge mortgage you can barely afford plainly isn't risky enough. You and Sophie got greedy. You want to play the big I Am and buy a holiday home, but there's only one place you can find the cash. So the company loans you, probably interest-free, and you make some payments as and when you feel like it – if at all. Is that about the long and the short of it?'

'I'm sorry.' Michael's words are barely audible.

'Pardon?'

'I'm sorry. It was Sophie's idea, really. I should have talked to you first.'

Guilty as charged. Now for the sentencing.

'Here's what's going to happen, Michael. You're going to sell that house. You'll probably lose money, but that's life. The company will then arrange for you to repay that debt over a sensible period. Fair?'

Michael nods.

'Then we're going to remove that stupid sign on this office door and you can make some space for another desk in here. I'm moving back in. And I won't be moving out again until I can trust you won't put the company in jeopardy ever again. Is that clear?'

Michael feels a burning at the back of his throat. He attempts to swallow, but it's difficult. 'Yes, perfectly,' he sniffs.

'Good. I'll be in at eight-thirty tomorrow morning and I'll

expect to see evidence the Barbados house is on the market, okay? Now pull yourself together and get the ball rolling.'

Michael sits back up in the chair. 'I never said those things, you know, about the inheritance. I don't even know anything about the company. It's not who we bought the house from.' He sounds so sincere Reg almost believes him, but he doesn't comment. He's already left the room.

The first thing Michael does is go to the Buy Barbados website. A message comes up: Page not found. He looks at the ad again and retypes the address in case he made a mistake. Same message. He's been stitched up, but by whom? And why?

Michael is unsure whether he's angry or upset or both. He feels like a five-year-old who's just been sent to his room. And he knows Sophie will be livid. No, make that apoplectic. She's boasted about it to too many people. Holiday dates are fixed, flights booked, and invitations delivered for Sophie's friends to stay.

How will he tell her? Perhaps she doesn't need to know yet? A part of him wants to take a break away from the office, away from Sophie, away from his parents. He wants them to know he's hurting. Then he thinks of the kids. His eyes well up.

―――

In the public gallery of the local magistrate's court the following morning, George looks down upon his attacker and hopes he's feeling the pressure too. White Car Man is asked to stand by the clerk and verify his name, address, date of birth and nationality. The brown pinstripe suit he's wearing appears to have been picked up in a charity shop whilst under the influence of alcohol in the nineteen-seventies. The jacket sleeves are too short, the lapels wider than is good for them, and the trouser legs incorporate the generosity of flare that could make shoes disappear. We discover the accused's name is Barry Andrew Briggs.

A magistrate reads out the charges and asks Briggs how he pleads.

Briggs' head droops. 'Not guilty,' he mumbles.

The other magistrate leans forward, a hand to his ear. 'Pardon?'

Briggs raises his head a few degrees. 'Not. Guilty. Sir.'

'Thank you, Mister Briggs.'

Briggs wears a smirk on his face that the utterly non-violent George would like to slap. The magistrates and clerk confer in whispers.

'Mister Briggs,' says the first magistrate finally, 'because of the seriousness of the alleged offences, and considering your past criminal record, we are referring your case for trial in the Crown Court.'

George is gobsmacked and wished he'd asked Angela or Ray to accompany him. They could have verified what he's just heard because his brain is refusing to believe it. How could this psychopath enter a not guilty plea? There were plenty of witnesses, after all.

He leaves in disgust and walks across the road to the library. He needs to focus on something mundane to rid his head of the nasty whiff of potential injustice. Something like thumbing through directories of local businesses and making a note of their contact details.

Despite his nagging anger, working on a new mission that doesn't involve complex actions and reactions feels quite liberating. He's decided to invest in printing a small brochure detailing his business services, and he aims to post or hand-deliver them. The cost would easily be recouped on his first job. He hadn't realised just how many small to medium-sized businesses there were in his locality. George had worked out he only required around fifteen hundred pounds a month to stave off having to sell the house. A couple of days' work a week at most. Surely that was doable?

As he flicks through the Building Services section, he feels rhythmic vibrations in his trouser pocket. He slips out the phone and checks the screen: Angela. Oh, how he wanted to answer the call, but an elderly woman sitting opposite glared at him. By the time he'd stepped outside, Angela had rung off. Now a text appeared on his screen: *Call me xxxxx*. Five, yes, five kisses. A sixty-seven percent increase, he calculated, on her last text.

The embryonic couple had reached first base the previous night. An onlooker would have noticed their body language becoming more intimate, the speech softer, the casual physical contact more frequent. This time something other than alcohol nourished the evening. The kiss didn't come until the last minute, on the doorstep, the waiting cab in the middle distance. They both leaned in, each head tilted at a sympathetic angle, mouths slightly apart. A microsecond after their lips met, mouths opened. Is this a good time for tongues, George momentarily questioned, or is it still too early? Before he had time to answer himself, Angela's tongue engaged with his and he was forced to defend his territory. To prolong the moment, one of her hands locked George's head against hers while the other hand pressed on George's bottom, pulling his groin against her pelvic area. The combination of this activity resulted in an almost instantaneous erection in George's trousers. This was not only embarrassing but uncomfortable. His penis was trapped in totally the wrong position and it needed to escape. While still engaging Angela's feral tongue, George attempted to pull his hips away from Angela without her noticing. Fat chance.

Angela pulled her head away, looked into his eyes. 'Are you okay with this, George?'

'Oh yes. Yes, I am. Yes.' He cleared his throat.

Angela resumed her offensive with some gusto.

It was with that image in his head that George returns Angela's call.

'Angela. Sorry, I was in the library.'

'And I thought you were you avoiding me. Were you avoiding me, George?'

'No, no, of course not. Why would I?'

'Who knows? Men are from Pluto, women from Venus.' Pause. 'You know, the book. That we're from different planets.'

'I think you mean Mars. Men are from Mars, Angela. And just another minor correction, if you'll forgive me. Pluto isn't an actual planet anymore. Since 2006 it's been designated as a dwarf planet.'

'Oh George, that's such a turn on.'

'Really?'

'No. Now are we going to talk about astronomy or astrology or whatever it is – George, do not correct me! – or do you want to hear my news?'

'I do. Very much indeed. Yes.'

'Reg is coming back, starting tomorrow. He just called me.'

George pogos on the spot like he's in the front row at a sweaty Sex Pistols gig in 1976. He's not sure why he's doing it now because he didn't do it then. A touch too young really, and he wouldn't have liked the aerial salvos of saliva, anyway. He stops when two passing boys laugh at him.

'He's coming back? It worked then. Our plan worked. We did it!'

Angela feels flattered that he's included her, but she knows this is a good time to further boost his confidence. 'You did it,

George. You. I only played a minor part. You're a genius. Imagine what else you could do.'

'You're right, there's a lot of good we could do – like superheroes, going incognito.' Not for the first time he pictures himself in a spandex Puppet Master costume. The image is not without appeal. 'So what happened to Michael?'

'Still going to be there, but I know Reg will keep him from doing anything silly. This is a champagne moment,' says Angela. 'My place or yours?'

Champagne. He'd drunk a glass or two at his wedding. Cynthia had enjoyed much more. Consequently, the first few hours of their wedding night were spent with George accompanying Cynthia to the bathroom to ensure she didn't choke on her own vomit.

'Er, when are you thinking of? Not that I have anything on.'

'Tonight, of course. Otherwise we'll miss the moment, see? And yes, I know we had dinner last night. Tell you what, I'll pick up a couple of pizzas on the way home, so come over to me. Do you eat pizza?'

'Yes, anything. You can surprise me this time.'

'I hope to,' she giggles. 'Get a cab and grab some bubbly on the way.'

George returns to his seat in the library. The glaring woman has left, and he's alone at the table. He scans through his notes but finds it difficult to concentrate. Angela's latest news has proved that his Intervention Theory actually works. From potential chaos at Finguish Fans, he's orchestrated order like a twenty-first century Zeus. Finally, something remarkable has happened in his life, just as he'd hoped. And now he has someone to share it with. He picks up his pad and returns the directories to the shelves. There's still more to do, but now is not the time. An evening with Angela beckons.

He returns home via a supermarket where he picks up some own-label, on-offer champagne, and a mixed bouquet of flowers with a ten-day guarantee. During what's left of the afternoon, he writes up the last notes on the Project Angela document and files it away with the Speeders project in a new folder: *Projects-successful*. While he's at it, he creates another: *Projects-failures*. He hopes he never has need of it.

With the admin completed, he starts pulling clothes from the wardrobe and laying them on the bed. Good quality brands, but old and tired. Shirts with worn collars and cuffs, and trousers stretched at the knees. George has never been a clothes shopper. To Cynthia's credit, it had been the one area in his life she'd involved herself. He guessed she didn't want to be seen with a man who looked like he didn't care what he wore – which is, in fact, a fair judgement. It would have been bad for her image, whatever that was. He selects a pair of taupe chinos and a burgundy, slim-fit shirt that's now one size too small for him. He slips them on in front of the mirror and nods. His phone beeps. The cab has arrived.

———

The Bell Inn, less than a mile from George's house, is so quiet when Goldtooth enters that the sound of the door opening causes the bored woman behind the bar and both of the pub's customers to turn around. Goldtooth's eyes scan the room as he walks towards the bar.

'Have you got lost, love, or can I get you something?' says the woman, suddenly more animated.

Goldtooth forensically scans the bar.

'Sorry?' he says, distracted as he spots a large glass jar not three feet away. It's exactly what he's been looking for after a frustrating search in seven other nearby pubs.

'What'll you have? You must be desperate if you're out on a wet Tuesday night.' She adds a laugh in the hope of creating some kind of connection.

Goldtooth pulls out his phone, pretends to look at the screen. 'Bloody mobiles. Even when you put them on silent, they still bother you.'

The woman looks bemused.

Goldtooth points to his phone. 'Emergency. Friend in need, apparently. Shame.'

He waves the phone in her direction as he walks towards the door.

'I'll be back.'

This is true. He has every intention of returning, but only when everything is ready. He's done what he came to do, and a wet Tuesday evening in an empty pub is the last place he wants to be.

―――

Angela, fancy underwear clinging tightly to her freshly showered skin, is checking out her reflection. Now she slides on the red dress, zips it up, and adjusts it to her body. She concentrates not on the dress but on the eyes staring back at her. She knows she's ready.

The doorbell interrupts her thoughts. It's a triple press, a sign of urgency. She takes a deep breath, licks her lips briefly, and heads downstairs to the front door.

'George, perfect timing. Come in.' She stands aside to let him enter.

He thrusts a shopping bag towards her. 'For you.' Angela takes the bag and peers inside.

'You didn't forget, then,' she says, lifting out the bottle. 'I bought one too, just in case. Lovely flowers. You're making me feel like a proper lady.' With one hand on his arm, she stretches up to kiss him. A quick kiss, then another, this time longer, deeper.

'You know where this is going, don't you?' she whispers in his ear.

George swallows hard and wonders if they'll ever make it out of the tiny hallway.

Angela has other plans. She takes him by the hand into the kitchen, puts the flowers in a vase and swaps George's bottle for a colder one in the fridge. 'Will you do the honours? It always makes me jump.' This is a lie. She's more than capable of opening the bottle, but she knows it's something men like to do.

Given George's history of alcohol consumption, it comes as no surprise that he's had zero experience of champagne since the days of Cynthia. That's why before he left home he googled how to open a bottle of sparkling wine. With some sensible advice to twist the bottle, not the cork, he performs a perfect decapitation.

'Glasses,' he commands, a man rightly proud of his latest achievement.

Angela pretends to be impressed. 'You've done that a few times. I didn't even hear it pop.'

'Totally unnecessary. It's all a question of ...' He pulls himself back from the brink of scientific explanation and pours the champagne.

'To us,' says Angela raising her glass for the second time on consecutive nights.

'George and Angela.'

'Angela and George.' Angela puts her glass down and wraps her arms around him. 'We deserve this, don't we?'

George agrees, but the time for words has passed. Such is his anticipation, the tip of his tongue emerges from his mouth before it makes contact with Angela. Not that she's complaining. Pelvises grinding together, George rises above the pain barrier of yet another erection trapped inside his underwear.

They're off, with any thoughts they have of Finguish Fans and intervention theories swiftly archived to a folder marked pending.

Somehow Angela prises her right hand between the two of them – it's difficult because George isn't thinking ahead like her – and opens his trousers, pulling them down as far as her arms can stretch. His underwear follows suit.

With George shuffling self-consciously while holding up his trousers, she pulls him into the living room. Unsurprisingly, preparations have been made. The curtains are closed and there's a throw on the sofa that hadn't been there on George's last visit. What's more, Angela's choice of a pizza dinner has allowed an infinitely flexible meal time.

George tries to calm himself down or it could be all over for him all too soon. And sex in the living room? Cynthia had been a traditional bedroom lover, "otherwise it gets messy". To be honest, it surprised George she hadn't insisted on using the shower as a more practical lovemaking nest. Especially after he'd caught her masturbating in there one Sunday morning. Perhaps she wanted to keep that particular venue to herself? It seemed fair.

Angela turns her back on him, takes hold of the zip fastener. 'Would you mind?'

George obliges with a trembling hand.

She slips off the dress and turns back, holding George at arms' length so he's forced to appreciate her underwear. After thirty seconds of ferocious foreplay, Angela leans back on the sofa, George inside her. He comes without warning barely a minute later.

'I've ... Have you ...?' He's cursing himself for not holding back, for being totally lost in the moment. For being, perish the thought, out of control.

Angela takes his hand and places it between her legs. 'Still got some work to do.' Previous experience moderates her disappointment. Most men found it difficult to dial back their passion, particularly on the first occasion. She re-focusses on the job in hand.

When it's over, they lie together saying nothing, but thinking everything. The oven beeps, announcing the desired temperature for pizza has been reached.

'Peckish?' says Angela.

———

Even though she's had less sleep than usual, there's a pronounced spring in Angela's step when she walks into the office the following morning. She pops her head into Michael's office. The door sign has gone and Reg is sitting at a new desk by the window.

'Morning Angela,' he says cheerfully. 'I was just emailing you with a list of things you can help me with. No rush. Get yourself a coffee and settle in first.'

'Welcome back, Reg. Where's...? Will Michael be in today?'

'Should be in by now. Probably sulking.' He leans forward conspiratorially. 'His, er, behaviour is between you and me, okay. Neville's the only other person to know about any of this. Well, he would know because he was the one who transferred the money for Michael to use. We've had words, so that won't be happening again.'

Angela is super-efficient today. Even the two mouthy sales guys, summoned earlier for a briefing from Reg, could spot something different about her.

'She's had a shag, I'm telling you,' says one to the other, enjoying a cigarette in the car park.

'Bit old for that, isn't she?'

'She looks tidy, though. Never really noticed before.'

'Ha, you fancy her.'

'Piss off, you prat.'

The lady in question would have secretly enjoyed this conversation. However, she's busy ploughing through the sales figures and employee records that Reg needed. As far as she's aware, Michael still hasn't turned up. All the proof anyone would need that he's a loser. Can't even take a dressing down from his own dad. Arsehole. The last word actually comes out of her mouth.

'Who's an arsehole?' says Mary, the accounts clerk who sits nearby.

'Sorry, just some idiot. No one you know.'

———

Reg, on the other side of the wall to Angela, is back to feeling useful again. In fact, he's thoroughly enjoying himself. The only blot on the landscape is the continued absence of Michael. Reg can't understand it. When he'd walked in that morning the vanity sign on the door had been removed and a printout of an email from a Barbados real estate agent agreeing to put the house on the market was on his desk. Michael had done everything asked of him. So where was he?

His mobile rings. A number that wasn't on his contact list. A spam call? He takes it anyway, prepared to give the caller both barrels for bothering him about an accident injury or internet issue he's never had.

'Mister Finguish?'

'Yes, who's calling?'

'Buckinghamshire Police. Constable Evans. Before I continue, can I confirm you're Reginald Finguish, father of Michael Finguish?'

'Yes, yes. What's this about? Is this something to do with Michael?'

'I'm sorry to tell you, sir, that your son is in Stoke Mandeville hospital following a suspected suicide attempt.'

Time stops for Reg, like he's in the aftermath of an enormous explosion.

'Mister Finguish?'

———

Eight

Michael had spent the previous day ticking off everything Reg had demanded. The Barbadian agent advised that if he wanted a quick sale, Michael would have to be prepared to lose up to twenty-five thousand dollars. Allow for forty thousand including the fees, the agent said. Michael calculated that the repayment of a company loan to cover that would mean some household cutbacks. Long-haul holidays would be the first item to be culled.

That's when he started to sweat, because it isn't Reg he's most afraid of. It's Sophie.

They'd met at a thirtieth birthday celebration of a mutual friend, Jed, at a local bar. Michael, accompanied by his long-term girlfriend, Sally, had arrived more than an hour after the party officially started, by which time everyone had loosened up. It was usual at such events for the couple to gravitate to those they knew best, but when Sally found herself embroiled in an increasingly heated discussion with some climate change deniers neither of them had ever met, Michael sneaked away on the pretext of needing a pee. What he really wanted was another drink and some levity.

Jed spotted him as he wove his way to the bar. 'Mine's a Vodka Red Bull,' he said, grabbing Michael's arm. Perspiration dotted his forehead, shirt half in and half out of his jeans. 'Happy birthday to me.'

'No worries,' said Michael. 'I need a break from your weird friends back there.'

Jed glanced over his shoulder and spotted Sally waving her arms around. 'You mean Paul and Chris? They're not weird, just focused on their own shit. They're flippers. Always buying, renovating and selling property. Sell it for silly money. We met them at ante-natal classes.'

'You met everyone you know at those ante-natal classes except me and Sal.' He turned to the barman and ordered the drinks.

Jed put his arm around Michael's shoulder. 'You meet a lovely class of people there, mate. Don't knock it. Might be you one day.'

'Not if Sal has anything to do with it. Precious job and all that. I live in hope.'

'You poor old fucker. Now where's my drink?'

As Jed turned to face the bar, a beautiful woman appeared behind him. Catching Michael's eye, she brought a finger to her lips. Already they were sharing a secret. Then she reached over Jed's shoulders and clamped her hands over his eyes.

'Guess who?' she said softly into his ear, her eyes still on Michael.

'By the smell of that perfume it's certainly not my wife.' He turned, took her hands in his and kissed them. 'Soph, you sexy minx. I thought you'd forgotten.'

'Had to pop into another do on the way. A mate from

work. Who's your friend then?' She appraised Michael in the manner she usually reserved for shopping for clothes.

'Mike,' Jed proudly announced, 'this is Sophie, someone else I didn't meet at ante-natal. She's in PR. We had a thing way back. Right, Soph?'

Sophie isn't interested in the past. The past is for losers. 'Pleased to meet you, Mike. I didn't realise Jed had any good-looking friends.' She'd never been one to waste time.

'Likewise, Sophie. Can I get you a drink?' And Michael, always a sucker for a strong woman, has been paying for her ever since.

They met again in her tiny flat two days later, and on each of the following four evenings while Michael was purportedly working late. Weekends were a little more awkward, but it wasn't long before he constructed a series of believable lies for Sally in order to extricate himself from the house for a few hours at a time. Next came a fictitious mid-week trade show in London where they managed two nights away together. That's when it dawned on Michael that an affair with Sophie wouldn't be cheap.

She'd insisted on a newly refurbed landmark hotel, an afternoon of pampering at one of the capital's most prestigious spas, and dinners at on-trend restaurants. They talked and boozed, and ate and had sex, then talked some more. Her eyes were constantly upon him, her hands rarely leaving some part or other of his body. The conversations invariably touched on the issues of Michael's relationship with Sally, and Sophie couldn't have been more understanding. Her mission wasn't about selling Brand Sophie to Michael. The aim was making him want to buy, and the finest sales people in the land couldn't have achieved a better result.

The more they talked, the less Michael seemed to care about the carnage being wrought on his credit card. There was never, ever, a question of Sophie offering to pay, the unwritten rule taken as read by both of them. Michael succumbed to this willingly, control over his life slipping away almost unnoticed as he became caught up in a shallow fantasy.

During those fateful few days, real life intruded only for a short time. He'd promised to call Sally on the first evening, taking advantage of Sophie's absence from the hotel bedroom. Lying half-dressed on the bed, a TV news channel burbling away in the background, he hit the call button.

'It's me.'

'Hello me. Are you lonely, young man?' Sally's usually cheerful voice took on a seductive tone. Michael instantly resented her crossing the line into his current mood.

'You're never lonely if you have room service. How was your day?'

'Not as exciting as your conference, I'm sure. Do tell.'

While Michael related the highlights of the conference that never was, Sophie walked in naked from the bathroom. She silently knelt down on the bed, slid down Michael's underwear and took his penis in her mouth, her eyes rarely leaving his. While Michael had the presence of mind to keep the conversation going, Sally's fate had been well and truly sealed.

Within a week she was history, within a month Michael and Sophie moved in together, within a year they were married and Sophie became pregnant. She never returned to work. The financial demands on Michael increased year after year as he worked to feed her lifestyle. But what Sophie lacked in work ethic and compassion she made up for in cheerleading. No partner could have been more supportive in his career – a Lady Macbeth but with a better wardrobe – and that gave Michael the confidence to succeed in business. When Reg had finally offered Michael the top job at Finguish Fans, and the increased salary and perks that came with it, Sophie revelled in her success. Next stop, Barbados.

But that was then.

After Michael had left the office on the day of his demotion, he'd sat in his car for some time thinking about what Sophie would say. Going backwards isn't something Sophie does. Nor is losing face to the very people she'd been desperate to impress. Selling the Barbados house would hit her hard. And that's before he'd have to confess to being in debt to the company with nothing to show for it.

He ran through the conversation he's about to have. It doesn't end well. It's not forever, he would say to her, give it a year or three and we'll be back on track. We're very lucky to have what we have already, more than many of our friends, when you think about it. Then she would get angry and a door would slam, and he'd shout out that he'd done it all for her.

He drove home slowly.

At the front door, Josh, his youngest, ran up to meet him.

'Daddy's home,' he shouted, then ran away again.

Michael dumped his bag on the hall table and wandered into the kitchen. Sophie was sitting at the table feeding Mia. She glanced up.

'Josh is uncontrollable,' she said. 'You'll have to speak to him. I've tried, but he won't listen to me. Look at this mess.' She gestured to splotches of food on the table and more on the floor.

'Leave him to me.' Michael thought if he helped deal with Josh it might deflect some of the sting from the news he's about to deliver. He takes a deep breath.

'It's been a bad day.' He thrust his hands in his trouser pockets and began circling the room. 'Like really bad.'

'At least you don't have all this to cope with.'

'This is worse, Soph. The new house.' He could barely bring himself to continue.

Sophie put down the spoon she'd been using to feed Mia and turned directly towards Michael.

'What do you mean, the new house?'

'It's got to go. Dad found out I'd used company money. I knew he would. God, I'm such an idiot.'

The silence that ensued was excruciating. Then Sophie opened her mouth a fraction and words flowed through expensively manicured teeth.

'Who's running the effing company? You or your old man? Jesus, Michael, just grow a pair and sort it.'

She never called him Michael.

'It's already done,' he mumbled, looking down at his feet. 'The house is on the market for a quick sale. Those were dad's terms. And don't think we can get away with another mad scheme – he's coming back to work tomorrow. To be honest, I'm lucky to have a job at all.'

Josh ran into the room waving a drawing of something indescribable.

'Josh, out!' said Sophie. 'Now!'

Michael waved Josh away. 'I'll come and play with you in a minute. Promise.' It's a promise he won't be able to keep.

Sophie stood up. Shorter than Michael, she now appeared bigger, stronger, a formidable opponent. Mia looked up at her and made a bleating noise.

'This is a fucking joke, right?' she said. Michael simply stood there, looking uncomfortable. 'Do you know what a fool I'm going to look? Do you? Really?' She turned away and addressed the ceiling. 'I can't fucking believe it.'

Then he made the mistake of using one of his rehearsed lines.

'But I tried to do it for us, for you.'

'What? Fuck things up so we lose the house? Letting your dad walk all over you? Christ. Listen to yourself.'

As it seemingly couldn't get much worse for him, Michael revealed some more information.

'There's something else.'

'What?'

'We're going to lose money on the house sale so we'll have to pay back the company.'

'Well, they can fucking wait for that. How much?'

Michael tries to swallow, fails. 'Forty thousand'ish. Maybe less. Dollars, obviously.'

Sophie's pale complexion turned the colour of a very nice bottle of premium rosé that lurked in the fridge door. Her pretty face convoluted into something grotesque, chest heaving as she fought for breath. They stood there for some time until Sophie exercised some control over her body. When she eventually spoke, the words came out calmly but firmly.

'Get out. Go on, get out. I can't bear to look at you.'

Michael still continued to stare at her.

'Pack a bag and get the fuck out.'

He started to say something, but then his head dropped again. He left the room, picked up his car keys, and opened the front door. Josh came running up to him from the living room.

'Daddy, you promised.'

Michael looked down at him. 'I'm sorry,' he said, wiping the snot dripping from his nose on the back of his hand. Then, closing the door softly behind him, he walked around the side of the house to the shed. He quickly found what he needed.

As he reversed down the drive, he saw Josh staring at him from the window. Michael waved and drove off. He didn't get very far, stopping a hundred metres down the street underneath the one streetlight that wasn't lit. The suppressed anger he'd felt had dissipated. Now he wept, and once his tear ducts had emptied he drove to the common and parked in the same space George had used only days before when he'd met Angela. Michael switched off the engine and cranked the seat back. An overwhelming wave of exhaustion overtook him, the events of the past twelve hours taking their toll.

He awoke before dawn. Sophie's contorted face is the first image he sees. Then Josh's face at the window, and Mia, blissfully unaware of the language that flew from Sophie's mouth. Words of wisdom came to him: *Sleep on it* and *it'll be better in the morning*. Well, he had, and it wasn't.

Michael started the engine and got out of the car. He opened the boot, picked up a garden hose and a roller of gaffer tape, and set to work.

At 6:00 a.m. a dog walker, making his way across the car park, spotted a solitary car at the far side, close to the trees. It was nothing unusual. The man later told the police he thought he could see someone in the driving seat of the Jaguar and assumed that there had been another person in the car. The common car park was, after all, a well-known spot for illicit liaisons before and after work. On his return, this time passing much closer to the car, the man spotted a hose taped to one of the exhaust pipes.

One of the western world's most successful clean air policies has been the mandatory fitting of catalytic converters to cut carbon monoxide emissions from vehicles. As a result, there was an unforeseen bonus – a huge decrease in the number of successful suicides thorough CO poisoning. If Michael had been driving a very old car, his attempt to escape Sophie would probably have succeeded. But when the dog walker pulled open the Jaguar's door, Michael was still semiconscious.

The ambulance crew who arrived shortly after told the dog walker that it had been the second such case in the past week.

The other had been the ex-boyfriend of a local lottery jackpot winner.

———

While Angela makes her mid-morning cup of coffee in the office kitchen, Reg appears at the doorway.

'Angela!' He beckons her to join him and disappears into his office. She nods and holds up two fingers, but he's gone.

'Be with you in a sec, Reg.'

Reg is soon back in the doorway, gesticulating wildly. There's something in his eyes she's not seen before. She follows him into his office.

'It's Michael,' says Reg, pacing the room. 'He's in Stoke Mandeville. Someone found him by the common this morning.'

Angela's body sways. 'Oh my God, is he okay? I mean, what's the matter?'

'The police said he tried to...' Reg is close to tears, but he will not cry in front of Angela. 'I need you to hold the fort, postpone the meeting with Jim, whatever. I'll be at the hospital with Anne. And keep all this quiet, okay?' He grabs his jacket and briefcase and starts to leave. At the door, he turns around to face her. 'Maybe if I hadn't said anything about the house, and just let it go?' Angela studies his face. It's aged ten years in a single hour.

In the moments after he leaves, she stares at the empty doorway and her brain is already reversing the sequence of events that led to this moment. A shiver runs through her. She needs to share how she feels, but the one person who'd understand is complicit in the whole ridiculous, tragic scenario. And not just complicit. She's all too aware that George is the one who set the whole thing in motion, and involved her, and Reg and Anne. Still, she reasons, Michael isn't dead. Yet. She gently closes the door to Reg's office, sits down in his chair, and pulls out her mobile.

———

George picks up Angela's call almost immediately. 'Angela! Are you missing me or something?'

'Something terrible has happened, George, and it's all our fault,' she says.

George detects a note of hysteria in her voice and is eager to clamp down on it before it gets out of control. 'Don't tell me,' he laughs, 'Michael threw a punch at Reg, and Reg has given him his marching orders. I could see it happening. Didn't I tell you that—?'

'Shut up and listen, for heaven's sake. Michael's in hospital. I think he tried to kill himself. Reg is in a terrible state.'

'Suicide? He only lost a holiday house he'd never even been to. What's the matter with the man?' Bravado is one of George's specialities. It's not one of Angela's.

'We did this, George. We made it happen.' He can hear her voice breaking.

'Hang on a minute. Look, I feel sorry for him, but he did it to himself. We just let Reg know what was going on. You can't blame us.'

'But if we hadn't done it, it wouldn't have happened. That's what I'm trying to say.'

'Angela, we're not going to take any responsibility for this. Who's to say this wouldn't have happened anyway? Please calm yourself down.'

'But what if he dies? He's got kids.'

'Then he should have thought of them first.' Even as he spoke those words, George was ashamed of them. 'That came out wrong,' he continued in an effort to salvage some humanity. 'What I mean is —'

'I should go.'

'Okay, maybe I should pop round tonight so we can talk about it.'

'I don't know. Everything feels a bit weird at the moment.'

George sees the call has been terminated. 'Shit,' he says. 'Shit, shit, shit, shit, shit.' The words spill out via a little-used synapse in George's brain that usually remains unconnected to his mouth. When he planned the intervention, he failed to take into account Michael's mental health history. And as a result, he's broken his own intervention code. Someone has been hurt. Did the end justify the means? Alone now with his own thoughts, he couldn't honestly say it did.

Perhaps more distressing is how Angela has reacted to this turn of events. Where would their relationship go from here? Has he blown it? Though sorely tempted, he declines to write out a sequence of events that led to this point, and where it might lead to. Already he can see how it might end for him, for them.

———

Angela sits at the desk, staring at nothing in particular, thoughts whirling around her head. With her tasks completed and Michael and Reg out of the office, she'd resorted to browsing a lengthy online blog: *50 ways to retire early*. Ironically, the first piece of advice is to keep working – at least in some capacity. This is not what Angela wishes to hear. She's had enough of working, of Finguish Fans. And now she's in that negative mind-set, Angela thinks she's had enough of men too. They show promise, then fail to deliver. They lie, cheat, control, embarrass. They weaken you. And then there's George.

A man, she believes, with the best intentions who's landed her in a situation she never asked for. A man who perhaps tries too hard. And that was the saddest part of all.

Her desk phone rings. She can see it's an external call.

'Angela Hayworth.'

'It's Reg. We're still at the hospital. Anything I need to know about?'

'Oh, Reg.' She lowers her voice to avoid being overheard. 'What's the news on Michael?'

'He'll live, silly bugger. Looks like they'll keep him in overnight, but he should be well enough to go home tomorrow.'

'Thank God. I'm sure Sophie's been frantic.'

'Well, you'd think, wouldn't you? She kicked him out, Angela. She damn well kicked him out. He'll be coming home with us. For now, at least.'

'Poor Michael. I hadn't realised there were, you know, problems at home. You shouldn't rush back. Jim's handling everything. You always said he's a safe pair of hands.'

'I'll be in at some point tomorrow. Better than moping around the house. Anne will keep an eye on Michael, anyway.'

As Angela replaces the handset, she feels her guilt and doubts subside. Michael is alive and Reg is still in the top job. And George? Could she really condemn a man who was only trying to help her? Surely that's better than one who barely cared.

She texts George: *Sorry, better now. Michael OK. Kicked out by Sophie. Evil witch! Xxxxxx.*

———

George stares at the message. With a mere twelve words Angela has efficiently supplied him with a critical update on Michael's condition, the name of the person directly responsible, her opinion of the culprit, an update on her current state of mind, an apology and a reaffirmation of her feelings for George in the form of six kisses, one more than the maximum to date. It was humbling.

He's got away with his dangerous game and Angela is back on track. Sure, he'd suffered a slight wobble, but Angela's text lessened any guilt he felt. Also, by twisting events around as he's wont to do, he thought that perhaps he'd done Michael a favour. That bringing to breaking point what must have been an already fragile relationship might prevent further suffering for all parties involved. What must the children have been going through, he ponders? So why did he feel more drained than elated?

He hadn't considered the effect his plan might have on others, people like Sophie and the children who might now be termed *collateral damage*. They would have to be included in his calculations for future interventions. That's if there were any. George realises he's reached another pivotal point.

———

Nine

'Already!?' Jackie is aghast at the news that Angela has, as she herself put it, *slept with George*.

'What do you mean already? We've been friends for a month, remember? You sound like Mum.'

'Well, it's a good job she's not here to see it. You're acting like a teenager.'

Angela wished she'd never mentioned George, but Jackie had been persistent. Besides, what was the harm in consensual sex between adults, particularly middle-aged ones? It's not as if she could get pregnant.

'He might have some dreadful disease,' continued Jackie. 'I read that sexually transmitted diseases are on the up in the over-sixties. Listen to me, Angela,' she paused for maximum dramatic effect, 'you don't know where he's been.'

'For a start, neither of us is over sixty. And I don't think George has been anywhere for a while, to be honest.'

'That's exactly my point. He sounds like the kind of man who might use prostitutes. Or worse. It's always the loners. I've warned you before.'

Angela is unsure whether Jackie is genuinely concerned for her well-being or if she's trying to infect the relationship out of some kind of jealousy.

'He's not that sort of man, Jacks, believe me.' Now, with a wicked smirk on her face, she delivers the coup de grâce. 'I've invited him to stay over tomorrow night.' She leaves it hanging there like a grenade with the pin taken out. Seconds tick away before Jackie can answer.

'Are you quite mad? He'll be moving in next ... Angela? ... Angela!'

———

Even though the sun had set an hour ago, Angela's house is in darkness. The dining table hosts a new arrangement of wild flowers in a crystal fluted vase. Sofa cushions have been plumped and carefully arranged. The dishwasher hums in the kitchen, the vibrations causing empty wine bottles on the worktop above to tinkle as they gently touch one another.

George's small canvas holdall sits in the hallway near the front door. It contains pyjamas, underwear, shirt, toothbrush, and a pack of cholesterol-lowering medication. Not that George needs any of this paraphernalia right now. He's concentrating on a particularly awkward quadratic equation as he continues to thrust into Angela. This climax-delaying tactic seems to work because he's been at it for a while, a considerable improvement on his abject, though forgivable, performance earlier in the week. Angela coos away in the background like a dove on heat.

To their credit, they hadn't leapt into bed the moment he arrived. Instead, Angela served a simple meal, and then, to the strains of Barry White's Greatest Hits Collection, they'd enjoyed an intimate coffee nestled in the sofa. Barry's baritone isn't to George's taste but let no one argue the man doesn't know how to set a lovemaking mood.

After the CD finished, Angela led him by the hand up the stairs to the bedroom. George was pleased to discover the décor was neutral, not Arabian-Nights-on-a-budget that had been Cynthia's choice. After she moved out, the sole survivors of George's bedroom revamp were a pair of Moroccan-style hardwood cabinets and the bed frame. The mattress had been disposed of. George was never sure, despite Cynthia's assurances to the contrary, whether she'd entertained Geoff in the marital bed. Whatever, he certainly wasn't prepared to take the chance.

In a gentlemanly fashion, he lets Angela climax first. Then – somewhat reluctantly, as he was close to solving it – dismisses the equation from his mind. A last push, a low grunt, and he collapses beside her, his biceps on fire. He makes a mental note to check out some fitness videos on YouTube and work on his upper body.

He wakes in the early hours of the morning, blinks his eyes a few times and props himself up in bed. Gentle breathing comes from the body next to him. The room smells of something sweet and comforting. Rolling his tongue around his mouth, he remembers he didn't clean his teeth. This is a heinous personal care crime, punishable by slow and expensive torture from his dental hygienist.

Naked, and still slightly woozy from the wine they consumed, he tiptoes downstairs to collect his bag from the hallway. He tries to remember the last time he'd felt so content. It was like the world had hugged him and now he was on the road to learning how to hug it back. On his return, he pauses by the open bedroom door to gaze at Angela's sleeping figure, and smiles a genuine smile. He would have stood there for longer, but clean teeth are more important than just about anything.

Especially these days, George having lost his valuable company health insurance perk.

When he slips back into bed, Angela stirs and turns over to face him. George assumed she was still asleep, but then he felt a hand softly take hold of his penis.

'Well, you don't need Viagra, do you?' whispers Angela, pulling him towards her.

———

While George was mulling over what the seemingly impossible duration of a Viagra-infused erection might feel like, a new order pinged up on a computer screen at MaxPrint, on a huge industrial estate on the outskirts of Wolverhampton. Alan, the night-shift orders manager, clicked a few boxes, made a cursory check of the artwork file, and sent it on its way to join a virtual queue for one of the three huge digital print machines on the floor below.

These days, it seemed, everyone wanted to be part of the start-up economy and that had been good for MaxPrint. Stationary, flyers, brochures and posters printed for all manner of micro-business entrepreneurs flew off the machines day and night.

The new order was nothing out of the ordinary. Just another business card for a company that would probably go broke in a few years, if indeed it ever really got going. But he liked the look of the picture on the back of the card. A beautiful Caribbean home surrounded by a tropical garden. All right for some, thought Alan, who could barely afford the rent on his dingy, net-curtained flat above a chicken shop that regularly hosted skirmishes between local youths.

———

Angela had been unsure of George's breakfast of choice so she'd covered all the bases: cereal, fruit, the full English, toast. Such is the choice, the tablecloth is barely visible. George has taken advantage of everything on the menu as if he was staying in a B&B. It makes sense to get your money's worth. And after the action-packed night they'd shared, he believed he'd earned it.

'Do you have any plans today?' says Angela, placing her cutlery down and dabbing her lips with a square of kitchen paper she's just ripped from the roll. George has already suffered a minor panic – he politely kept it to himself – when he realised on a normal Saturday his weekly supermarket shop would have already been done and dusted.

'Haven't thought about it, really,' he lied, 'other than perhaps doing some shopping. Nothing that can't wait.' He finds the words hard. Breaking a routine is tough for him. 'Do you want that sausage,' he says, pointing to her plate.

'Be my guest,' she says, spearing it and dropping it onto George's plate. Then she catches his eye and giggles. 'I think I've had enough sausage for a little while.'

George's face reddens, but there's a wild glint in his eyes.

'Let's do something,' she says. 'Something different. We could drive somewhere. Perhaps a country pub or a stately home and you could stay over again or...' She stops herself. Is she being too pushy? George is silent. 'Or you might want some time to yourself. We all do sometimes, don't we? I'm easy either way.'

George cuts the remnants of the sausage in two. He spears the penultimate morsel and is about to put it into his mouth when he says, 'Angela, your sausages are truly first class. I can't abide a cheap sausage. All that rusk to bulk it up and those vile additives they put in to make it taste more porky.' He chews away. 'Mmm, first class.'

'Thank you, George. I'm pleased you find them to your satisfaction.'

What was the matter with the man, she thought. He's had the opportunity to comment on her ideas, yet changes the subject. What Angela is failing to consider is that you can't hurry a George. His conscious mind may be processing the contents of a sausage, but in the background the options are spinning around his head like the reels on a fruit machine.

Kerching! Three cherries. It might not be the jackpot, but a win's a win.

'Good idea, Angela,' says George, returning to the unanswered question. 'I really ought to pop in to the supermarket later, but why don't we drive over to the Black Swan at Aldbury for lunch? Maybe a stroll too? I know a nice four-miler. Nothing too strenuous.' Like many of his plans, they come out fully formed. And Angela likes people who know their own mind. But then George remembers something.

'Oh no.' George's face is fraught with anguish. 'Ray. I'm supposed to be meeting him for chess at eleven. He always looks forward to it.'

Angela's head drops. 'Up to you, of course.'

In a rare move, George capitulates before he has time to evaluate the positives and negatives. Ray has been demoted in life's pecking order.

'I'll text him. He'll understand.'

Although they don't discuss it – probably through fear of upsetting what might be a delicate situation – both of them feel the dynamic in their relationship has subtly changed. George and Angela are now an item.

It was reinforced later, during an afternoon walk in the Chilterns. On a steeply sloping section of the footpath, George had looked back and offered his hand to Angela. She took it, and when the path levelled out, hadn't given it back. At that moment, he wished he'd met her years ago, before the ridiculous Cynthia had got her claws into him. Perhaps he and Angela might have had children? He wiped away an intrepid tear at the thought of the wasted years, the unfulfilled dreams.

'You're quiet,' she said.

George gently squeezed her hand. 'I'm only thinking about … about what a lovely day this is.'

―――――

While Michael naps on the sofa in Reg and Anne's conservatory, Reg drives to Michael's house on the pretext of collecting some clothes and other personal effects. His real agenda is to interrogate Sophie. When she opens the door, he notices a slight recoil.

'Sophie, sorry to arrive out of the blue. Michael needs some things.' She continues to stand in the doorway. 'It wasn't like he packed when you … when he left. Is it okay to come in?'

She moves to one side, avoiding his gaze. 'Yes. Yes, of course.'

'Josh and Mia okay? Missing their dad, I expect.'

'Mum's looking after them until the morning. They're fine.'

'So what have you told them?'

'Just that Michael is sick and had to go to hospital. Kids are very resilient, you know.'

'Will you talk to him? I know he'd like to hear from you.'

'I don't know, Reg. First there was the house fiasco, and now the suicide nonsense. I didn't sign up for this, you know. I had to cope before, you know, when he went all weird. Now I've got kids who need looking after. He's being selfish.'

On a different day, Reg might have lost his temper. He'd never been keen on Sophie. Nor had Anne, who'd been the first to assign the "gold-digger" label. Still, the two of them had invested a lot into Michael's marriage: time, effort, kindness, and of course some money. And Reg won't ditch a long-term investment just because the markets are shaky.

'None of us signed up for it, but there it is. What can Anne and I do to help?'

Reg has cunningly put the ball into Sophie's court.

Her voice hardens. 'He broke his promise to me, Reg. About the house.'

'But it wasn't his money to use.'

'He's the CEO and it was his decision to make. You even gave him the job. Anyway, it's only a loan. It's not just me he's let down. It's the kids. Josh was looking forward to going to Barbados. We'd showed him which bedroom would be his and everything.'

'Listen Sophie, Anne and I would be happy to pay for a holiday there. I think it would be good for you all to take a break and clear the air.'

'A holiday? It's not exactly the same thing, is it?' she says. 'And who's to say Michael won't do something like this again, eh? Maybe in front of the kids next time. Imagine that, Reg. Imagine that.'

Reg tethers his anger remarkably well, knowing that if he responds in the manner he'd like, there'd be no going back. Instead he says wearily, 'Please show me upstairs so I can collect those things for Michael.'

———

Monday. George wakes to the sound of beeping from the alarm clock. He rolls over and notes with a pang of regret that the other side of the bed is empty.

The alarm beeps again. George swings his legs out of bed.

He makes up for Angela's absence by catching up on all the tasks he should have done over the weekend. He starts by trimming the back lawn and cleaning the house, which allows him thinking time on a more critical matter: making money.

After lunch, he calls Ray. Surely Ray's planning job would mean he came into contact with plenty of builders and developers, and they may have use of George's services. A personal intro goes a long way. What was it those marketing people in the office kept banging on about? Word of mouth. The best kind of advertising. It had been the only thing they and George agreed on, mainly because word of mouth was free.

'Ray Smith.' says a voice devoid of enthusiasm.

'Ray, it's George. Sorry again about Saturday. I would have called but Angela was hovering.'

'Think nothing of it. How is the dear lady?'

'Very well. We've been seeing rather a lot of each other, actually.'

'I bet you have, George. Hope you like what you saw.' Ray sniggers.

George chooses to ignore Ray's out-of-character smuttiness. If Ray's in that kind of mood, he won't update him on the success of Project Angela. He'd probably make fun of it. Ray, though, is ahead of him.

'So, what else is happening? Did you ever get a result on that intervention thingy you were doing for her? I thought that was terribly clever.'

George decides not to put a gloss on things. He needs to get Ray's take on what happened.

'Maybe not so clever. In fact, it nearly ended in disaster. Her boss tried to commit suicide after his mad wife kicked him out. He's back with his parents now.'

A low whistle from Ray.

'And then Angela had a bit of a wobble because I involved

her.'

'Just shows playing God is complex stuff,' says Ray. 'Imagine if that guy had died? I'm sure you're worried he might try it again.'

This is not what George wants to hear. Ray has eloquently summarised his fears and he doesn't want to be reminded of them.

'Sorry, George. That was insensitive of me. I'm sure it'll work out okay. Most suicide attempts are just a cry for help. What you need is a few games to take your mind off it.'

'That would be nice, but what I really need is some work. Like freelance accountancy and book-keeping. I thought you might know some likely candidates. Small developers and the like. It was just a thought. Before we know it, those winter fuel bills will stack up, and I need to replace my old TV.'

'Built-in obsolescence. China's revenge. Nothing you can do about it either. Happy to do what I can with my contacts. But book-keeping? Seriously? It's a bit of a comedown from what you're used to.'

'Needs must, Ray. It seems I'm not exactly employable in corporate land. They want young and cheap these days.'

'Leave it with me. Hate to see a friend in need.'

―――

Nestling in a sparsely populated valley, and surrounded by expansive gardens and mature trees, sits a large detached house. Dating from 1905, it's built in the Arts & Crafts style of dark brick and tile with sturdy oak-mullioned and latticed windows. A structure that gives the impression of having always been there. A house inhabited by thinkers, artists, writers. Where ideas happen, where movements are born, where titans make time to prune their own roses.

A white delivery van, engine running, stops by a pair of black iron gates that defend the entrance to the property. The driver gets out and presses the button of an entry phone set into the brick pillar.

'Yes?' says a nervous voice through the speaker grille.

'Delivery for Wakefield,' says the driver who may be Spanish or South American.

'From whom?' says the voice.

Silence. Then from the driver: 'I sorry?'

The voice again: 'Delivery. Where ... from? Who ... sent ... it?'

'Ah.' The driver flips the small package over and reads from the label. 'From MaxPrint. For Wakefield. You not Wakefield?'

'Proceed through the gates. Leave it on the doorstep. The. Door. Step.'

The gates soundlessly swing open before the driver can ask another question. The van moves slowly down the gravelled drive, the driver marvelling at the setting. Every tree, every shrub, path, and bench has been meticulously positioned to form the most perfect vistas from any angle. When the driver considered it later, he noted the entry phone was the only thing that appeared out of place. Almost reverentially, he places the package on the top of three wide stone steps by the front door, and backs away as if he's had an audience with royalty.

Checking his mirror as he drives back through the gates, he spots a figure, package in hand. Male, bald, and in contrast to the grand doorway, slight of frame.

———

The mahogany pedestal desk with its worn bottle-green leather top would dwarf most rooms, but here, in the cavernous oak-panelled space, it looks right at home. If it wasn't for the three computer screens lined up along one edge and the leather and steel office chair, the room could be a snapshot of another era. There are one hundred and three other items on the desk. A wireless mouse, an A5-size hardback spiral-bound notebook, and a small translucent plastic box containing one hundred freshly printed business cards.

Goldtooth angles back in his chair, locates a pair of plastic catering gloves from one of the desk drawers and puts them on. From another drawer, he removes a cheap ballpoint pen. Now he opens the box of cards and takes out the top one. He checks the first side, then flips it over and examines the reverse. Satisfied, he looks up at one of the screens, finds the section he's looking for, and copies it onto the card in tiny handwriting: *Boys and girls: himagzi4xcrr2vdfx0osk.onion.* Next, he holds the card up to the screen and double checks what he's written. Underneath he writes: *M1!s23gh0_1RH*. Perfect. He puts the card into his inside jacket pocket. That's the first job done.

On another screen, he brings up the contents of George's laptop and dives into its pristine depths. Locating the spreadsheet of television specs and reviews he discovered earlier, he adds some text he's copied from the internet and saves the changes.

One hour later, at the Bell Inn, he orders a large whiskey. While the barman who looks too young to work behind a bar is busy pouring him a single malt, he extracts the card from his pocket and pops it into the glass jar next to him on the bar. The handwritten label on the jar reads *LEAVE YOUR BUSINESS CARD. WIN GREAT PRIZES! NEXT DRAW FRIDAY 1.30PM.*

Goldtooth sinks the whiskey in one and leaves the pub. He heads towards the only phone box left in town that actually functions as a phone box. Of the remaining two boxes, one is solely for internet access, the other contains a defibrillator. He thinks George might need one soon. The phone box stinks of urine and he wishes he'd brought the gloves with him. He stuffs a pound coin into the slot and punches in three digits.

'Thank you for calling 101,' says a female voice. 'We are connecting you to Buckinghamshire Police. If you require a different police force, please press hash.'

Five seconds of silence, then a ringing tone.

'Buckinghamshire Police, can I take your name please?' says another female voice.

Goldtooth clears his throat and assumes what people now call an Estuary accent. He feels it will add more of an edge to what he's about to say.

'No, you can't. Now just listen—.'

The voice interjects. 'I really would like your name, sir, and the number you're calling from.'

'You're not going to get it so shut up and listen. And don't hang up on me. You got a pen? ... A fuckin' pen?'

'I can't really—'

'Paedo. Claremont Avenue, Aylesbury. You got it?'

'Well, I—'

'Did you get it? Paedo scum, Claremont Avenue, yes?'

'Yes.'

'Good.' He rings off.

The 101 switchboard operator is used to emotional people. She's had extensive training to deal with them. And all the cranks, too. But there was something about the tone of this caller that unsettled her. As it wasn't an emergency, she'd discuss it with a supervisor on her next break. But now, as every call is logged, she types a brief note on her screen, and clicks onto the next call.

———

Ten

George flicks through the detritus that has just washed up on his doormat.

A menu for a local pizza delivery company featuring perhaps the worst food photography he's ever seen, a low-cost cremation plan flyer offering a free toaster with every policy, a credit card leaflet with guaranteed acceptance and an annual percentage rate that causes him to wince, and an envelope with a black portcullis icon in the top left-hand corner and the words House of Commons next to it.

Only the latter is saved from the graveyard of his recycling bins.

He stares at it for some time, admiring its sheer understatement. It looks and feels valuable, a missive of import. He carefully slides a finger under the flap, not wishing to tear it – it might be framed later. The letter inside has been neatly concertinaed into perfect thirds. George nods admiringly. He flattens out the heavy cream sheet, settles himself in the bay window chair, and starts to read.

Dear Mr Sanderson,

Thank you very much for your recent letter. I fully appreciate your determination to improve the road safety of our local area (and beyond, as you say). If it weren't for concerned citizens such as yourself, our great nation would be all the poorer for it. And I can only applaud the sheer creativity of your project and the obvious enthusiasm with which you carried it out. Marvellous!

Up to this point, George is revelling in his own glory. Then he reads on.

Unfortunately, issues like these are out of my control. Such matters are under the jurisdiction of your local council. I've taken the liberty of notifying your local councillor, Dianne Ackroyd. She will be in touch soon, I am sure. Have you talked to her before about this matter? I notice you also copied in the local police authority. Far be it for me to say, but I believe you will receive a similar answer from them. The police are not responsible for traffic management initiatives such as road humps or setting speed limits, merely enforcing the law, and so it is the council with whom you must discuss the matter.

On a more positive note, you say you are currently unemployed, and for that I am deeply sympathetic. However, I feel sure that an employer will very soon look upon your considerable talents and give you the position you so richly deserve.
I wish you the very best of luck in all your endeavours.

Yours sincerely

RT. HON. JAMES RAYNESFORD MP

The fingers that hold the letter gradually contract into a trembling fist. George is vaguely aware of the sound of crumpling premium-quality paper, which makes a deeper sound than the cheap stuff. He lets out the bellow of a wounded beast.

'You patronising...' He wants to say tosser but can't. '... arse.' It's the best he can do, and even now he feels a little ashamed for letting himself down. Moron would have been perfectly satisfactory. Mostly he's annoyed that the elected representative, who he only recently voted for, has failed to see the benefits of his intervention for the whole of the country. Speeding in urban areas is a nationwide problem. What was the matter with the ignorant man?

George pulls himself together. With his anger subsiding, he flattens out the letter and re-reads the first paragraph. And then reads it again. And finally, he reads the last paragraph. Between the two of them is a virtual character reference, and a pretty good one at that. One or more of Raynesford's phrases on his CV or ad or flyer, or whatever medium he markets himself, would add some weight. '... *Sheer creativity of your project ... considerable talents ... Marvellous!*'. The middle section of the letter is almost forgotten already. That's George for you. And he's not done yet.

On the local council website, he finds the contact details of Ms Ackroyd and sends her an introductory email.

Subject: Teddy Memorial – a new traffic-calming initiative

Dear Councillor Ackroyd

I gather James Raynesford has talked to you about my concept of slowing urban traffic, and the experiment I carried out on my local street. I hope you are as enthusiastic as him about it!

FYI when I wrote to James I also cc'd Brian Sexton, the head of the Highways and Transportation Dept at the county council. I've heard nothing from him to date. Very odd. Perhaps the letter didn't arrive? I know the quality of the postal service is far from that of its heyday.

When would be a good time to meet? I'd like to take you through my thoughts and research to date and perhaps show you the location where the 'magic' first happened. (You'll also be able to see there's plenty of space on the outside of the house for a blue plaque! Ha, ha.)

Yours most sincerely

George Sanderson
Accountancy • Bookkeeping • Financial Consultancy

Having added his new email signature – George hopes that the councillor may have contacts who have need of his services – his thoughts turn to business. He extracts a folder from a nearby cabinet and pulls out the contact details of the local businesses he copied in the library the previous week. He picks up the phone and keys in the first number on the list.

It takes him the entire day to get through his initial list of calls. Only around half picked up and many of those asked him to call back, write or email. Soul-destroying work, but he gamely presses on. He now emails everyone, a task that consumes another day because each one has to be personalised to the recipient. He'd read that was important. By Thursday night the task is done, and he sits back and awaits the results.

A night with Angela had been the only chink of light during a tedious week. She came to George's on Wednesday, bringing a small trolley bag that had the vague odour of antiseptic, and a bottle of expensive Chablis that Reg had given her as a thank you. The bag was last used on a low-cost weekend break to Marbella three years ago with Jackie and Jackie's next-door neighbour. It was the latter who'd vomited over the bag in the departure lounge on the return leg after a night of suckling pig and industrial sangria.

For George, the best thing about being with Angela, even better than the sex, was simply knowing she was there.

———

Friday lunchtimes at the Bell Inn are always busy. There must be fifty or sixty customers, predominantly male. The majority are eating, others necking a speedy second or third pint fast so their blood alcohol levels will have returned to a semblance of normality by the time they drive home.

The landlord, Justin – polished skull and pregnant belly – checks his watch. He's done this a few times, like a football referee when the game's approaching full time. 'Time for the draw,' he murmurs to Kathy, the bartender nearest him. 'You get the jar, I'll shut 'em up.' Kathy disappears round to the other end of the bar. Justin grabs a knife from the lemons and limes cutting board and bashes it against a pint glass. A hush falls over the room.

'Ladies & gen'lemen – and just for the record I'm ain't sure if the ladies are really ladies, and I know for certain there ain't any gen'leman 'ere (a titter amongst the men) – it's time for the Amazin' Business Card Draw! I call upon my esteemed colleague and all-round sexy brunette, Kathy – I couldn't afford a blond – to make the draw (admiring whistles).' He turns around. 'Where are ya, darlin'?'

Kathy steps up next to Justin and presents the jar to the gathered audience like she's modelling it on a catwalk.

'The runners-up prize which is a free lunch right 'ere at the Bell, Monday to Thursday, goes to ... Pick one out then, girl.' Justin rolls his eyes.

Kathy delves a hand into the jar and pulls out a card. 'Jamie Simpson from ETC Electronics.'

A whoop from the crowd.

'That's Jamie Simpson from ETC Electronics,' repeats Justin. 'Looks like he's 'ere, Kath. I'll let you sort him out.' He grins. 'Just go easy on him.'

Jamie staggers forward after a hard slap on the back from a colleague and spills some of his lager.

'Next up, the main event. The lunch for two at the Bell on a Friday. Yes, on a Friday, gents, so you can pick someone you fancy from the office and rub your mates' faces in it. Kathy, do the business per-lease.'

With a grand flourish, Kathy pulls out another card. 'David Winslow, Vulcan Logistics.'

'He's not here,' someone called out. 'Fell out of his cab yesterday. Broke his ankle.'

'You seein' him anytime soon?' asks Justin.

'Nah!'

'D'you want to be David Winslow then?' says Justin. 'I won't tell if you won't. See Kathy when we're done, all right? And finally, a new prize, as suggested by my lovely assistant. For the best-lookin' card of 'em all. She's 'ad 'em all out over the bar and I 'ave to say there's some pretty grim ones here. You can use a bit of colour, you know. It don't cost any extra. Anyway, Kath, tell us who's goin' to get a £20 voucher to spend right 'ere at the Bell.'

Kathy displays one side of the winning card. To be honest, it's a little dull: just some text and a logo. 'Yeah, I know what you're thinking,' she says. 'It's just like any other card. But then you turn it over.' She flips the card. 'Who wouldn't want a piece of that?' she says, displaying a lovely image of a tropical home. People peer at it from afar.

Justin says, 'What's the name, love?'

'Sorry,' says Kathy, 'forgot that bit,' she giggles. 'It's – tadaaaa – George Sanderson, Buy Barbados dot uk.'

'Well, let's hear it for George. George, you 'ere?' No answer. 'Maybe he's a virtual George, only exists in the world-wide web? That's all then, ladies and gents. Thanks for your attention and don't forget to drop your card in for next week's, alright?'

Justin takes the card from Kathy. 'Nice one, Kath. Not only do we have their email addresses, we're now encouragin' the bleedin' Arts. Should get a grant for doin' that, surely? I'm runnin' a bleedin' charity here as it is, so the cash would come in 'andy.' Kathy looks pleased. 'Better call this guy before I forget.' Justin flips the card over for George's contact details and notices some tiny handwriting running perpendicular to the printed text.

Goldtooth didn't bother going to the pub. He's worked the odds and knows that whether or not they picked the card out for a prize, someone would probably spot the handwriting. How many people would put a soiled business card into a competition? And what's the worst case? Well, there was always next week or the week after.

Back in school when Goldtooth had learned that, one way or another, almost everything in life is a lottery, he became a gambler. And once he had money, he gambled with that too. He invested everything in five internet start-ups before the term *dotcom boom* was even coined. His virtual net worth increased ten-fold in just a few years. Re-mortgaging his home, he then ploughed cash into those companies' competitors. All the bases were covered. Sell up in a couple of years and he wouldn't just be rich, he'd be powerfully rich.

By 2002, boom had turned into crash and his sure-fire investments were worthless as company after company filed for bankruptcy or was sold off for a pittance. The champagne lifestyle was over and his home repossessed. His parents believed that this was an important life lesson and, despite his pleas, they decided against a rescue plan. Goldtooth's drinking continued and his mood darkened. Within a year, there was nowhere for him to go but the streets or, if he got lucky, the night shelters.

Salvation came in the form of a private detective, hired by a firm of solicitors. He delivered what he considered would be a bittersweet message to Goldtooth: his parents had died in a plane crash off the coast of Indonesia some months ago and they'd bequeathed him some money. He shed no tears at the news of their deaths. He hadn't seen them for two years. And what little warmth he felt towards them evaporated when he was told that their business empire was given to a charitable trust in south-east Asia. Though the sum left him was still considerable, he felt short-changed. Nevertheless, he'd become a wealthy man again and he vowed only to invest in himself from now on.

There was no one else he could trust.

―――

George checks his emails for the umpteenth time that day. Finally, at 3.25 p.m., the email he's been waiting for pops up in his inbox.

Subject: Re: Teddy Memorial – a new traffic calming initiative

Dear Mr Sanderson,

Thank you for your email. James Raynesford did indeed contact me about your interesting idea. I have given it some thought, talked with colleagues, and also done a little research into the traffic history of your area. It appears that there has never been a reported accident involving injury in your road since comprehensive records began some fifteen years ago, and whilst I applaud your determination to make a difference to our community, I'm wondering if we aren't jumping the gun a little here.

May I suggest we review things in, say, twelve months? Of course, if the traffic situation worsens in the meantime, please don't hesitate to contact me.

Yours sincerely

Dianne Ackroyd (Cllr)
Two Valleys Council

'You've missed the point, haven't you?' says George to his laptop screen. You've totally missed the point. Why can't you see it? You've missed ... Oh, what's the use?!' He slaps the palms of his hands down on the desk. Not hard – more of a token effort really because it might be painful – but his body language says everything. Gone is the chin up, chest out, bullish George of late. Now, as he stands up and walks over to the sideboard that holds the gin and the tonic, arms lie loosely at his side, back stooped, the head flopping downwards. Back to the old George. Except this old George wants to partake of gin, even though it's not Friday evening. He pours himself a large measure followed by a splash of tonic and downs the glass in one. The Speeders Intervention has not only turned out to be disappointing. It's embarrassing. At some point, he'll have to tell Angela that one of his projects has failed. Maybe even Ray.

He sloshes some more G and T in the glass, grabs a biography of Richard Branson – smart but too full of himself, thinks George – and heads for the sofa. Maybe he should take a break from interventions? He would have liked to have seen Angela, but she was going to a local bar with some workmates on a hen night. He felt a pang of jealousy. What if she met another man? Younger, better-looking. Employed. Anything can happen when people have a few drinks inside them. What George really means is anything could happen when Cynthia had a few drinks at a party. The bodies of men of any age became super-magnets for her semi-precious metal-encrusted fingers. She couldn't stop herself.

He puts the book down after a single paragraph, switches on the TV and searches for a quiz. There's always a quiz whatever the time of day, so it didn't take long. He needed something to take the focus of his thoughts off Angela and the contemptible Dianne Ackroyd.

———

'Spritzes all round,' squeals Rochelle, attempting to place a loaded tray of drinks on the table without spilling anything.

'What's a Spritz?' shouts Angela in Mary from dispatch's ear.

'Italian thingy. You never had one?'

'I should get out more.' They both laugh and take glasses from the tray. 'Ooooh, that's nice,' says Angela, chugging it back. 'What's in it?'

'Prosecco and, and, and … Aperol,' says Mary. When the name finally comes to her, she makes it sound like April. Angela looks confused. 'Ap-er-ol. You can get it from the supermarket. S'what makes it orange.'

Rochelle raises her glass. 'To Jade, who's going to have to put up with Darren for better or worse.'

'That'll be worse, then,' slurs Jade. She downs half the drink in one. 'God knows what state he's in now, silly arse.'

God does know, and might now be wondering if the creation of homo sapiens was a worthwhile enterprise, even though they'd been knocked out from scratch on day five. That's because forty-year-old Darren is currently in a London Soho bar thrusting his tongue down the throat of a considerably younger brunette he doesn't know, nor is particularly interested in knowing.

Oiled by lager and tequila, he's on a mission to complete five challenges set by his mates and is finding each one easier than the last. Darren's tongue is not satisfied with his brunette's mouth. There is so much more to explore. Gripping her back with his left hand, he coats her neck, ears, shoulders and cleavage with his particular vintage of forty per cent proof saliva. His right hand, feeling left out of the action, inches awkwardly up her thigh and beneath her dress. She pushes it down without conviction.

'Oi, not in 'ere,' she grins.

Darren, who has never lacked tenacity, grins back and continues where he left off.

The ladies, considering they are now three hours into their evening, are comparatively well-behaved. Rochelle, the organiser, is under strict orders from Jade: no silly dress code, no stripper, cabs home at 1.00 a.m. I'm thirty-five, she'd said. I did all that stuff last time and look what happened.

The most riotous part of the evening so far has been a game of Truth or Dare. They may as well have called it Truth, everyone apparently happier to come clean on some concealed aspect of their personal lives rather than risk certain ridicule.

Jade flips over the card for Angela and smirks. *How many orgasms have you had this week?* The twenty-something receptionist sitting opposite, and who doesn't know Angela very well, stifles a laugh.

Mary looks at Angela, raises her eyebrows. Angela looks up at the ceiling, but all the action was going on in her fingers. One ... two ... three ... four ...

'Five,' she says.

A hush falls over the table.

'What the fuck!' mouths Jade. That's way more than she'd managed with Darren recently, and she was marrying him in seven days' time. Perhaps more likely, she thought, the old lady's describing a different route to orgasm. She leans across to Angela who has an embarrassed grin on her face, puts a hand on her forearm.

'Masturbation is nothing to be ashamed of,' she says, a face so earnest it's impossible for Angela to tell if she's taking the piss or not. In the best interests of the evening, she decides to take Jade's words at face value.

'I wasn't masturbating.'

'Yes, of course,' says Jade, her arm still attached to Angela. 'Poor Angela.'

'Well, you're a bit of a dark horse,' says Rochelle, who knows all about George. 'Is he, you know, good? You know.'

'He must be,' says a middle-aged lady called Anne, 'otherwise she wouldn't have gone for the five.'

Everyone except Jade howls with laughter. And that's the moment the table receives a visitor.

Male, tall, handsome. Firefighter's uniform.

'Ladies, good evening.' He removes his helmet and bows. 'I'm Sam, Fireman Sam. Which one of you beauties is Jade?'

'Oh Jesus,' groans Jade, giving herself away.

The man smiles, clears a space on the table for a portable speaker, and presses a few buttons on his mobile. It's that Barry White again. A hush descends around them.

'Fuckin' 'ell, Roch!' Jade's not amused. Everyone else is, except Rochelle.

'Don't blame me, I never got him.'

She didn't. Nor did anyone else around the table.

Fixing his eyes on Jade, Fireman Sam (actual name Gerry Blunt) sheds his jacket, revealing a shaved and oiled torso.

Rotating his hips with the music, Gerry rips apart his Velcroed-together trousers, revealing a posing pouch that would burst at the seams if it had any seams. He beckons to Jade, but she refuses to extricate herself from the far end of the booth. Huh? He's used to hen nights, and usually his victims are game for a laugh. On this occasion, though, he's not too bothered. Gerry has special instructions from his anonymous client to concentrate his efforts on another woman – the oldest one in the group, and easily recognisable from the photo he'd been sent.

Amidst whooping from the entire bar, gyrating hips are now in full swing. Angela, who's now had two drinks too many, looks up at Gerry's glistening pecs and bursts out laughing. He takes her free hand and places it gently on his chest, moving it side to side over his right nipple. Then he picks up his phone from the table, flicks it into camera mode and takes a selfie of them both. Angela tries to hide her face, but it's too late.

Ten minutes later he sends the image to Goldtooth.

———

'The Magna Carta.' George is now on his fourth quiz show of the day and Angela has only broken into his thoughts during the commercial breaks. So that's sixteen times, then. Luckily, this hasn't affected his recall for historical facts.

'Habeas Corpus,' says the contestant.

'Idiot,' says George.

The screen flickers, fades to black. The sound mutes.

He fiddles with the remote. Changes the channel, turns the TV off and on, hits buttons at random. It's dead. He stands up, walks over to the TV socket and removes the plug, replaces it. Switches on the TV. Nothing. He replaces the plug fuse. Last chance. The TV's ten years old and has served George well. Now it wants out, over two hundred minutes of continuous quizzing possibly being the final straw. Who can blame it? But what a heroic way to die, with your last words in a dead language.

———

Two beeps from a desk drawer. Goldtooth reaches down and slides it open. Light streams in to reveal a dozen mobile phones, some smart, some basic. He rummages through them and selects a large smartphone with a green notification bubble on its screen. A message. Goldtooth accesses it in a single click. Only it's not simply text message. It's a photo, and he's not happy with it.

Fireman Sam has been paid top dollar, plus a bonus for sending the picture, yet the image is quite tame. He expected Angela to be on her knees, clutching Gerry's well-developed thighs, his pouch a smidgeon from her mouth. Still, there was flesh-against-flesh contact and it would have to do. He immediately made a note on his pad to create a short, sharp shock for Gerry for failing to comply with his instructions.

He considers how to deliver the photo. He could email or text it to George from one of his many mobiles, but decides to post it. A big photo would have more impact. And George would need to sully his hands on it as he removes it from the envelope – the kind of psychological game Goldtooth enjoys. He downloads the image, prints it and pops it into an A4 envelope.

———

George wakes up on Saturday morning with a smile because tomorrow he won't be waking up alone. He closes his eyes again, turns over, and puts his arm around an imaginary Angela. Any remaining anxiety over her potential for adultery has faded.

The first task of the day is to order a new TV. Yes, his dwindling cash would take a hit, but good ones were not as expensive as they used to be. And he didn't need a huge 4K model, just a sensible size with good picture quality. Anticipating this appliance's end-of-life some time ago, he'd already compiled a list of the top-rated TVs in his budget range. From a folder named Appliance Reviews on his laptop, he pulls up a spreadsheet of TVs, their attributes, ratings, prices and retailers. At the top of the list was a brand name normally associated with poor quality appliances, yet today he notes the reviews and ratings are excellent: 'Five stars. This brand has turned itself around and shown the big boys how to make great technology on a small budget. If you can find one, buy it!!'

George would normally consider only premium brands, so he's a little puzzled this item had even made his list. But there it is: everything he needs in a TV, for less. It must have slipped his mind. He does a quick web search for availability and latest prices, and finds an obscure retailer who can deliver as early as Monday.

Police Community Support Officer, Yasmin Patel, studies the writing on the business card the Bell Inn's landlord has just handed her.

'See what I mean?' said Justin. 'It's a bit sus, ain't it? One on the 'ouse, Yas?'

Yasmin declines with a practised shake of the head, carefully picks up the card by the edges, and slides it into her pocket. Pats it. 'The world is full of vile and dangerous people, Justin, and we might have one here,' she says, a smug smile on her face.

The reality of life as a PCSO is not quite what she signed up for. Lots of community meetings, home security advice, reprimanding nitrous oxide-imbibing teenagers. Very little action. It's no surprise she grabs at whatever slim pickings there are. And this piece of evidence might be the catalyst needed to crack a huge paedophile ring. In her eyes, it doesn't get much bigger than that.

'Thanks for being so observant,' she says, regurgitating a line she's used countless times. 'Sadly, in these days of budget cuts we have to rely on help from people such as yourself.' The word *sadly* is unfortunate. She's just lucky Justin hasn't noticed this unintentional smear on his character.

Back at her office, a tiny room in a local community centre she shares with Malcolm and Ryan, her regular PCSO partners, Yasmin messages her boss. She attaches scans of both sides of the business card and sits back to await a special commendation.

Eleven

While George checks his pockets for a pound coin for the supermarket trolley before he leaves home, Goldtooth is pacing the morning room, screaming fluent Mandarin into his mobile. He gesticulates at nothing in particular, slaps his head, and ends the call with a syllable so long his mouth appears to be stuck open. Then he laughs. Laughs so hard tears slide down his cheeks.

He's still laughing thirty seconds later when he enters the panelled room, his office. Hitting a random key on a computer keyboard, a screen wakes up revealing a bank account statement. His eyes track down a column of numbers to the total: $2,214,000. He refreshes the page. Jackpot: $2,314,000.

His good intentions of letting work take a back seat had lasted little longer than a month. He'd missed the excitement, the deadlines and challenges of his usual work. To have more power than entire armies with the touch of a few keys.

Goldtooth's rather impressive work session is not over. He opens an email app on another screen and plugs in a new keyboard. The keys are in Russian Cyrillic. After making a few adjustments in the computer's settings, those delicate hands start dancing across the keyboard as if it's his first language. The message is curt: Просто говорю. He likes the understated tone of *just saying* for what he's about to send his client. Finally, he attaches an image directly into the body of the email. It's a photo of a current US presidential candidate talking to another man in a restaurant. Someone with links to the Kremlin will soon become very excited.

Even in Goldtooth's world of international espionage, George has not been forgotten. He logs into George's laptop and searches the emails for the word 'TV'. There's one result. An email from AZ Electronics of Swindon. He clicks on it.

ORDER REF: BSF560110BDS - NIHAOMA KC11220-42 TV

Hello
Thanks for your custom.
Your order will arrive on Monday, 6 September 2021.

It's hard for Goldtooth to suppress a look of unadulterated smugness. And, to be fair, we can hardly blame him. The delivery date couldn't have been more perfect.

Poor George. He has absolutely no idea of the triple whammy that's about to hit him.

Black Monday is just forty-eight hours away.

———

In George's expert hands, the supermarket trolley is like an extension of his own body. Because he knows where everything is, he plays a little game where he attempts to complete the entire Saturday shop while keeping the trolley moving. Eyes scan ahead, zeroing in on his targets, hands grabbing items as he glides past the shelves, avoiding potential hazards such as lost children, breakages on the floor, conversing couples, and reversing shoppers who suffer from a lack of spatial awareness. It's like a beautifully choreographed dance.

His mobile rings. What is it with people, he grumbles, always calling at the most inopportune times? He knows the caller is probably Angela, but still. He's due to see her at 2 p.m. and there's still much to do.

How will he negotiate the challenge of keeping the trolley moving yet answering the call? He requires one hand to hold the phone, the other to flip open the pseudo-leather case, the cover of which is closed by an unnecessarily powerful magnet. He achieves the feat by pushing the trolley along with his stomach but, now distracted, fails to spot an elderly lady crossing from one side of the aisle to the other. No hand signals. The trolleys meet. George's trolley bounces off the lady's and ricochets into the shelving. It's stationary.

He takes a deep breath to compose himself. Hits the green button.

'Angela. How was last night?'

'Morning George, I think. Let's just say I'm too old for girly nights out like that. I'd have been happy to leave at ten but didn't get in until after one. That's why I'm calling. Can you come over later this afternoon now, please? Say, four? Sorry, I'm running a bit late.'

George has been diligently working to their mutually agreed deadline, and now the deadline has moved. And he has to sort out his own lunch. And his trolley has stalled in the cereal aisle. Could the day get any worse? He grits his teeth.

'Of course. Whatever suits.'

With an extra two free hours in his day, he calls Ray from the car park with an invitation to meet up. It's a long shot at such short notice.

'Ooh, is that my long-lost friend Georgio?' says Ray, with an unnecessary impersonation of a rather camp Italian. 'The one who hath forsaken me for a lady? She has let you down, I am thinking?'

'Ha ha. In a manner of speaking, yes. She has a hangover.'

'Out with the girls, I bet.' says Ray, returning to his more familiar voice. George is thankful. It was getting a little embarrassing.

'Very perceptive. Younger girls mostly, from her office. She's paying the penalty. I don't think she gets out much.'

'Probably more than us, eh, George?'

———

Ray sits at a window table in the Earthmother Café looking like he's posing for a photograph, side-lit and all moody. The chess board is already set up, each piece perfectly placed within the squares. He stands as George approaches the table, holding out a tanned hand. George, not wishing to crush such an elegant appendage, gives it little more than a stroke.

Ray pulls two digital timers from his leather shoulder bag.

'Thought we'd play some Speed,' he says. 'Should be able to get half a dozen under our belts before you need to leave. I've ordered you a coffee.'

While George feels a frisson of excitement as he looks down at the board, he's been rather looking forward to a good chat as well. He has plenty to talk about. And that's why, half an hour later, they still haven't got around to moving a single chess piece.

'Good Lord, George,' says Ray, 'your exploits make me feel quite exhausted. I'll tell you something though, for what it's worth. Despite my initial scepticism, I think you're on to something with your intervention thingy.'

George looks pleased.

'I mean it.' Ray strokes his scalp as if flattening imaginary hair. 'Makes my addled grey matter look quite pedestrian.'

George self-consciously bats away the comment with a flick of his hand. 'Chess?' He's feeling confident.

They play five manic ten-minute games: Ray 4, George 0, with one lucky draw. There's nothing addled about Ray's mind.

As they're leaving, George remembers he hasn't after Ray's wife. Now it seems like an afterthought, but at least he's remembered her name.

'Martha. How is she? There's me waffling on and you kindly listening to my nonsense.'

'Erm…' Ray looks sheepish. 'Well, there is a bit of news. She's back in hospital for the next couple of weeks at least. For the best, really. They assure me this procedure will help, at least in the short term. And, to be quite honest, George, I needed the break. Selfish I know but…'

'Don't be silly. It must be terrible living on a knife edge all the time.'

'That's why I jumped at the chance to get out of the house, to see you. Takes my mind off things. You don't know the half of it.'

George has an idea. 'Listen, why don't you, and feel free to say no … Why don't you come over for dinner one night?'

'I couldn't possibly impose on you two lovebirds. It's very kind but—'

'You wouldn't be imposing and anyway it would just be the two of us. Angela and I aren't married, you know.' He laughs nervously. 'Please say yes. I don't know what I'd have done without you these past few months.'

Ray pats him on the shoulder. 'Thanks George, that means a lot. I know what it's like when you need a friend.'

Inspector John McKinley, who's on his second weekend shift in a row, checks out the business card scans from PCSO Patel. In order to read the handwriting properly, he rotates and zooms in on the reverse side of the card. He's no internet expert, but he knows enough to realise the handwritten website address relates to a platform of content on the murky dark web. And he's not authorised to access that. He pings the image over to a colleague in the Paedophile Unit with a brief note: *Might be nothing but ...* He's not expecting to get a response until Monday, so he's surprised when he gets a call two hours later.

'Rob Tyler here, sir, about your dodgy business card. You were right to punt it over. Dark web. Very graphic material of adults with children. Where'd it come from?'

'One of our PCSO's got a call from a publican in town. Apparently, someone had put it into a pub prize draw.'

'Bit careless. Listen, I've done a bit of checking on the company. It isn't one.'

'It isn't one what?'

'Buy Barbados doesn't exist. The website domain licensee info is protected, but I pulled in a favour. It belongs to a guy called George Sanderson. Lives in Claremont Avenue. No record, but he popped up as the victim of a road rage six weeks ago. However, just because it's Sanderson's card doesn't mean the writing on it was his.'

'True, but who else would bother to put his card into a prize draw. They wouldn't be up for the prize, would they? Looks like we need to dig a little deeper,' says McKinley furiously scribbling some notes. 'Leave it with me for now then. I'll be in touch.'

McKinley is happy. He likes it when his PCSO's unearth something interesting. It keeps their morale up.

In less than a minute, he's pulled up George's statement from the road rage incident. Then he does a wider search on reported offences in the Claremont Avenue area in the past three months. There's a list of five: one case of domestic abuse, one attempted burglary, two reports of speeding cars from a Mister George Sanderson, and an anonymous 101 call reporting an unidentified paedophile living in the road.

―――

Overnight bag in hand, George stands by Angela's front door at 4.01 p.m. He's never early. If someone wanted you earlier, they would have stated an earlier time. He doesn't like to be late either, because that would be rude. He's never quite got to grips with the meaning of fashionably late. Exactly how late would you have to be before your tardiness was unfashionable?

In his peripheral vision, he catches a neighbour peeking at him from a bay window. George turns his head to face the elderly woman and smiles. As he does so Angela's door opens, a hand grabs his arm and pulls him inside. The neighbour returns the smile, and for good measure, adds a pair of raised eyebrows.

'Looks like you have an admirer,' says Angela, waving to the woman.

'Oh, I like an older woman,' says George in a rare attempt at humour.

Angela stretches up to kiss him but moves her head away at the last moment. 'Naughty boy,' she giggles, and smacks his bottom.

Before dinner they walk hand in hand around the local park and stop for tea at the little café. It's about to close and they're the sole customers.

'I needed that,' says Angela. 'The fresh air. I've felt muzzy all day and I'm still hoarse from all that shouting.'

'Shouting?'

'Well, you know what it's like in those bars. Loud music, jam-packed full of youngsters on the pull.'

'Not exactly my scene,' says George.

While she relates the events of the evening in chronological order, George's mind drifts back to a time when he and Cynthia went to a Town Hall Christmas Dinner & Disco with a friend of Cynthia's and her husband. The girls danced all evening while the two men sat side by side, casually glancing at their watches between truncated attempts at conversation.

'So Cynthia tells me you work at blah blah blah.'

'Yes.'

'I expect that's a very interesting job?'

'Has its moments.' Pause. 'You and Cynthia been together long?'

'Four years, three months and two weeks.'

'That's good.' Pause.

'This is not really my kind of music.'

'Pardon?'

'I said, this isn't my kind of music. Too loud.'

'I don't like music.'

'No.'

When Cynthia and friend returned to the table, George whispered in her ear, 'That man you were dancing with. Who was he?'

'You mean Geoff? Never seen him before. He's a right laugh. I said he should come round for dinner.'

'Dinner?! Looked like he was trying to pull you from what I saw.' George blurts this out loud just as Angela gets to the part about the arrival of the stripper.

'What?' she says, striving to make sense of his words.

'Nothing. I got a bit distracted, that's all. I think things might be getting on top of me.'

'Careful what you wish for,' she grins.

The momentum of her story is broken and she forgets to tell George about Fireman Sam.

———

Lazy Sunday. George potters around Angela's kitchen in a white tee shirt and grey jogging pants that have never been, and would never be, used for jogging. He's now knows where the tea bags and sugar are secreted, and hopes to surprise Angela who's pretending to be asleep.

While the kettle boils, he argues with himself about what to do with Michael Finguish. Guilt has lodged Michael firmly in his head and he won't go away. Could a new intervention repair his marriage? Perhaps even make him a better person? But then could he really put one hundred percent effort into helping – how did Angela put it – a tosser? He's not unaware of the irony. If he'd left well alone in the first place, he wouldn't be in this position now. There are more important projects on which he could spend his precious time. He doesn't know what those might be yet, but he knows they were out there somewhere, waiting for the Puppetmaster to come to the rescue. It all seemed such an immense responsibility.

The kind of roar a jet fighter would be proud of brings him back to the task in hand. He reminds himself to recommend a new kettle to Angela. The decibel level of the current one when it's close to boiling is quite unacceptable. He stirs half a teaspoon of sugar into Angela's mug, ensuring it's fully dissolved. There are few things worse than drinking a mouthful of super-sweet tea when you get towards the bottom of a mug.

He walks upstairs, places the mug carefully on Angela's bedside cabinet, and tiptoes around the bed. He wishes she'd had the forethought to buy another cabinet for his side, then reminds himself that she's always lived alone in this house. He puts the mug on the floor and slips under the duvet.

'Where've you been?' Angela fibs. 'I woke up and you weren't there.'

'Tea. I brought you a cup of tea.' George comes across like a little boy trying to please his mum on Mother's Day.

'You're spoiling me. It's not even my birthday,' she says.

'I was thirsty,' says George, spoiling any kudos he'd just earned.

Angela finally moves, props herself up on her forearms. 'It's raining. Whatever are we going to do with ourselves?' She gives him the eye.

After breakfast and between rain showers, George walks down to the local corner shop to buy a newspaper. He rarely reads one during the week, but the quality Sundays were especially good value, with enough magazines and supplements to feed his appetite throughout the week. He always discards the sports section. At school, George had learned about team-playing the hard way. Whilst he'd been an adequate sprinter and swimmer, any sport involving balls was a disaster. On the football pitch, even his own team would give him a good kicking if they could get away with it.

'Do you really read all that?' Angela says, looking at the dining table awash with papers. George is so engrossed in an article about a Brit incarcerated in a Texan prison, he doesn't hear her.

'Could be years, you know. This man in Texas waiting to be executed,' he says finally. 'Imagine that. Not knowing when you're going to die.'

'Like the rest of us, you mean,' says Angela. 'What's the difference?'

'Well, it's a particularly nasty death, isn't it? Lethal injection.'

'I'm sure there are worse ways to die. George, why are we having this conversation on a Sunday morning? Have you been to Texas and done something very bad?'

George laughs. 'I'm too scared to do something bad.' He thinks for a moment, the smile slipping from his face. 'But it always seems like bad things happen to me.'

'That's enough of that kind of talk,' says Angela. 'Did you book The Bell for lunch?'

'One thirty. Strange, isn't it? I've lived here for thirty years and never been in there. I'm quite looking forward to it.'

―――

'You being served?' asks the baby-faced bartender as George hovers at the bar looking around him as if it's the first time he's ever been in a pub.

'I booked a table for one thirty. Sanderson, George Sanderson. Table for two.'

'I recognise you, mate. You had a Chinese. Claremont Avenue. Thirty-two. Never forget a face, innit.' He winks. A wink without the customary accompanying smile.

For a second, George is at a loss. Then it clicks. 'The delivery boy. On the scooter.'

'You shouted at me.'

'No, I didn't. I gave you a generous tip and you drove off.'

'No mate, you shouted something.'

George stares at the ceiling, squints his eyes, willing his memory to help him out. It had something to do with the tip. Angela looks a tad embarrassed.

'The tip! That's it. I said you should open a savings account. Saving makes sense, you know. A pound saved at your age could be worth fifty when you retire.'

'I got one. Got loads in it. Work three part-time jobs, see?

Chinese, the Bell, Artima mag delivery. Ain't got time to spend it.'

'I can see you didn't need my advice after all. Well done. Carry on like that and you could be a millionaire by the time you're forty.'

'Thirty,' says the boy, consulting the bookings sheet. 'I ain't waiting 'til I'm old. Your table's over there next to the alcove. Number five.' He passes George some menus. 'Drinks?'

After they've ordered and settled themselves at the table, Justin, the manager, calls Scooter Boy over.

'What did he say his name was, that bloke you were talkin' to?'

'Sanderson. Funny geezer. Thinks I'm thick or something.'

'Sanderson, thought I heard right. First name?'

'George, I think.'

'Fuck me,' he whispers to himself. 'It's 'im with that woman, right?' He points to the table.

'That's the one, boss.'

'Tell the kitchen to call me when his food's ready. I'll take it over.'

Angela is glad she'd dragged George out for lunch. She's already worked out that he's a man who needs distractions. And George is feeling quite at home in The Bell, despite his dislike of pubs. He guessed the average age of the diners was around fifty, and there were several multi-generational tables. A family pub, he concluded. A pleasant atmosphere and no loud music or fighting. He peered over at one of the nearby tables.

'The portions look huge,' says George.

'That's why I ordered the tuna salad.'

'Angela, I've been thinking.' Her shoulders imperceptibly droop. 'It may be a little presumptuous ... I've been thinking about a ... Shall we go away for a weekend? Nowhere expensive, of course. Just somewhere nice. Obviously, I'd quite understand if you, er ...'

'Yes.'

'Would you? Really?'

Angela reaches over and cups George's hand in hers. The warmth of it reaches his toes.

'Yes, really.'

Meanwhile, at the bar, Justin gets the nod from one of the kitchen staff that George and Angela's meals are ready. He collects the plates and strolls over to their table.

'Sanderson?' he says, slapping the plates on the table like they're too hot to handle.

'Yes, that's—' A simmering Justin cuts across George.

'Eat up and get out, mate. We don't want your sort in here.'

George, mouth half open, glances up at the towering form who's casting a shadow over the entire table. He's so dumbfounded by what Justin has said, he can't find any words. Angela doesn't have that problem.

'What do you mean, your sort? This won't look good on TripAdvisor, you know.' She thinks George would be very proud of her name-checking one of his favourite review sites.

Justin ignores her, leans in to George's ear. 'Want me to spell it out, you dirty dog? You got twenty minutes, then I'm throwin' you out.' He stomps off.

'What does he mean?' Angela looks pale. 'Have you been here before? He seems to know you.'

George's mouth still hangs open.

'He called you a dirty dog, George. I think we should go. I don't want to be here any longer.'

George stands up. He hasn't been humiliated in front of a woman since a Tenerife hotelier insulted him, and Cynthia cried out of self-pity. Words strive to find a way out of his mouth, but there's an invisible barrier in his throat behind which they're piling up. The moment he and Angela reach the pub car park, the barrier is breached and a flood tide of supressed hurt bursts through.

'The man's mad. I've never even seen him before. I should sue him. It's slander. We were having such a nice weekend and then that man... Why would he call me a dirty dog? I'm not a dirty dog. And now we'll have to find somewhere else. We don't deserve this, Angela. It's not fair. I'll write to the brewery. I'll do an intervention. He'll wish he never insulted me ... us.'

He's close to tears. The ignominy, the unfairness. Angela moves closer, puts an arm around his waist and guides him towards the car.

'Let's get away from this place,' she says. 'I'm sure it's all a terrible mistake.'

She doesn't sound too sure.

―――――

Sanderson update: possible serious crime. Specialist unit looking at it now. Thought you ought to know.

Goldtooth scans the text message again. The more he thinks about it, the less like a game this feels. Perhaps he's overstepped the mark this time? One thing's for sure, now the police are involved it's too late to pull the plug.

―――――

Home is George's sanctuary from the threat of the outside world. When he arrived home later that afternoon, he breathed a sigh of relief. Since he and Angela had left the Bell Inn, a disturbing atmosphere descended over them. They'd ended up at a pub on the edge of town. Angela had been quiet and apologised for it. She told him she was a little shaken up and for him not to worry about it. But George did worry about it. And when he'd dropped her home and picked up his overnight bag, he detected an awkwardness from her he'd never felt before. He thanked her for a lovely weekend and pecked her on the lips. Angela's hands barely touched him, as if he'd succumbed to some super-virulent disease.

He puts on the radio for company, settles in the armchair, and opens up his laptop. Life goes on. There's an email from a bed shop in town enquiring about his services. He writes back, suggesting they meet up next week. At least he might salvage something from the wreckage of one of the most embarrassing days in his life.

Tiredness washes over him. He fights it for a few minutes before succumbing to sleep. When he wakes up, the room is in partial darkness, lit only by a streetlamp. He checks his watch: 9.00 p.m. He has a sudden urge to call Angela but what would he say? He'd said it all earlier. And it was then he realised that Angela is as fragile as he is, and he's yet to fully earn her trust. Today's events have tarnished their relationship.

Feeling helpless, he seeks solace in his go-to comfort snack of toast and marmite. Come on George, he cajoles, tomorrow is another day. And Mondays often set the tone for the rest of the week.

―――

Twelve

Light streams through a crack in the bedroom curtains and contours across George's sleeping figure. When the alarm sounds, he does something quite out of character. He presses the snooze button and snuggles down in a duvet cocoon in a bid to recoup some of the sleep he lost in the early hours replaying the Bell Inn fiasco. Then he remembers it's Monday. His new TV is due to be delivered between 8.00 a.m. and 10.00 a.m. And since every new TV is better than the previous one, it's enough to get him out of bed and downstairs in less than ten minutes.

The first thing he does is check his emails. Nothing from the bed shop, but it's still early. The only other response to his business emails had come from a 'quality' used sports car dealer. He suggested George join his local networking breakfast club. It's like a fry-up with the Masons, the man wrote, but without the dodgy handshakes. George isn't too sure about joining clubs. Already he barely had enough hours to fit in everything, but he promised to think it over.

The fact is, he's getting stressed by juggling all the elements of his life. There was the court case to come, a new woman in his life, a bank account with a short use-by date, marketing his financial talents, and the interventions. It was like having five important jobs. And Angela was taking up more and more of his time. Maybe that's why he couldn't win a game against Ray? He knows that patients in hospitals can become institutionalised in days. Is that what's happening to me with Angela, he questioned?

The TV arrives at 9.58 a.m. in the arms of the kind of man who probably could have used one arm quite easily. 'Mister Sanderson?'

'Yes. Skin of teeth, eh?'

'Sorry?'

'Just made the time slot, ha ha.' Secretly, George is pissed off because he could have had an extra two hours' sleep.

'That's good then,' says the man, oblivious of George's sarcasm. 'Never quite know 'til we get the delivery list at seven. Where's it going?'

George leads him through to the living room where the old TV still sits.

The man puts the box down. 'Want me to set it up for you?'

'Yes please,' says George. 'I could do it, but you're the expert.'

Within ten minutes, the TV is connected and tuned in.

'There you go,' says the man. 'You're good to go.'

George studies the screen. 'Hmm. I think there's something wrong. It's not very sharp, is it? And the colours ... they look a bit washed out.'

'Well, you're not going to get the best image at this price. Or sound quality. Not like your old TV.' He nods towards the sofa where it's reclining as if waiting to pass judgement on its replacement. 'I bet that was quality, right?'

'But this is supposed to be a quality TV. The reviews said so. It's on my list. The Best Buy List.' It looks like George is pleading with the man to change his mind.

'Nah, won't find this on Best Buys, but then you wouldn't expect to at this price.'

George has heard enough. 'Can you take it away please. Sorry. I don't understand how this could have happened.'

'Should do your research, mate, before you order. That's what people do.'

That's a massive slap in the face for George. Of all things to be criticised for. He knows so much he could start a consumer magazine or host a YouTube channel on what to buy and what not. Something in his system had broken, and that troubled him.

One-nil to Goldtooth.

―――

With his feet on the desk, the man responsible for George's consternation is enjoying a protein-packed smoothie and listening to the unfolding events through the mic in George's laptop. The voices are faint –the laptop must be in a different room, he concludes – but the words are clear. And when the installer had said "should do your research, mate" he spluttered into his glass sending globules of pink smoothie flying. This is more like it, he thought. The practical joke. Very refreshing. He tried not to think about what might happen to George later.

―――

How could I have got it so wrong? George is forensically investigating his Best Buys list. He searches online for current reviews of the TV which is now on its way back to Swindon. None of the reviewers have a good word to say about it: "Avoid", "Don't Buy", "Poor". Am I going mad, he thinks? Maybe I confused it with a brand of a similar name? Dementia! Is this the start? Ridiculous. Much more likely to be the road rage incident, the subsequent head injury. Perhaps I have bleeding on the brain? Before he has time to thoroughly check the symptoms online, there's a knock at the front door.

A shadowy movement behind the 1930s stained glass panel. Even before George reaches it, there's another knock, like someone's in a hurry. He opens the door wide. A postman in shirt, shorts and well-worn boots that may have seen military service, hands him a large hardback envelope.

'Sorry, wouldn't fit,' he says, already walking back down the path.

'Thanks,' George calls out 'Have you run out of junk mail, then?' but the postman has already disappeared behind the hedge.

He finds a sharp knife in the kitchen and carefully slits the envelope open. He'll keep it with the others he saves because they're expensive to buy. At first, he thinks there's nothing in there. Then his fingertips find an edge and he pulls out a single sheet of paper. It's blank. He flips it over.

His right hand starts to shake so much he calls upon his left hand for back up. Now he sits down so slowly there's a question mark over whether his bottom will ever touch the seat of the chair.

Angela. Glazed eyes. Her hand. A nipple. A young man in a thong. A leer on his face. George averts his eyes. Then glances back to the photo again. He takes it outside and tosses it into the recycling bin. He wants to know who the man is, and who sent the picture. And why. There's no accompanying note, no "From a well-wisher" sign-off. In George's experience of the whodunit genre, the sender rarely wished the recipient well, the intention usually cold and calculating. He'd like to un-see the picture, but he knows he never will.

Returning to the recycling bin, he removes the photo, and texts a picture of it to Angela with the briefest of messages: *?*

He's under no illusions that this will probably cause some kind of confrontation, but so be it. If Angela is untrustworthy, then she can't be a part of his life. His eyes moisten at the possibility.

Two-nil to Goldtooth. And the day has barely begun.

Around the world, forty-nine thousand earthquakes a year cause some kind of disturbance, but rarely damage anything. One hundred and twenty may cause substantial damage. Eighteen can be devastating. Even if George could have predicted something so potentially destructive is coming, there's nothing he can do about it. What's done is done.

A few minutes later, the door knocker sounds again.

George wonders if it's the postman returning, having found more mail in his bag for number thirty-two. Ready to deliver another junk mail witticism, he opens the door. Two men stare back at him. The one closest to the door is considerably shorter and younger than George, and wears the kind of clothes a man who hates shopping for clothes buys. Colourless, shapeless, hopeless. A man who could disappear in a crowd of Brits at a racetrack. Only his eyes display energy. Behind him is an even younger man. Light jacket, tee shirt, jeans, a supercilious smile. As George sizes them up, two uniformed police officers walk up the drive from the road.

His only thought is of Angela. Has she been in some kind of accident?

'Mister Sanderson? DS Tyler.' He pulls out his ID and pokes it in front of George's face. Then jabs a wayward thumb over his shoulder. 'Detective Constable Bryant. May we come in?'

George is confused. Why would it take four people to tell him that something's happened to Angela? And that young one wouldn't be smiling, although he couldn't be sure about that. Young people these days were a different species in his opinion. You can't second guess them.

'Yes, come in, come in,' he says, stepping to one side. 'The living room, on the left.' The two detectives squeeze past him, but the uniforms hold back. 'Are you coming in?' asks George.

One of them grins good-naturedly and says 'We're okay, thanks.'

'Well, I'd rather you did, please. It doesn't look good to have police on your drive.'

'As I said, sir, we're okay here.'

George stares at them, then starts to follow the detectives inside. He pauses, turns around and says, 'I'll leave the door on the latch so you can come in if you want. It's a bit chilly this morning.'

'Very thoughtful, sir,' says the other one.

In the living room, the eyes of Tyler and Bryant are everywhere, as if they're making a snap assessment of George's character from the objects in the room. As he enters, their heads turn towards him.

'Please have a seat,' says George, voice wavering and mouth dry. *Seat* comes across as *Sheet*. He doesn't know why he's nervous, but he feels guilty all the same. 'What ... How can I help you?'

Tyler speaks up. 'I'm sure it's nothing, Mister Sanderson, but we have reason to believe you may have been engaged in child pornography.'

George laughs. It's his silly, frightened laugh. The one he perfected at school.

'I'm not sure it's a laughing matter, sir. Do you find it funny, DC Bryant?'

Before Bryant can answer, George interjects. 'It's not funny. It's ridiculous. I ... I have a girlfriend.'

Bryant smothers a laugh in a closed fist.

Tyler continues. 'I'm sure we can clear the matter up quickly. Do you own a computer? Or a smartphone, tablet, anything with access to the internet?'

'Of course,' says George, pointing to his laptop on the unoccupied armchair. 'My phone's in the kitchen.'

'Would you mind ...?' says Tyler. He nods to Bryant who follows George into the kitchen.

'It's just charging,' George says. 'Forgot to do it last night. Probably only 60% on it at the moment.'

Bryant takes the phone and ushers George back to the living room.

'Any other devices, sir?' asks Tyler, who's holding the laptop.

George, now hunched on the sofa, shakes his head.

'Absolutely sure?'

'Yes.'

'Mind if we take a look around, Mister Sanderson? You're within your rights to say no, but should anything come to light later it wouldn't look good, would it, Bryant?'

'No, sir, it would not.'

'And I should tell you that anything we do find and anything you say may be used in evidence. Is that understood, Mister Sanderson?'

George stands up, a little unsteady on his feet. 'I can show you around?'

'That's all right, Bryant is quick, careful and tidy, aren't you, Bryant?'

'I am all of those, sir.' He leaves the room.

'I don't understand why you think I'm this ... person,' says George. 'I'm normal. I've never seen any pornography in my life. It's for perverts.'

'As I said, we're only checking. If everything's okay, we can eliminate you from our enquiries. I have one last favour to ask you. Would you mind coming back to the station with us for a formal interview? That way you can put your side of the story.'

'Do I have to?'

'No, sir, but it will make things a whole lot easier for all of us. Then you can get back to whatever it was you were doing. What were you doing?'

'Me? I was just about to reply to some emails. I'm looking for work. Accountancy, that sort of thing. Money's a bit tight.'

'Tough for many people at the moment, so I believe,' says Tyler. 'Let's wait for DC Bryant and then we can go. Mind if I'm nosey?' He motions to the room. George waves his hand.

After Tyler's done looking through the bookcase and TV unit, they sit in near silence for ten minutes. George offers to make tea but it's declined. Periodically he hears the sounds of footsteps above him, drawers and doors opening, closing. And all the while, he's thinking of Angela, even though he thinks he can't trust her anymore. How can he? Then his mind rewinds to everything that's happened to him in the last twenty-four hours. It's as if a stack of dominoes has been set in motion. As it, and he quite can't get his head around this, he's at the centre of an intervention.

Bryant steps back into the room. 'Nothing else. At least, nothing I can find.' He puts the laptop and mobile into plastic bags, pulls out a pen and makes some notes on the labels.

Tyler stands up. 'Shall we?' he says with a smile.

'I'm not being arrested, am I?' asks George.

'Just helping us make sense of this, sir.'

George stands, walks out to the hallway and picks up his jacket from the hook. 'Well, if it helps,' he says to Tyler, who's right beside him.

Three-nil to Goldtooth.

―――

Goldtooth sifts through his impressive collection of mobiles, pulls one out and checks the screen. Another text: *Your man was picked up. I'll keep you posted when I can.*

He wonders how George is feeling right now.

―――

The faint smell of paint fumes suggests the interview room has been recently painted. A very poor job, George observes. Roller splashes on the tiled floor and white brush marks encroaching onto the grey door frame. If Tyler and Bryant were in the room, he'd bring it to their attention. Get the contractors back in to make good their shoddy work.

He feels the need to talk to someone, but how? He has no phone but supposes they'd let him use a landline. But who? Angela's off his list now. Ray? What would he tell him? It's too embarrassing. The Samaritans? Perhaps too early for that. And the only solicitor he knows charged him a not inconsiderable sum to prepare his will.

It's lunchtime, but he has no appetite for food. In front of him, on the laminated table, stands a plastic cup filled to the brim with water. He can't trust his still-trembling hands to pick it up without spilling it. The only option is to bend his head over the cup so he can take sips. As he does so he's reminded of those kitsch, faux-perpetual motion toys from the nineteen-sixties – a pivoting bird that continuously dunked its beak into a glass.

DC Bryant spots George's eccentric take on it through the window in the door. He motions to Tyler who shakes his head in disbelief.

'Everything alright, Mister Sanderson?' Tyler says as he enters the room alone. He's used to witnessing bizarre behaviour in a pressurised environment and has been trained in risk assessment of mental instability.

George's head flips back up. He licks his lips.

'Okay if I call you George? It all seems a bit formal otherwise, doesn't it?'

'Sure.'

Tyler sits down opposite him and places a thin folder on the desk. He looks at his watch. 'Fancy a sandwich? I'm sure our dwindling reserves will stretch to that.'

'No, thank you. I don't seem to be hungry right now.'

'Okay,' says Tyler, 'Let's make this as painless as possible.' He presses a button on the interview recorder. 'Just so you know, this interview is being recorded. Present are DS Tyler and George Sanderson. George, you have agreed to attend this interview voluntarily. Also, you have divulged your device passwords voluntarily. You are not under arrest, you may leave at any time, and you may have a legal representative present. Are you happy that you don't have a solicitor here with you? We can arrange one for you if you choose.'

'I don't need one. I haven't done anything wrong. Except that speeding offence a few years ago. And that —'

Tyler interrupts. 'Please stop there, George, I need to read you your rights before you tell me anything else, okay?'

'Yes.'

'You do not have to say anything, but it may harm your defence if you do not mention when questioned something you may later rely on in court. Anything you do say may be given in evidence.' Tyler looks George in the eye. 'Is that clear?'

George nods. Under the desk, the nails of his right hand are digging into his left palm. He doesn't realise he's doing it. Despite Tyler earlier making light of the chat they were about to have, the words defence, court, and evidence tell a very different story.

'Then let's move on.' Tyler opens the folder before him. 'And just to let you know, George, your laptop and mobile phone are being investigated right now by our computer forensics team. Because the offence I referred to is very serious, the investigation has jumped the usual queue. That's good news all round. It means we may have some results soon, maybe even later today. I can't promise anything, though.'

'But what if someone calls me? I don't want the police answering.'

'Relax, we're very discreet. Now tell me about BuyBarbados.uk.'

How on earth does he know about that, thinks George. Nevertheless, it's a subject he's happy to talk about. 'Well, it's all down to something I invented called Intervention Theory.' And he's away for the next twenty minutes – a soliloquy broken up by occasional prods and queries from Tyler.

So why,' asks Tyler eventually, 'did you bother to print business cards if you were doing everything on your website and by email?'

'I didn't. Print any cards, that is.'

'But we have one in our possession, George.'

'That's impossible. What would be the point? I've said it wasn't a real company. I don't meet people and try to sell them fictitious homes, you know.'

From the folder, Tyler pulls out photocopies of both sides of the card, pushes them across the table.

'So you don't recognise this, then? A card with your name and contact details on?'

George's first thought is that the card looks very attractive. Just the kind of graphics he'd have used if he'd ever needed cards. The effect was partially spoilt because someone had scribbled on it. His second thought is more sobering. Why the hell would anyone want to print some? He felt like he was in some parallel universe and another George had actually created a real company.

'Never seen it before. Where did you get it from? Looks like someone's copying me. There must be a law against that surely?'

Tyler sighs, presses on.

'Do you go to the Bell in the High Street often?'

'We were there yesterday. A terrible experience and I won't be going there again. Why?'

'Because that's where your business card was found. And written on that card is the address and password of a website that contained pictures of a man and young children.'

George makes the vital connection. 'That's it. Why that man was so rude to me and Angela. It was very embarrassing, you know.'

'I'm sure. And the time before that?'

'Never. I don't really like pubs. It was Angela's suggestion. Plus I checked it out on PubAdvisor and they gave it four stars. No point wasting time and money on a sub-standard meal.'

'You sound like a very astute man. You realise you were verging on fraud when you devised this, er, intervention?'

'But there was no material gain for me,' says George. 'It was simply a way of allowing information to get to the right person to stop someone else being an idiot and playing with the livelihoods of others.'

'A bit like Robin Hood, then?'

This cheers up George. He even smiles. 'Except the robbing part,' he says, warming to the role. 'And the hood. And I don't have a band of merry men, just Angela sometimes.'

'Hmm, yes. Tell me about Angela.'

George's first reaction is to tell him that Angela is a filthy adulterer, but he thinks that might complicate matters. So he starts at the beginning and tries to describe Angela in a fair and honourable fashion. It's hard.

'She sounds like a lovely lady. Many of us don't deserve them, do we?' It's a leading question and George is having none of it.

'I think I do. It's not been easy for me. When your wife runs out on you, when you've been made redundant, when ... when you're my age. I think it's my turn to get some luck.'

Tyler turns to a sheet of paper in the folder.

'George, is there a reason you've been lurking in your street?'

'Lurking? I don't lurk.'

'We had a report a few weeks back of a man standing in your street with a notepad, often at the times of the school runs. He answers to your description.'

'Oh, that. It's another intervention. I wrote to your Chief Constable about it, actually. You'll find it on my laptop in the Interventions folder. He's not responded, which I think is rude. I'm sure he's a busy man but—'

'An intervention about what exactly?'

'Speeding cars. Your colleagues are obviously too engaged with drug dealers and knifings to do anything about it, despite my complaints, so I came up with an idea involving a teddy bear and flowers. It was moderately successful. I could send you the spreadsheet if you like?'

DS Tyler believes himself to be a good judge of character and takes pride in being able to see through a fog of waffle. What he sees in front of him is a most unlikely candidate for the offence under discussion.

'Are you sure I can't get you anything?' says Tyler. 'God knows I need a coffee.'

George has regained some confidence. 'I'll have that sandwich, please, if it's not too late to ask. Ham and cheese perhaps? And a tea. Earl Grey, if you have it. Just a tad of milk and absolutely no sugar. Thank you.'

DS Tyler pulls his fingers through his hair. 'We'll do what we can, George. Interview paused at fifteen-fourteen. DS Tyler leaving the room.' He presses a button on the recorder and leaves the room.

Outside, he bumps into Bryant.

'You know, Steve, nothing about this makes any sense. He's a bit of an oddball, but I really don't think he fits the profile. And why DCI Howard in Fraud is involved, I've no idea. Just said he was a person of interest. How are they doing on the devices?'

'They said there's not much on it so shouldn't take too long.'

'Good. Can you get him a sandwich please, and a tea, no sugar, and the usual for me.'

Tyler re-enters the interview room, presses the record button.

'Interview with George Sanderson by DS Tyler resuming at fifteen-seventeen. Moving on. Let's talk about your friends.'

Luckily for Tyler, it was the one section of the interview that George keeps mercifully short, mainly because he only has one real friend. He extolls the virtues of Ray – very supportive and a wizard chess player – and explains the situation with his very poorly wife.

The door opens. In walks Bryant carrying a tray. He puts it down on the table and distributes the contents.

'Boss, a word,' he says to Tyler, flicking his head towards the door. Tyler pauses the machine once more and follows Bryant from the room.

He can barely keep his excitement in check. 'We've got the dirty bastard. Just had the call. About a hundred photos and videos. We've fucking got him.'

Tyler looks confused, rubs his chin. 'Is Sanderson in any of them?'

'Who cares? He's got the pics, hasn't he? That's enough to hold him. They're running through everything else now to see if they can find where he got them from.'

Tyler nods.

Bryant isn't finished. 'And there's something else, boss. That DCI left another message. Seems super keen to see our progress on this. Sounds like this could be big. Can I come in with you now? I want to see his sorry face.'

George, on the other hand, is quite chipper, even thinking he'll be able to leave soon. DS Tyler has been called out to be told that they've found nothing illegal on his laptop and phone. His full and honest answers appeared to have left Tyler quite satisfied. Should be home in half an hour.

He bites into the very thin, chemical-ridden white bread sandwich, a portion of which immediately glues itself to the roof of his mouth. It's very irritating. His tongue can loosen the bit at the front, but the back part is still stuck. He resorts to sticking an index finger in his mouth to loosen it. He sloshes some lukewarm tea around his mouth to clear any residue and gives up on the sandwich.

Tyler reappears with Bryant in tow. The latter is trying to

perfect a look of disgust. It's actually a thin veneer hiding the world's biggest grin. Tyler appears drained. George stands up, ready to leave. Tyler walks past him, restarts the recorder.

'Sit down, Mister Sanderson. We haven't finished yet.'

George wonders why Tyler didn't call him George. They were getting on so well.

'Forensics have found over one hundred indecent images and videos involving minors on your laptop.' He leaves it there. Waits for George to respond.

George's eyes blink. Once, twice, three times. For some psychological reason unknown to him, they won't stop blinking. His lips and teeth are glued together, but it's not the bread. Were they actually talking to him, or another George in a nether world known only to sci-fi authors and scriptwriters? Were Tyler and Bryant real? That bang on the head?

'Mister Sanderson.' Tyler's voice cuts through George's musings.

'Yes?'

'Tell me about the images on your laptop. Please.'

'I don't have any. I don't really take pictures.'

'But they're on your laptop. Did you take them? Or download them? Or did someone else give them to you?' Tyler's voice is sharper now. He's lost faith in his normally reliable judgement and George is to blame.

'No.'

'No to taking them or no to receiving them?'

'No, no, no to them all.' George sounds desperate, his voice breaking. 'You're making a mistake. They've been looking on the wrong laptop. Or...' George can't look at them because of what he's about to say. 'Or you're framing me, and I don't know why.' His voice trails off into a mutter.

Bryant is loving this. He's slumped in his chair, legs splayed in front of him, hands clasped behind his neck. Tyler leans forward, takes a deep breath.

'George Sanderson, I'm arresting you for the possession of indecent images contrary to Section 1 of the Protection of Children Act 1978. You will now be held here pending further investigation, after which you may be charged.'

No one speaks for a few seconds. Then George stands up.

'I'd like to make that call now, please.'

———

Thirteen

'You've been what?' Ray's voice booms out of the landline receiver.

George tries to explain his predicament as calmly and succinctly as possible, which right now is anything but calm and succinct. He's rambling.

'George, if I may, let me summarise so I know what we're dealing with.' George notices the "we're" and that comforts him a little. 'They've found some dodgy images on your laptop and some writing on one of your business cards that you didn't have printed. Yes?'

'Yes.'

'And they haven't charged you?'

'No. They said they might.'

'Well, that probably means they don't have enough evidence yet. And they can't hold you for long either so they'll need to work fast before they have to release you. Only get a solicitor involved if the police charge you. They're expensive. There's a copper I know. I'll call them now and see what they suggest, okay?'

George is impressed at Ray's knowledge of such things.

'George? You there?'

'Sorry, yes I'm still here.'

'Just keep calm and don't worry. We'll try to sort this mess out.'

'Will we? I don't know why any of this is happening, Ray, but thanks for being a good friend. I know you've got enough troubles of your own to deal with.'

―――

Three hundred and eighty-two, three hundred and eighty-three. George appears satisfied. It's the third time he's counted the tiles lining the walls of his cell, and this time the result is the same as on the previous occasion. He can now move on to his next self-imposed assignment. To flick through some random magazines they've given him to read: Cosmopolitan, Inside Soap, Gardeners' World, Country Homes & Interiors, and What Car?. He can think of few titles less relevant for the situation he finds himself in. The lack of Accountancy World or Chess for Beginners won't stop him, though. Any distraction from the miserable situation he finds himself in is welcome.

Following his arrest, and bolstered by Ray's calming words, George had followed Tyler to the custody suite where he was signed in. The extremely polite custody sergeant explained George's rights and reaffirmed his right to speak to a solicitor. George again refused, on the basis that his arrest was simply a terrible mistake and he'd soon be exonerated.

The sergeant appeared to made a note of this, then took a large buff envelope from under the counter.

'Would you mind emptying your pockets please, sir. The contents will be quite safe in here.'

George pulled out his wallet, watch and keys, and passed them over.

'No loose change?'

George gave him a look of incredulity. 'Who carries change these days? Do you know it's predicted that coinage will be obsolete by 2026? Not before time, in my opinion.'

'A date, I'm sure, that will be welcomed by many, sir,' said the sergeant. 'Now can I have your belt and shoelaces. Just a precaution for health and safety. I'm sure you understand.'

George was about to comment on the bizarre necessity to remove his laces but, unusually, couldn't find the right words. In fact, try as he might, he couldn't find any words because the reality of his plight had sunk in. And did they really think he might try to self-harm? Did they know something he didn't? Maybe people do bad things to themselves in a cell.

'Before we show you to your accommodation, sir, we just need to take a few photos. My colleague will do the business if you'd like to follow him.'

A constable stood up from his computer screen and motioned George towards a door. Meekly, George followed him into a tiny white-painted room. A static camera on a tripod stood close to one wall.

'If you could stand on the red x, please.'

George complied, adjusting his hair and jacket collar as he does so. He didn't want to look like a madman.

'Now relax and imagine this is for a passport. I need a neutral expression, so no smiling, okay?'

The smile, in George's repertoire of expressions, was currently absent without leave, so the request required no effort whatsoever. Thankfully, the photo session was over in less than a minute. The constable even complimented him on the quality of his poses, and that gave George some solace.

His cell, though, brought him back down to earth again. A

distinct aroma of bleach, and not George's favoured lemon-scented variety. A bed so narrow a restless night could result in a broken limb or concussion. And a toilet without a seat. That was the final straw.

'I'm sorry to be a pain,' he said to the constable, 'but would it be possible to swap cells for one with a complete toilet. I suppose your budget cuts mean it's difficult to replace broken seats?'

'They're designed that way, sir. Health and safety. A seat be used as an offensive weapon.' The constable shrugged. 'You get all sorts.'

George wondered what kind of person might see a potentially offensive weapon in a toilet seat, but then he remembers White Car Man.

'I'll bring you a selection of magazines. Helps to pass the time. Any questions?'

George shook his head and started to hum. That's when tile-counting seemed beneficial to his wellbeing.

Now he regards the magazines with a forensic eye. All manner of hands will have touched them. Had they licked their fingers to turn the pages? How long did diseases last on paper? The fingerprint team would have a field day, he thinks. Perhaps one of them belonged to a notorious criminal? The magazine in the worst condition is What Car. Probably, he thinks, because miscreants wanted to know the best vehicles for a quick getaway, yet had low running costs and sensible fuel consumption. The least thumbed copy is Gardener's World. George suspects that many criminals either didn't have gardens or didn't have time to tend them – perhaps because they spent too much time in prison. He delves into an article on Delphiniums, in his opinion a particularly obstinate plant to nurture.

A hefty slam on the door startles him. The hatch slides back and a voice calls out, 'Everything okay, Mister Sanderson? Just a brief update for you. Forensics are still examining your devices. That means you'll be our guest for the night.'

'I'll have to sleep here?' The thin blue, plastic-covered mattress George is sitting on is barely comfortable enough for his bottom.

'Well, it may not be much, but it comes with full board. Can I offer you one of our finest microwaved two-course dinners?'

He lists the diet options available. George considers choosing the vegan option. It might make him appear less of a threat. Ultimately, he plumps for cottage pie, an old favourite.

It arrives on a tray through the hatch ten minutes later, steaming in its original container, and accompanied by a small cup of fruit salad and two plastic spoons. George studies the tray. He's really not hungry but feels it would be rude not to at least make some kind of effort. He digs in to the brown mush.

It's not only his appetite that's missing. All sense of time has disappeared. The cell has no windows and appears to be acoustically detached from the rest of the world. He wonders if Angela is still at work, or whether she's preparing dinner. Maybe she's thinking about him this very minute? Maybe she's in bed with that other man?

He places the tray on the floor, lies down on his side facing an imaginary Angela, and closes his eyes. Tears trickle down his cheek and pool onto the plastic-covered mattress.

The summer of nineteen sixty-seven. The flower children on the west coast of America are basking in the Summer of Love. But any semblance of peace and love and poetry had yet to reach the occupants of 113a Chiltern Street, in the London borough of Enfield.

'If you're not out of that bathroom in ten seconds, we'll bloody well leave you here,' screamed George's mother, banging on the door. 'Ten ... Nine ...

The sound of a flushing toilet. Soft footsteps. A tiny hand reaching for the door handle. Click. The door opens. A hand reaches in and yanks George's arm.

'If we miss that ferry, you'll be sorry.'

George looks up at his mother. 'Sorry,' he whispers.

'Too late for that now.'

She propels him from the back of the house through the kitchen to the narrow hall where his father stands by two battered junk shop suitcases. One big, one small. She takes George's coat from a hook and thrusts it at him.

'Daddy,' says George, 'do I have to go to Auntie Eileen's? Why can't I go to the island with you and mummy? Is it really white?'

George's father looks like he'd rather be somewhere else. 'Well, er, you see ...' He looks to his wife for help.

'I'll tell you why.' She stoops down, grips George's shoulder. 'Me and him need a holiday and you're too much trouble. You're lucky I could find someone to take you.'

George's bottom lip quivers, but he will not cry.

'Pull yourself together, you ungrateful little sod.'

———

The cell is so hot, George's tears have evaporated. The dimmed lighting is too bright to allow sleep. He misses the bark of a neighbour's annoying dog, the wind and rain lashing against the window and, as the town awakes, the first cars of the day.

His thoughts are now focussed on his potential fate. With no pen and paper to hand, he mentally compiles a chronology of the worst-case scenario.

Forensics can't find any clues to how the images came to be on my laptop.
They'll charge me with a serious offence.
I'll need a solicitor and they cost money I don't have.
The media will report it.
No more Angela, no more chess with Ray.
At the court hearing, I'll plead not guilty.
Bail denied.
At the court case months later, I'll be found guilty.
How many years do paedophiles get? Five? Ten? More??
I'll be drawing my pension when I get out.
Do they reduce the state pension for criminals?
Poverty in old age, shunned by everyone.

Even as George runs through the possibilities, he feels anger growing inside him. Someone somewhere is responsible for his current situation. Who and why? And how? The laptop has barely left his side since he bought it brand new two years ago from a reputable store. There's never been any evidence of a break-in at home in order to plant the material, and in any case, they'd need his password in order to do so. In search of an answer, he paces the room. Even this simple act is inconvenient because after every three paces he has to turn around.

On his seventy-third lap, the door hatch slides back and another tray is pushed through.

'Morning,' says a cheerful voice George doesn't recognise from the other side. 'Mister Sanderson, isn't it? Breakfast for you. Hope you like toast and tea.'

'I'm not hungry, thank you, but I'll take the tea if I may.'

'Don't blame you for passing on the toast. I tried it once. It's rubbish bread. Budget cuts, see? Just so you know, we should have some news for you later this morning, okay? It's a bit early yet.'

The hatch slides shut. George continues pacing for a while.

He's no nearer coming to any conclusions about the photos. What he can't fathom is how he hadn't noticed them. In which folder had they been hiding? And how long had they been there? Nothing made any sense.

———

The DCI in Fraud is enjoying a leisurely breakfast in the kind of kitchen well above a DCI's pay grade. As she considers the options of how to spend her day off, her mobile beeps.

Sanderson's been hacked. Check his emails for a free book offer. I'm sure you'll want to pass this on ASAP.

———

A new aroma has infiltrated George's cell. Gone is the acrid bleach to which his nasal passages have become accustomed. Now it's the sweet smell of his own sweat. He'd declined the use of the shower room last night, anticipating there'd be security cameras, and he wasn't about to display his naked body to all and sundry. Who knows, the footage might even end up on the internet as some kind of revenge porn, or become part of a Christmas compilation of the year's most laughable events at the police station?

He sips tea and turns to Cosmopolitan and an article titled *Sex Outside the Bedroom*. It featured testimonials from couples for whom a bed appeared to be the last place they enjoyed making love. Kitchens, bathrooms, moonlit conservatories, stairs, woodland, hot tubs and swimming pools. George's mind floats off into a fantasy world starring him and Angela and a granite worktop. The scene is suddenly paused for three reasons. First, George suspects the worktop may be too cold for naked flesh. Second, he's not sure how much he likes Angela any more. Third, he's disturbed by the sound of a key in the lock.

The door swings open, squeaking on its heavy-duty hinges.

'DS Tyler requests the pleasure of your company, sir. Follow me, please.'

George's pulse accelerates faster than the Audi R8 he'd read about last evening. His mouth dries, breaths become shallower, legs feel shaky. He shuffles towards the door.

The young constable leads him to the same interview room as yesterday. On the way, they pass DC Bryant who gives George a look of contempt.

'I'll let him know you're here,' says the constable as he leaves the empty room.

George wonders if this is some kind of mind game. To make him, as he thinks the expression goes, sweat. To force him into a confession. And, with another psychological trick known only to the police, the CIA and Mossad, get him to sign it. He'd always had the highest regard for British justice. That confidence has been severely dented now, and he wonders how many other innocents have sat in this very chair staring at the prospect of a false conviction. He's barely passed the opening scene of The Shawshank Redemption when Tyler and Bryant enter the room.

'Morning George,' says Tyler, 'hope we've looked after you. I have some news.'

George tenses, ready to take both barrels from Tyler's mouth.

'You've been hacked, my old chum.'

As if a bolt of lightning had generated life into a broken body, George shudders, feeling more alive now than he's ever been.

'I've been what?! Are you telling me someone's—'

Tyler makes an intervention of his own. He hasn't got all day to listen to George.

'Lucky break. Do you remember responding to an email about a free book?'

George tries to slow his breathing by holding his breath for twenty seconds. He points to his closed mouth, then his chest.

Tyler looks concerned. The beginnings of a heart attack, perhaps? There's a protocol for that. 'You okay?' he says.

Holding two fists in the air and looking Tyler in the eye, George pops up a finger every second until both hands are splayed. He breathes out.

'Jeeesus,' mutters Bryant.

'How could I forget?' says George, taking in another deep breath but, mercifully for Tyler, exhaling immediately. 'Very odd, it was. I clicked the link to order the book and there was Maggie Thatcher, God bless her. Then I tried it again on my phone. Was that it then, how they did it?'

'Looks like it. The team had a nod from another department. An informant apparently. We might find out more but these investigations are very time consuming. Sorry George, but we'll need to keep the laptop for a while. Your mobile too. Might be able to track the person down.'

'But what about my emails? I can't work without email.'

'Looks like you'll have to borrow someone's then. The library has some computers you could use.'

'But all my intervention folders are on it. And household accounts. Important stuff.'

'You don't have it all backed up?'

'Well no, I purchased a very reliable brand.' George is inwardly kicking himself for his naïve faith in technology.

'Listen, I'm going to wrap this up for now. As far as we're concerned, you are no longer a suspect, but you're still helping us with our enquiries. Please don't leave the country.' He smiles at George.

'I don't even have a passport any more. You don't need one for Dorset.'

'I'll call tomorrow to arrange for you to come back in for a chat. It's pretty obvious someone's got it in for you.'

George, being more concerned about his lack of devices for the foreseeable future, has barely started to consider this. Who hates me enough to do such a thing, to go to all that bother? Have I done something bad to someone?

Tyler accompanies him to the front doors of the building. 'You okay getting home? We could order you a taxi, or there's a bus stop along the road.'

'I'd like to walk, thanks. Get some air, eh?'

'I'm sorry you had to go through this.' says Tyler, 'If you notice any other suspicious activity, let me know pronto. Lock your doors. I'll be in touch.'

He shakes George's hand and leaves.

George is so desperate to leave he clean forgets to mention yesterday's other mysterious incidents. As he hits the fresh air, he feels like a man who's cheated certain death. He knows he wouldn't do well in prison. Unless his cell mate was an accountant, or Ray. And they had a chess set.

He makes it along the pavement as far as a firm of funeral directors before his legs sag and the world turns to black. He's unconscious before he hits the ground. Three people immediately surround him.

'You alright, mate?' says a young Asian man peering into George's now blinking eyes. 'You went down like a ton of bricks.'

George pulls himself up slowly to a sitting position. He scrapes the dirt from a minor graze on his hand.

'Thank you,' he says, 'I've just been a bit stressed, that's all.'

———

The news of George's release comes through to Goldtooth at 11.30 a.m. He clicks off the call with a feeling of relief. The project was over, the mission accomplished. George had received a short sharp shock and his life had temporarily been turned upside down. No lasting harm done.

Nevertheless, something still bothers him. The way Angela had stolen George's attentions, that they were building something together. It didn't seem fair.

Perhaps one last game?

———

Fourteen

Angela is more than a little angry with George.

It's now Tuesday evening, and it's been thirty-six hours since she'd heard from him. When she spotted his message with the photo yesterday morning, she texted him back. As she had nothing to hide, her response was upbeat.

How on earth did you get that silly picture? It's a good job you've never seen a hen night. This one was quite tame compared with some others I've been on! The stripper's called Fireman Sam, but he's not my type. Might have been thirty years ago lol. Anyway, call me. I don't like silences. Bye xxxxx

Silence from George. She sent another two messages. Nothing. Then she'd tried to call him. It went straight to voicemail. Why was he being so childish?

Angela could have sworn none of the group took that picture. Weren't they all at the table behind her? And anyway, where on earth would they have got George's address from? Even those who knew he existed didn't even know his surname. And why would they do it anyway? Nothing made sense. To gain some insight, she shared the photo with the hen night group.

OK, own up. Who sent this to George?

Later that evening, following blanket denials of responsibility from her friends, she attempted to reach him again. As she searched for her mobile in the jumble of sofa cushions, she heard it ring. At last, she thought, suddenly aware of her heartbeat.

'Angela? Jackie.'

In some perverse way, the fact that it wasn't George came as a relief.

'Random person here,' she said. 'Who's speaking again?' Why does Jackie always query who it is when she's the one who called?

'Don't be silly. It's not clever, you know.' Clearly, Jackie is in no mood for fun. Angela surrendered to the probability of a long, tedious call and nestled down on the sofa amongst the cushions with her half full glass of wine.

'What's up, Jacks?'

'I keep telling you not to call me that. Mum too, on many occasions, but you never listened, did you?'

'Oh, for God's sake, what's happened?'

As Jackie rambled on about the latest instalment of her seemingly complicated life that isn't really any more complicated that anyone else's, Angela drifted back in time to her teenage years and her mum. To the time when she'd been on the receiving end of a complication that would trump anything that happened, and would ever happen, to Jackie. The day she returned home late from school with a note from her doctor.

At the time, her mother was alone in the house, Jackie and her father still at work. She walked through the front door into a haze of boiling vegetable fumes and misted windows. The atmosphere had the solidity of night air in a rainforest. Her cheeks were moist with tears, but it would have been impossible to notice them, such was the heat and humidity. With her head down, she passed the note to her mum.

'What have you done now?'

Angela had asked the doctor to write it down because she knew she could never say it. Not out loud anyway. Her mum read the note. It was short, to the point. There were no extraneous words. The small square of paper dropped from mum's fingers to the floor, landing silently as if attempting to downplay its importance.

Mum screamed. 'What have you done?'

She gripped her sixteen-year-old daughter in both hands. Shook her. 'What have you done, what have you done, you stupid, stupid girl?'

'Sorry.' More of a breath than a word.

The situation didn't improve when Jackie arrived home. Mum held up Angela's predicament to Jackie as an example of how not to behave. Jackie's initial reaction was to laugh about it, but a feeling of envy lurked beneath the surface. Angela had achieved a particular milestone before her.

Shortly afterwards, when they heard the front door open and close, the kitchen fell silent.

'Don't mind me,' dad said, walking into the room, picking up on the tension.

When no one responded, he tried again. 'Talking about me, were you?' The gun was loaded, but no one wanted to pull the trigger. 'Happy days,' he mumbled.

Mum could contain herself no longer. 'Your daughter's pregnant.' Her disownment put the inference of blame upon him.

Dad looked from Jackie to Angela and back again.

'Not me,' squealed Jackie. 'Her.'

Dad took a step towards Angela. Slapped her across the face.

'Get rid of it,' he said quietly before leaving the room.

The abortion didn't go well. An infection resulted in a minor but necessary procedure. Damage was done, but Angela wouldn't find out for nearly two decades.

When she did, it was too late to do anything about it. She would never have children. It had already cost her one boyfriend, and Angela resigned herself to a life of broken relationships. Or perhaps none at all. At first, she'd been angry with her dad, but as time went on she came to the conclusion that it was her mother who'd let her down so badly. Another woman. Mum became a dirty word in Angela's world.

'Angela?' Jackie has come to the end of her diatribe against Peter, who's taken up golf, allegedly to get away from her. Unbeknown to Jackie, the truth is somewhat different. Peter, who recently took early retirement from the police, leaves the house twice a week with a set of ancient and unplayable clubs he bought on EBay for twenty pounds. He drives to the flat of an unemployed ex-school friend called Brian. Here they chat about old times, drink tea and lager, and smoke. It helps to while away a few hours.

Angela yawned. Reg had dumped a lot of work with a tight deadline on her today. What she really wanted was to curl up and snooze.

'Was that a yawn?' said Jackie. 'I'm so sorry if I'm boring you. I'm sure you're rather be talking to your boyfriend.'

Angela caught the laugh before it came out of her mouth. 'Boyfriend? You make it sound like I'm fourteen again. Actually, he's gone on the missing list at the moment.'

'Good riddance. You're better off without him' said Jackie unknowingly hitting a nerve.

A beep from the oven timer. George, now revived after a vigorous shower, pulls out the grill pan. Such was his hunger, he'd made a most uncharacteristic decision to have dinner at lunchtime. He squeezes the rest of the lemon juice on top of the pork chop and scoops it onto his pre-warmed plate with a spatula. After adding steamed broccoli, roasted cherry tomatoes in olive oil and basil, and mashed potato with a pinch of nutmeg he sits down at the kitchen table.

To avoid distraction from the pleasure of eating, he pushes the barely-read newspaper to one side. It's time to enjoy the character of each ingredient, its favour, aroma, texture, and the subtleties of different combinations in his mouth. This simple joy is short-lived as his thoughts turn elsewhere. Despite learning in the past few hours that someone in the world wanted to see him incarcerated, it was Angela and the oiled Adonis who have his foremost attention.

Perhaps he'd been a little hasty sending her that briefest of texts? It wasn't like she and the toy boy had been locked in some passionate embrace. But then why didn't she mention it if it had been nothing more than a light-hearted joke? As far as George is concerned, the jury is still out.

There was little doubt in his mind who'd sent it – the same person who'd set him up for a crime he'd didn't commit. And who'd amended his sacred best-buy TVs spreadsheet by adding a rubbish brand at the top of the list. That was criminal in itself. He mentally scrolls through all the people who might have taken offence to something he'd said or done in the past year. The list is short, but then this is George's assessment and he really has no idea how many people he's pissed off.

Michael. The man who lost control of his company, forced

to put his new holiday home on the market, thrown out by his wife, attempted suicide. What a motive!

White Car Man. He damaged his BMW and is now awaiting trial for serious offences. He wouldn't dare. Or would he?

Angry speeding drivers in Claremont Avenue hell-bent on revenge. But does shouting and gesticulating at them really count?

Supermarket customer services lady. She regularly has to refund items he'd judged to be substandard and he could see that her patience was wearing thin. But as it wasn't her own money she was refunding, why would she care?

He stops at this point, rightly concluding he's now scraping the barrel of enemies. And he doubts any of them would have the creativity or technical knowhow to pull off such a complex task. More worrying, though, is the knowledge that a very dangerous person knows where he lives.

After he loads the dishwasher, he retires to the living room to watch a half hour quiz show. It's been four days since his last fix. He's greeted by a space where a TV should be. His old one sits on the floor, ready to be taken to the recycling centre. He curses his absentmindedness, then forgives himself because it's not every week you've had to question your own sanity, been framed for a serious crime, and then subjected to rigorous interrogation and locked up by the police. And it's still only Tuesday afternoon.

Probably for the best, he thinks. Better to spend the time checking his emails at the library. He checks his watch. Still two hours before it closes. As he leaves the room, his eyes alight on the barely used landline phone that sits on a small table beside the sofa. The pull of the phone is strong and, while George does his best to resist, he weakens. He needs a verbal hug. Putting it off no longer, he calls Angela.

Her voice, when she answers, perks him up. 'I've not been in an accident, and I'm happy with my computer thingies, thank you very much.'

'Angela, it's me.'

'George? Why aren't you using your mobile? I've been texting you. A lot. And I left a voicemail.' George thinks she sounds a bit put out.

'Actually, I think you've been texting some police forensics people.'

Angela replays George's last words. They make little sense to her. 'No, I haven't, I've been texting you. Why would I text the police?'

George runs Angela through the events of the past twenty-four hours. He would have liked to leave out the sordid reason for Tyler's visit. Being associated with something like that was bad enough, and who knows how Angela might react? Still, he feels compelled to make full disclosure.

'So they didn't charge you, then?' she says.

'No, I'm just helping them with their enquiries now,' George says with an element of pride.

To many people, that's code for he's still under investigation. But not Angela. Jackie may have a different view. 'Is there anything you're not telling me? I mean, why would someone want to do this to you?'

'I really don't know. And it's not only those pictures. They made me buy the wrong TV. I had to send it back.' Even George admits this might be stretching Angela's credulity. How could anyone make someone buy something they didn't want?

'And then they sent the picture of you and that...' George forces the words from his mouth. '...that man. That wasn't the best start to my day. Luckily, it got a whole lot worse so I forgot about it for a while.'

'Well, it certainly didn't come from me and the girls. I asked them. I'll tell you something odd though. None of us arranged for that stripper to turn up. At least, no one owned up to it.'

The provenance of the hiring, George thinks, is hardly the issue here.

'But why you were touching him? Why did you touch him like that?'

'Haven't you heard any hen night stories before, George? This is what ladies do. It doesn't mean anything. It's just a laugh. Nothing ever actually happens.' She pauses, and then says brightly, 'He was quite fit though.'

George hopes for a compliment himself, a sign that Angela is still interested in him, but it doesn't come. That's because she's currently considering whether he's some kind of gang member or spy, or perhaps a blackmailer. To her, the entire story had the smell of revenge.

Disappointed, George continues to interrogate her about the events of the hen night. 'So, you're not stepping out with him?' This vintage phrase would be laughable coming from anyone else, but George manages to bring an air of respectability to the potential liaison.

'For God's sake, he's young enough to be my grandson, if I had any. You think he'd look at an old bird like me?'

'Well, he might. I did.'

'Thank you so much. It's good to know you appreciate an old bird.'

George realises he's suckered himself into a trap. The tables have been turned. 'I meant,' he says, sucking in air through his teeth, 'you're a very attractive woman.' He was tempted to add *for your age*, which he thought was both accurate and a compliment, but wisely discarded the idea.

'We're not going to get very far if you can't trust me.' The edge has returned to Angela's voice.

George grits his teeth.

'No toilet seat? Good God,' says Ray. 'To be honest, George, I think you were lucky escaping their clutches so quickly.'

'Very inconvenient. I had to hover over the top and that really hurt my thigh muscles. You don't realise these things until you've experienced them. On the plus side, at least I know what muscles I need to work on.'

George is enjoying his call with Ray much more than the one with Angela. Two men with no agenda chewing the cud. It's refreshing.

'Perish the thought I ever get caught up in a web of intrigue,' Ray says. 'And you've no idea who's behind it all?'

'None, but I'm seeing the police again tomorrow. It's worrying, Ray. Who knows what this person might do next? If it hadn't been for your wise words, I don't know how I'd have coped so far.'

'Keep the faith. No point concerning yourself over something that might happen. The worst is over. Time to move on. You still okay for a game on Saturday? That'll help take your mind off it.'

In all the recent madness, George has forgotten about it. He'd like to say yes but he's supposed to be Angela's plus one at Jade's wedding. Now he wonders if Angela in her current mood still wants him to come. And he feels he owes a debt to Ray for his moral support. This is not the kind of dilemma he's used to dealing with. He decides to play it straight because he's more scared of Angela than he is of Ray.

'Well, um, I'm supposed to be going to a wedding with Angela but I'm not sure she likes me very much at the moment. She didn't mention it when I spoke to her a few minutes ago. By the way, do you know what happens at hen parties?'

'Hen parties? You're testing the limits of my knowledge, old man. Lots of shrieking and drunkenness so I gather. Are you thinking of gate-crashing one, then? Takes a brave man to do that, I'd imagine.'

'It's a long story. I don't know why I mentioned it really.'

'How is the dear girl, anyway? Have you told her? About why the police pulled you in?'

'As soon as I could. She knows it wasn't me.'

'Hmm, I think I would have kept that quiet. She might think there's no smoke without fire. It's a very distasteful business, George. There's no denying it. And until the police find the real culprit, there'll still be an element of suspicion. Have you thought of that?'

Of course he'd considered it, but he felt he was being paranoid. But now Ray has come to the same conclusion, he wishes he hadn't called him at all. Would Angela stand by him? So much for Ray's advice to move on.

'What else could I do?' says George. 'Lie? I'm not very good at that sort of thing.'

'Don't ask me, old man. I've led a very sheltered life. Wouldn't say boo to a goose, me. Perhaps you have to wait it out until the police have caught this man.' There's a pause. 'Or woman, even. Stranger things have happened. Hell hath no fury, et cetera. Know what I mean?'

'I don't go around upsetting women. I quite like them.' George has a sudden realisation that none of this started until after he met Angela. And he's upset her a few times already. But this is a woman who barely uses one per cent of the capability of her smartphone, who's frightened of online banking and shopping, who calls George whenever she has a minor issue with her laptop or mobile. How could she possibly have the specialist knowledge to hack computers? Then he remembers the double-glazing salesman, who he thought had become a friend. Geoff had no qualms about bedding and subsequently stealing his wife. Proof you never really know someone.

'I think you need to sit tight,' says Ray. 'Wait for it all to blow over. We could meet up, chat it over if you like.'

'Thanks, Ray.' George hopes he hasn't pushed Ray into helping him. The man had enough on his plate. 'And before I forget, how about next Wednesday for dinner over here? Shall we say seven?'

'You sure you're up for it, George, after all this nonsense? I don't want to put you to any trouble.'

'I'll take that as a yes, then. I'll get back to you later in the week about meeting on Saturday. I don't want to let you down. Oh, and before I forget, I probably won't be able to make the weekend after. I'm planning on taking Angela away. It's a surprise.'

'Of course. You do what you need to do, George. Don't worry about me.'

George gets the feeling that's code for the exact opposite.

———

Other than a few primary school kids with their mothers, George has the public library to himself. Staring at an ancient computer screen, he's wondering whether to try out the networking club on Friday morning at a nearby hotel. It's not really George's thing, but the potential benefits are obvious. A decent breakfast, at the very least, will help offset the cost.

Just email me, the organiser had written, and be prepared to give a one minute presentation about what you do and how you can help the network's members. It's all very relaxed, he continued, so no need to be nervous. George snorted when he read this. Nervous is for under-prepared people, for situations you have no control over. Engaging presentations were the result of hard graft and rehearsal, not some genetic gift for blagging. He pings the man a reply saying he'd be delighted to attend and looked forward to his sixty seconds of fame.

George notices the bed retailer, Mr Appleton, had responded yesterday, suggesting he pop into the shop to see him today. He rattles off a short apologetic note citing extenuating circumstances and offers to meet up later that afternoon. He's about to send the email when he realises he won't be able to check any replies unless he stays in the library. And he can't be contacted by phone either. He could buy a cheap phone and load it with credit, but wonders about the value of that. There was a chance he could get his devices back from the police tomorrow. No guarantees, though. What to do? He deletes the email and decides to call into the shop unannounced and hope the owner would have time to talk to him. He isn't entirely happy about this. If the situation was reversed, he'd want someone to make a proper appointment so he'd be prepared. Still, what did he have to lose?

The shop is a quarter mile away, just off the main street. The matt black fascia is adorned with the name in a gold, classic font: *PERCHANCE TO DREAM*. George thinks it's a strange name for a bed shop. Surely it should have the word "beds" in it to attract passing trade? The owner had probably read a book by a marketing witch-doctor who was always rubbish at marketing but saw a niche in selling books about it. The Shakespearean reference escapes him because he only studied *The Merchant of Venice* and *The Tempest* at school and hadn't much cared for either. However, he has to admit the shop front has a degree of sophistication that most other shops in the vicinity lack, with their brash colours and clunky typography. And when he looks closer at the sky-high prices of the two huge beds in the window, he can see that the shop isn't catering to people like him.

An old-fashioned bell rings as he walks through the door. He wishes he'd worn his best grey suit. First impressions count, but it's too late now. At the rear of the shop sits a man of similar age, hunched over a computer screen. He glances up.

'Can I help you?'

George smiles his best smile. 'Perhaps it is I who can help you, Mr Appleton, perchance to compile your annual accounts.'

The man's eyebrows register confusion.

'George Sanderson, the accountant who emailed you?' George reaches out his hand. 'I was passing by.'

During the hour George is in the shop discussing business terms and the work required, there are only two potential customers, both of whom walk out without buying. He wonders if the business is on the rocks, and he'd be left chasing Appleton for an unpaid bill for his services later in the year. Perhaps *Perchance to Dream* is a metaphor for the owner's fantasy of a successful entrepreneurial career? George needs more info.

'May I ask what your current turnover is?'

Appleton looks ceiling-ward. 'Last financial year end, we did close on half a mill. We're twenty per cent up on that already this year.'

George is shocked but hides it. 'And your margin?'

'Somewhere around forty-five per cent. Less during our biannual sales, obviously.'

I'm in the wrong business, thinks George. A quarter million gross profit from a little shop off the high street while I'll be scrabbling around for as little as two hundred a day.

'So can you fit me in, George?' asks Appleton. 'I'm sure my old accountant missed a few tricks on tax avoidance.'

'Absolutely,' says George. 'I'll get a quote back to you in the next couple of days.'

He leaves the shop knowing that this client alone would cover a couple of months of his household expenses. Just a few more and he might be able to start saving again, maybe even add to his pension fund.

On the whole, it's been a good morning, he thinks, striding purposefully down the high street. The police are on the case to find his stalker, he'll have some actual work to do if he pitches his quote for the bed shop perfectly, and Angela ...? Well, he feels he owes her a proper apology for doubting her allegiance. What was he thinking?

He stops at the florist and orders a dozen red roses to be delivered early the next morning. This comes at a considerable premium, but he thinks it's worth it. He mulls over the accompanying message for some time before writing: *Sorry. Gxxx*

'That'll be fifty-five pounds, please. You been a bad boy, then?' says the harsh-featured female florist, flicking back a pony tail so exceptionally long that it wraps around her stomach before unfurling itself.

'Pardon?'

'You reckon these'll do it? Keep the fire burning?'

'Oh, I see what you mean. Yes, hope so. I've been a bit of a fool.'

'So you might want to upgrade to the two dozen. Makes a big statement, you know. Says, I value you.'

'Probably to the tune of a hundred pounds, I'd imagine,' says George, looking her in the eye. 'We'll stick with the dozen, please.'

———

'No smoke without fire, Angela. And don't say I didn't warn you. Blundering into things without thinking.'

Angela had been thinking about George ever since he called

earlier. Although he'd appeared to be totally open about his arrest, there was definitely something he wasn't telling her. Why were the men she met so problematic? Even Jackie's Peter, despite his faults, must be pretty decent just to put up with Jackie's interminable whining. She'd like to have a good heart to heart with a friend, but most of them were younger or happily partnered up and probably wouldn't understand. That's why she'd called Jackie, craving some female companionship, and perhaps even compassion. It was a long shot.

'I didn't blunder,' Angela says. 'And we don't know if he's guilty of anything yet. He's just helping them with their enquiries. They let him go, you know, so he can't be a risk, can he?'

'Ha!' Jackie's derision is so loud Angela involuntarily moves the phone away from her ear. 'They obviously let him go for a reason. Probably being tailed as we speak, waiting for him to trip up. They all do eventually. It's only a matter of time.'

Angela ponders her sister's authoritative words. She's seen enough TV crime series to know Jackie could be right. 'He's supposed to be coming over tomorrow, and we've got a wedding to go to on Saturday.'

'You carry on with him and you could be an accessory. After the fact. I'm not sure what that bit means but it's serious. Get shot of him, Angela. Get shot.'

'I don't know. I still can't believe he's the kind of—'

'That's what Mrs Hitler thought when young Adolf came back from school with a painting of the Nativity. Really, you're living in a fantasy world. Now I must get on. Peter's had a skinful. Had to get a taxi home again. Said he got another hole-in-one and it was drinks all round.'

———

George's flowers arrive early the following morning. The florist didn't get an answer when she rang the bell and left them on the doorstep. Angela nearly trips over them as she leaves the house to go to work. The last time she'd received a flower delivery was from Finguish Fans when she turned fifty – mildly embarrassing at the time because for a decade she'd pretended to her colleagues to be five years younger.

She stoops down to pick up the bouquet, anchored in its own water bag and packaged in a pink and white box. Roses. Expensive. Beautifully arranged. And there, a note tucked into a ribbon. She reads it and is immediately confused. What did George mean by *Sorry*? She's forgotten she'd reprimanded him for thinking there was some kind of liaison with Fireman Sam. So now she thinks he's apologising for something much bigger. She takes the bouquet inside and places them on the kitchen worktop.

As she walks to the car she texts him: *OK, what have you done? xxx*. Then, too late, she remembers the police have George's phone. As she drives to work, it occurs to her the police might misconstrue her message. Suddenly life has become complicated. She's mixed up with George, and he's mixed up in something she doesn't understand. And Angela can't live like that. She needs certainty.

———

Goldtooth, on the other hand, requires confusion, so when he sees the text Angela has sent he can't help but applaud her for muddying the waters. Half an hour later, he opens his desk drawer, selects one of the pay-as-you-go mobiles, and sends her a text: *Still hanging with that filthy paedo?*

There's always fun to be had with a George.

Fifteen

George's patience is being tested. He's been waiting half an hour for a call on his landline from Angela. Surely it wasn't every day she received flowers. He like to call her but he feels it's her duty to make the first move now. And he still hasn't heard from Tyler. Despite Ray's advice to move on, he's finding it difficult to concentrate on anything when it's apparent he's a sitting target for an unknown adversary.

He busies himself with still more mundane chores. Washing down the exterior paintwork, trimming the wisteria and ensuring the hedge is a now a perfect bevel-edged rectangle. As he sweeps up the debris from the pavement, he hears the distant sound of his phone ringing. He'd like to answer it but health and safety is more important. The last thing he wants is for someone to sue him for slipping on his shiny yew cuttings and getting whiplash or some other nefarious reason to claim. When he's finished, the section of pavement in front of his house is noticeably cleaner than his neighbours. He hopes it shames them into action.

Back inside, he checks the landline's phone log. The last missed call is not a mobile number he knows, but he calls it out of courtesy. It goes straight to voicemail.

'DS Tyler. Please leave a brief message and your phone number.'

George's heart lifts. 'George Sanderson. Sorry I missed you. I was out trimming the...' He stops himself, remembering the word *brief* in Tyler's message. 'Call me anytime. I'm in until seven.'

The call is returned two minutes later.

'Mr Sanderson? George? DS Tyler. Good news. Your laptop and phone are ready for collection. When can you pop in? I still have a few questions for you.'

'Thank God. Now?' says George. 'I never thought I'd say this, but I really can't function properly without them.'

At the police station, he's shown to a waiting area. Tyler arrives promptly, clutching a folder. It pleased George that the pugnacious Bryant isn't accompanying him.

'Come through,' says Tyler, waving a pass over an electronic lock and pushing the door open. They walk down a dimly lit corridor and enter a tiny room with no windows or air conditioning. It's been furnished on the cheap: a small sofa, two plastic chairs, and a coffee table upon which stand George's confiscated devices and a miniature cactus. Tyler gestures towards it.

'Supposed to make the place feel more homely. It's a bit random, but there you are. Take a seat.'

George sits at one end of the sofa, removes his jacket, and undoes a button on his shirt, rolls up his sleeves. It's no wonder the cactus looks so healthy. Tyler sits next to him, a pad and pen at the ready.

'So George, we know how the stalker got into your laptop and your phone, but so far we haven't been able to identify the location of the device that sent you the malicious piece of code. And without that, we can't begin to identify the owner. In other words, he's not stupid. And no one at the Bell remembers the person who dropped the business card into the jar. No CCTV for that area of the bar either. That would have been helpful. I've got someone checking on which company printed them but that's a huge task so I'm not holding my breath. What does all this mean? In the short term it means we're going to have to rely on you to give us any information you think may be useful. Understand?'

'Yes, but I don't think I know anything. I made a list of people who don't like me.' He produces a folded piece of paper from his jacket pocket with two names written on it: Michael Finguish, and Barry Briggs. Tyler takes it from him. He scans through his notes.

'Finguish. He's the guy you stitched up, right?'

'Well, I wouldn't say—'

Tyler cuts him short. He's wise to George's waffle by now. 'Please let's not get pedantic. I've got a stack of work and we need to press on as fast as possible, okay?'

George mumbles a barely audible apology of sorts.

Tyler continues, studying his notes again. 'How much do you know about Finguish? Does he know you did this thing to him?'

'I didn't do anything, his father did. I was just—'

'George!'

'No, no one knows except Angela. And she wouldn't have told anyone. It was all a bit embarrassing in the end, when Michael got kicked out of his home and tried to commit suicide.'

'And that happened when?' asks Tyler.

'Must have been about three weeks ago, I suppose.'

'So, months after that dodgy email came in then. That's him off the list, then.'

George inwardly kicks himself for not spotting such an obvious fact.

'We can discount Briggs too, the guy who attacked you. Anyone else you can think of, maybe someone way back in your past?'

'There are other things, bad things this person has done to me.'

Tyler's ears prick up. 'What do you mean, other things?'

'He made me purchase the wrong TV and sent me a picture of Angela with some hen night stripper. It must have been him.'

Tyler stifles a laugh. 'Forgive me, George, but how can someone make you buy the wrong TV? It's difficult to believe someone like you could make an error like that.' He smiles. 'By the way, that's a compliment, not a criticism.'

George explains the Sanderson method of purchasing electronics and white goods and how the stalker must have added an extra item in the list.

'And I guess the photo was meant to make you jealous, right?' says Tyler. 'He's playing games with you, isn't he?'

'I'm a bit worried about what he might do next. And, worse, what if he starts targeting Angela?'

'You'd better let me have that photo and the name of whoever organised the hen night.'

'I don't have it anymore. I put it in the bin and it was collected yesterday morning.'

'Would anyone else have a copy? And I need the name of the stripper.'

'Angela said none of her friends sent it. There a photo of it on my phone. May I?'

George takes his phone from Tyler, finds the last photo he took, and hands the phone back to Tyler.

'Wow, he's a big boy, isn't he?' says the detective. 'Is that your Angela all over him?'

George's face reddens. Now the photo feels like porn.

Tyler can feel the tension. 'Okay, why don't you let me have Angela's number so we can sort this out. Cut out the middleman, eh?'

This is a concern for George. 'Really, I'd rather keep her out of all this if possible.'

'I'd rather talk to her myself if you don't mind. By the way, she's been texting you. I couldn't help reading the last one.'

George opens his texts.

Tyler looks him in the eye. 'What have you done, George? Anything we should know about?'

George hangs his head. 'I kind of asked her what their relationship was.'

Tyler shakes his head in disbelief.

'She wasn't at all pleased so I sent her roses,' George continues. 'Do you think it'll help?'

'It never worked with the first Mrs Tyler. I haven't dared try it on the second.'

As George leaves, Tyler gives him strict instructions to call if he spots any other suspicious activity. Then he hands over the laptop and phone, and takes a piece of paper from his jacket pocket. 'A note from the lab boys. Basically, it says you should chuck them. But if you don't do that, then at least back up the important files, wipe everything and get yourself a new email address. Same goes for the mobile.'

George hugs his devices all the way to the car where he texts Angela to expect a call from Tyler. He doesn't want her to have any more surprises. She pings back a reply immediately: *OK, I think. xxx.* George notes her lack of enthusiasm and wonders if he needs to purchase more roses, or perhaps another variety of flowers. Were roses old-school now?

Back home the first thing he does is scroll through his best-buy TVs spreadsheet, picks a model, triple-checks its current pedigree on the review sites, and places an order. Then he copies all his files onto the memory stick he purchased on the way home. He deletes everything on his laptop and reinstalls the software. Finally, he buys some top-notch anti-virus software. By the time he's finished, it's almost time to change for his visit to Angela.

As he deliberates on which shirt to wear – is striped too formal? – he mulls over the events of the last three days. It's barely believable that on Sunday morning his future had seemed so bright, so hopeful.

The words *Why Me?* reverberate in his head.

———

The following day, while Angela's eating a diminutive tuna salad at her desk, the call comes in from Tyler. She slips out into the car park for some privacy. She corroborates George's version of the events of the hen night and tells him Rochelle had circulated some pictures Fireman Sam sent. The one George sent her hadn't been among them. Tyler notes Rochelle's number.

'You know George's laptop and phone have been hacked, don't you?'

'Yes, he told me.'

'Well, you need to be careful too. They could have got your number and email address from George's phone.'

'They've got my number already. I had a text yesterday. About George being a ... one of those kind of people.' She reads out the number the text came from.

'Probably a pay-as-you-go mobile. Difficult to trace. George never mentioned this.'

'I haven't told him. He's angry enough as it is.'

'Listen, my advice is to block that number right now. If you still get unwanted texts then you'll need to change your number. No other option.'

Angela has no idea about blocking, and she certainly doesn't want a new number for herself. It took her years to memorise this one.

Tyler continues, 'Do you own a laptop or other computer?'

'Yes, a laptop, but I don't use it much.'

'Any suspicious emails lately? That's how they hacked George.'

'I'm always very careful. There are so many scams these days preying on older people.'

'Good, so let me know if anything crops up in your inbox that looks odd. And don't click any links.'

To Angela, the call had felt bittersweet. On the one hand, she might be more involved in all this than she imagined. On the other, the straight-talking detective seemed to be in no doubt that George was a victim here.

For the past few days, she's been debating whether George should accompany her to Jade's wedding. What if he came and everyone liked him, and then he turned out to be a paedophile after all? But thanks to Tyler, her confidence is restored, and she felt she was now ready to commit to George. If anything, she was now more attracted to him than ever.

She'd given him a bit of a hard time yesterday evening when he came around. Now she feels guilty. Back at her desk she texts him: *Police called. They were nice but told me not to click anything. I'm a bit worried now. xxxxx*

George answers it immediately, having noted that there are

five kisses in the text, two more that her earlier text: *Don't worry. Call me when you get home. xxxxx*

When George finally clicks off the call with Angela, he feels more at ease. Despite his trepidation of the wedding where he expected to be a Subject of Interest as Angela's new partner, he was experiencing something quite rare in his life. A sense of belonging to the world at large, and not some eccentric lurking at the margins.

Early the next morning, he bravely broke his weekday routine and headed off to the networking breakfast with renewed vigour. In his pocket were a dozen shiny new business cards. The design was simple, the typography conservative – exactly what you'd expect and require from an accountant and business consultant. Only money-launderers want an accountant with a sense of adventure. He took with him a plastic folder containing a notepad, pen and a single folded A4 sheet which contained the key points of his sixty-second presentation. He'd rehearsed it numerous times and doubted he'd need to refer to it.

At 7.28 a.m. George, suited up, walks through the door of the Westgate Hotel. A sign by the reception desk directs him to a large room at the far end of the foyer with a long table laid for thirty people. Three men drinking coffee are stood chatting by the window. One of them turns as he enters.

'Ah, a newbie. I'm Gerry, Gerry Mandelson.' He stuck out a hand.

George assesses him. Forties, casual but probably expensive clothes, tanned face. He looked successful. 'George Sanderson. Pleased to meet you.'

'Likewise, George. You're the accountant, right? We had

one in our network but he left recently. Dementia. Now he's fond of reciting spreadsheet formulas to anyone who'll listen. Very sad. Coffee?'

George scans at the table. 'I'd prefer a tea?'

'Looking after your heart, George? Very sensible. Me, I need three coffees to get me going in the mornings.' He moves to the table, pours George a tea. 'I have to drag myself here for this, to be honest. Let me intro you to some people.'

Over the following thirty minutes, the room fills up and George gets stuck in. He hadn't realised what a disparate crowd it was going to be: young entrepreneurs, middle-aged tradespeople, professionals. Or, as George notes, from ridiculous hairstyles to no hair at all. And so many obviously capable women, verbally jousting with men twice their age. It was a revelation. He began to enjoy himself. It had been a long time since he'd been in a room with so many people. When the breakfast arrives, Gerry escorts him to a seat in the middle of the table.

'Everything going okay, George?' he asks. 'This lot can be full on despite the early hour.'

'Good thanks, Gerry. They're a friendly bunch. I hope I'll fit in.'

'Fear not, you are already. I can tell.' He winks. George feels pleased with himself.

The breakfast, as rated by George, is good and large. The only let-down is the fried egg. He likes a solid white and a runny yolk but his had been overcooked. What would he dip his sausage into now? To compound matters, he can see that the eggs on some other plates are perfect. It's a small niggle and something he will only mention if asked. He won't be.

The middle-aged solicitor and a young female recruitment consultant sitting either side of him are more interested in explaining why he should recommend their talents to others than discovering what George has to offer. Despite this, he thinks they're pleasant enough. Besides, he'd get his chance to shine once the plates have been cleared away.

During a lull in the chat, he scans the table. He'd always found it fascinating to match the way people consume the food on their plates with their personalities. He, for example, would eat a fry-up in a precise way, with at least two different food elements on his fork before it entered his mouth (control freak, though George would term it adventurous). Some people dive in as if they'd not eaten for days, using their fork as an inefficient spoon to shovel the food into their mouths (reckless, poor attention to detail). Others appeared to be focused on eating one element at a time, dipping everything into a pool of brown sauce (methodical, unsophisticated, smokers?). A small minority, including the lady next to him, had opted for what's commonly called the healthy option – croissants and a bowl of fresh fruit salad with yoghurt that she explored with her fork but rarely ate (sensitive, easily led). George watches with interest as tiny flakes of pastry adhere to her top lip. He didn't think he knew her well enough to point it out. Maybe he's being judgemental, or perhaps he's subliminally searching for someone who eats exactly like him.

Gerry raps a teaspoon on his empty cup.

'Girls and boys, time's getting on so I'd like to welcome our new member, George Sanderson. That's him with the exceptionally clean plate opposite me. Being an accountant, I'm sure he wanted to get his money's worth.' A titter of laughter from the assembled. 'George gets the newbie intro slot and hopefully, if he comes back for more after you lot have pestered him, then he'll tell us how we can get one over Her Majesty's tax inspectors. You're on, George, and your sixty seconds starts now!' Gerry flashes him a wide smile.

George stands up. Even without the benefit of caffeine, his mind is as sharp as his freshly honed chef's blade. Talking about himself comes easily because George is his specialist subject.

'Good morning, everyone. I don't think many kids growing up set their sights on being an accountant. Excitement is to be found elsewhere – on the railway track, in outer space, up a fireman's ladder. And that's exactly why I chose to work with money. I don't want excitement. I'm risk averse. What I want is the satisfaction of making money work better. Before my redundancy from the head office of a high-street retail chain, I controlled millions of pounds every day.'

This is not entirely accurate. George's boss controlled the money, but George would say he did all the hard work.

'Now I want to offer my services to the very people who'd really benefit from them: small businesses. I want to save my clients money, make sure they operate within the tax laws, and give them advice on how to make a company valuable – to help where I can. To put something back. And the best bit is, my rates are very competitive.'

It's going very well at this point. The room is nodding with approval. They can see George was once a serious corporate player, and there aren't many of those in their midst.

'And to prove people like me aren't totally boring, I'll leave you with a joke. How many accountants does it take to change a lightbulb?'

Nervous glances. The clearing of throats. They've heard newbies tell jokes before.

'Three. One to change the bulb, and one to note down it's a tax-deductible expense. Thank you.'

There was a pause while everyone tried to work out the joke within the joke. George has unnecessarily tried to crowbar a gag about accountants who can't count into a perfectly reasonable lightbulb joke. Gerry comes to the rescue.

'Ha ha, very good, George. I think I can say on behalf of everyone here that was an excellent intro into what you do.'

George nods enthusiastically.

'Just don't pack it all in for the stage yet, eh?'

Everyone laughs. The solicitor pats George on the back and tells him he did a good job.

Later, as the networkers file out of the room, George feels a hand on his shoulder.

'Nice to meet you, mate,' says a tiny, spindly man with glasses. 'I'm Alan Mills the builder, commonly known in these parts as Lofty 'cause loft conversions are my speciality. We should have a chat. I've just taken on another team and it's getting complicated.'

George shakes his hand and thinks he's never seen anyone who looks less like their job description. Except his height. That would be an obvious benefit in loft working.

'Now?' said George, hopefully.

'I'm late at a site already. Don't want 'em fucking things up. Gimme a card and I'll call you.'

George hands him his last but one card. 'You must know Ray Caldwell. Works in the Planning Department. Lovely man.'

'Never heard of him, George. Maybe he's new?' Alan starts walking off, then turns around and shouts, 'You got any influence over him, then? Might be useful. Laters.'

He gives George the double thumbs up and disappears.

George is on his fourth tea of the day and it's only 10.30 a.m. Back home now, he's already booked his place for the next networking meeting, having considered his earlier appearance a resounding success. A cost estimate for the bed shop work sits on his laptop screen. He mulls over whether to add an extra ten per cent for contingency. After all, when he gets his hands on the shop's accounts, who knows what mess they'd be in? Then he worries he might price himself out of a job. These are the kind of decisions he's never had to make before. He goes with the courage of his convictions and clicks Send.

Lofty calls. George can barely hear him above a cacophony of drilling.

'George? Alan Mills. You know, Lofty. What did I tell you? They fucked it up. Muppets. Anyway, I'll be passing your way this afternoon. Can I pop in? Quick chat.'

'Alan, er, Lofty. Yes, of course. I'm in all afternoon. Actually, not all the time. I have to go to the dry cleaners. Emergency visit. A wedding, you know. Can't turn up in a crumpled—'

Lofty is a busy man. He doesn't have time to listen to George.

'Three fifteen? That's when I'm passing.'

George detects this really isn't a question if he wants the job.

'Perfect.' And then he feels the need to address a niggle in his mind that won't go away. 'Er, Lofty, are you sure you don't know Ray Caldwell in Planning? He's been there for years.'

'Like I said, George. And I thought I knew 'em all. Never forget a name, me. First rule of business.'

George, deep in thought, drains his mug and walks over to the sink to rinse it out. Just because Lofty doesn't know Ray isn't any cause for alarm, surely. He suspects Lofty's kind of work only requires the attention of the more junior staff in the department. He shrugs his shoulders and turns his attention to home security.

Until the police arrest his mysterious stalker, as George now refers to him or her, then his home may be at risk. In twenty-three years, his home has never been burgled, and crime in the area is low. Nevertheless, he feels exposed without any form of protection. And protection, he's finding, can be very expensive. He looks at monitored alarm systems, extra heavy-duty locks, floodlights and cameras. The latter seemed to come highly recommended by an ex-burglar on a security blog. In the end, he settles for an internet-connected outdoor camera that lets him know, wherever he is, if anyone approaches the door. It isn't cheap, but he orders it. He'll feel safer. But safer from whom?

He googles the phone number of the local council.

Sixteen

Angela leans across to George and whispers in his ear.

'We must be two of the oldest people in the room. Even Jade's mum and dad are probably younger than us.' She then points out some of the ladies from the hen party. Because it was a night George is trying to forget, her words drift into one ear and evaporate.

He surveys the room. It's not the most convivial place for a wedding ceremony, but then he'd rarely been in a nineteen sixties-built municipal office block that had any character at all. Pale green walls, poorly installed cheap white cornices, a table with huge vases of faded dried flowers at each end, rows of stackable chairs with scuffed seats, and a panoramic view over the busy car park to a block of sorry-looking flats from a similar era.

'Seventy per cent of the population is younger than us now.' says George. 'Actually, it's sixty-nine point five but I rounded it up. That's because it's only a projection based on the previous year's actual figures.'

Angela gives him a look he knows only too well.

'This is a wedding, George, not a conference with one of those PowerPoint thingies. Look, here's the registrar.'

A navy blue-suited woman strides into the room and stands behind the table. When she smiles at the assembled, she appears to George every inch a local government servant. Willing yet unenthusiastic, homely yet somehow disconnected, smart, but on closer inspection, a tad shabby – rather like the room, George thinks. A hush presides over the guests.

It's all over in twenty minutes, ten minutes too long as George remarks to Angela when they stand up. He starts to massage his buttocks until he remembers people are sitting behind him.

His own wedding ceremony had been equally brief. The guests were rather one-sided in favour of Cynthia. Only his mother – resplendent in a knock off suit and cloaked in cynicism – and two colleagues from George's office represented the Sandersons. As they left the reception in the saloon bar of his new father-in-law's local, a male friend of Cynthia's shouted, 'Give her one for me, George!' Another male guest, clearly more knowledgeable about Cynthia's history than the groom, responded with, 'We all have, haven't we?' The catcalls, whistles and laughter that followed triggered a self-conscious smile from George. It may have been forty-five years since the Valentine's Day card incident, but some things are never forgotten. Cynthia dealt with the situation better, giving her friends the finger.

Angela nods to a few people as they make their way out. They return the nod and raise it with a wink.

'I think they like you already,' Angela says, as she negotiates her precarious heels down the concrete steps to the car park.

'Mind how you go, Ange,' shouts a giggling voice from behind. Rochelle appears beside them, clutching the hand of a young man who's plainly not at all comfortable in this company.

'So,' she says, flashing chemically whitened teeth at George, 'you must be Gentleman George.' She pokes George in the chest, to emphasise the *you*. She holds up her right cheek to George's face. After pecking it briefly, George's head resumes the upright position. Rochelle isn't finished. She's European through and through, especially the Costa del Sol, except when it comes to its languages and food and immigrants. She bares the other cheek. George glances at Angela, perhaps for affirmation, then bends down again to finish the job.

Angela's gritting her teeth in a half smile. Rochelle has let George's nickname, shared only with the girls, out of the bag. She has no idea what Rochelle might say next, but at least the drinking hasn't started.

'Oooh, isn't he lovely,' says Rochelle as if she's talking to a baby or a puppy. 'Here …' She propels her man forwards. 'This is Paul. He's lovely too, aren't you, Paul?'

Paul nods sheepishly. George has some sympathy with Paul. They shake hands. 'Aren't you going to give Ange a kiss, Paul?' Rochelle tries to push him forward.

'Yeah,' mumbles Paul, who stays rooted to the spot, wiping his nose with the back of his hand.

The reception is held in the King's Suite at the White Hart Hotel, a crumbling seventeenth-century coaching inn. Although critical works over the centuries have been serially bodged, it's a testament to the craftsmanship of the original builders that the place is still standing at all.

Following a lukewarm lunch, there's a scandalous and potentially litigious speech from the best man who claimed to have bedded two of the bridesmaids on behalf of the groom. Everyone bar the groom and bridesmaids thinks this is hilarious, but the fact is it's true.

Now eighty guests are letting their hair down. Curtains have been drawn, lights dimmed, ties discarded, and a nineties mega-hit throbs through the DJ's speakers. This is not a place for George.

'Excuse me,' he says to Angela, rising from his chair, 'I really must, er, you know, the gents.' It's George's plan to engage in conversation with a random guest out in the hotel lobby, a legitimate excuse for not returning to the dining room-turned-nightclub for a while.

'I might be gone when you get back, if you don't hurry. Who knows which of this drunken bunch will ask me to dance?' She's winding him up, of course, but George's sensitivity knows no bounds. He's back at the table in less than three minutes.

'Have another glass of wine, George.' Angela's hoping a few more will loosen him up for the moment when she eventually drags him onto the overflowing dancefloor. He's already tapping a foot, so there's hope.

―――

Fireman Sam, in full costume, sits in A&E, blood leaking from several wounds on his face. His right hand nurses bruised ribs. He's been there for three hours, watching a succession of children and the elderly move ahead of him in the queue. When he arrived, the welcome had been warm and efficient. Then a nurse discovered he was impersonating a real fireman, a person of actual merit, and any kudos disappeared.

Anonymously, Goldtooth had sent him to a supposedly gay bar in a large town nearby with specific instructions to perform for the whole clientele. It was a common request. The bar was unexpectedly rough, full of the sort of people he'd normally cross the street to avoid because they were usually looking for trouble. So not like a gay bar at all. But he bravely carried on anyway, the true professional that he is. Fireman Sam may not be the brightest, but he is reliable.

His act lasted less than a minute before someone got upset and hit him. He'd tried to protect himself, but others piled in to exact punishment for daring to thrust his ample pouch in their direction.

He looks down at his broken helmet and wonders if it's time to hang it up for good.

———

Pushing the duvet away from her neck, Angela turns over. Simultaneously, her right arm curls around George's chest. Her mouth, inches from his right ear, pushes slow, regular breaths against his face. Her eyelids flicker but remain closed.

George, unlike Angela, is wide awake. He's been lying on his back for three hours, eyes open, watching the ever-moving silhouette of a tree behind the curtain. He covers her hand with his. She stirs, swallows, relaxes again. George closes his eyes, knowing sleep won't come easily, even with the protective arm of Angela to reassure him.

They'd left the wedding reception at ten o'clock after Angela finally dragged George onto the dancefloor for a slow dance that didn't require him to execute any complex moves. For Angela, the event had been a success and her friends remarked how good she and George looked together. It was the endorsement she needed to hear.

When the taxi pulled up outside Angela's house, it had been George's intention to deliver Angela to her front door, then take the taxi home. She hadn't invited him to stay over so he assumed that, because of recent events, she still hadn't entirely made up her mind about him.

Angela had other ideas. 'Stay,' she'd said, grabbing the lapels of his jacket and looking him the eyes, 'please stay.'

'I don't have a toothbrush or anything.'

She raises her eyebrows.

'Well, if you're sure it's okay.'

Angela sucked him inside and double-locked the door.

But even the safe haven of Angela's home couldn't stop George from worrying about his predicament. He's an i-dotter, a t-crosser, a triple checker, a plan for the worst and hope for the best kind of guy. And he can't function efficiently if his future is compromised.

What's keeping him awake right now are the weak spots in his life could be manipulated. The critical areas were Angela, his finances and his freedom. All three have already been compromised one way or another. Could it happen again now the code had been wiped from his computer? He supposes if the stalker is that clever then nothing is beyond them. After all, the stunt with the salacious images and the Buy Barbados business card was, he grudgingly admits, a work of near genius and he knew it would take some equally brilliant thinking from him to thwart his hidden enemy. It felt like a challenge and the very thought quickened his pulse.

And then there's that niggle. The one that won't go away. When he'd called the council yesterday he wasn't prepared for what he heard.

'Ray Caldwell, did you say? Let me see.' There followed a long pause. 'We have a Ray Thomas in Environmental Health and a Raymond Booker in Highways. No Caldwell. Are you sure you've got the right district council? Or maybe he works for the county council?'

'I'm certain he works for you.'

'Not unless he started today. Sorry.'

George extracts himself from Angela's arm and slips quietly

out of bed. Taking his mobile, he slips downstairs and leaves a voicemail for Detective Sergeant Tyler.

When he returns, Angela is sitting up in bed.

'Who were you talking too?'

George adheres to his resolution of total transparency. 'That detective. I left a voicemail for him.'

'And?'

'It's Ray, you see. He's been lying and I don't know why. I just thought the police should know. I didn't mention it before because I wasn't sure I believed it myself.'

Angela clears her throat in the way people do when they're about to make a confession. 'I got a nasty text a few days ago. I told that detective when he called me.'

George is more than a little put out. Here he is trying not to hide anything from Angela and she'd kept vital information from him.

'You could have told me. No secrets, right? Isn't that what we do?' George stops before his snappiness turns into something stronger.

'I didn't tell you because it wasn't very nice and I wanted to forget it, that's all.'

'So tell me now.'

Angela appears to be concentrating on picking at her fingernails. Her reply is so mumbled it's barely audible, let alone comprehensible.

'Pardon?'

Those fingernails are still receiving maximum attention. Eventually she says quietly, 'He asked if I was still going out with ... that paedo. Actually, he said filthy paedo.'

'Paedo? He called me a filthy paedophile? Good God! I hope you texted him back and put him right.'

Angela has had enough of this. 'George, he tried to frame you so why are you so surprised?'

'Yes, yes, of course. Silly of me.' He flops back on the bed. 'You know what he's trying to do, don't you? He wants you to leave me. Why would he want to do something like that? Why would he want to hurt us?'

Angela nestles her head against his, grips his hand as tightly as she can.

―――

A note is lying on the doormat when George arrives home from Angela's. It's from a courier company explaining a package for him had been left with Robert and Mary. He'd forgotten about the impending delivery of the security camera and reckons he'll have just enough time to install it before it gets dark. That's if his neighbours even hear him when he calls round to collect it. They're a little deaf these days.

He attacks their door knocker with gusto, waits, then gives it another couple of thumps, hoping to break through whatever radio programme they were listening to. A shadowy figure appears behind the door, opens it a crack.

Robert, wearing a stained checked shirt, corduroy trousers, and muddy slippers, greets him with a raised eyebrow. In the background, the radio is forecasting a north-westerly six to gale eight for Cromarty, moderate to rough with poor visibility.

George finds it less than riveting.

'Hello, Robert. Called to pick up my package.'

Robert purses his lips, releases them with an audible smack. Sucks in some air. 'Package.'

'Yes, Robert. The couriers gave it to you at three-fifteen. A medium-size box, I expect.'

'Package. Hmm.' He holds up a finger and disappears.

'Mary, it's that man from next door again.' A muffled reply from the depths of the house. Then, 'No, Mary, the one who had that awful wife ... Yes, that's the one ... Why have we got it, then?'

George, still on the doorstep, mutters to himself. Now he can hear movement and more muted voices.

'It's not in the kitchen or the living room, Mary ... No, I haven't checked the lavatory.'

George pushes open the door wide. He can see what looks like his package in the hallway under what must be one of the world's last telephone tables actually in use.

'Robert!' he calls out. 'It's right here, in the hall.'

Robert ambles back into view and picks up the box. 'Should have said. Would have saved a lot of mucking about if you'd told me earlier.'

———

A walk around the grounds hadn't helped Goldtooth's mood. He stares into the sitting room through the glazed terrace doors as he passes, but all he sees is the reflection of a loser staring back. After everything he's done, Angela still took George to the wedding. She still sleeps with him. Worse, he can see their relationship has become even stronger, probably as a result of his skulduggery. He knows this because he still has access to Angela's phone. He can read between the lines, see the narrative. It's painful.

———

Monday morning, and DS Tyler has arrived at his desk early, ready for another busy shift. For the past year, his workload had been steadily increasing due to the reallocation of staff onto higher priority work: gun and knife crimes, sexual assault, and robbery. Now, as he absent-mindedly stirs the coffee in his cup, he considers the cryptic voicemail he'd received from George: *I may have something of interest for you*. He's sceptical. Victims often conjure up the most ridiculous theories. So far, no one has been hurt, no theft has occurred, and no serious threats have been made. The forensic team's investigation of the hacking had stalled and would probably never start again. The case was simply too low level to demand the resources required.

But despite George being one of the most frustrating people he'd ever interviewed, he'd warmed to this eccentric man. And besides, the case intrigued him. He could have asked Bryant or another on his team to return George's call, but decided to do it himself.

George picks up Tyler's call immediately and tells him about his call to the local council.

'I know it sounds ridiculous,' says George. 'I pay chess with him and he's rather good, actually. And he's my best friend.'

Tyler screws his eyes up, rubs them with his fingers. He knows the next part of the conversation could be painful. 'And what might his motive be, George, this best friend of yours?'

'I've no idea. He almost always wins, so I don't think it can be him getting his own back. In fact, I think he lets me win sometimes so I don't get too disillusioned.'

'Is that it? No other ideas?'

George casts his mind back to something Ray said and before he knows it his mouth opens and the words spill out. 'Well, the only other person I've come into contact with recently is Angela.'

'Do you really think Angela has a motive, George? Have you upset her? I mean, we all have our tiffs, don't we?' Tyler is thinking that Angela must have the patience of a saint to put up with George. He instantly regretted mentioning her name, even in jest.

'Are you quite mad? Angela, a hacker, a stalker? It's laughable. She's hopeless with tech and software. I even had to help her set up a household expenses spreadsheet, for goodness' sake. And she didn't even want me to do that.'

Tyler isn't at all surprised.

'And, anyway, we met at the scene of my assault. She was driving the car behind. Totally random.'

Random. The word echoes in George's mind because more than anyone he knows, some events that appear to be random can actually be cleverly manipulated set-ups. But surely Angela couldn't be …

Tyler interrupts his terrible thought. 'I was joking, George. I wasn't seriously proposing that your Angela is the culprit. Give me your friend's full name and address and I'll do some digging.'

'It's Ray Caldwell. Charlie, hotel, alpha, delta, whiskey, echo, lima, lima.' Teeth are grinding at the other end of the line. 'And er, it may sound silly, but I don't know the address. The Hedley Park area, I think he mentioned once. Never been there. He has a wife who's at death's door. We usually meet at the Earthmother Café. It's very comfortable. Good cappuccino. Do you know it?'

Tyler sighs the third and deepest sigh of the conversation. 'Anything else you can tell me about him?'

'Only that his wife – she's called Martha – is very ill. In and out of hospital a lot. She's there now, I gather. He's got grown up kids too. I don't think he sees them much.'

―――

'About your friend.'

It's only twenty-four hours since George talked to Tyler, so he wasn't expecting an update so soon. He grips the phone in anticipation. 'Ray, yes?'

'We've contacted every council in the county. Ray Caldwell doesn't work in any of them and there are no marriage records for a Ray and Martha Caldwell. Of course, they might not actually be married. He doesn't appear on the local electoral roll either, nor does he pay council tax. You sure you he's local?'

'Perfectly sure. Does that mean you'll look into his background?'

'Let's just say it's interesting. Of course, he may have a good reason to lie about where he works or whether he's married. People lie about the most mundane things for all kinds of reasons. You'd be surprised.'

'But I'm his friend. He's even coming to dinner next week.'

'So you've invited to dinner the person you think may have hacked you?'

It did sound a little odd when expressed that way.

'Well, I didn't think it might be him when I gave the invitation. And I can't back out now. That would be rude. Anyway, if the stalker really is Ray, then he might slip up and give something away.'

'George, whoever this person is, they're not stupid and they're not very nice. He's a professional, and I'd like to put more resources on it. However, as I'm sure you understand, there are more pressing cases. To be honest, right now it's more a bad joke than a serious crime. My advice is to give your friend a wide berth. I'm afraid you're on your own for now.'

'You could bug my house, put a team outside to listen in. That would be easy. Or I could record the conversation on my phone. Ask a few probing questions.'

Tyler steels himself. 'Just keep me informed if anything else happens, okay?'

'So you don't think my idea of—'

George realises Tyler has ended the call and presumes the police are now dispensing with such niceties as friendly sign-offs for efficiency reasons. It made sense. If a few seconds could be trimmed from each call, the time savings could be huge. George takes a minute or two to search online for the number of police officers and support staff in the UK: 150,000. He estimates an average of ten calls per day with a five second saving on each by omitting greetings and sign offs. His hands fly over the worn keys of his ancient LED calculator, an unusually useful gift from Cynthia. Over two thousand hours per day, or the equivalent of the salaries of an additional two hundred and fifty officers. He makes a mental note to check with Tyler next time they speak whether this is now official policy or whether he's stumbled on an amazing idea that could increase clear-up rates at no extra cost.

A calendar alarm on his phone beeps. It reads: *Book weekend away – last chance!*

He'd meant to organise it before but he worried about whether Angela might think him presumptuous. Then on Sunday morning Angela had said she wished they could "get away from all this nastiness". Given the modern connected world, George wasn't too sure how effective that might be. Still, he thought Angela deserved a treat, given everything he'd dragged her through. And it was a perfect opportunity to show how romantic he could be. A weekend in Bournemouth perhaps. Or Brighton? A bit livelier. Nearer too, so he'd save on petrol.

He books a room in what's described online as a boutique hotel close to the seafront. The rooms looked bright and comfortable, and it appeared from the map they might have a sea view if they leant out of the window.

He texts Angela: *I'll pick you up from the office at 5pm on Friday. Bring an overnight bag with you. xxxxx*

Re-reading the message, he realises it might sound as if

they're going away for only one night. He texts again: *FYI pack for 2 nights xxxxx*

And then, to manage expectations, he sends another: *You won't need a passport or water purification tablets xxxxx*

———

'Oh, this is nice,' says Angela, flinging open the door of room six at the Dreamcatcher Hotel. She walks over to the window, testing the firmness of the bed on the way. George stands by the door, looking admiringly at her. The bed test is the first thing he would have done. His mind segues into the possibility that Angela is wearing her special underwear. He pushes the thought from his mind. Everything in its own time.

'Well, the review site should take most of the credit.' He moves further into the room and checks out the bathroom. 'Yes, it is a little pokey as two of the reviewers mentioned, but it'll do for a couple of nights.'

Angela now has the TV remote in one hand and the hotel guide in the other. She flicks through the pages. 'What a lot of channels they have here. We could watch a film later or...' She studies the channel guide intently, a wicked smile on her face. 'Or perhaps,' she teases, 'they have an adult channel.'

'Adult channel? Oh, I see. Well, I ... I don't think it's that kind of hotel. God, I'm starving. You?'

They find a small Sicilian bistro just up the street. It's early evening and the place is already busy.

'A good sign,' says George.

As they study the menu beside the door, Angela notices him tapping on his phone.

'What are you doing?'

'I'm just making sure. Checking the reviews. Won't be a minute.'

Angela opens the door and walks inside without him.

She'd been thrilled with George's surprise invitation and is looking forward to enjoying a light-hearted weekend without George having to think too much. No internet use, no talk of the stalker or the police, or George's assault case which comes to court in seven weeks. Just the two of them enjoying simple pleasures with no unpleasant distractions.

'Do you think they have wi-fi here?' says George as he sits down opposite her at a corner table.

'Is it a problem if they don't? I thought we came here to eat.'

'Point made, Angela.' He pockets the phone, starts tapping his fingers on the table top.

'Relax, George. You'll feel the benefit.'

'Sorry. I'm not very good at that.'

Angela can tell he's thinking.

'Unless I'm playing chess with Ray. That's quite relaxing. At least, it was. Maybe I should start investigating him myself. You could help and—'

Angela places her hands on his, looks him in the eye. 'Please choose something from the menu.'

George's phone chimes. He looks at Angela in horror.

'It's him!'

'Who him?'

'Him. The man who's out to get me.'

He pulls the phone from his pocket, flips open the case, and clicks the notification on the screen. A full screen image of an almost bird's-eye view of his front door pops up. An elderly man is attempting to stuff a magazine through his letterbox. Because of George's draught excluder on the reverse side, the man is having difficulty pushing it all the way in.

George pushes a button and speaks into the phone. 'Push harder.'

The man looks all around him for the disembodied voice.

'I know it's tight, but other people seem to manage. Go on, give it a proper push.'

The man shrugs his shoulders and walks out of view.

'Hey!', says George. 'Don't leave it like that!'

'Idiot,' he says to Angela whose nose is buried in the menu out of embarrassment. 'Sorry. It works though, eh? Should have remembered they deliver that Artima magazine today.' Still nothing from Angela. 'I'll look at the menu, shall I?'

Over the next two days, George masters the art of pretending he's in the moment while simultaneously thinking about something entirely different. In this instance, revenge.

———

Many homes have a room too small for a double bed, or too dingy to serve any useful purpose other than as a dumping ground. Usually for un-ironed laundry or items that apparently can't be thrown away, yet have no specified home elsewhere.

George's third bedroom is just such a room. He once used it as an occasional study but found the lack of light quite depressing. Musty old clothes in the wardrobe add to the dreary atmosphere. An ancient and rarely used computer printer sits on a cheap oak-veneered desk by a small north-facing window. Against one of the adjacent walls are three stacks of cardboard boxes of varying sizes, all from online retailers. George keeps them because in his experience fifty per cent of the goods he orders will be returned for failing to match their over-embellished and often farcical product descriptions. The opposite wall is unencumbered by anything. It's about to become a blank canvas for George to weave his logic.

He enters the room humming. When he and Angela arrived back in town late last night, they'd arranged to meet up again midweek. George is happy about this. He needs some time alone to construct a plan. Not simply an intervention plan, but a full-blown investigation. To discover if Ray is his stalker and, if so, how he can escape his clutches and bring him to book. Interventions require a laptop and internet access. Investigations require something more dynamic. A Crime Wall.

He's seen them in TV shows. He's seen them in movies. He knows how it works. Everyone does. You assemble all the facts, pin them to a board and link them with coloured string. That's why he's carrying in cupped hands a roll of adhesive tape, coloured pins, some green garden twine he uses to attach clematis to a trellis, a pad of fluorescent yellow sticky notes, and two marker pens, one black, one red. He lets them roll off his hands onto the desk.

Picking up the red pen, he writes one large character on each of seven sticky notes, then sticks them in a horizontal row on the wall, just above eye level: *WAR ROOM*. He would have liked to put it on the outside of the door, but he knows Angela would see it next time she sleeps over. He's now under strict instructions not to take on the stalker. Ignore him, said Angela, and he'll go away. Sound advice, but George has his pride to protect.

He tweaks the positioning of the sticky notes until they're equally spaced and level with each other. Satisfied, he returns downstairs and brings back his laptop. He connects it to the printer and prints off pictures of himself and Angela. The most recent one of him is a few years old. He'd asked one of his colleagues to take it after he was awarded Head Office Manager of the Month. In it, a coy George is seen pointing to a framed certificate on the wall behind his desk. More recent photos of him are on Angela's phone, but he can't ask her. For an image of Angela, he's spoilt for choice. She's quite photogenic in her own way, he thought. He picks one where she's laughing, at her most relaxed.

Now he tapes them to the wall under the War Room header. Next, he pulls a sheet of paper from the printer tray, folds it in half, then tears along the crease. On the top sheet, he draws the outline of a man's head and shoulders, and writes *Stalker* at the top. He does the same with the second sheet but this time he titles it *Ray?* He places it close to the stalker picture and runs a piece of twine between the two.

George continues to build the wall until lunchtime. He steps back and admires the collage onto which he'll add his logic. As well as the photos and drawings there are maps, slivers of paper with text and accompanying question marks, newspaper cuttings – the road rage attack, the lottery winner – and a timeline he's drawn on four A4 sheets stuck together, end to end.

He has fifty-six hours to make some sense of it before Ray comes to dinner. He works into the evening, making notes, fiddling with the elements on the wall, and standing by the window, staring out into the middle distance, deep in thought. He even forgets about dinner. It's only when his mobile rings at 8.30pm he realises just how immersed in the plan he's been.

It's Ray.

A shiver of excitement runs through George.

'Ray, I was just thinking about you,' says George in all honesty.

'Evening George, hope you weren't about to cancel me, ha ha. I'm just checking we're still on for Wednesday.'

'Of course. I was wondering if there's anything you don't eat,' he lied. 'You're not one of those vegans, are you?'

'Relax, my friend. I'll eat whatever you put on my plate. Or if you're pushed for time I could pick up a takeaway?'

'Certainly not. I've been looking forward to cooking for you.' You really don't know how much, thinks George.

'Very kind. Everything else okay? No nasty surprises, I hope. Police found your nemesis yet?'

George doesn't know how much to divulge at this stage. He still hasn't completed his plans for Ray and, whilst the police have put the investigation on hold, there seems no advantage in letting Ray know that.

'Not yet, but I gather they have a whole cybercrime team on it.' It sounded confident and he hopes he's left his possible adversary something to think about.

He goes downstairs to the kitchen, fixes himself a sandwich and texts a *how are you* message to Angela. Then, a moment of absolute clarity. Ray's mention of a takeaway has planted the seeds of an idea.

———

Seventeen

George wakes at the crack of dawn to the sound of raised voices. Robert and Mary are in their drive arguing about what rubbish goes in what bin, and which bins that week should be put out on the pavement, ready for collection. This is not an unusual situation, and one he could have easily ignored. Of course, he can't. He knows that if some people don't adhere to the rules, everyone could suffer. Slipping on some clothes, he makes his way downstairs and out into the cool air.

Mary is sporting an ankle-length nightgown of indeterminate age and material. Robert's maroon pyjamas are too long for his short legs. Rising damp from the dew has already reached his ankles. Their nightwear is topped with trademark identical sweaters. George assumes Robert has been knitting again because he doesn't recognise today's style – a large "Ban the Bomb" icon emblazoned in fearsome red on a vivid lime green background. It's enough to have people running for the nearest nuclear shelter.

'Worry ye not, the cavalry is here,' says George, keeping his voice down in a bid not to disturb any more neighbours. Neither Robert nor Mary hear him approach.

He taps Mary on the arm.

'It's him again,' she shouts to Robert.

Robert grunts, glances at George, then resumes his rubbish sorting.

'It's quite easy when you get the hang of it,' says George. He fishes a piece of plastic out a bin. 'See this?' he says, 'You can't recycle it. Wrong kind of plastic.' He crushes it in his hand, puts it to his ear. 'Makes a crinkly noise, see?'

Mary takes the plastic from George's hand, crushes it close to her ear. Then she passes it over to Robert who does the same. It's like watching a long-lost archaic tribe inspecting a mobile phone or a mirror.

'Arsehole,' she says to George, flicking her head towards Robert. 'He never listens. Never did, mind.' Now she holds up a dog-eared hardback book, *Archaeology of the Sonoran Desert Tribes*. 'Where does this go?'

George isn't listening. He's seen the illustration on the book cover, a woodcut of a lone Native American standing proudly on a rock. Behind him, storm clouds roll in over a barren landscape. One man standing fast against impending doom. It gives George cause for hope, but also for sadness. He knows he must press forward alone. And that means without Angela.

———

In the kitchen, George gazes at the rain lashing against the patio windows. It's a bittersweet moment. God knows the lawn could do with the water and the thought lifts his heart. On the downside, the lawn isn't his biggest problem. He knows he must talk to Angela, and she's not going to like what he has to say. It's not something he can do over the phone either. It has to be face to face.

He texts her, asking if she can meet him at lunchtime. Gets an almost immediate response: *Ooh, I am honoured. Pick me up at 1. Must dash, running late. xxxxx.* Hmm, thinks George, it's not quite what she thinks it is, but it will be better for both of them in the long term. He's convinced of that. At least, he thinks he is.

The clunk of bins, the whine of hydraulics and hiss of air brakes. Refuse collectors shouting in an unknown patois only they understand. George checks his watch. 7.05 a.m. He silently congratulates the men's efficiency. You can set your clock by them.

Robert and Mary, now calmer and having already forgotten everything George taught them earlier, silently eat their porridge and prunes against a background of popular classical music on Radio 3. It's their version of civilisation, and a world away from the Sonoran Desert where lizards outnumber people by a significant multiple.

Right now, George would probably swap the Home Counties for the desert, knowing he could hide away forever with little chance of discovery. What he has up his sleeve is ambitious. It relies on certain people playing their roles effectively. But so far, he's never really trusted anyone to live up to his very particular standards. Still, he's up for a challenge.

When he pulls into the Finguish Fans car park dead on 1.00 p.m., he sees Angela waving at him from the office entrance. He circles around and stops beside her. She jumps in enthusiastically, pecks him on the cheek.

'Dark, handsome professional picks up top middle-aged bird and takes her to lunch. I could get used to this.' She squeezes his hand which sits on top of the gearstick. Gives him a huge smile.

'Me too,' says George as he drives off. Angela silently excuses him for his lack of enthusiasm. She knows he likes to focus fully on driving.

Ten minutes later, they're sitting in a town centre café George is unfamiliar with. It's Angela's choice. They reminisce about the weekend, chat about the sudden change in weather, and then Angela makes the mistake of suggesting a day trip at the weekend.

George can put it off no longer.

'Angela,' he says.

'George,' she says.

'I've been thinking.'

Angela's posture slumps.

'I can't go on like this,' he continues. 'What I mean is, I can't go on not doing anything, knowing there's someone out there doing me harm. Doing us harm. It's obvious to me that what he really wants is to split us up. Hence that vicious and, I have to say, libellous text he sent you.'

He pauses. Takes a breath.

'We need to have a break.'

Angela's mouth is open, and just about to say something when George holds up the palm of his hand.

'Don't worry, it's just a pretend one. All part of my plan. Trust me. If we can fool the stalker into thinking we've split up, they'll think they've won. And it gives me time to find out who's doing this. Then the police can take over.'

So far, Angela has no idea what George intends to do about Ray, and George wants to keep it that way.

'Split up?' says Angela.

The words carry to customers on the surrounding tables. Ears perk up. Winks are exchanged.

'You know what, I'm smelling a rat,' she continues, oblivious to the rapt audience. 'Why can't you be honest and tell me it's all over? Have done with it. I'm a big girl now.'

With her relationship history, it's unsurprising she's sceptical of his words. George tries to put his hand on hers, but she flinches. He notices her eyes are watering.

'I am being honest, Angela. Please, please believe me. All we have to do is take a break for a month or so. Maybe even less if we're lucky. No emails, texts, calls, nothing. But remember, it's just a charade. He'll know we've separated because he somehow seems to find out everything. Then, maybe, he'll leave us alone, get bored, move onto someone else.'

'Hmm, well, it was nice while it lasted, but I won't miss the hacking and the stalking and the police and that nasty child porn business.' The ambient background volume in the café drops to zero. There's an atmosphere of expectation.

Angela doesn't disappoint. She stands up and collects her handbag from the back of the chair.

'I'm sure you won't mind picking up the bill,' she says to George as calmly as she can.

'But I'm trying to help both of us.'

Angela walks out.

George sits there, semi-stunned. Should he follow her? Should he plead with her? Would it do any good if he did? He blames himself. He knew it wouldn't be easy but what's done is done. He consoles himself knowing that after a good night's sleep she'll come around to the idea. Logic and good sense usually win in the end. Then he realises that in affairs of the heart sometimes they don't.

In the War Room, George has added some bullet points under the Action section on the crime wall.

1. The split
2. Who is Ray Caldwell?
3. Mission: Obfuscate

He picks up the red marker and reluctantly draws a tick next to number one. Let the stalker think he's achieved his goal. Take the sting out of his tail. George is aware, though, it probably won't be enough.

The next step is to investigate Ray so, at the very least, he can be discounted. Tomorrow evening's dinner may provide further clues, but if his best friend is indeed his adversary, then it's doubtful Ray will let anything slip. That's why George has realised he needs help, and why at 7.00 p.m. tonight he must order a Chinese takeaway.

———

'Well, don't say I didn't warn you,' says Jackie. 'Dinners, dirty weekends away, sex on tap. You gave him everything too quickly and he lost respect for you. It's what you've always done. And that's what men like that always do.' It's easy for Jackie to say. The very patient Peter had to make do with covert fumbles in darkened rooms until he and Jackie married.

On the other end of the call, Angela is silent.

Jackie, feeling she may have over-egged her sermon a little, relents. 'Listen, I'm sorry, I really am. I know you invested a lot into this ... this ... person. And he couldn't even come clean and say it was over for good. Wimp, Angela. He's a chicken-livered wimp.'

A sniff from Angela. 'But what if he's telling the truth? What if he's actually being quite brave and trying to protect me too? I think I might have overreacted.'

Jacki's having none of it.

'What kind of cloud cuckoo land are you living in? You've watched too many films. The land of make-believe. Take a leaf out of my book and find a man who's uncomplicated. They might not be the best company, but you can trust them to be there for you. Unless they're down at the blooming golf club. And now they can play at night. Not sure how that works. Giant floodlights, I think he said. Still, keeps him out of trouble.' A wry laugh.

Peter's life is actually becoming quite complicated, and he's finding it exciting. While Jackie talks to Angela, he's in Brian's flat enjoying the flattery of a Welsh alcoholic called Sheila. Brian has left them temporarily for the corner shop after a whip-round to buy more supplies. Peter has never met anyone quite like Sheila, and Shelia thinks Peter is a bit posh and had once remarked how nice he smelled. Peter wished he could reciprocate, but Sheila had been drinking since breakfast. When she arrived, there was a definite whiff of mature bedclothes and cheap vodka about her. Still, he thinks, after Jackie's ban on bedroom activity, it's nice to have some attention. And Sheila is good at that. Direct, animated, very touchy-feely. Peter's mind races off into a bedroom scenario featuring him and Sheila after she'd showered and, for good measure, Jackie. Sadly, exciting as these images are, he feels he's not only letting himself down. It's unfair on Sheila, too. She's obviously quite drunk and he'd be taking advantage. Also, there's her lack of teeth.

Angela finishes the call. She envies the stability of Jackie's marriage. Plainly, love wasn't everything. She puts a single slice of bread in the toaster. It's all she can stomach tonight.

Three rings on the doorbell in quick succession, followed by three knocks. George runs down the stairs from the War Room, opens the door.

Scooterboy.

In his left hand, a large brown paper carrier. In his right hand, the key to his scooter. He looks up.

'Ain't seen you in the pub for a while,' he says, handing over the bag.

'Do you want to earn some money?' says George, glossing over an incident he'd rather put behind him. 'What do they pay you at The Lantern House?'

'Twelve pound an hour,' lies Scooterboy, adding fifty per cent as a starting bid. 'Plus tips, so maybe twenty. Plus petrol.'

'Good grief, no wonder the food's so expensive these days. I'll pay you the same rate for an hour or two's work tomorrow night.'

'Depends innit. I'm delivering 'til ten. What d'ya want me to do, anyway? It ain't drugs, right?'

George sighs, gives him a does-it-look-like-I'm-a-county-lines-dealer expression.

'I can guarantee it's perfectly legal. You can start as soon as you finish your other job. You'll need your scooter. And ...' George lowers his voice. 'There's a touch of danger about it.'

Scooterboy instantly gives him the double thumbs up. 'I'm your man.'

'Come in for a minute. I want to show you something.'

———

Goldtooth sits in front of his bank of screens. He opens a piece of software and clicks on Angela's phone number. Up pops a collection of icons, similar to those on her mobile. The cursor hovers over *Messages*. Click. He scrolls through the most recent, the personal ones. That's when the smile returns to Goldtooth's face. A text from lunchtime today to her sister. *It's over. Speak later and don't say I told you so xx.*

Finally. He mentally thanks Jackie for being an unwitting ally for so long – always there to put the knife into George, and into her own sister, come to that. It may be a meagre result considering the hours invested, but a win's a win.

If he was honest, the drama of the entire project had disappeared the moment the police let George go free. It was a shame he'd had to punish George again. He was actually starting to like the guy before that woman got her teeth into him. He hopes George will gain something from the experience. He certainly has: stick to what you know.

Then he wonders if his original game plan had contained a fundamental flaw. In retrospect, it may have been better to pick a few likely candidates for a retribution game and do his usual due diligence first. Perhaps choosing George had been a little rash.

He walks over to the oak cabinet and pours himself a brandy. 'To George,' he says, holding up his generously filled glass, 'it was nothing personal.' But, of course, he knew it was.

―――

In the War room, Scooterboy checks his watch. For ten minutes, George has been explaining the background behind the task he wanted him to perform. It seemed barely believable. Hacking, cyber-stalking and framing. Like something from the movies. But such was the level of detail presented by George, together with the equally impressive crime wall, he's totally bought into the story.

He pleads with George to get to the point. Mister Huang would have other deliveries waiting for him. But George will not be hurried. He believes it's important to explain the reasons a task is important. That's how you get the best from people.

When Scooterboy finally leaves – having called Mister Huang to explain he'd had to stop at the scene of a traffic accident to give a woman mouth-to-mouth resuscitation – George discovers the food requires reheating.

While his meal circulates on the microwave turntable, his thoughts turn to Angela. If only he could allay her fears. He's desperate to call her, text her, email her, call round even, but he realises any of those methods of communication could compromise the charade and, in turn, his next steps.

The microwave pings. He removes the plate and sets it down on the breakfast bar next to his latest energy statement. The bill wasn't particularly expensive, but as winter approached he knew the next ones would be steep. Another reason to end this stalker nightmare quickly and properly focus on getting paid work. He forks into his mouth a large mouthful of Kung Po Chicken and glances at the bill again. Of course, the old-school method of the postal system. He could write a letter to Angela. The stalker would never know. Unless he'd bribed Angela's postman, and George thought that unlikely. But there's a problem. Using the Royal Mail would take too long, and he wants the letter to be in her hands tomorrow. There has to be another way because no one is going to come between him and Angela. No one.

———

Eighteen

Dear Angela

By the time you read this, my situation may have changed. You may remember Ray is coming to dinner tonight. I have a plan to find out more about him and I won't go into the details because I know it irritates you. I don't think it's dangerous, but if I haven't texted you by 8am tomorrow morning, please call Detective Sergeant Tyler. My text will read: *Please, please reconsider. Life is unbearable without you. G xxxxx.*

Do not answer it or attempt to contact me in any way. It may spoil the illusion.

That's my next point Angela. As I said to you in the café, I'm doing this because I need to be rid of the stalker, not you.

He pauses. Blinks. Breathes in deeply. A once-impenetrable shell is starting to crack. For the first time in his life, he's going to write from the heart. To tell Angela what he's wanted to say for some time, but always lacked the courage.

The past few months have been the best of my life. Truly, they have. Now I can see my road rage assault as a serendipitous event without which I would never have met you … every cloud etc. If only I'd found you decades ago before wasting so much of my life with another. I know I'm not the easiest person to be around but there is so much we can do together – if you'll still have me.

Please be patient for a little longer.

I love you.
George xxxxx

He puts down the pen and quietly weeps. Weeps for the unfairness of it all. Weeps for his past, his present, and a future that's been compromised. And, perhaps most of all, he weeps from frustration because there's no sense in why any of this is happening. It's like he's been picked out at random to be the subject of a sophisticated prank.

He folds the letter into three and carefully inserts it into the envelope. Then stares at the address, thinking of the fun and laughter and the sometimes-awkward sex he and Angela had enjoyed there. The strangely scented room fresheners, the soundless way he could walk through the house on the thick-pile carpet. Even the irritating things like Angela's gallant attempts at cooking, her trivial gossipy stories about Jackie and assorted work colleagues he barely knows. And he smiles. In a sudden epiphany, he realises that he actually enjoys those too, because they're a part of who Angela is. Slices of a life that makes him a part of something much bigger.

He puts the letter in his jacket pocket, picks up his keys and a shopping bag and leaves the house. He wants to make tonight's dinner with his friend extra special. If he discovers some useful information about Ray that might help the police, that's all well and good. If not, then at least they'll have enjoyed a fine meal and maybe he'll still have a friend.

He stops the car at a nearby taxi office, kisses the envelope like a child sending a request to Santa, and arranges its delivery. As he leaves, he has a sudden crisis of confidence. Had he bared too much of his soul to Angela? Or worse, had he sounded like a lovesick teen? It was too late to rewrite it now.

Fish and crustaceans are on tonight's menu because he wants to show off his sophisticated palate. He imagines Ray is expecting a retro menu from him as befits a man of his era. Like steak and kidney pie or beouf bourguignon, possibly preceded by a prawn cocktail or cream of tomato soup, and finishing with a black forest gateau. He'd scrolled through his internal compendium of recipes. Perhaps some pan-fried scallops on a bed of watercress to start, followed by baked sea bass with salsa, roasted peppers and courgettes. It all depends what the town's only remaining fishmonger has to offer. It's a relatively simple meal and he can do most of the preparation in advance, leaving plenty of opportunity for conversation. Or, as George would have it, probing and fact-finding.

Sharon the Fish does not disappoint. But the price does.

'Are you sure?' says George. 'I'm only feeding two people.'

'Global warming,' says Sharon. 'When was the last time you bought scallops?'

'Today,' says George.

Various rags and metal objects are scattered all over the pavement, as if some of the contents of a skip had fallen from a lorry. Scooterboy is on his knees oiling a chain. When he's done, he'll adjust the tensioner and put everything back together again. He's very much looking forward to tonight's activities. That's why he's stripped down the scooter to ensure every moving part is working at the optimum level. It's not so much that he doesn't want to let George down. More that he doesn't want to let himself down. A road warrior has pride.

When the rebuild is complete, he pulls on his freshly polished helmet and bikes over to the nearest petrol station to fill up. He hopes his journey tonight isn't too far because his tank range is only 200 miles. Along the way, he tests the throttle, brakes, and steering by playing a cat-and-mouse game with a lone cyclist who's weaving dangerously in and out of the traffic. By the time he gets home, he's satisfied the scooter is ready for whatever action comes his way.

———

Short, machine gun-like bursts from a vicious-looking knife fill the kitchen. Red onion, garlic, coriander, and tomatoes all fracturing into a thousand pieces. The ingredients join each other in a glass bowl. Lime juice is squeezed on top, followed by a splash of white wine vinegar. The mixture is lovingly stirred. This is a chef at the top of his game.

Behind the island stands a person with George's face and the semi-naked body of a male bodybuilder. In one of Cynthia's lighter moments, she'd spotted this novelty apron in a gift shop and thought it would make an amusing birthday present. He took the joke on the chin but subsequently failed to enrol at the local gym which is what Cynthia had been hinting at. George rarely wore it, but tonight was different. He found the well-formed pecs and the flat, toned stomach strangely empowering – and even caused him some amusement when he went to the bathroom to relieve himself and spotted his impressive torso in the mirror.

He runs through the evening's cooking schedule. Everything is timed to the minute. A bottle of Sauvignon Blanc sits in the fridge door, but he hopes Ray will bring something decent so he won't need to use it. The table is laid, with the Australian cork placemats – a cheap and, George noted, derisory wedding gift from Cynthia's tight-fisted parents – coming into service for only the fifth time in their history.

For background music, he plumped for a popular classical station. Low volume. There, but not there, like a movie soundtrack. Ray appears to have as little interest in music as him. George can't remember a time when the subject had come up at their chess meetings. In fact, when he considered this, there'd been a minor eureka moment. Didn't the principal topic of conversation almost always revolve around him? Ray is always quick to bat away questions about his own life because, as he once put it, nothing much ever happens to a man who cares for a terminally ill spouse. And that one-way flow of information fitted neatly into his latest theory that Ray might have no spouse at all.

With an hour to go, he calls every hospital within a twenty-mile radius. And each call ends in exactly the same way. Sorry, we don't have a patient of that name here.

―――

'I can't tell you how good this feels, George. To leave everything behind for a few hours. Most grateful, really most grateful.'

Ray's cultured voice from the living room reaches George who's popped into the kitchen to cook the starter.

'Think nothing of it,' George calls back, placing the scallops in the sizzling oil and setting a one minute timer on his phone. He'd had an attack of nerves just before Ray arrived and wished he'd taken the advice of DS Tyler. Alone with a potential madman – who knew what might happen as the evening progressed? But from the moment Ray arrived, the atmosphere seemed perfectly normal. Relax George, he told himself, if Ray wanted to murder you he'd be too smart to do it himself.

'Smells good,' comes the voice from the living room again. 'You going to give me a clue?'

George smiles as he sprinkles watercress on the plates. 'Let's just say tonight's a bit fishy.' He's pleased with his *double entendre* response. The timer beeps. He flips the scallops. 'Nearly there, Ray.'

They sit opposite each other at one end of the dining table, the starter before them. George pours two glasses of his Sauvignon Blanc. The disappointing room-temperature rosé Ray had brought was cooling in the fridge door.

'I must say, George, this looks most impressive. You really shouldn't have gone to so much trouble just for me.' He spears a fat scallop with his fork and crams the whole thing in his mouth. 'Mmm. Has the legendary Angela sampled this yet? To be honest, I rather thought she might be here. Is everything alright between you two?'

George attempts some acting. He sensibly decides to make use of micro expressions and significant pauses to express his emotions like the best film actors do. It would be all too easy to ham it up.

'George?'

'It's ...' George counts to three. There's a hint of a quiver at the edges of his lips. 'We're ...' He forces himself to count to five. 'I, er, won't be ... I won't be seeing her again, actually.' He blinks three times. Overkill?

Ray puts down his fork. Looks genuinely concerned. 'Good God, that's awful. I'm so sorry. Are you, you know, okay? I'm sure you don't want to talk about it, but if you do ...'

George silently acknowledges that Ray's no mean actor himself. He takes a deep breath, holds it, lets it out slowly through pursed lips. It's an impressive gesture, perhaps not Hollywood quality but a decent stab in the right direction. He intuitively knows this and has to stop himself from overdoing it by pretending to cry.

He looks Ray in the eye. 'It's this weird stalking business and those photos. She doesn't know what to believe and it's all been too much for her. The trust is gone.' Now he's talking about Angela, George detects an actual tear aching to break out. After all, he knows he has some way to go to win her over again.

'You poor fellow,' says Ray. 'There's me wittering on and you're having another crisis. We could have postponed. I would have understood.'

'No, no, no. I need to – what's the expression they use these days? – move on. Yes, that's it. No point in self-pity. Got a life to live, et cetera.'

'Damn right. Plenty of other, er, scallops in the sea, eh? She'll regret it, you know. Her loss.'

George sniffs once. Silence. 'You know, Ray, I'd rather not talk about it anymore if it's alright with you. Trying to move on, right?' A faint smile.

'Of course. Insensitive of me. So, any news of your man? What stage are the police at now?'

George adopts the kind of relieved smile he believes is appropriate at this change in topic. 'Not a lot to report, really, but you might have some thoughts. Give me five minutes in the kitchen and we'll continue.' He stands up and takes the plates.

As we know, George doesn't do dancing, but in the kitchen right now there's a little leg shuffle going on as he pulls the fish from the oven. He knows he's on top of the situation and any qualms about violence from Ray have evaporated. In fact, he's been so polite and caring, so *Ray* really, George wonders if his suspicions are unfounded. Then he reminds himself that Ray has lied about his job and his wife. He plates up the sea bass, adds the salsa and greens and returns to the dining room. Ray is standing by the window, staring out.

'Lovely place you have here. Quiet. Like what you've done to the hedge. Must have taken a few years to create that chamfer at the top so perfectly.'

'A labour of love.'

After a lengthy chat on the art of winter pruning, George swings the conversation onto the progress of the police investigation. He omits to tell Ray that it's stalled and may never be restarted.

'The good thing is,' George concludes, 'they're taking it very seriously.'

'Quite right, too. It's enough to give a man a nervous breakdown.'

George laughs. 'It'll take more than that. I've toughened up a lot over the years, you know. If only Angela…' A pause while he appears to be lost in thought but is actually counting seconds silently again for maximum effect.

'Have you thought it might be someone you know,' interrupts Ray, 'or maybe someone you've met, even fleetingly? I mean, why pick on you? It always sounded like a revenge thing to me.'

George screws up his face as if he's in severe pain. It's an unnecessary gesture, the result of someone who's had one glass of wine too many.

'That's what I first thought, but surely I'd remember if I'd upset someone so much they'd be prepared to go to these lengths to get even.'

'Well, there was that idiot who smashed into you. And didn't you say that company director fella lost his job after you exposed him?'

George slowly shakes his head. 'The hack was well before those two came on the scene.'

'Hmm. Anyone else you met prior to it all kicking off, as it were?'

'No one else I can think of. Apart from you, obviously.'

Ray's eyes flick up towards the ceiling like he's working something out. 'Angela?' He says it so quietly George is unsure whether he caught the name at all.

'Sorry, I didn't quite catch what—?'

Ray lets out a hollow laugh, waves his arm as if to expunge his comment. 'No, no, no. Forget it. Sorry.'

But George isn't going to ignore him. 'Did you say Angela?'

'Yes, well, I did, but of course it can't be her. Although, George...' Ray leans forward. 'You hear these stories about the most unlikely people doing crazy things. I mean, there was a man I knew in Environmental Health who bred fighting dogs. Lovely man, he was. Quiet, friendly. But behind it all ... He got an eighteen-month suspended sentence.'

George isn't listening. Ray's clumsy attempt at driving a wedge between him and Angela is no different to the hacker's insidious tactics. Surely this confirmed they were one and the same? But then might it be a simple case of jealousy?

Ray rouses George from his ruminations by waving a hand in front of his face.

'What? Sorry, Ray. It's this Angela business. Tell me, what news of your wife? I feel like I'm monopolising the evening.'

'Oh, same old, same old. Looks like she might be back home by the weekend but you never really know until it happens. I live in hope they'll find a cure. Do you know, her disorder is so rare it doesn't even have a name?'

George thinks this is very convenient. 'How terrible. And frustrating. The kids, are they helping out a bit more now?'

'Got their own lives to lead, George, and I can't blame them. I'm sure when things get critical they'll show their faces more often, but for now it's just me.'

'So what happens when she's not in the hospital and you're at work? That must be problematic? Do you have carers coming in?'

George is warming up to attack the job charade in a minute, and he's feeling confident again.

Ray responds convincingly.

'When she's at home, someone comes in every lunchtime to make sure she's okay, but it's still a worry. Doesn't come cheap, either. Wish I could take a leave of absence, but we need the money.'

'Tell me about it,' says George. 'I've started getting some work in the nick of time. By the way, do you know a local builder – well, he calls himself a developer – called David Williams? I met him at a networking breakfast.' George is pleased he had the foresight to change Lofty's name to a fictitious one.

Ray is silent.

'Nice guy,' continues George. 'Seems to be very busy doing loft conversions.'

Still nothing from Ray.

'Huge guy. Broad Welsh accent. Talks with a lisp.'

Ray is thinking.

'Williams, Welsh ...? Yes, of course I do. Makes me look small. Very professional, so they say.'

Gotcha, says George to himself.

Ray puts down his knife and fork with a clatter on the empty plate. The sound breaks the flow of the conversation, perhaps as Ray intended. 'Wonderful, really lovely. A man who can cook. You've spoilt me. I'll be back to ready meals tomorrow.'

'Ha ha, and probably beans on toast for me.'

George stands up and takes the plates. 'There's something I've been meaning to ask you, Ray.'

'Fire away.'

'I'm thinking about moving, downsizing I suppose, to realise some cash. Just wanted to pick your brain. Let me grab the desserts and I'll fill you in.'

In the kitchen, George is basking in a reality reserved solely for people who have planned meticulously and seen some very positive results. He pulls an identical pair of summer fruit meringues from the fridge and waltzes back to the dining room.

'There's a possibility, and it's just a possibility, we might become neighbours.'

Ray's not looking too comfortable. 'Really?'

'I spotted something in your neck of the woods. Those new-build flats about to go up in Drummond Road. Wanted to get your thoughts on the developer. I worry that it's such an enormous project they might be knocked up on the cheap.'

The next fuse has been lit. There's never been a planning application for flats in that road. It's the last place you'd get permission to build them, given the exclusiveness of the neighbourhood. But if there was, it's certainly something Ray would know about, even if he wasn't personally dealing with the project.

'Oh, that one. Not on my list, more's the pity,' says Ray with a sigh.

Bingo! Yet another confirmation of Ray's lies.

'Rather a sore point, actually,' Ray continues. 'I've been pushing for a move up the ranks for years. I thought I had a chance. Then they bring in this guy from London. Thinks he's the bee's knees. And those flats are his baby.'

'That's tough on you. And the developer?' George won't let Ray's sob story create a diversion.

'Also from out of the area, I believe. Their top man knows the planning committee chairman from what I've heard. There are rumours ...' Ray leaves the words hanging there for George to make sense of as he sees fit.

'Ah, it's like that, is it? Still, probably worth investigating. Sorry you were, er, overlooked for that job though. Rotten luck on top of everything else.'

'Thanks for the sympathy, George.' Ray looks at his watch. 'You know what, I really should be going. Planning committee tomorrow so it's an early start. I'm sure you understand.'

George surreptitiously glances at his watch. It's only 9.55 p.m. Scooterboy could still be on delivery duty, and the most important part of his plan hangs in the balance. He has a delaying tactic up his sleeve but is he brave enough to carry it out?

———

Two miles away on the other side of town, a trio of noisy teenagers who've been drinking minimart vodka all evening in a nearby park are now playing a game of jumping the stripes on a pedestrian crossing. Thankfully, the road is almost devoid of traffic. Such is the group's focus on the challenges they've set for themselves they fail to hear the high-pitched buzz of a

125cc engine with a custom exhaust growing increasingly louder.

With a long run up across the wide grass verge, one lad takes off from the kerb and clears four of the white stripes. He lands poorly, falling forward onto his hands.

The other two fall about laughing. 'What a muppet!' says one.

'Fuck off,' says the jumper. 'Fuckin' four stripes, you losers. Four!'

He picks himself up and dusts down his hands and knees. Just as he notices a small tear in his trousers, there's a deafening beep of a dual-tone horn. Scooterboy flies past him with only inches to spare and causes the boy to jerk backwards and fall over again.

'Oi! It's a fucking crossing, you fuck.'

While Scooterboy doesn't hear the actual words, he instinctively knows he's being badmouthed. He rams on the brakes, turns the scooter at right angles to the road, and looks back towards the crossing. Silhouetted by a nearby streetlight, even the diminutive Scooterboy is an intimidating sight. For added drama, he revs the engine. Once, twice, three times. He knows what works. A bit of front is everything.

'Shit,' says the jumper who scampers off into the night closely followed by his friends.

Satisfied with his revenge movie tactic, he resumes his adventurous journey towards the penultimate destination of the evening. He calculates he'll be at George's house by 9.58 p.m.

———

George dabs his mouth with a napkin, carefully places it on the table, and looks his guest in the eye. All the business leadership manuals say that eye contact is essential in the search for truth and George isn't going to argue with the renowned ex-CEO who wrote it. He's even rehearsed what he's about to say in front of the mirror.

'Ray, I'm worried about you.' Despite his heart thumping against the overtight shirt, George's voice is dripping with concern. 'I mean, is there something going on you're not telling me?' He leans in. 'I tried to call you at work a few days ago.'

Ray eyes dance around. He shifts in his seat.

George goes for it. 'The switchboard told me no one of your name works there. It's been worrying me.'

Ray sits back in the chair, throws his arms wide. 'It's embarrassing,' he says with a weak smile. 'But I guess you should know the truth. You won't like it.'

George surreptitiously scans the table for the best weapon available to him, should the need arise. The pepper grinder looks to be the best bet. Or a fork, perhaps?

'I've never worked for the council but I thought you'd judge me if I told you what I really do.' He looks down at his empty plate. 'I write stories with a sexual content. You'd call it porn. I made a lot of money from magazines in the UK and US in the days when people bought magazines. Now, of course, it's all on the internet and no one wants to read porn, they want to see it. It's a famine out there for people like me.'

George empties his glass, pours another one. A porn writer? The idea is so ludicrous it could be true. Perhaps Ray is simply a lost soul?

'So you thought I wouldn't want anything to do with you, then?'

Ray returns George's gaze. 'Let's be honest, who wants a friend who does that?'

George knows that Ray's initial assessment of him was

correct and it's not something he feels good about. Nevertheless, he's not finished. He stands up and goes for the jugular.

'And your wife's illness? I imagine that's not true either?'

'Cards on the table, George. There is no wife. I live alone in a tiny flat on the Frobert Estate. My income is pitiful. My once top-of-the-range car is ten-years-old, and I barely turn on the heating in winter. That's why I could never invite you round. There. Now you know.'

'Good God, Ray. I thought we knew each other better than that. You could have told me before. We're chess buddies.'

George looks down at the anguished figure in front of him and feels pity. Then his mobile beeps from the kitchen. 'Do you mind?' he says, before leaving the room.

He checks the screen: *Outside*.

'Business network,' says George, returning to the dining room. 'Cancelling tomorrow's breakfast. Shame.'

Ray is already out of his seat and putting on his jacket. 'I should go. He holds out a hand. George pauses before offering his. 'I'm so sorry, George. I really am. Please forgive me.'

George tries to smile.

'And good luck with finding your stalker. You might get a medal.'

He gives the briefest of laughs, revealing a hint of gold in the shadow of his mouth.

———

Nineteen

The narrow country lane twists and turns. The powerful headlights of the high-performance VW Golf sweep across the tall hedges that appear to block the road on tight bends. Ray is in no hurry. He doesn't particularly want to hit an errant badger or intrepid fox. It might put a dent in his car. Besides, he's deep in thought.

George himself confirmed that Angela had finally been scared off. *Project Angela: The Revenge* was over. It had been messy, but the path to success is rarely smooth. So why, he asks himself, aren't I jumping for joy? He had to admit he'd developed a certain admiration for the man. Despite everything that had been thrown at him, George appeared to shrug it all off. He'd even noticed a distinct aroma of self-assuredness at dinner. It was quite depressing. One thing's for certain, he'll never have to put up with George's relentless prattling about his beloved Angela again. Or sift through her inane texts to Jackie with their laughable responses. They'd all worn him down. Yet, even in that moment, he knew he'd miss George in some strange way.

He'd surprised himself by enjoying the evening until George made things awkward by bringing up the subject of those new flats. Still, he blagged it without missing a beat. That was before he realised George had been testing his backstory. He hadn't bargained on that. Or the way he was made to feel stupid. But he was proud of the way he'd turned things around with the writer story. George had looked positively shocked, flustered even – that he'd forced his friend into making an embarrassing confession. But, critically, was George simply being nosey or was he trying to link him to the stalker? If it was the latter, he might reveal his suspicions to the police. And that could have serious repercussions. He'd underestimated his adversary more than once already. Now was not the time to repeat those mistakes. He needed to put some physical space between him and George as quickly as possible.

He turns up the volume of Wagner's Tristan and Isolde to drown his fears.

———

In a much more positive frame of mind is Scooterboy. He's seen plenty of movies with unmarked police cars or private detectives following criminals. There are rules. Like not following too close, and perhaps even overtaking the target vehicle, then pulling over to let it pass before resuming the chase.

When Ray had left George's house, Scooterboy had the engine running but his lights off. Once the Golf signalled a left turn near the end of Claremont Avenue, he made his move, driving without lights until he reached the junction. Keeping two hundred metres between them, Scooterboy followed Ray out of town and onto a B-road heading north-west. After eight miles, the Golf made a right turn onto a road signed *Single Track with Passing Places*.

Scooterboy knows the road well. Early on Saturday mornings, he drives the route to go fishing for a few hours in a nearby river. He finds the peace therapeutic. Already, though, he's realised that the twisting road has both advantages and disadvantages. On the plus side, it's unlikely the man in the car ahead would spot him in his rear-view mirror. The downside would be if the Golf suddenly turns off and he might miss it. He resolves to get a little closer. The ultimate destination can't be that far. The road would eventually join a dual carriageway that Ray could have easily accessed from town without driving down this particular road.

He twists the throttle and speeds up slowly to avoid a sudden change in engine noise. Though everything looks different in darkness, he remembers there's a hill at the end of this stretch of road. As he turns a corner near the top of the rise, the Golf suddenly appears. It's parked half on the road, half on the verge. Just fifty metres away. It's too late to brake. As he passes the Golf, he catches sight of Ray talking to himself.

When Ray's mobile rang, he'd had no intention of answering it. He'd be home in less than five minutes and the caller could wait. But then he studied the number and recognised the country code: Saudi Arabia. And it wouldn't do to fuck with those guys.

'Marhabaan.' He isn't fluent in Arabic, but knows the basics. It pays to be respectful.

He heard a click. Almost certainly a call being transferred. The big guys wouldn't key in the numbers themselves when they had resources.

The next thing he heard was the rasp of a scooter passing by, ridden far too fast. He wished the rider a premature death.

'Mister Wakefield.' The voice could have been any one of thousands of foreigners coached in the very best received pronunciation and manners at an expensive English public school. Ray was unsurprised. Many of his dubious clients had enjoyed the finest education over here. 'Thank you for taking my call,' the cultured voice continued, 'You come highly recommended.'

Ray wasn't sure he actually wants another job right now. Maybe not another job ever. But he feels he should listen to the proposition before turning it down. Respectfully, of course.

———

Scooterboy is parked beside a field gate less than a quarter mile down the road. The interior of his helmet is wet with perspiration. Had the man in the Golf noticed him following and deliberately stopped to allow him past? He knows that's an old trick. And if so, had his target been on the phone calling for reinforcements? He walks the scooter back a few feet to hug the side of the thick hedgerow. The scooter's lights are off, the engine idling quietly.

He thinks it unlikely he would be noticed when the Golf passes him but he has to be careful. Should he be seen, and the car stops, then Plan B is to make a rapid escape back towards town, knowing it would take the Golf valuable time to turn around on such a narrow road, by which time he may have found a better hiding place. If there was such a thing. No guarantees. He wishes he'd paid more attention to the road earlier.

He times his breaths, slow and regular, just as he'd read Special Forces soldiers do in stressful situations, and waits. And waits. A handful of other cars pass by and still no sign of the Golf. He checks the time on his mobile. Ten minutes have elapsed, and he thinks that perhaps the Golf has turned off somewhere between where it had stopped and where he's waiting now. But he'd checked for that eventuality on the way and doubts he'd missed anything. He puts the phone back into his jacket pocket and focuses on his heart rate.

A few minutes later, he hears the sound he's been waiting for. Scooterboy can detect a Golf R at a hundred paces. And pretty much every other performance car. He flicks down the visor on his helmet. The Golf passes him at speed, as if the driver suddenly had an urgent appointment. Scooterboy pulls back onto the road, lights still off, and follows the Golf. There's no need to get too near. He can see flashes of the car's headlights way ahead as it weaves its way to its destination. Two miles further, as he passes through a tiny hamlet of a dozen homes, the road widens and a car approaches from the opposite direction. Scooterboy flicks on his lights for safety and flicks them off again once the car has passed. Now he glimpses the Golf's brake lights, glowing red in the thin low mist that floods the valley. He notes the location and continues. When he arrives at the last known sighting, he slows. Just up ahead and on the left-hand side are a pair of tall cast iron gates. He inches forward just as the gates click shut. The car can be seen speeding down the drive towards a large country house.

All the pent-up adrenaline is released from Scooterboy's nervous system. He punches the air and flicks the finger at the Golf's receding rear end. Then he checks his location on his phone map and saves it. Job done.

———

10.35 p.m. George's mobile rings. He's been pacing the house, waiting for this moment ever since Ray left. He clicks on the call and holds his breath.

'Sorted,' says Scooterboy in a masterclass of brevity George could only dream of, if only he knew what he meant.

'Sorted?' says George.

'You should see his house, mate. It's a bleedin' palace. Must be worth a few mill. Big gates, gravel drive. Should be drivin' a Range Rover 5.0 P525 Autobiography, not that Golf. Mind you, it's the R version, so it shifts like a demon. Wouldn't mind one of them my—'

George cuts across him before he launches into a full review of the model.

'Well done. Really, well done. What's the address?'

'Dunno. Says Blackwell House on the gates, somewhere near Bilston. I can send you a photo and a map link. You gonna transfer the money to my account first? Not that I don't trust you, right, but...'

'Of course. I'll do it right now. Then you'll send me the map, yes?'

George is a tad annoyed at this lack of confidence in his credit-worthiness but forgives Scooterboy. He may have had a tough upbringing and, as a result, developed trust issues. But he can't help but be impressed with the boy's business sense.

'That's the deal,' says Scooterboy. 'Pleasure doing business with you. Gimme a shout if you need anything else. Rates might go up a bit, though. This is professional work, you know. Like bodyguards in Iraq. They earn five hundred quid a day.'

'Well, I'm not sure if the two jobs equate, but I understand the point you're making. And in recognition of your sterling service tonight I'm going to give you a bonus.'

Scooterboy's ears light up.

'Yes, I'm going to give you a free two-hour financial advice session. Purely friend to friend as I'm not officially qualified to offer advice, but I know everything those people know. Could be useful for an enterprising young man such as yourself.'

There's a silence on the line. It's not the bonus the boy had in mind.

'Hello?' says George.

'Still here, mate. You couldn't see your way to bunging me another twenty, could you? It's a nice offer and all that that, but cash is king. You should know that.'

George sighs wearily. 'And that's why we need to discuss your financial affairs. I'll guarantee you'll make a lot more than twenty pounds if you follow my advice.'

Scooterboy is thinking. And as we know, he's not stupid.

'Go on then,' he says. 'But I'll keep count. I will. I'm not stupid.'

'Give me one minute,' says George. He opens up his bank app and transfers the money to Scooterboy. 'Done. By the time you get home, it should show up in your account. You can send me the link then.'

He clicks off the call and texts the agreed safe message to Angela: *Please, please reconsider. Life is unbearable without you. G xxxxx.* He hopes Angela will be pleased he's still alive.

His phone beeps again. *Here's a pic and a map. Ta for the cash. Blackwell House near Bilston. https.//mapster.uk/skk67y-w2yTZul*

He opens the image, stares at the iron gates, then clicks the link. A map appears with a red marker in the middle of a lot of green space. Next, he hits the Directions button and a wiggly blue line connects his house with Ray's. Journey time 23 minutes. Distance 10.5 miles. So nowhere near where he said he lived. A lie upon a lie upon a lie. He wonders if there's a name for that. And he bets that the almost surreal porn writer story is pure fiction. To think he almost bought into Ray's pathetic confessions.

He pushes himself out of the sofa, pours himself a glass of water in the kitchen, and runs upstairs to the War Room. It may be past his bedtime, but vengeance is a powerful stimulant.

A quick property search on Blackwell House reveals it changed hands three years ago for £2.8 million. There were also a few photographs of the exterior. A house George could only dream of owning, though his first thoughts, typically, were more practical. What kind of income would it take to maintain a home like this? Money down the drain, he concluded. Better to invest it in a good pension plan and live somewhere more sensible.

Next, he opens the Land Registry site hoping to find the name of the owner. He doubts Ray Caldwell is his actual name. The police, of course, would have easy access to this kind of information, but they're faffing about, aren't they? He needs to do as much legwork as possible so his findings will prompt Tyler to kick-start the investigation. He signs up and begrudgingly pays the £25 fee. It's been an expensive evening, what with the land ownership data, Scooterboy's fee, and those scallops priced like they were a species in imminent danger of extinction. It's even cost him what he thought was a good friend. And for a moment he wishes he'd never questioned Ray's honesty, never employed Scooterboy to trail him. Ignorance is sometimes kinder.

The site reveals a name: David Raymond Wakefield. He stares at it for so long it takes on a life of itself. He puts the name into a search engine. No exact results. He deletes the middle name and repeats the process. Over ninety thousand results. Hopeless. He's gone as far as he can with the resources he has. Time to move on to his backup plan.

While he now has some useful info for Tyler, he's can't rely on him to use it. So that's where the payback part comes in. Even if the law can't bring this man to justice, the least he can do is to make Mister Wakefield's life a misery, to give him a taste of his own medicine. There's no time for an elaborate intervention. What's needed is direct action with, George decides, an unhealthy side portion of chaos. It's always good to have something special to look forward to. As he heads for bed, the clock downstairs chimes 1.00 a.m.

The following morning, he spends far more time in the shower than usual, dispensing with his own credo that recognises that the whole point of a shower is that, unlike a bath, it cleans the body more efficiently. Ten minutes go by and it's as if the sensation of water rippling off his body has created a hypnotic effect that affects time and place. He's transported to a lovely house he doesn't recognise. In the lush garden, he sees himself drinking tea. A dog is stretched out at his feet. Feeling a slight pressure on his forearm, he turns to see Angela standing beside him. Her arms wrap around him and a warm, cosy feeling floods through his entire body. The image flickers and disappears, and George realises he's totally alone.

The kitchen still stinks of fish. As he unloads the dishwasher, he remembers something. He picks up his mobile and texts Ray. *Morning Ray, hope you got home OK! Sorry I had to ask those questions. You know I'm feeling a bit paranoid at the moment! Thanks for coming and let's do it again soon. G*

George has sensibly kept the tone breezy and affable. It wouldn't do for him to get any more suspicious than he probably already is. It's important Ray believes he's been forgiven. Otherwise, heaven knows what he might do.

Then he calls Tyler. It goes straight to voicemail.

'DS Tyler. Please leave a brief message.'

'George Sanderson. About my so-called friend, Ray. I think his real name is David Raymond Wakefield, and he lives at Blackwell House, near Bilston. He's lied about everything. Let's talk.'

He likes the sign off. It feels like he's taking back control.

Across town, a bleary-eyed Angela is cramming down a quick breakfast. She puts the blame for her insomnia squarely on George's shoulders. Now she's running late for work. Her mood isn't helped by the discovery of George's text from the night before. And unhelpfully for George, she's totally unaware of its context. That's because the cab driver delivered George's plaintive letter to the wrong address, mistaking the number *9* in George's handwriting for the number *8*. After she'd spent the last two days trying to banish all thoughts of George, he's reopened the wound. Should she even grace the message with a reply? After consideration, she decides it is. Better to nip this nonsense in the bud. The message is terse.

Please don't contact me again.

Her doorbell rings. As she heads towards the door, it rings again.

'Yes, I'm coming,' she calls. 'Jesus!' she says under her breath as she unlocks the door.

A vaguely familiar woman stands on the other side.

'Hello, are you Angela Hayworth?' The woman smiles.

Angela nods, trying to remember where she's seen the face before.

'I'm Alice. I live opposite. Not been there long.' She thrusts a letter into Angela's hands. 'Sorry, I only spotted it last night. Must have been hand-delivered because there isn't a stamp. I think someone misread the address.'

Angela looks at the envelope and recognises the writing. Good God, will the man never give up? She returns a somewhat forced smile.

The letter is consigned unopened into the kitchen bin, joining other detritus deemed unfit for recycling.

George reads Angela's text. Her words are unequivocal. Even after his passionate and exquisitely composed letter, their relationship is dead in the water. Hope evaporates in an instant. Ray has destroyed his already sorry life. And for that there would be a reckoning.

He pulls an A4 lined pad from the War Room desk drawer and starts writing. Hours tick by. When at last he reviews his seven pages of notes, he concludes that his plans are not without an element of risk. He circles what he considers are the best options, chuckling to himself at their sheer audacity. If only he could share them with someone like ... like Angela.

———

Twenty-four hours pass before George hears from Tyler. The buzzing from his phone on the bedside table wakes him at 9.30 a.m. When his alarm had gone off at the usual time, George groaned. Still with closed eyes, his hand crept out of the duvet and finally located the off button. After a second night of disturbed sleep, and in a shocking change to his normal routine, he'd stayed in bed. Just one extra hour, he'd pleaded to any omnipotent powers who may have been listening. Plainly they were feeling sympathetic as he'd been allotted an extra two.

'George? Rob Tyler. I see you took my advice and left well alone.'

'Ah, hello,' says a yawning George, noting Tyler's unnecessary sarcasm. 'Yes, well, I couldn't help myself, really. Sorry.'

'And dare I ask how you came by this information?'

George tells Tyler the story, chronologically in handy bullet points.

'I'll need to take it further up the chain,' says Tyler. 'Available man hours etc. I'll be in touch soon. You don't have any plans to meet him again, do you?'

'Certainly not. It's a trust thing, see?'

'Good. Please, please, don't play the private detective again. You don't even know if he's the actual stalker, do you? This Ray person hasn't been violent, he hasn't tried to con you out of money, has he? He might just be a lonely soul. World's full of them.'

'But why would he play this silly charade if he isn't. That would be one hell of a coincidence, wouldn't it?'

'I've seen bigger ones. Now leave it with us please, George.'

George has no plans to meet Ray, and the investigative work is over. He's been truthful to Tyler, but that won't stop his new Confuse & Harass plan. He glances at today's to-do list. It contains a single item: *Pizza*. More money to splash out but it couldn't be helped. Pride is a powerful motivator. He bolts down some breakfast, grabs his car keys and leaves the house. He's already behind schedule and that makes him feel uncomfortable.

———

At Finguish Fans, Reg notices a change in Angela's usual demeanour. She appears distracted, her responses to his requests curt. He lets it go. It doesn't do to pry, he thinks. Women are an anomaly to him, and in his experience, prying might open up a can of worms he's ill-equipped to deal with. However, when her mood had failed to improve by late afternoon, he plucks up the courage to speak.

'Angela, is everything okay? I noticed you've not been yourself the past few days. If there's anything I can do to help? God knows you've helped me enough over the years.'

Angela bursts into tears.

It's not something she does, and Reg is taken aback. He's also unsure how to comfort an emotional woman. Usually, when Anne gets upset, he pats her gently on the back and asks her to cheer up. But here in the office he knows he has a duty of care.

He walks over to the office door and closes it.

'So, what's it all about then?'

Angela dabs at her eyes, careful to avoid displacing her mascara.

'Sorry, Reg, I'm being silly.'

'Tell me anyway.'

It takes a good half hour before Reg has pieced together a semblance of the story from the disjointed fragments Angela has told him. He can barely believe it.

'I've got to hand it to you,' he says, 'I didn't realise you were going through such a stressful time. And far be it from me to comment on your relationship with, er, George, but it does rather sound as if he's protecting you from further anguish. Has he actually said he doesn't want to see you anymore?'

Angela thinks back to their last meeting in the café. 'Well, not exactly, but I can't be doing with this temporary separation thing,' she sniffs. 'I've been there before with people blowing hot and cold, and what they really mean is let's break up. God, this all sound so childish. Sorry, Reg.'

Reg leans over and tentatively pats her back. 'And the letter you said he sent. What did it say?'

'I don't know. I don't want to read it.'

'Then I think you should. You need all the facts before you can make a decision. I would. From what you've told me in the past, he sounds a decent enough sort of chap.'

Angela winces at the comment, thinking of what happened to Michael, and George's part in his downfall.

'I'm being pathetic, aren't I?' A laugh escapes through the sobs.

'I think,' says Reg with a smile, 'you're being rather defensive. What you and George have been through would put a strain on the strongest of relationships. Now cheer up.' He sits back in his chair, quietly pleased with his words. He thinks Anne would have been proud of him.

Twenty

At Blackwell House, plans are underway for Ray's retirement. He'd made the decision just hours after his dinner with George. He found it hard to accept that the primary catalyst for this sudden life-changer had been a middle-aged nobody. And he hadn't counted on George's regular company having another effect on him. The part of his brain that processed guilt and locked it away for expediency appeared to be malfunctioning. How would George survive without Angela? Could he survive?

He casts his mind back to their first meeting in the café. What was George's crime, other than to bring his particular brand of logic to a situation where empathy would have been more appropriate? What had he said to the homeless guy? It's all about value for money? Wasn't he simply saying what many people think? Isn't that how capitalism worked?

His light entertainment project, far from energising him, had turned into a last and somewhat deflating hurrah. It was far from being a glittering end to his career, and he'd thought long and hard about whether to do a final job. After all, the Saudis were still waiting for a definitive answer. But his heart isn't in it anymore. He'd reflected on his early wins, and the sheer joy and excitement they generated. It all seemed such a long time ago. Now it was time to move on, to live with a single identity and perhaps make some friends. He might even find a partner. If George could do it...

The decision had felt liberating, but it was tinged with sadness. He'd lose the home he loved. While the UK had made a practical base from where to conduct his business, it was not the best environment for living in anonymity. And who knows what George might tell the police after last night's fiasco? He'd acted quickly lest his resolve crumbled and throw his life into further jeopardy. Arrangements had been made for the contents of the house be taken into storage. The house itself would be mothballed until he decided what to do with it.

There were still many arrangements to make. Critically, where to go? A man has to have roots, and he felt he was still young enough to put some down before old age and infirmity made decisions for him. The squabbles in Europe would lead to divisive and unstable governments, and the USA would fare no better. The cultures of Asia and Africa were too alien. Where could he become anonymous yet live the lifestyle of a man of some considerable means? So, South America? It had worked for the escaping Nazis after the war. Or perhaps an island in the Caribbean? There was money enough to buy a small one. But such choices required time and research. He settled on spending a few months on the Cote D'Azur before committing to anything.

His phone chirps. Someone at the gate. He taps a button.
'Yes?'
'Pizza.'

'Pardon?'

'Pizza for Wakefield.'

'I didn't order a pizza.'

'Wakefield, Blackwell House. Four Seasons pizza, extra jalapenos, coleslaw, large Coke.'

'Who ordered it?'

'Guess you did, sir?'

Ray's palms start to sweat. As far as he can remember, that name has only ever been used to pay his council tax, and energy and internet suppliers. The gardening and cleaning companies were paid in cash. And they would hardly send him a free pizza, despite the astronomical amounts he pays them all. The situation didn't feel right.

'I'm buzzing you in,' he says. 'Drive slowly.'

He reaches into the bottom drawer of his desk, takes out a revolver. Checks the magazine and pushes it, barrel first, down the back of his trousers. Then he walks to the front door.

A Toyota Prius is slowly advancing down the drive towards him. It's an old model, so likely to belong a driver from a local taxi firm. The car swings in an arc around the fountain in the centre of the drive and stops.

A middle-aged Asian man gets out, opens a passenger door and picks up a large insulated plastic bag and a sealed plastic cup. He pauses beside the car, taking in the house and gardens. He's clearly impressed.

Ray relaxes. The guy looks genuine.

'Sorry, sir,' says the driver. 'It has taken me much time to get here, so I do not know if it is still hot. It is a very long way from my customer.'

He pulls open the flap and hands over the contents of the bag, then the drink.

'And who is your customer?' says Ray.

'Magic Pizza. They are excellent friends of mine when they are busy.'

'And you don't know who ordered it?'

'I do not, sir, but you must be a very lucky man to have such a friend.' He beams. 'Now I must leave. Thank you very much, sir.' He starts to walk back to the car, then stops and turns back. 'You have a most gracious home,' he says with a sweep of an arm, as if pointing out something Ray hadn't seen before. 'Oh, silly me.' He puts his hand into his inside jacket pocket and pulls out an envelope with the name David Wakefield on it.

'For you,' he says, holding it at arms' length. 'Very sorry.'

Ray walks over to retrieve it. As the Toyota drives out, he takes the pizza and drink into the house and bins them.

Now he studies the envelope. The neat handwriting is unfamiliar, and it's so well stuck down it's difficult to open it without potentially ripping the contents. He can feel from the weight there's not much inside. He holds it up to one of the powerful LED bulbs in the kitchen ceiling. It appears there's a small slip of paper inside. Nothing dangerous then, but he can't be too careful in his profession. He carefully slices the top edge off with a sharp knife and shakes the contents loose. Annoyingly, the small piece of paper lands on the blank side so he can't read it. He flicks it over with the knife blade in case it's contaminated. A message.

The next delivery won't be so tasty.

He calls Magic Pizza.

'You've just sent me a pizza by taxi. Wakefield, Blackwell House, Bilston.'

'Is there a problem then?' says the young-sounding girl.

'No there isn't. In fact, I wanted to thank the person who ordered it. Can you check for me, please?'

'Hang on a minute.'

He hears low voices, some clattering of utensils, coughing.

Now the girl's voice again. 'Sorry, he says we can't tell you the name. Something to do with data protection. You can't be too careful these days, you know, what with spammers and hackers and stalkers and—'

Ray has heard enough and cuts the call. If he didn't know better, he'd think the girl was taking the piss.

———

If George could have heard the conversation, he'd realise it was money well spent. The plan was within a hairsbreadth of being cancelled when he called into Magic Pizza yesterday. He was told they didn't normally deliver as far out as Bilston. Then they hit him with the cost of a taxi delivery: eighteen pounds. He did the maths. A total cost of close to thirty pounds. On top of Wednesday night's scallops and sea bass. Ray or David or whatever his name is, is eating well at my expense, he grumbled to himself.

———

Angela pours a large glass of wine, turns on the oven and pulls a small pizza from the freezer. After a rollercoaster week, she was in the mood for finishing the bottle, watching some mindless telly and having an early night. George's letter remains in the bin, just a few feet away under more rubbish and food leftovers.

For all that Reg said, and she had to admit he'd been quite convincing, it was a point of honour not to take advice from a man about another man. They always stand up for one another, right? But as the evening wore on, her steadfast position begins to weaken.

Finally, more than two days after George cabbed over the letter, she delves into the bin and removes it with a pair of tongs usually reserved for turning bacon slices under the grill. The envelope is damp and stained with tea and leftover pasta sauce. It looks repulsive, and there's little hope that the contents are much different. Given that it was delivered to the wrong house, perhaps that was fate's way of protecting her? But then, why would fate have directed her neighbour to call on her yesterday morning? Fate can't be that stupid.

The envelope is so well sealed, edge to edge, she can't get a nail underneath to tear it open. And she curses George for being so bloody meticulous in absolutely everything he does. It's exhausting. She reaches for some scissors.

Carefully trimming off the top edge, she pulls out the letter and unfolds it.

The tears come quickly. And now she curses herself and everyone else who helped create the person she'd become. The one with the brittle interior who couldn't trust anyone to be loyal.

She pulls off a sheet of kitchen roll and dries her eyes. What can she do? George specifically asked her not to respond, and yet she had.

Please don't contact me again.

And while she realised her message had done nothing to spoil George's charade of a relationship gone bad, what must he think of her? Is it all too late? Her text seemed so definitive.

―――

'No!' squawks Jackie. 'No, no, no, no! You're so gullible, Angela.'

Angela has told Jackie about the letter. And how she's treated George unfairly. At the best of times, Jackie's response would be pessimistic. Tonight, it's worse. Peter arrived home smelling of cheap perfume. All men are liars and cheats, and that's an end to it. Her pride forbids mentioning this to Angela, though.

It wasn't Peter's fault that the ambitious Sheila had turned up at Brian's in some tatty old party gear she'd found outside a charity shop one night. Makeup slathered on and reeking of a supposedly famous brand of eau de toilette she'd swapped for a kiss and a fleeting grope of her breasts from a market trader. When she'd slipped her arms around Peter from behind and nuzzled her face into his neck, the damage was done. Now it's touch and go whether poor Peter will be dispatched from the spare room to the street. Jackie hasn't made up her mind yet.

'I'm going to talk to him,' says Angela. 'I owe him that, at least.'

'You owe him nothing.'

———

Raindrops sprinkle onto puddles that dot the supermarket car park. A mother and toddler splash through them as they run laughing towards the entrance. Angela smiles wistfully at the woman.

Despite Jackie's misgivings, Angela is more determined than ever to get a message to George. She'd spent the rest of the evening working out how that might happen without endangering him. A letter posted on a Friday night wouldn't be delivered until Monday morning at the earliest. And the idea of using a taxi to deliver it anonymously hadn't occurred to her. It was only when she wrote out her shopping list for the next day did the solution come to her.

As a creature of habit, George was sure to make his usual supermarket visit at 9 a.m. the following morning. A perfect opportunity to meet him away from their respective homes. Even that was fraught with difficulty. George's letter had alluded to a potential threat of violence. What if his stalker is part of a bigger setup with huge personnel resources? Perhaps he's being followed, or even filmed? Perhaps she is?

That's why, before leaving home earlier, she'd adopted a rudimentary disguise, tying back her hair, wearing sunglasses despite the overcast sky, and a thick winter jacket, the collar of which she could pull up around her face.

She now stands some distance from the entrance, sheltering under an umbrella – close enough to see George when he arrives. Nine o'clock comes and goes. Nine-fifteen. Nine-thirty. Shoppers she'd noticed entering the store are already coming out. Where the hell is he? Of all the days for him to switch routine. It must look, she thinks self-consciously, like I've been stood up. Then, at nine thirty-two, she spots a familiar car. George's Mondeo passes within twenty metres of her and turns into a section of the car park with the most vacant spaces.

George has every reason to be late. He's had some extra-curricular shopping to attend to first. At the exact moment that Angela had assumed her stakeout position, he'd been close by, on the far side of the retail park, entering a large DIY store. There were very few customers inside, and that's what he'd been banking on. He needed some advice, and finding the relevant staff at busy times is nigh on impossible.

Checking the signage as he worked his way along the huge aisles, he found what he needed at the far end of the store: security/padlocks/chains. He scanned the shelves for the biggest padlock, flinched at the price, but put one into his basket anyway. Then he turned his attention to the chains. There was plenty of choice, from cheap to eye-wateringly expensive. George thought one of them might give gold a run for its money. A small notice invited him to contact a member of staff to cut it to his chosen length.

The length wasn't something he'd considered, and he berated himself for the oversight. Opening his phone, he scrolled through his photos until he found the right one. He stood the phone on a shelf and pulled off some heavy-duty chain from a roll, referring to the photo to estimate the necessary length. Then he doubles it and adds a bit more. It won't be cheap, he calculated, but now was not the time to cut corners. Better to have too much than too little.

He left the aisle in search of the information desk. When he arrived, there was no one there. He waited for a few minutes, drumming his fingers on the countertop, cursing the store's inefficiency. He checked his watch and noted he could have completed half of his supermarket shop by now.

'Can I help you?' said a tiny voice from behind him.

George swivelled around to see a figure as diminutive as the voice. At first, he thought it was a young boy, but on closer inspection, he estimated from the contours, it could actually be a girl. Short spiky hair, nose stud, tattoos on both hands.

'Ah, er, I need someone to cut me a length of chain.'

'No problem, I'll do it now for you,' she said with an accent more common in PR or publishing than DIY sheds.

She leads him back to the chain aisle. The only thought on George's mind is whether she'd be strong enough to do it.

'Which one would you like?' she said.

'How much do you know about chains?' said George.

'More than you think, I suspect.'

He feels like he's been rapped over the knuckles. 'Well, I want the strongest one. One that would be difficult to saw through.' He didn't hold out much hope for an answer.

The girl points to a flat-faced black chain. 'This is the one you want, 100 Grade cut-resistant steel. Most bolt-cutters can't even get through that. What you chaining up, then? Your Harley, perhaps? An adventurous partner?' She flashes her dazzling teeth.

George thought he couldn't look less like a Harley Davidson owner, nor some sexual deviant, but was nevertheless impressed at the girl's knowledge of hardware miscellanea. He declined to answer her unnecessary questions.

'I'll take that one then,' he said. 'A metre should do it. How are you going to cut it if it can't be cut?' George thinks this is a clever question.

'With one of these.' At full stretch the girl reached up to the shelf above and with both hands pulls down a large cutting tool. She handled it like it weighed nothing.

'Hydraulic. Costs a fortune,' she added. She measured out the length, put the chain into the jaws of the cutter. Thunk.

She made a note on a label and handed the length of chain to George. 'What padlock are you using? No point having a chain like that if the padlock's rubbish. You should have one like this. The best combi lock we sell.' She moved down the aisle and picked one out. 'It's nearly fifty quid, but it's worth it. Last you a lifetime.'

George mentally totted up the price of the two items, added it to the cost of the pizza stunt, and felt his blood pressure rise. He thanked her and headed for the nearest empty checkout, manned by a nervous-looking youth accompanied by a middle-aged man wearing an Assistant Manager's badge.

'Good morning, sir,' said the manager. 'Did you find everything you wanted today?'

'Yes, yes I did, thank you.'

The manager isn't actually listening. He's distracted. The youth is dithering over the keyboard.

'Darren,' he said, wearily, 'it's like I said. Once you see the total, just hit the Enter button again and ask the customer to present his card.'

He turned to George. 'Unless you're paying cash? Are you paying in cash, sir?'

George wondered who would carry around that amount of cash.

'Card. By the way, I must commend one of your staff members. Short girl, young, spiky hair with red bits in. She was very helpful.'

'Ah, you must mean Olivia,' said the manager. 'She is a they, but you weren't to know.'

'Pardon?' George's internal grammar-check searched for meaning and came up short.

'They're non-binary. It's no secret. They'd want you to know.'

'Yes, I see.' George didn't see at all, and he wasn't about to waste more time trying to see. At least, not right now. Chaos called, but not before he'd replenished the contents of his fridge.

———

Neatly folded colour-coded bags in hand, George marches towards the supermarket doors. Such is his focus, he probably wouldn't have spotted Angela even if she'd dispensed with her disguise.

She waits a few seconds and follows him inside. She walks past the store security man feeling naked without a trolley or basket, and fears she may look like a shoplifter.

George stops at the front of the Bakery section. He's only ten metres ahead. Angela stops, opens her handbag, and pretends to look for something while sneaking glances in his direction. Then, serendipitously, he walks away, leaving his trolley unattended. Angela inches closer, pulse racing. George is at the far wall picking out a freshly baked loaf. It's probably now or never. She pulls an envelope from her bag and drops into the empty trolley as she passes.

One minute later, she's back in the car worrying about whether George will even notice her note. Did it land with his name face up? Or down? She can't remember. If she'd written his name on both sides, she wouldn't be feeling so anxious about it.

When George returns to the trolley and drops the bread inside, he spots the envelope and ignores it, assuming it to be the reverse side of a shopping list left by a previous customer. It's not unusual. In fact, it's another of his bugbears. The way people just dump their rubbish in trolleys: crisp packets, chocolate wrappers, fruit drink cartons, the contents of which they must have consumed whilst they were shopping. Blatant stealing, and that impacts on prices for everyone. He continues his shop.

At the checkout, he unloads the trolley. As he pulls out the last item, a large bag of frozen peas, he sees the envelope has stuck to the bottom of the bag. He flicks it off with his finger, not wishing to infect himself with someone else's germs. It lands the opposite way up.

There, in large capital letters, is his name. Another George? It was one hell of a coincidence, he thought. As he starts to open the envelope, a voice interrupts him.

'Sir?'

The conveyer belt is on the move and items are being

scanned. A backlog is already building up in the bag loading area.

An impatient man in the queue behind coughs loudly.

'Yes, of course,' says George, noticing the problem.

George stuffs the envelope in his jacket pocket and fills the bags. Green for fresh fruit and vegetables, red for frozen and chilled produce, yellow for packaged dried food, blue for non-food. When he first invented his packing system, he'd spent some considerable time debating in which bag he should place the bread. It was neither fresh produce nor frozen, or packaged or non-food. In the end, he made the painful decision to put it in the bag with the most room at the end, hoping such organisational anarchy wouldn't insidiously infect the rest of his life.

As he wheels the trolley out of the store towards his car, the mysterious envelope is far from forgotten. Who is the writer and how did it get into his trolley? Is it the catalyst of an intervention, primed to blow his life apart again? The closer he gets to his car, the more he believes this must be the work of Ray. His heart sinks. Just when he's on the offensive, along comes another attack of some kind. He can barely summon the courage to read what's inside.

He loads the boot of the car with the bags, puts the key into the ignition, and sits there quietly staring out of the windscreen for a few minutes, wishing the envelope would somehow dematerialise. On the contrary. As he drives out of the space into the exit lane, the envelope, an edge of which is poking out of his pocket, appears to be growing, to be gaining weight. It's now too big to ignore. He pulls into a vacant space. With the engine still running, he gingerly tears open the envelope, fingering only the edges. There might be useful fingerprints, he thinks.

Ten seconds later, the security camera close to the car park exit will have caught a stationary Mondeo rocking up and down on its suspension. If the camera angle had been lower, it would have captured the image of a middle-aged man bouncing up and down on his seat. And if audio capture had been available, it would have heard George thanking fate and a God he'd previously never had time for.

The enclosed note was succinct. *Be careful! I love you too. Axxxxx.*

———

Twenty-One

When George had flown over Ray's country house on an online 3D map, his plan had appeared quite doable. But now the eight-feet high brick wall is proving to be a problem. He'd banked on being able to hide behind it and peek over. To check for other options, he pulls a satellite-view printout from his pocket.

Earlier, he'd parked his car in a shallow pullout. After grabbing a small backpack from the boot, he jogged the quarter mile to the gates of Ray's house. The journey, though short, was potentially hazardous. What if Ray drove past him? And if so, what would be his excuse for being there?

The backpack contained his office leaving gift. The Head of Finance had asked him, in view of his many years of loyal service, if there was anything he particularly wanted.

'I think we can stretch to around three hundred ponds value,' he said. 'What about a framed art print, or travel vouchers, or something for a hobby?'

George immediately discounted the first two options. He

knew nothing about art, though he quite liked Constable because you could understand what he'd painted. And he didn't think travel vouchers would apply to somewhere like Dorset. And hobbies? Well, he was too embarrassed to say he didn't have any of note. Were chess and cooking hobbies? A new set of saucepans might seem a little unimaginative. Instead, he invented something that sounded cool.

'Perhaps a new camera?'

'Didn't know you were an amateur snapper, George. Me too.' said the boss. 'Landscape? Wildlife? Portraits?'

'Well, er...' Flustered, George picks the genre he thinks makes him appear more interesting. 'Wildlife. Yes, wildlife mainly. Great fun. Birds, bees, everything in between.'

Despite the small talk, his boss really couldn't care less. Since inheriting him when he'd taken over the department three years ago, George had been thoroughly competent, occasionally brilliant, but mainly a massive pain in the arse. He would have been happy to single-handedly fork out for a camera of George's choice just to be shot of him and his constantly questioning ways.

'Wonderful,' he said. 'Consider it done.'

And that's how George ended up with a digital white elephant with wide angle and telephoto zoom lenses. He'd used the kit once, the day after his redundancy, photographing a show-boating squirrel doing acrobatics in his garden. Since then, the kit had remained at the bottom of a wardrobe.

George scans the printout. It appeared he could get a decent view of the house from a neighbouring field. He walks back in the direction of the car and climbs over a dilapidated post and rail fence. Hugging the ancient hedge that separates the grounds of the house from the grassy field, he scurries to a midway point. Crouching down, he looks through a small gap in the hedge. The front door of the house is little more than a hundred metres away. He knows it's the closest he'll get.

Snapping the telephoto lens into the camera body, he peers through the viewfinder. Zooming in as far as possible, he's pleased to discover that anyone in the grounds between him and the house would appear quite large in the frame. He knows there's a chance Ray won't make an appearance, but he's prepared to wait for as long as it takes. Well, at least until darkness falls. After that, he has another job to do.

He beds down in his sniper's nest for the next two hours with nothing to entertain him bar trying to find faces in the passing clouds. But they're travelling so slowly the opportunities are limited. He switches to visions of sex with Angela which are more satisfying.

The light dims suddenly as the sun dips behind a distant line of trees. A chilly breeze whips up out of nowhere. George wishes he'd worn another layer. Come on, he silently cries out to Ray, you must need to venture outside for something!

Very little traffic has passed by on the road, but now he can make out the sound of a car slowing, stopping. George perks up. Seconds later, an Aston Martin cruises down the drive and comes to a halt close to the front door. He readies the camera, zooming in through the hole in hedge towards the front of the car.

Now his mobile, zipped into the anorak pocket, rings. The ringtone is set, as always, to maximum volume. Panic. He lets go of the camera, hands desperately pulling at the pocket's zip. The camera swings back and forth like a pendulum around his neck counting the time before Ray becomes suspicious.

Ray steps out of the car, mobile to his ear. Starts walking slowly towards the house. Then he stops, looks around.

George swallows. His desperate hands take on a life of their own in a combined mission to relieve the phone from the anorak before it's too late. Fumbling fingers tear open the case and flick down the silent mode switch. Eyes pick up the caller's name: Ray Caldwell.

Ray's gaze turns towards the hedge and away again. Moving off, he starts speaking into his phone.

George drops his phone to the ground and frantically takes a few shots of Ray before he closes the front door behind him. No time to refocus or adjust the exposure. This is shooting from the hip. He checks the results on the tiny camera screen. Not perfect but the images look sharp enough, despite his trembling hands. As he picks up his mobile, it vibrates. A new voicemail.

'I've been rushing around today, George, and forgot to respond to your message. I just wanted to say it's me who should be sorry. I let you down. Deplorable really. And after all the trouble you went to. Please forgive me. There's one more thing I wanted to say. It's about Angela. I wouldn't give up on her too easily if I were you. Must go, old man. Catch up soon, eh.'

George sniffs. Words are cheap. Yet the mention of Angela seemed sincere. And doesn't that disprove his theory about Ray trying to break them up? Then he reminded himself that the man's a serial liar. And possibly a sociopath. It didn't make any sense and he isn't going to waste time figuring it out. There's work to do.

He sidles back along the hedge towards the road, hoping Ray hadn't recognised his car as he drove past. When he reaches the Mondeo, he stuffs the backpack in the boot and jumps into the front. For the next hour, he listens to a talk radio station – all the while passing judgement on the intelligence of some of the station's callers – in an unsuccessful attempt to relax. It's a relief, then, when it's dark enough to leave the car again and execute the next part of his plan.

This requires walking back down the narrow road in dark clothes on a moonless night. The kind of unnecessary risk-taking George abhors in pedestrians. He rummages around in the boot and finds the collapsible warning triangle. It would have to do. In his other hand, he picks up a sturdy carrier bag and puts it down beside the car. It clunks heavily as it comes into contact with the tarmac. He pulls up his anorak hood, holds the reflective red triangle to his chest, and heads back towards the house. The triangle looks and feels incongruous, but George doesn't care. There have been many occasions in his life when he's looked sillier.

When he reaches the gates, he pulls a heavy chain from the bag and wraps it around the ironwork. Then he secures it with the padlock. The whole process takes seconds. Ray isn't leaving his home anytime soon. As he turns to leave, he notices a blinking red light high on the left-hand gatepost. A tiny security camera. How could he have missed it earlier? Has he triggered an alarm?

George runs.

'I'll need to see some ID,' says a man with a gruff voice over the phone. It's early, and he'd rather stay at home in bed on a Sunday morning, but the payoff of an emergency callout was too tempting.

'What?' shouts Ray into his mobile. 'It's my house, my gates. I can't even get my car out!'

'The locksmith's code, sir. I can't be cutting a security chain on someone's property without proof of ownership. A utility bill and driver's licence would do it.'

Twenty minutes earlier, Ray had driven up the drive and waited for the sensors to activate the gates. When they didn't open, he took a remote control from the glove compartment and pointed it at the gates. And when that failed to work, he left the car and walked towards the manual override button on the same post as the security camera. It was then he'd noticed something odd about the gates. Something in the centre that shouldn't be there. He'd pulled the chain through until he was holding the combination padlock.

'Fuck it, fuck it, fuck it!' he'd screamed, hands balling into tight fists. First the pizza, now the gates. An entirely different tone to each incident, like someone had been pulling ideas from a hat. It was then he knew instinctively there would be more to come, each one more unsettling than the last. Whoever was behind them probably wouldn't stop until their agenda, whatever that might be, was completed. It only reinforced his decision to get the hell out of there.

Back in his office, he brings up the security camera video screens on his computer. There are six, two rows of three, each covering a wide section of the grounds. In the top left window are the gates. He clicks a button to enlarge it to full screen.

There'd been a twelve-hour window during which someone could have fixed the chain, but he knew it was most likely done under the cover of darkness. That potentially cut his task by a third. He rewinds the footage, first at three-times speed and then, becoming impatient, increasing it to ten-times. The night flew past in reverse all the way to 8.45 p.m. when his keen eyes picked up a fleeting movement. He stops the video and runs it forward at normal speed.

There, a man with a carrier bag and, bizarrely, a reflective triangle around his neck. The man fitting the chain, clipping on the padlock. Now walking away. Pausing, looking directly up at the camera. Although the image is sharp, the facial features are unclear, the eyes two ghostly white holes beneath the hood-shrouded head. But. But. There's something familiar about the way the man moved.

His phone beeps twice. A message. The locksmith has arrived. Ray jumps into the Aston and drives to the gates. Without any greeting, he passes the required ID through the gates to a man who, he thought, looked nothing like a locksmith. Surely they were older, with greying hair, shabby clothes smeared with oil? Not someone with the physique of a bull, wearing jogging bottoms and tee shirt, with a hefty gold chain throttling his neck.

'Yep,' says the man, scanning the documents, 'all good.' He picks up the chain, fondles it lovingly. 'Quality. Nice lock, too. You forgot the combi then?'

Ray looks ready to implode.

'Just get it off. Please.'

'Easier said than done. Not worth spending time on the combi lock. And the bolt-cutter I'm carrying probably won't do the chain either. Hydraulic might, but there's not much call for those in my business. Normally rescuing old ladies locked out of their houses or fitting new stuff after a burglary, know what I mean? Let's have a look, eh?'

He returns to the van, pulls out some heavy-duty bolt-cutters and returns to the gate. There's a minor struggle as he attempts to cut through the chain.

'100 grade steel, this is. No chance.' He lets the cutters hang by his side.

'So?' says Ray.

The locksmith detects more than a hint of aggression in Ray's tone. He sucks in a breath.

'So,' he says calmly, 'we go to Plan B. That'll do it.'

If Plan B is so fucking good, then why wasn't it Plan A, thinks Ray.

Plan B turns out to be lengthy and noisy, and not without

some danger. Plan B involves the locksmith wielding a large battery-powered circular saw and attempting to cut through something that's not held firmly in position.

'Might scratch the gate, but I'll do what I can,' says the man after a few seconds. 'Happy for me to continue?'

Ray nods reluctantly. He's way more concerned about who's behind these incidents and what they might do next.

———

The printer clicks, whirs, and spits out three sheets of photographic paper. A hand pulls them from the tray. The pages are placed side by side on the desk. Ray's face in various poses, the house in the background. The pictures are so clear it's like the photographer had been standing just a few metres away. An invasion of privacy Ray couldn't ignore.

George studies them intently, trying to find meaning in the facial expressions, but ends up only making himself angry again. With his index finger, he flicks each of the three heads in turn as if they were flies on a dinner plate. Childish, he admits, but the act gives him considerable pleasure. He pins the pictures to the crime wall and returns to his laptop where he copies the images onto a memory stick.

Unsurprisingly, George has thought through the next stage with due diligence. He has a choice of either posting the images to Ray which would mean he wouldn't receive them until Tuesday at the earliest, or adding to his project expenses by paying someone to deliver them, or emailing them to the address Ray gave him so they could play remote chess. Suspecting he has multiple email accounts, George covers himself by emailing the images today and posting them tomorrow. Keeping up the momentum is important.

He realises he can't use his own email account or even his

own computer. An experienced hacker like Ray would probably find it easy to trace the email back to him. What he needs is a new email account and the use of an anonymous computer. And on a Sunday that may prove challenging. The library would have been a good option with its four ageing and rarely used work stations, but that would be closed. And the two internet cafes which briefly graced the local high street had closed nearly a decade ago. A web search reveals only one within a twenty-five-mile radius, in a convenience store in North London.

George hates driving in London. Drivers are a different breed there. Constantly looking for the smallest opportunity to speed up their journeys. Assessing the timings of traffic lights in order to take off first. Estimating lane congestion and constantly weaving in and out to gain the most meagre of territorial advantage. A city inhabited by people like White Car Man. To George, it appeared to be a giant, reckless video game where the skill level was high yet the rewards pitifully small – perhaps measured in seconds saved over an entire journey. It seemed less about getting from A to B and more about X getting one over on Y. With some reluctance, he makes the trip.

The store is cramped, a one-stop location packed with goods that cater for almost any eventuality. A strange, unidentifiable aroma permeates the air, a heady mix of machine coffee, joss sticks, and microwaved pies. A grimy PC sits on a raised stand next to the counter. George doubts it had ever been dusted, let alone disinfected. There's no chair either, but what he needs to do won't take long. He pays a surly-looking man for a half-hour session.

'No porn, okay mate?' says the man, 'Get kiddies in here.'

George wonders what kind of person would watch porn in a shop.

First, he sets up the new email account. He'd thought about

the name on the journey down: *theendisnigh@cheetahmail.uk* had a nice ring to it. Simple, impactful. Other alternatives occurred to him – *thejapesofwrath@, ticktockticktock@, thelastsupper@* – but were discarded on the grounds of being perhaps too obtuse.

He punches in the chosen name as directed and is disappointed to find it's been taken. The site thoughtfully suggests an alternative, *theendisnigh116@cheetahmail.uk*, which he grudgingly agrees to, barely believing that at least one hundred and fifteen people had got before him. Is nothing original anymore?

He types in Ray's email address and attaches the images from the stick. Should he add a message? George plumps for less is more. His email address would do the job for him. He hits the Send button and pockets the stick.

As he walks out, he spots a lottery promotional screen on the counter. He's never bought a ticket in his life, knowing he may as well throw away the money, but George believes his luck is on a roll. He invests four pounds in two random-numbered tickets.

At the end of the street, close to where he's parked his car, he spots a post box into which he deposits an A4 cardboard envelope. Other than his fingerprints, George has left no trace of his involvement in the entire operation.

He drives home, the anticipation of his release from purgatory steadily increasing. The moment he's through the front door, he calls Ray on the pretext of setting up a chess game. What he really wants to know is Ray's state of mind following the pizza and padlock incidents. The phone, disappointingly, goes straight to voicemail. He leaves a message on the off-chance Ray might listen to it.

'Ray, it's George. Chess next week? Call me. Thanks.'

In the country house, the desk that housed multiple computer screens is bare, together with the drawers of mobiles, hard drives, memory sticks, and notepads. Almost everything has been packed carefully into boxes and sealed with gaffer tape. Other than a single mobile in Ray's jacket pocket, the only other piece of tech now available to him, a laptop, sits on the kitchen table. The display reveals an email confirming a short-term lease on a large house in a village twenty miles north of Nice. Money helps to speed up almost everything.

A large suitcase packed with clothes lies open in the dressing room of the master suite. It's been organised so neatly it looks like a publicity shot for the luggage manufacturer.

Ray stands outside the French windows of the dining room surveying the grounds, and the fields and woodland beyond. The day after tomorrow he'll be gazing out over distant mountains. It seems like a fair trade, he thinks. It's not the first time he'd found it necessary to move on, but he hopes it would be one of the last.

He hasn't yet listened to George's voicemail. The old-school mobile rang as he had been clearing out the drawers. As George was the only person to ring that phone, he knew who the caller was immediately. But he's already consigned George to the past. Out of necessity as much as any other reason. Even though George was rubbish at chess, he'd miss the routine of their Saturday sessions. Routines meant not having to make decisions and that had been another revelation.

Upon reflection, he decides to send George a final message, simply to bookend his time with him. There's a moment of hesitation. The mobile labelled "George" is packed away, so does he really want to use a phone with his personal number to contact him? Does it matter? He could always block him later if he became a pest.

He writes: *Ray here on a new number. Sorry for everything and good luck. I don't think I'm the kind of friend you need.*

He presses the green button.

Twenty-Two

'George?' Tyler's voice sounds softer than usual.

'Speaking.' George barely recognises the voice. It's familiar, but he can't put a name to it.

'Detective Sergeant Tyler.'

Gone is the mildly sarcastic tone. George thinks he can even detect a rare element of enthusiasm.

'Quick update on your mate Caldwell or Wakefield, or Dzamic as he's sometimes known. He's only wanted by the FBI, isn't he? You won't believe the shit-storms he's caused. Last place he was known to be living was Serbia. That was three years ago.'

'So you've arrested him, then?' says George, his chest fluttering.

'Steady George, we're pulling together the paperwork now. Probably tomorrow. It's complicated. A lot of vested interests so we can't go in half-cocked. Have you had any contact with him since we last spoke?'

'Er...' George wonders how much to tell Tyler, given that he's not meant to be meddling. Considering the critical nature of the current situation, he decides it's better to be transparent. 'I've been playing some games with him, actually.'

'Games?'

'A kind of revenge, really. I know it's childish, but I wanted him to feel threatened. Just like I did. I thought he was my friend.'

Tyler buries his head in his hands.

'Sweet Jesus, George, what have you done now?' The world-weary tone has returned. He listens as George relates tales of pizza and chains and paparazzi stakeouts. After he finishes, there's a silence as Tyler considers the ramifications of George's exploits. The pause is brief.

'What the fuck?! You could have compromised everything. Did you stop to consider you might drive him away?'

George had considered this. In fact, it was the whole point of the exercise. Anything to break free from the man who was ruining his life.

'I had to look after myself. And Angela. You said you were under-resourced.'

'Do you think he knows it's you who's behind these ... these ... stunts?'

'I don't think so. There was a camera on the gate, but it was dark and a hood covered my face. And he left me a nice voicemail at the weekend. Apologising for lying to me, mostly. And quite right, too.'

Tyler is clenching the phone like he's wringing the life out of it. He's about to deliver a powerful rebuke, but decides against it. This is George he's dealing with and Georges, apparently, aren't like other people.

'Stay where you are. Do not move. It's possible you may be in danger. I'll try to arrange for someone to stay with you, but don't hold your breath.'

Suddenly George feels important.

'Well, if you feel it's necessary. I'm happy to give them lunch. Perhaps a sand—'

'Shut up, George. I need to make some urgent calls. My boss isn't going to like this,' says Tyler, suppressing his anger as best he can. 'This conversation stays with us, okay? No telling anyone, understand? Not. Even. Angela. You got that?'

'Mutti's the word.'

'What?'

'Mutti. It's mum in German. It's just a silly—'

Tyler has hung up.

As George puts down the phone, he notices a message notification on the screen. It's an unknown number, but the first line of text tells him it's from Ray.

While he's tempted to respond, he knows what Tyler's opinion would be.

———

The removal vans had arrived at first light. Three of them. Eight cheerful men, looking fresh and capable, exited the cabs. Ray had paid a substantial premium to procure them at such short notice. But that would be nothing compared with the massive long-term storage costs. Still, it was only money, and making more was easy if you were desperate. After an exhaustive briefing, during which he was pleased to see the men taking detailed notes, the team had set about the task quickly and efficiently. One van appeared to be half full already.

Ray pours himself half a glass of water, downs it in one hit, and leaves it on the bare quartz worktop. He checks his watch. Fifteen minutes before the sales rep from a local Aston Martin dealership is due to arrive to make an offer on the car. The Golf too. Both were surplus to requirements. A taxi to a Heathrow hotel this evening would be his last road trip in the UK. In his current state of mind, it couldn't come soon enough.

Yesterday evening, he was shocked to see the candid photos of himself in the inbox solely reserved for messaging George. To his knowledge, no one else knew of that email address except George. Unless George had passed it on to the police. But if that was the case, why would they have sent him the photos? For that matter, why would George? It didn't seem like one of his interventions. What would he have to gain? Besides, George had left him a cheery message only two days ago wanting to set up a game for Saturday. Only one possible conclusion remained. Despite his sophisticated software, he'd been hacked. That would be a first.

He'd scrolled through the previous twenty-four hours' CCTV footage. Two cameras captured overlapping views of the area from which the photos had been taken. It was a pointless exercise. His video revealed only a small movement in a tiny gap in the boundary hedge. The campaign of intimidation was clearly ramping up. The pizza had been a joke, the padlocked gate a considerable inconvenience, but the candid pictures of him by the house felt more invasive. Even so, despite having no clue to the identity or motive of the sender, he found it impossible to let the email go unanswered. It was a matter of pride. He sent an immediate reply: *Ready when you are, big man*. You have to stand up to bullies.

Twenty-four hours. One day without incident. That's all he needs now.

―――

Starved of ambient air pressure for the past thirty minutes, Tyler's right ear is throbbing. He transfers the phone to his left ear, but the position feels awkward. He yawns. His right ear pops.

Since talking to George the previous day, he's been in a constant loop with his superiors and the National Crime Agency, the operation involving more and more people by the hour. A surveillance team had been dispatched within minutes of his call with George. The idiot's meddling – which he grudgingly admired for its sheer audacity – had the potential to precipitate a hasty escape by the target.

The team on the ground, some of whom are hiding out close to where George took the photos, reported the presence of removal vans but have yet to discover if Ray is actually at home. Tyler clicks off the call and speed dials another number. Before the call clicks through, there's a shout from across the room.

'We've got 'em,' says a young detective constable.

The hush in the room is extreme. Only the hum of computer hard drives adds substance to the atmosphere. Everyone knows what those three words mean. The search and arrest warrants have been secured. Tyler makes a brief call to his DCI. Then he stands up and grabs his jacket.

'We're on,' he says to a room of expectant faces.

———

By lunchtime, the removal team is nearly halfway through its task. The men sit in the back of the only empty van, taking a break.

Ray is more relaxed now. The way things are going, he might be able to get to the hotel in time for a late dinner. His mid-morning flight to Nice, followed by a thirty-minute drive, meant he'd be in his new rental tomorrow afternoon. Every hour here now seemed a drain on his energy and spirit. He'd miss the house, though. The rental, a twenty-year-old villa, would be soulless by comparison.

His travel bags sit in the hallway. Window and door locks have been checked. The fridges turned off, their doors left open. The heating system shut down. He would turn off the water and electricity at the last moment. To kill time, he takes a final stroll around the grounds.

A single prolonged ring on George's doorbell. Simultaneously, his phone chimes.

George freezes. He's deep into composing a long letter to Angela, apologising again for dragging her into this mess. His newfound brevity has been forgotten, the word count already standing at nine hundred and forty-six. Ever since the call with Tyler, he's been on edge. His new security camera now felt woefully inadequate against an international hoodlum. Writing had seemed like a good distraction.

Taking a deep breath, he checks the video feed on his phone. A middle-aged uniformed policeman stares right back at him. George goes to the front door. He still isn't going to take any chances. He clicks the door chain into place and opens the door a crack.

The policeman has an amused expression on his face. 'Mister Sanderson? Constable John Irving. We shouldn't need to be here too long, apparently.'

'May I see your ID please? Dangerous times and all that.' A weak laugh from George. 'I expect you can buy those uniforms on eBay.'

The policeman isn't at all surprised by George's manner. Tyler had warned him. He wearily reaches into a pocket and pulls out his warrant card.

'All bona fide, sir. We're here at the request of DS Tyler.'

'You said we?'

'I did?' The policeman scratches his neck.

'Yes, you said *we* shouldn't need to be here for long.'

'Oh yes, my colleague. He's in the car. He'll be staying there for the duration. Extra protection. Very visible. Can I come in?'

George clocks the red stripes of a police car beyond his hedge. Nods his head as if acknowledging the gravity of the situation. He closes the door, releases the chain and opens the door wide. He makes an instant assessment on how effective his bodyguard would be in the event of a violent attack. Constable Irving must be close to retirement, likely armed with little more than a stick and possibly a Taser, and the man is plainly unambitious due to his lowly rank. Not exactly the criteria for the job if George had written them. He tries to put the thought from his mind, but the feeling in his stomach betrays his fears. Where was the Tactical Firearms Unit?

'Any other access to your house?' says the constable. 'You'd better show me the garden, anyway. Can't be too careful.'

George watches as his guardian walks slowly around the perimeter, looking over the garden fences. He makes a quick call on his radio and returns to the house.

'Only one rule, Mister Sanderson. If I say go upstairs, you go upstairs. Lock yourself in the bathroom. Other than that, you can go about your business, okay?' He clears his throat. 'Any chance of some tea? I'm parched.'

'Builders or Earl Grey?' says George. 'I find the subtlety of Earl Grey most refreshing. Did you know it's flavoured with the oil of the Bergamot—'

'Builders, please,' says the officer, wishing to arrest a lecture on the science of tea before it gets out of hand. 'Two sugars in one, none in the other, thank you. I'll be in the living room.'

He checks his watch and turns back to George. 'Mind I switch the telly on, sir? Nothing like a quiz to pass the time.'

'Be my guest, officer. It's brand new. The latest tech. I'll join you if you don't mind. Biscuits? I think I have some Garibaldis. Named after—'

'General Garibaldi,' cuts in Constable Irving. 'If memory serves me, hero of Italian unification. Not sure why, though.' He grins.

George returns to the kitchen and finds a rarely used teapot. As he's making tea for three, it seems to make sense. It feels good to go back to the old ways once in a while. While he's waiting for the kettle to boil, his eyes lock on to his mobile. It's sitting on the breakfast bar and appears to be radiating a hypnotic attraction.

Pick me up, George, it's saying. Pick me up and call Ray. It might be the last chance you have. To get to the bottom of all this. You have to find out *why* for your own piece of mind.

What harm can it do, thinks George. I'm protected. Tyler's operation is underway. I might even be helping because Ray will be distracted.

He delivers the tea and heads for the back garden.

―――

Ray wanders aimlessly through the small stand of oaks at the west end of the grounds when his mobile rings. His first thought is the removal men have an issue. Then he sees the caller's number. To answer or not to answer?

'George, I'm a little pushed for time. What can I do for you?'

'Why did you do it, Ray or whatever your name is? I thought we were friends.' George's tone is calm, the words measured.

Ray stops walking. A visual mashup of locked gates, free pizza and illicit photos strobe through his head in a microsecond before screeching to a halt at an infra-red image of a hooded man wearing a triangle.

'Have you been sending me pizza, George? I'm afraid I'd just had lunch, so bad timing.'

'Shame. I'm sure it was perfectly good. But why me? What did I ever do to you?'

'You sure you want to know?' An embarrassed laugh from Ray. 'Okay, this is going to sound silly. Remember the day we first met in the cafe? The way you treated that homeless guy? Have you ever given a thought for what it must be like to give up your dignity? To beg for crumbs from people who mostly pretend you don't even exist?' Ray's voice has an edge George wouldn't have recognised. 'I do, because twenty-five years ago that was me, George. Difficult to believe, eh? Well, you caught me at a time I was bored, and looking for someone to play a little game with. And you'll especially love this part. It could have been anyone. Simple as that. You just happened to piss me off before anyone else did, demanding that guy became a performing monkey for your entertainment. That got to me. To be honest, I wish I'd never started the whole thing, but you can't turn back the clock.'

'All this for a game?!' George realises his voice has become raised. He looks back towards the house. His bodyguard doesn't appear to have noticed.

'Haven't you ever found yourself in a rut?' says Ray. 'Wanting a change, some light relief? Of course you have. You of all people.'

A distant sound interrupts his flow. A helicopter. It's not uncommon. Heathrow is little more than twenty miles away.

'Often, Ray, but I don't go around hurting people because it makes me feel better. The sea air on the Bournemouth prom usually does the trick. Or scarifying the lawn. You should try it one day. Listen, I had no idea about what happened to you, and I'm sorry, but you know things haven't been exactly easy for me either. If it wasn't for Angela—'

Ray cuts in. 'I feel especially bad about that part. I could see how she helped you. Changed you, even. I was – don't laugh – a bit envious. You and Angela this, you and Angela that. It was hard to take. Yes, I know it's pathetic.'

'Ha! That'll be the first time someone's jealous of me. I'm disappointed in you, Ray.'

'Ouch, but fair. And here's something ironic. You helped me realise what's missing in my life. I'm proud of you, George. Really, I am. In another universe, maybe we'd be real friends. In fact, there was a point where I wanted to call the whole thing off but it was too late. The best I could do was to get you released early. I'm not expecting you to thank me.'

'I'm not about to. You nearly ruined everything for me.'

It's time, Ray thinks, to head back to the house. He feels he's left the removers for too long, even though they'd managed perfectly well without him so far.

'As I said, I'm a bit pushed. Here's a bit of advice to save you from wasting your time with the boys in blue. Nothing I've done can ever be traced back to me. So good luck, George. Be grateful for what you have and have a nice life. It's not all about money. Oh, and protect your king better. It can be powerful in attack too.' He clicks off the call.

The helicopter continues on its trajectory along the valley towards the house.

Skirting around the formal garden, Ray heads back to the driveway. Two of the men are loading an enormous sofa.

'Everything okay?' says Ray. 'Tea? Coffee? There's still some milk left.'

'We're okay, ta.'

Ray can barely hear the voice above the now deafening clatter of helicopter blades. Surely there's some law about flying at such low levels. He cups his ears. 'Sorry?'

'Gotta push on,' shouts the older man who looks way too frail to be doing heavy lifting. Then he points skywards, above the roof of the house.

Ray turns around, walks backwards towards the removal van. A stiff downdraft suddenly whips up the air around him. The helicopter appears over the house as if in slow motion. It's so close he can see the pilot. He spins around to face the gate. Movement. Then the gates swing open.

As he runs back to the house, he sees half a dozen black clad figures running towards him from the hedge on the south side. They're screaming at him. Twelve seconds away if they run fast. He darts into the lobby. On a clothes hook is a jacket, the hem on one side hanging lower than the other. He pulls out the handgun he would have kept until the last possible minute before burying it somewhere in the grounds. He's never shot anyone in his life and doesn't intend to today. However, a gun makes a loud noise and that might be the diversion he needs to make a swift exit via the back door. Just one problem. He's already locked it. Now he hears sirens.

As he crosses the entrance hall, he sees through the open door four police vehicles speeding down the drive. They'd reach the house in twenty seconds, maybe less. Grabbing a large bunch of keys from the kitchen table, he heads through the utility room to a side door. He fumbles through them, identifies the correct one, unlocks the door.

A dark figure dressed in full combat gear, semi-automatic Heckler & Koch rifle readied, steps sideways from behind the wall to block his path.

'Shit,' says Ray, his Provençal bolthole evaporating in an instant.

'You've made me look good.'

George had soaked up Tyler's words and basked in them for the past hour. His bodyguards left the moment they received the call that Ray had been apprehended. George has been in a state of shock ever since. He hadn't expected the situation to move so fast. Or the operation to be so large. Tyler told him over forty personnel were involved. And when he mentioned the helicopter, it dawned on him just how important a catch Ray was.

He replayed his friend's last words and knew then he'd never be able to move his king ever again without fondly remembering those games in the cafe. Or that Ray had said he was proud of him. No one else ever has been. Well, maybe one other person. He isn't quite sure.

He picks up his car keys, checks his hair in the hall mirror, and leaves the house. He's humming his own version of Abba's *The Winner Takes It All*, though Benny and Bjorn would take out an injunction were it ever to reach the public domain.

He drives smoothly and with no great haste to an industrial estate on the edge of town and pulls up in the visitors' car park of Finguish Fans. He sits quietly for a few minutes, composing himself. Then he pulls the mobile from his pocket and texts Angela.

Look out of your window xxxxx

Then he realises her desk might be on the opposite side of the building. He rapidly texts again.

Into the car park! Not sure where you sit xxxxx

He's barely hit the Send button when Angela appears at a ground-floor window. She's motionless at first. Then she waves. Less of a wave really, more a raised hand, like she isn't quite sure who he is. George steps out of the car, waves back vigorously.

Angela disappears. As the seconds tick by, he becomes more and more anxious. Maybe it isn't a good time? Maybe she's reconsidered? Perhaps she's still scared?

The double doors slide back, and she's there, standing at the top of the short flight of steps. She looks back at the building, the windows now revealing other faces. Now she turns towards George. He walks towards her.

'It's over,' he says, as if the final whistle had been blown on a football match of little importance. 'Italian or Chinese tonight? I'm thinking Italian, as I've noticed some pretty poor reviews of the Chinese lately. Of course, it's entirely up to you. Or perhaps we could—'

'Shush, my lovely brave man. Come here.'

———

Twenty-Three

The list of Ray's villainy ran to over forty pages.

Multinational companies and the governments of the USA and Israel had all been victims. Judiciaries the world over would seek Ray's extradition for offences ranging from cybercrime to blackmail and multi-million-dollar fraud. China and Russia wanted their pound of flesh too, but were reluctant to detail exactly why. Ray's actions against George, microscopic in comparison, were relegated to a one-liner on the last page. When Tyler broke that piece of news to George, he'd taken it well. Others were ahead of him in the retribution league. But, as Tyler pointed out, George would always have the knowledge he'd been instrumental in his capture.

After the national and international newspaper reports of Ray's arrest, word had filtered out that George had been a key element in his downfall. The story immediately had a new angle and the media were going to bleed it dry. The headlines were generous to him.

ACCOUNTANT BEATS INTERPOL TO UNMASK WORLD'S MOST WANTED

HACKER THWACKER!
UK HERO MAKES WORLD A SAFER PLACE

George enjoyed his fame for precisely two days. Owing to the large number of reporters and TV crews camped outside his house, parking for residents and visitors became problematic. Neighbours were quick to complain and they organised a petition. George signed it too. A local newspaper revealed his feelings.

'I WANT A QUIET LIFE' SAYS LOCAL MAN WHO FOILED HACKER

As a result of his now near-legendary status in the local area, many potential clients on George's email list came calling. His workload increased exponentially. He gave a special breakfast presentation to the business network entitled "How bold creative thinking can keep you one step ahead." They would talk it about for many years. Not least because George overran and had to be strongly encouraged to get to his summary before the Women's Institute arrived for lunch.

One of his new clients is a small chain of estate agents. The job came out of the blue. Literally. An electric-blue Subaru Imprezza with a throaty exhaust had appeared in his drive one morning. As George peered out of the living room window, a sharp-suited young man got out. It took him a second or two to recognise the face. Scooterboy saluted as he walked confidently up to the door.

'Like my wheels?' he said. 'Got a new job selling houses. Salesperson of the month already. Raking it in.'

George laughed. 'I'm happy for you. Must be time we had a chat about your investments, then.'

'Yeah, maybe. No rush, eh?'

'No,' said George with a pasted-on smile. 'No rush at all.'

'I told 'em you were a genius so don't let me down.'

'I never let friends down.'

Scooterboy looked pleased.

———

A throbbing bass line of a pop classic leaks through the doors of the Westgate Hotel's largest function room and finds its way into the men's toilets. George zips up his trousers and turns towards the wash basins. The door opens. Michael Finguish walks in, a necklace of magenta tinsel around his neck. He smiles at George.

'It's George, isn't it. Angela's partner? I'm Michael, her boss. Enjoying the party, I hope?'

'Pleased to meet you, Michael. And congratulations on getting the top job back. I know things haven't been easy for you.'

Michael has come to terms with everyone knowing his business. And, in a weird way, it had made the turmoil in his life easier to manage. No secrets.

'Thanks. You know, George, I sincerely believe that everything that happened was for the best. I learnt some valuable lessons.'

'Still, it must be hard work juggling the company and two young kids.'

'You do what you have to do, don't you? Once my wife decided motherhood wasn't for her, she had to make a tough decision too. Angela's been a real help to me. You should be proud of her. We all are. Dad said to me he'd only agree to step down if she stayed. I hope you're not going to whisk her away into the exciting world of espionage?' He claps George on the shoulder, laughs.

After many months, George at last feels vindicated for creating Project Angela.

———

The hottest ticket in town today is the public gallery of the crown court. Many onlookers are regulars, mostly pensioners with a fondness for schadenfreude and crime thrillers. Others are single women of a certain age who fancy their chances with the biggest celebrity in town. Angela knows which ones they are because they're always bothering George in the street. The press enclosure is full-to-bursting. A small crowd of disappointed people, unable to get in, wait outside. It may not be an important case, but the victim is a national treasure.

George stands in the witness box, suited and booted, his new burgundy tie acknowledging the solemnity of the occasion. Angela looks on proudly.

'And yet in your statement you say you did nothing to provoke the actions of Mister Briggs?' says the counsel for the defence, a middle-aged man with such a dark beard shadow George assumes his testosterone count must be huge, and that could have serious health repercussions later in life. He makes a mental note to mention it to him afterwards.

'Correct.'

The prosecution counsel breathed a sigh of relief. Having experienced George's predilection for verbiage at their pre-court chat, he'd pleaded with him to be concise in his answers.

'But,' continued the defence counsel, 'as we have heard from Mister Rowley, the driver of the Toyota in front of you, he had been braking slowly and smoothly as the traffic in front of him was coming to a gradual halt. Yet what he saw in his rearview mirror was, and I quote, "a terrifying image of a black Ford bearing down on me". Therefore, is it not the case that the emergency stop you performed would have been unnecessary had you been concentrating properly at the time? And by that token, the accident would never have occurred?'

The prosecution counsel jumps to his feet. 'Objection. Mister Sanderson is not the person on trial here today.'

'Overruled.' The judge turns to George. 'Please answer the question, Mister Sanderson.'

George thinks for a moment. This is awkward and he knows he's under oath. But he also knows the law.

'Whatever my state of mind at the time, it wouldn't justify the vicious assault on me. I would have had some sympathy for him over the collision, but couldn't we simply have exchanged names and addresses? Like civilised people?'

He looks over to the jury to see their reaction and is pleased to note a few nods.

'So you admit to not being in full control of your vehicle, Mister Sanderson?'

'Let he who is without sin cast the first stone,' says George.

'So you do admit it. Thank you, Mister Sanderson.'

George isn't finished.

'Can any of us honestly say we've never been distracted whilst driving? Can you?' He fixes his eyes on the defence counsel. There's a titter of amusement around the court.

'Thank you, you've answered the question,' barks the counsel. 'We're not here to discuss the philosophy of driving.'

George is a little disappointed in this. He'd be quite happy to air his take on the moronic habits of many of today's motorists. And bikers and cyclists and e-scooterists. They were perhaps worse.

'You were amazing,' Angela says in the lunchtime recess. 'Put that jumped-up man in his place. The jury were laughing.'

George grins. For the first time in his life, he has backup.

The jury takes less than thirty minutes to reach a guilty on all counts verdict. The judge cites Brigg's actions as both despicable and potentially life-threatening before remanding him into custody pending psychological reports. George thinks hiring a psychiatrist would be a waste of hard-earned public money.

It had been the driest spring for over a hundred years. Not that you'd know it from the vibrant green of George's lawn that would probably have been visible from the International Space Station. Raked, seeded, fertilised, irrigated, and precision mowed, he'd put a lot of love into it. The rest of his spare time he saved for Angela who'd moved in temporarily at Christmas and never returned.

Somewhat reluctantly, he'd agreed to accompany her on a week's winter sun break in Lanzarote. He tentatively suggested Weymouth, but she put her foot down. He rather enjoyed it, although Angela had needed to confiscate his laptop from time to time.

While they were out of the country, White Car Man was sentenced to three years' imprisonment. George would have given him ten at the very least, but let it go.

Back home, the couple celebrate with Angela's cottage pie – a little overcooked and under-seasoned in his opinion – shortly followed by a bout of enthusiastic lovemaking during which George made a valiant attempt to subdue the effects of severe acid reflux. He makes a note to always allow a suitable digestion period after meals before exerting himself like that again.

Recuperating in bed afterwards, George brings the small talk to a halt.

'Angela?'

'Yes?'

'I know you probably haven't considered this, and it might be a little early in the day, so to speak, but ...'

'Yes?'

'Angela, would you marry me?'

Downstairs, the dishwasher signals the end of its cycle with a beep. Then another. And another.

Under the duvet, Angela's hand finds George's. Squeezes it gently.

'Dear George,' she murmurs.

His hand twitches. Angela continues.

'It's not that I don't love you or want to be with you. It's just ...' She's struggling to find the right words. 'Maybe we will get married one day, but why put ourselves under any pressure now? We're okay as we are, aren't we?'

'Of course, but ...' He stops short of reminding her of the tax benefits. Now is not the time.

———

Dear Mr Sanderson,

I have been instructed by my client, David Wakefield – I believe you know him as "Ray" – to offer you a proposition.
He would like you to manage a charity – yet to be formed – to assist homeless people get back into employment by starting their own businesses. The cause is something close to his heart and he thinks you will understand how important this is.
As you may be aware, incarcerated people cannot set up, nor be

a director of, an enterprise so it would be, as he puts it, 'your baby'.

I'm sure you may be wondering where the initial funding for such a venture will come from. I'm pleased to say that my client is the beneficiary of a significant trust fund of clean cash and assets that he inherited from his wealthy parents but never took advantage of.

Mr Wakefield tells me his offer will, understandably, come as quite a shock to you, but he begs you to give it due consideration. He believes you'd be a very safe pair of hands. Messrs Fermer, Larter and Hope would be happy to help you put the project in motion. On a personal note, I think that a person with a profile such as yours would add considerable cachet to this enterprise and I echo Mr Wakefield's desire for you to be the figurehead.

Please contact me when it's convenient for you.

Yours very sincerely,

Robert Hope
Senior partner, Fermer, Larter and Hope

George puts down the letter and stares out of the window at nothing in particular. Angela is out for lunch with a friend. And, today being a Saturday, George wishes he could rewind twelve months and have a few games of chess with Ray (he still referred to him by that name), and a coffee and a sandwich and a chat about the world. Back then, it was something to get out of bed for. And, he admitted, he still missed it ... missed him. Despite Ray's terrible crimes, he knew they had a lot in common.

He casts his eyes over the letter again. He'd have to talk it through with Angela but he knows she'll be happy if it's something he really wants to do. Especially if it doesn't involve interventions.

A rustling in the bedroom.

Angela opens her eyes, yawns. 'What are you doing?' she mumbles at George, voice dry from sleep.

'I've just remembered something,' he says, rummaging through the pockets of a jacket he hadn't worn since the autumn. 'Got 'em.' he says, pulling out two pieces of paper. 'Those lottery tickets I bought months ago. Do you think I could still claim on them?'

Angela closes her eyes and turns away, pulling the duvet over her head.

George potters into his office, mostly a repository for Angela's clothes now, opens the laptop and brings up the lottery website. He finds the claims section and keys in the numbers.

Angela, who's fallen back into that agreeable state of half sleep, hears her name whispered repeatedly. She feels pressure on her shoulder. A gentle rocking motion. The voice becomes more urgent.

'Angela! Angela! Karma's come knocking.'

George's face looms above hers.

'Who?'

He thrusts a lottery ticket so close to her eyes the text is blurred.

'It's a winner,' he beams. 'And I can still claim.'

Angela shifts in the bed, pulls herself up.

'How much?'

'Forty pounds!'

Angela sees the face of a child who's unwrapped the present they've always wanted.

'Forty pounds,' she repeats, without a hint of emotion.

'Yes. Yes!' His enthusiasm is undimmed by Angela's lack of excitement. 'That's a two-thousand per cent profit on the investment. Okay, it was a gamble, not an investment, but still ... Tell me, why did I choose to buy those tickets at that point in time?'

Angela slumps back against the pillow. George starts pacing the room.

'Perhaps that's the key. To only do things when they come into your head. No planning. It isn't about yin and yang at all. Maybe fate rewards people who live their lives on the hoof.'

He stares, unfocused, out of the window.

'In fact, that gives me an idea ...'

'George!'

―――

Acknowledgements

Hacking George would not have been published without the help and support of many people. I'd like to thank my author wife Berni Stevens for her encouragement and advice, and my son Sam Palmer who's on his own writing adventure. My editor, Sara Starbuck, added some much-needed structure and a beating heart to the story. Thanks to best-selling author Tony Lee for his encouragement and much-needed technical support. Critically, the incisive feedback from my early readers gave me the confidence to press on and get the job done – so thank you David Osborn-Cook, Tony & Helen Blin-Stoyle, Chip Mellor, Ian Wilson, and Lorna Kerry.

Most of all, I want to thank you, the reader, for taking a chance and investing your precious time reading this book. I hope you enjoyed it as much as I did writing it.

Bob Palmer—Hertfordshire, April 2022

About The Author

A former town planner and rock drummer, Bob Palmer finally found his niche as an advertising creative in London, winning numerous UK and international awards. A pioneer of book trailer marketing, he has extensive experience in the publishing industry.

He co-founded the television production company and emerging talent showcase *HYPtv*. Bob has mentored numerous young filmmakers, helping them take their first steps into commercials, TV and film. More recently, he co-produced the New York Times Critics Pick feature film *Us & Them*.

Bob shares a creaky 400-year-old cottage on the edge of London with a black cat, rampant woodworm, and his infinitely patient author and cover-designer wife Berni Stevens. When he's not working, you'll find him hiking canyons in south-east Utah searching for ancient ruins and rock art. To share his passion, he created the popular website reddirt-blueskies.net.

Hacking George is his debut novel and a labour of love. His next novel, *The Last Boy in America*, is scheduled for release in autumn 2022.

What did you think of Hacking George?

If you enjoyed my book, please recommend it to friends and family.

And perhaps you could post a review on Amazon? Go to ***mybook.to/HackingGeorge***

Your feedback is important to me.

Thank you.

Subscribe to my mailing list and get the first chapter of my next book, *The Last Boy In America*.

bit.ly/3KGEryJ

Printed in Great Britain
by Amazon